T.M. SMITH

EVERNIGHT PUBLISHING ®

www.evernightpublishing.com

Copyright© 2025

T.M. Smith

ISBN: 978-0-3695-1225-3

Cover Artist: Jay Aheer

Editor: CA Clauson

T.M. SMITH

DEDICATION

For Mike, who was there to support me through all my books, bragging about them to anyone who would listen. I miss you.

In the incipient galaxy, the Siblings came to be, at first bewildered and then awed by the potential. An explosion broke the silence, darkness gave way to light, and matter blasted across nothingness. With his own hands, the OneCreator formed planets and dimensions. Chaos abstained for fear his power was in destruction. Lumia sprinkled the skies with stars. Melodia breathed, sweetening the worlds with flora and fauna, while Prima's tears of joy flooded into lakes, oceans, and rivers. Behold! It was good.

T.M. SMITH

DARK SHADOW OF GUILT

The Winged Assassin Series, 1

T.M. Smith

Copyright © 2025

Chapter One

Angor, OneWorld, Present Day

What the hell?

Madeline slid her sandpapery eyelids open. Closed. Blink. Blink. She drew a deep breath and coughed. The air was stale, dusty, and sour with the faint odor of garbage left too long in a trashcan.

When reality trickled into her brain, pain rocketed through her shoulders. Her arms were stretched overhead, her full weight on them because her knees had buckled. She wiggled. No give.

Madeline straightened her wobbly knees to relieve the ache in her arms. She widened her eyes, trying to see in the dim room. She twisted her head from side to side. Down. Up. No wonder. Above her, ropes bound her wrists to a bolt in concrete. She was a damn bug pinned to a wall. Swallowing the hard lump in her throat, she struggled against the bindings.

No go.

Think. Think. Don't panic.

She and her older sisters used to listen to a radio talk show psychiatrist from New York, Lizette Lee. The woman doled out advice, some of it helping them cope with their shitty home life.

What did Lizette say? Yeah. Step one—identify the problem.

At the moment, though, Madeline couldn't concentrate. Her chest popped in and out as panic bubbled to the surface.

Fight it. Check out the surroundings. Identify the problem.

Staring straight ahead and fluttering her lids to clear the blurry vision, she took in a cavernous room with unlit bulbs hanging from the ceiling on cords. Windows, the only light source, were small and high off the ground. The place was damp, with moisture seeping from the floor and walls. She shivered. A chill passed through her body.

"Hello. Hello," she called out. When no one answered, she shouted, "Help me."

Madeline pulled against the bindings, tearing the skin on her wrists. Blood dripped down her arms, and her eyes watered.

"Hello," she yelled again.

She was alone.

Pressing her chin to her chest, Madeline glanced down. Buttons on her blouse were ripped off, exposing part of her bra. Her skirt was torn and dirty, but at least her clothes were on. Her feet were bare. No Uggs.

So, in the best imitation of Lizette Lee, she'd identified the problem.

She was in a shitty situation. Hogtied to a wall in what looked like a warehouse.

Madeline licked her cracked lips. Thirsty. How long had she been here? Long enough to need water.

How the hell did she get here?

She focused on memories that came to her in hazy bits and pieces.

Getting ready to close up the St. Louis Central Library, which she did each night, she grabbed her coat from the hook and slipped it on. Trading her comfortable pumps for warmer footwear, she slid into suede, shearling-lined Uggs. She took her purse from a desk drawer and stuck the pumps in its place. After pulling out her keys, she slung the bag over her shoulder and went from room to room shutting off lights. Once outside she closed and locked the door, checking the handle twice, even though the cleaning crew would come in behind her.

After donning warm gloves, she pulled her coat tighter. It got cold after the ice storm moved in earlier. She maneuvered carefully down the steps to the sidewalk. On the street, she stared over her shoulder at the library.

At the bottom, she began her six-block walk home, using the time to think about reheating a good soup and tossing a salad. After dinner, she'd call Fia or Darya to catch up and, afterward, crawl into bed with a half-finished book.

Madeline pulled straight down on her arms despite the torn skin under the ropes. She couldn't free herself.

Another memory drifted into her mind.

Once Madeline had crossed the street, a man bumped into her. She mumbled, "Sorry," her head down, burrowed into the warmth of her coat collar. Instead of going on his way, he grabbed her shoulders. Before she could use the martial arts tricks she'd perfected, he...

She had thought if he planned to mug her, he was out of luck. She carried little cash, much preferring her debit card or Apple Pay. Then ... then what?

Nothing. She'd blacked out. He must have drugged her before he brought her here. Wherever here was.

No. That wasn't the entire memory. She had first awakened elsewhere. In a bed. Not tied up against a wall. A woman fed her soup. A strange woman with... No... Impossible.

That recollection was too fuzzy. Maybe not real.

Rocking her body from side to side and tugging on the ropes ravaged more of her tender flesh. She sucked back tears, swallowing the screams in her mind. Not only was crying useless, but it was also a hindrance. She needed a clear head to think. Madeline drew a deep, calming breath in through her nose. Pursing her lips, she exhaled through her mouth.

Focus.

She was bound to a wall in a room that looked like an empty warehouse. She couldn't get loose.

Yet.

But the calm she had won vanished. Once again, panic set in.

No. No.

When Madeline was young, she had wondered if she had a touch of OCD. Her sister Darya had said, "So what! You're seriously hooked on lists and order." *True.* She organized clothes in her closet by type and color. In her kitchen cabinet, all the cans of chicken soup were side by side. Vegetable soup was with vegetable soup. And so on. Anything that could be grouped was.

She blamed her needs on growing up in the out-of-control home of an alcoholic. It drove her desire for order. She became a librarian because of the structure.

Each book had its proper place.

Now was the time to call on tried-and-true relaxation methods. When stressed, she recited the Dewey Decimal Classification Chart. Since she could use some tranquility, she mumbled, "Computer Science, Information, and General Works. Philosophy and Psychology…"

A door banged open, interrupting her mental recitation. When the light switch flipped on, most bulbs came to life, though a few flickered and dimmed. Madeline slammed her lids shut against the painful brightness. The ominous sound of boots thudding across the floor caused her heart to nearly burst out of her chest. Someone was coming.

Managing rapid, shallow breaths, she prepared to face her assailant.

Calm. Think. Steel yourself.

A deep voice punched through her quiet. "Good. You're awake."

Inching her lids open, Madeline stared at the man before her. Her gaze traveled up his long legs to a trim waist and broad shoulders. His sandy hair was tied back. She judged him to be a bit over six feet. What met her next was the stuff of nightmares. His eyes were cruel, uncaring, murderous.

And solid white. Irises. Pupils. The works.

Breath shot from her chest. She shuddered, stifling a scream. He was a monster.

Her kidnapper jerked his fists to his hips while he scrutinized her. "We're going to have such fun. Well, at least I shall." His laugh was deep, loud, hollow.

Madeline cleared her throat twice, finally squeaking out, "Who are you?"

Leathery, veined charcoal-gray wings popped from his back.

Unable to control herself, she screamed.

Fucking bat wings. Impossible. Like the woman she dimly remembered, the one who had fed her.

Madeline couldn't stop herself. She tugged on her arms and tried to kick her feet clear of the ties. Blood dripped onto her shirt. What her captor did next, however, led her to gravitate from scared to pissed in seconds.

He laughed, and she wanted to bitch slap him. She may be a librarian, but she didn't fit the stereotype. No shy, retiring demeanor for her. She was more inclined to rip out your throat if you didn't obey the posted quiet signs.

Not really, but sometimes the urge was there. She was a librarian for the lists and order, not to hide behind the bookshelves.

Years with her mother's erratic, drunken behavior had taught her well. Never let the enemy see you sweat. She wiped the fear from her expression and stared at the monster, her gaze devoid of emotion.

The nightmare vision in front of her tapped his chest. "I'm Praevus."

Latin for *evil, perverse.* Uselessly tugging on her wrists again, she asked, "Where am I?"

"Angor."

Hmm. She didn't know where Angor was.

"Why am I here?" She drew breath in through her nose and exhaled through her mouth.

"You were my gift to me." His white eyes shone like twin full moons.

"What do you mean?" Madeline bit her lower lip, using the pain to center her thoughts.

Praevus's wings disappeared from view as if he had retracted them. "That is none of your concern."

She hated the sound of his hollow voice. "Turn

me loose. You don't want to hurt me."

The guy was a nightmare, but she wasn't dreaming. He was in focus. Too sharp.

She stifled sobs, reminding herself that crying did no good. And terror was incapacitating. It muddled thoughts, preventing her from forming a game plan. That was step two of Lizette Lee's strategy. After clarification of the problem, came solving the problem.

Madeline began reciting the Dewey Decimal Classification system again, a focus for her concentration. She whispered, "Religion. Social Sciences. Language…"

The monster's hollow voice interrupted her recitation. "But I do want to hurt you. Besides, if I turn you loose, there is nowhere for you to run in Angor."

Madeline slowed her breathing, struggling to form thoughts. She stopped her mental relaxation technique. "Where is Angor? What part of St. Louis is it in?" But she already suspected this monster wasn't human. Nor was he from Earth.

The white-eyed, bat-winged pervert chuckled. "St. Louis? Earth? These are places of your past. They will mean nothing to you. Not even a memory. I shall be your place, your reason for living, the center of your universe."

He's a fricking psycho villain from a bad melodrama. A megalomaniacal serial killer. If he were a book, she'd file him under Philosophy and Psychology. She'd shelve him with other parapsychology and occultism works in the Mental Derangements section. Of course, the label no longer existed, but it fit Praevus. She shook her head. Back to reality. "You're going to kill me."

He shrugged. "In a way. Your body will live on. Your mind, though, will belong to me. Its only thought will be my pleasure. My approval. If I want you to kill for me, you will. If I want you to fuck me, you will. If I want you to walk into a blazing fire for me, you will." He rubbed his hands together.

Yep.

A B-movie villain.

He continued with his bad-film dialogue. "I have never had a human. I hope your flesh and mind are not too weak for my plans."

Madeline and all of Earth had watched the shocking news several years ago. Humankind's illusions had shattered like glass when TV anchors reported on Aeternals, a superior species living in another realm called Scath. We were not alone.

Hungry for knowledge, she'd studied the tons of newspapers that came into the library to get a clearer picture of these unknown beings. Though St. Louis hadn't been attacked like other cities, she learned the American military had fought beside a group who called themselves … what? Firebrands. Their common goal was to save the world from an organization determined to enslave humans. They won.

Once the good guys defeated the bad guys, Lizette Lee began broadcasting again after a long hiatus, telling how she'd been kidnapped, taken to this other realm, held prisoner, and saved by a Firebrand. Madeline had been happy to hear of her return.

Could Praevus be with those terrorists who wanted to enslave humans? Reporters had announced they'd been rounded up and killed or incarcerated, but he may have escaped.

"Are you an Aeternal from Scath?" she asked.

He rolled his white eyes as if he resented the accusation. "Those weak bastards? No. I told you. I am Praevus. I'm an Immortal. Well, I was. Now I am called a Scourge."

"What's an Immortal? What's a Scourge?"

Keep him talking.

As long as he talked, she was safe. Besides, questions were an occupational hazard for a librarian and a big part of her personality. Madeline needed to know as much as possible about her problem before formulating a successful escape plan.

"I am an Immortal whom the black-winged assassin Dominion wrongfully threw into Angor. Because I have certain ... um ... tastes, they call me a Scourge. Someday, I shall find a way to extinct him or make him suffer an eternity of torture as I have. Perhaps the latter is better." Her captor's upper lip curled into a sneer.

Madeline didn't understand what the hell Praevus was rattling on about, but she figured it was bad. Scourge? Immortal? Assassin? The last two rang a bell. She'd read something.

Think. Think.

The only thing she could connect to his rants were news shows where talking heads had discussed another being they called an Immortal. What was his name? *Yes.* Angel. *No.* Ohngel. They identified him as a winged assassin. They'd even flashed pictures of him on the screen. Despite his title, they said he was a good guy who had helped the Firebrands save humans.

None of this explained how she was here or why he chose her. When the answers to those questions eluded her, she trembled, her calmer thoughts scattering. She swallowed the bile rising in her throat, determined not to upchuck.

When she was young, Maddy and her sisters had played what-if games. What if one of their mother's gentleman callers visited the wrong room? What if they had no money for food? What if their mother fell against the edge of a table and died? But the current dilemma with Praevus was worse. Scary. Not a game.

Her captor stepped closer. He tangled his fingers in her hair and yanked her head down. She turned her cheek to the cold concrete wall but could not escape his oily touch.

"Wait here, my pet. Don't leave before I return," he whispered. Stroking her lower lip, he chuckled as if he had made a joke. "Our time together is just beginning."

She listened as the pounding of his boots faded, the lights went out, and a metal door slammed shut. "Control," she murmured, again ticking off major classes of the Dewey Decimal System. "Science. Technology. Arts and Recreation…"

Madeline clenched her fists, commanding her fear to dive deep into her heart where she buried it. One thing was for sure. She refused to break. Her sisters had prepared her well.

Chapter Two

Dominion shoved his way through the crowded bar, patrons scurrying out of his way and his entrance causing a brief lull in the noise. He pulled alongside his fellow winged assassins. Deep in conversation, Ely greeted him with a nod and Remi a slight smile. Dom cocked his foot onto the railing, his usual grim frown in place.

The Angor Management Club was the only sleazy tavern in this dimension where the Feard, aka the winged assassins of the OneCreator, could find a good drink without being hassled.

Elysium perched beside Dom on a barstool, his hand cradling an imported Demon Brew, his icy wings snapped tight to his spine.

On the other side of Ely sat Remiel, drinking a local rum. Leaning forward to include Dom in the convo, he said, "I need to kill something." His jittery fingers tapped on wood marred by centuries of use. The bronze spike-winged assassin was high-strung, always seeking action, never satisfied unless he was fighting or buried cock-deep in a female.

Just then a dominatrix decked out in leathers, ankle-breaking thigh-high boots, and a shit-ton of metal strolled by their stools. With rumpled blonde hair and eyeliner that would do a raccoon proud, she was dressed for a little BDSM play later that night.

Remi winked at the female, halting the *tap, tap, tap* on the bar. The eternal playboy.

Returning his admiration, she cracked her whip overhead and grinned, her tongue sweeping across black lips. Then her eyes widened when she spotted Dom. The dolled-up Scourge shuddered and scurried on her way, putting distance between herself and the grim onyx-winged assassin who enjoyed his rep.

Ely studied the female's retreating backside as she shot a nervous glance over her bare shoulder. In a delayed response to Remi's need-to-kill-something statement, he said, "Downtime. Killing. It's all the same now. Ho-hum."

The ice-winged assassin was struggling with the boredom of eternity again. The last time he got bad, he sought stasis for a millennium. Dom had missed him, but if it was something his brother-in-arms needed, well...

Dominion, able to launch sharp obsidian-bladed feathers from his wings with little more than a thought, didn't bother to track the dominatrix rushing off. He was accustomed to patrons giving him space and speaking in whispers. Maybe it was the patch over one eye. As a rule, Immortals were not scarred. Not on the outside.

Yep.

He knew how to keep a party lively.

Pushing three hundred pounds, all of it solid muscle, Dom was a full head taller than most of the patrons. His long hair flowed to the middle of his back, as black as the darkness that surrounded his soul. He was the biggest, though not the oldest, of the Feard. That honor went to Ely. *Yeah.* Kudos to him for being a bit younger than dirt.

Dom tightened his rock-hard jaw, donning his stone-cold-killer expression, while he adjusted the intimidating leather patch over one eye. He didn't mind the flaw. Goddesses in Vast and female Scourges in Angor told him that the savagery it implied made him an enticing hunk of meat. That fact got him laid. A lot.

His true love, though, was his work as an assassin for the OneCreator. Whether it was a capture or extinct assignment, he lived for the job. One and done. Brush that asshole off the list.

When the bartender came through a rear door, he spied Dom and attempted a hasty retreat. Too late.

"Hey, there, asswipe. Get me a drink," Dom growled, daring the barkeep to disappear into the back room.

The guy stayed put. He knew better. "What kind?" he asked, his voice quivering.

"Surprise me."

Scourges came in four flavors—Flesh Eaters, Blood Leeches, Mind Rats, and Soul Suckers. The one behind the bar was an Immortal condemned to Angor by the OneCreator. His malady? Well, the pearly white fangs and taste for a vein were dead giveaways. He was a Leech. Not a vamp, though. Immortals didn't swing that way. He craved blood but didn't need it to survive. He just enjoyed it and the pain he caused when he took it.

Nobody knew why some of their kind contracted a malady, developed an unhealthy obsession, and changed physically. Not even the OneCreator. Rumor had it that Chaos, the boss's now-extincted brother, was the cause. Something about how that Sibling's destructive powers altered Immortal DNA, forever making the species vulnerable to the affliction. Another rumor claimed the cause was the pressure of eternity.

So-named Scourges, who succumbed to a malady, met one of two fates. If they were beyond saving, the OneCreator issued an order to extinct them, to end their existence. The justice was deserved, swift, bloody, and legit. If the OC deemed the malady-infected Immortals salvageable, an assassin dropped them in Angor where they had a chance to redeem themselves. Happy times and job security.

If Harmony, Angor's head honcho in the OC's

absence, or the OC pronounced a Scourge rehabilitated, they returned to Vast, reformed and their physical perfection restored.

While some Immortals contracted maladies, others successfully fought the disease or remained uninfected.

The bartender looked as if he might piss his pants. "Fuck no, Dominion. The last time I prepped a surprise drink, you broke my jaw." His mouth dropped open, showing two yellowed fangs peeking below an upper lip.

Dom didn't feel sorry for the guy who had swept through Vast on a rampage when he succumbed to his malady. In a haven, a home for newly-created Immortals and a supposedly safe place for the young from infancy to maturity, the Blood Leech bartender had drained four toddlers. The only evidence left behind was their withered skins. When he was found, his victims' blood still dripped down his chin onto his soiled shirt. The OC condemned him to Angor, believing he would truly reform after doing penance for his crimes. Dominion had delivered the sentence, bagging him and dropping him off in the dimension where he would be punished.

Though mature Immortals could be extincted only at the hand of the OneCreator, Michael, or the Feard, toddlers were not so lucky. They had not settled into their eternal form yet. So, the bartender's victims had died slow, terrifying deaths. Shouldn't happen to kids.

Dom uncoiled from the barstool, his movements fluid. He leaned on a bent, thickly muscled forearm, his good eye freezing the Leech. "Punishment is part of the gig here. What's your complaint, wuss?"

"You never appreciate my choices." The guy shook, imitating a willow in a strong wind.

"Not true. I just enjoy breaking your bones. Any Scourge who is in here for your crimes deserves a constant reminder of his sins." Dom continued his intimidation while Ely and Remi looked on.

The bartender groaned. "Isn't it enough you confined me in this pit where I'm regularly tortured at the Ordeals?"

Once in Angor, Scourges were assigned to different Ordeals for their punishments, each specializing in a torment. Drowning. Fire. Limbs torn off or chewed on by predators. Strangulation. Whips. Knives. Fun times, fashioned specifically to fit each malady.

In between torments, the OC, or Harmony in his stead, gave the Scourges brief stays, believing that downtime increased their fear. They got to think about what was coming. A little icing on the cake of agony.

But not all punishment occurred at the Ordeals. For grins and giggles, wicked malady-stricken attacked their own on the streets or dragged them out of their quarters for impromptu pain.

Trustees, those Scourges who were nearly rehabilitated, got to be the punishers at the Ordeals or moved into management positions, running a restaurant, a shop, or a bar.

"No biggie," said Dom, answering the bartender's question. "By morning, you heal. Refreshed, hearty, and eager to start a new day."

The barkeep continued his sad story. "I get no reprieve. When my daily dose of torture ends at the Ordeals, I go home to the pits where it stinks like backed-up sewage."

"Invest in air freshener," said Dom.

"There's noise, too. Screams. Pleas. Never-ending cries for help."

"Boo hoo," said Remi. "Have you tried Air Pods and heavy metal?"

"Can we get that stuff here?" asked the Scourge,

his eyes lighting with excitement.

Ely took a swig of his brew. Afterward, expelling a loud sigh. "You can't. Like we're gonna buy you an iTunes account and some Apple shit. Do you think about the babes? You shoulda fought your thirst and stayed in Vast. It smells good there, and the sounds are mostly giggles. Some guitar music. Beaches. Blue waters. Rolling hills of green. Sunlight. Stars at night in a clear sky."

Remi added his two cents. "Of course, we prefer to live in Angor where we can watch the Scourges suffer. Besides, no politics here. No games. No kissing the OC's perfect ass. We do fly to Vast to shag a goddess now and again. Though we have no qualms about doing the females here, too."

"My drink," reminded Dom. He perched on the stool, his working eye glaring at the bartender.

The guy shuffled off, returning with a goblet filled with a dark amber liquid and fruit. He slammed it onto the worn bar.

Dom guzzled the entire thing. He swiped the back of his hand across his lips. "What's it called?

"A Dead Manhattan."

"Excellent." Dom rose, hauled back a fist, and let go at the bartender's jaw. The guy flew into a rack of bottles. Only a few crashed to the floor and shattered as he slid onto his ass, legs out straight, his head lolling on his shoulders.

"Good one. Looks like you cracked his mandibular again. Got that out of your system, Dom?" asked Remi.

"Yeah. I've been feeling a little down. That helped."

"I was just saying we need a KOC order," Remi said, clapping his hand onto Ely's shoulder.

"Even kill-on-contact extinctions have become boring. We need an interesting assignment," said Ely.

Peeking over the bar, Dom said, "Get the fuck up, asswipe. Pour me another Dead Manhattan."

Leaning forward on an elbow, Remi asked, "Where's Ohngel? I thought you were on assignment with him."

Ohngel was the fire-winged assassin, one of the Feard. He had mated an Aeternal, a witch named Indigo. The OneCreator, being a sap for true love, allowed their brother-in-arms to travel between here and the realm of Scath with his mate. The OC also permitted her to accompany him anywhere in OneWorld.

"Nope. I was flying solo. He and his mate are on something Indigo called a honeymoon," said Dom.

A stranger interrupted, slapping a mottled hand on Ely's upper arm. "Hey, aren't you guys the Feard, the OneCreator's winged assassins?"

Ely brushed off the guy's misplaced palm and glared over his shoulder. "So what?"

The Scourge lowered his voice as if letting them in on a conspiracy. "I've got intel. What can I get for it?"

"Your teeth get to stay in your mouth," said Remi.

When the guy buttoned up, Ely said, "One free pass when you do something stupid. And you will."

The male thought for a moment. "This is worth more. What's the one steadfast rule we must all obey?"

"Never run from the Feard," said Dom.

The guy puzzled his brows, a wrinkle between them. "Another one."

"Do not tell the OC to fuck off," said Ely.

The guy sighed. "No. Another."

"Do not bring an outsider onto Angor," said Remi.

"Bingo." The Scourge scratched his arm. A chunk

of skin peeled off and fell to the ground, a sure sign he was a Flesh Eater.

Ely snapped out his wings. The ice-bladed feathers unsheathed and nearly decapped the stranger. "Oops. Not sorry." Obviously having found the exciting assignment he was looking for, Ely glanced at Dom and Remi. "Here we go again. How long has it been?"

"Not long enough," said the black-winged assassin. "Maybe three centuries?"

Ely tossed back what was left of his brew while Remi scrubbed a hand across his eyes.

Dom pushed off his stool, fisting the front of the informant's ragged shirt. "What's your name, Scourge?"

"Ike."

"Well, Ike, tell us about the outsider." Dom's upper lip curled into a sneer, his no-nonsense, do-what-I-say expression.

"I want to negotiate."

Remi asked, "What do you expect for the intel?"

"I want time off from all Ordeals."

Dom answered the Scourge. "Not happening. Besides, we have no say-so. That's up to the OC or Harmony. If your shit is important, we'll negotiate to keep you out of a few Ordeals of your choice."

Ike looked as if he was thinking about the deal, but that assumed he was capable of rational thought. He scratched his arm again, opening a sore. "Deal. Time off from three punishments of my choice."

Dom nodded. "Spill."

"The outsider's a human."

The news exploded like a bomb blast. OneWorld was restricted. Vast was for Immortals. Angor for Scourges. Never. Never. Humans. And for good reason. Earthers were weak creatures who would be easy prey for Immortals and easier prey for Scourges. Besides, the

OneCreator had a very protective fondness for them.

Ely's eyes pinged from Remi to Dom. "What the fuck?"

Dominion guzzled his Dead Manhattan and jacked onto his feet. "Time to earn our pay. Shit just got very interesting, huh, Ely?"

T.M. SMITH

Chapter Three

On the street in front of the Angor Management Club, Dom released his grip on Ike, the Scourge-dash-snitch. "Well, where is this human?"

Rubbing the back of his neck hard enough to slough off skin, Ike stuttered, "I-I-I have to show you."

"We have trust issues," said Remi, speaking for everyone.

The Feard warriors finished the convo telepathically.

What's the worst that could happen? Dom shifted from one foot to the other as he pathed his brethren.

A bored Ely rested a hand on the hilt of a short blade in his hip holster. *A shitload of Scourges could be waiting to jump us.*

And that would hurt us how, Ely? Dom frowned, not sure what the problem was. They were Immortals, and other than themselves, no one except the OneCreator or Michael could extinct them.

His ice-winged brethren turned an empty gaze to Dom. *They can't kill us, but we could be laid up for a while if there were enough of them.*

When did you get to be such a wuss? asked Remi.

Ely's eyes narrowed to angry slits. *Not. I could use a real dust-up to keep me awake. Just throwing out a possibility.*

Dom scrubbed a fist across his jaw. *I'll fly above the Scourge, keeping pace with him. You two stay on his ass. Be ready for a surprise once we land.*

"Let's go, Ike." Dom's ebony wings spread wide as he pounded into the air. The Scourge popped off the ground next with Remi and Ely following him. They skimmed the rooftops, taking a route toward the industrial district.

Newly arrived inmates in Angor or those who were too stupid to move up in status worked in the factories here in Stupool. No safety standards. They breathed chemicals, sooty air, and toxic fumes. A dark cloud of smog enveloped the area, a thick, nasty haze vomiting from smokestacks. Not that it could kill them, but getting air in the zone was like breathing underwater and had them hacking up black spit.

After Ike signaled below, he angled toward the ground, coming in for a soft landing on a street. "She's in this d-d-district, but the alleyway gets n-n-narrow. We have to walk."

Dom snagged his upper arm, nearly yanking him off his feet. "She? You didn't tell us the human was a female."

"Does it matter?" The Scourge's cheek twitched.

Dom distrusted beings with nervous tics. They weren't reliable. "Where we goin'?"

Ike pointed straight ahead, leading the way.

Dom's gaze took in both sides of the alley. What a dump. Course that assessment pretty much held for all of Angor, except where the assassins lived. The largest city, Stupool, was a dismal industrial jungle of factories, flesh bars, BDSM joints, roads clogged with cars emitting carbon monoxide, and streets ripe with smells and things you didn't want to think about. Whenever possible, he avoided strolling the avenues, wading through sewage that leeched onto the street.

Beyond the city were the Ordeals—Blood Volcano, Slough of Despair, Blades Forest, Violence Village. And more. Each spot was a punishment zone for Scourges.

Angor was often shrouded in fog and storm

clouds, the sky dim, a palpable gloom that ranged from shadowy to inky. Yet the fickle weather would change in an instant. Gentle breezes turned to gale-like winds and tornadoes, light mists transformed into monsoon rains, and black skies heralded sunshine. One moment, you slapped on sunscreen and dark shades on a hot, bright day. The next, you buttoned up your fur-lined jacket against the stormy skies and intermittent light, a cold, icy, stark place as cruel as those it contained.

Nonetheless, centuries ago, the Feard had elected to live in the White Mountains of Angor rather than among their kind in Vast. Each winged assassin had a different reason for the relocation. Ohngel had grown weary of the politics of Vast, the OC's favored dimension. Ely, bored with immortality, was game for anything new. Dom wanted to distance himself from those he might have to capture or kill another day, as he'd done with Gareth. Remi? Well, who knew why the bronze spike-winged assassin did anything.

The Feard had built their homes on cliffs high in the mountains, open to the air and overlooking the ocean and Scutter Shoals Bay. In that territory, they thrived in the unpredictable environment, far from Vast's politics, other Immortals, and the ennui of eternity.

Though they lived among the Scourges of Angor, the same detritus the Feard tracked, captured, or extincted, there was an honesty to this dimension that Vast lacked. The OneCreator's home base was a place of disguises, platitudes, and intrigues. And it had its own miscreants, sometimes as dangerous as Scourges.

Behind Dom, Ely cleared his throat. *We're heading into a warehouse zone. Keep sharp.*

Dom answered by flicking out his onyx-tipped wings, some with sheathed razor-edged feathers. Then he swooshed them into his spine. "Ike, we better get there soon. I'm getting itchy. When I get itchy, shit dies."

The Scourge pivoted around, his eyes wide with fear. "Just a little farther. H-h-honest." He resumed walking forward.

Dom listened as Remi rambled on about his kinks. *This place smells like the ass-end of a pig. Not my favorite perfume. I prefer a nicely showered female Scourge wearing a leather garter belt, fishnet stockings, and nipple rings. She's carrying a whip and chain.*

Remi had a thing for fucking Angor inmates. The more pain, the more pleasure. For someone who could light up a dimension with his broad, dimpled smile and deep amber eyes, he could be dark and destructive.

But Dom was in no position to judge. He enjoyed a weekly visit from the Scourge Mora, and he dabbled in other local females as well as several in Vast. He had one steadfast rule, though—no emotional connections. Sex for the sake of sex. If a female got too clingy, too demanding, she was history.

Ike halted. He gestured toward a tall metal door. "H-h-here. I'll wait outside."

"You wish," said Dom. "You'll be keepin' us company. In fact, you'll be first through the entrance. Thanks for volunteering to be target practice."

"But Praevus is mean."

The Feard flicked their gazes from one to the other. "That fucking Mind Rat," said Remi. "Is he our mark?"

The Scourge nodded.

Dom grabbed the handle, jerked on it, and, grabbing the back of Ike's ragged tee, shoved him through the door. The Scourge stumbled, falling to the ground. The Feard stepped over him, Ely and Remi racing forward to flank their brother assassin.

Nothing.

The place was empty. Dom's nostrils quivered as he picked up a faint scent beneath the stale air of the warehouse. The female. She had a rich, layered aroma. He had sensed something similar before. It was when he had been in the OneCreator's library in Vast. *Books.* Ancient ones. Classics. The boundless array of learning had appealed to his senses. And floating just above that scholarly bouquet was the spice of the skies beyond his home, the free territory between Vast and Angor. Also, OneWorld's oranges. He drew a deep breath, wanting to remember the complicated smells. Wanting to roll around in them. Books, oranges, and fresh, free air.

Boots echoed across the massive warehouse as the Feard searched.

Ely paused beside a back wall. "We got ropes here. Looks like she was cut loose." He eyed the ground. "The only footprints belong to a male. No female has feet that big. He must have carried her off."

Rummaging in boxes scattered throughout the cavernous space, Remi shouted, "Looks like Praevus boogied out in a hurry. Nothing good here."

Dom stroked his chin. "Ike, get the fuck over here."

The Scourge pushed off the ground and raced across the warehouse. "This is where she was. I swear. You owe me."

"Yeah. Yeah. She was here. We'll pay what we owe. But part of the deal is you report whatever you hear. If I find out you're holding back, I'll put you through a meat grinder. Literally. First pain, followed by non-existence at the end of my blade."

The Feard most often extincted because of an order from the OC. But not always. Faced with a situation, they could use their own judgment.

"I-I-I'd never ch-ch-cheat you, Dominion."

"Get lost. We'll be checking on you."

As Ike hustled out the door, disappearing into the alley, the assassins confabbed. Ohngel was on his fucking honeymoon. But to Dom, the Feard would always be short a member. He stared into space, missing his friend Gareth and their adventures. They'd raced across the sky to see who was faster. Challenged each other to sword fights. Shared willing Immortals in bed. Tossed back drinks at a bar, enjoying the camaraderie of friendship.

Ely interrupted Dom's memory-lane trip. "We could use Ohngel. This is shaping up to be more than a three-man job."

"Damn straight," muttered Remi. "Their honeymoon is over. We need him. The search for Praevus and this human female requires a full crew to tear Angor apart."

Dom hesitated because Ohngel had insisted that he and Indigo have some alone time, free from business in Angor or Vast. Screw their me time. This was serious. "I'll call him in, and we'll divvy up the tasks. Ely, you hit the hot spots, the clubs, the hangouts, the joints frequented by Scourges. Remi, you see what you can learn at the Ordeals. I'll be on the ground, scouring streets and alleys. We'll assign Ohngel to flyovers, stopping any place that looks promising."

After Ely and Remi headed off on their assignments, Dom rubbed his sightless eye. It ached today. Pain in his barometer was never a good sign, a signal something bad was about to happen.

He strolled out of the alley. Stretching his midnight wings, he shot into the air, his flight taking him into the passageway that led out of Angor. From there, he traveled to Scath, the realm of a species called Aeternals, where Ohngel's mate resided.

First stop, Indigo's office. Dom could have pathed

his brother-in-arms, but he was certain Ohngel would cut him off. This situation required a face-to-face and, perhaps, muscled persuasion.

Not long ago their fire-winged assassin brother had saved Scath's Aeternals and Earth's humans. But the OneCreator had a non-interference rule. When Ohngel violated it, he was put in stasis. Eventually he'd been forgiven and offered his old job back.

In a surprise move, the OC reinstated Ohngel and allowed Indigo to travel with him in OneWorld. For some reason, the boss was soft on the mouthy witch from Scath. And the couple fascinated Dom. He couldn't understand the bond they had formed. Anyway, they were still on what the witch called their honeymoon. His assassin brethren said it meant he didn't have to chase asshole Immortals and could fuck the days and nights away.

Time's up.

Ohngel needed to clock in on the job, but Indigo's office was empty. Since Dom knew the witch spent hours at the River Am, reading the water for images of possible futures or hints of trouble, he winged his way there.

Dom spotted the couple swimming in a calm pool, dammed by boulders and fallen trees. Hovering above them, he watched their riveting play for a while before he floated to the bank of the river.

Laughing, Ohngel dunked his mate under the water. Then his head snapped around. "What the hell, Dom? Indy, stay put." The fire-winged assassin strode up the incline, naked, threatening, muttering something like, "Fucking intruders. Fucking up my fucking good time."

Once Ohngel was out of the river, he fashioned clothes with a flick of his wrist, faster than re-donning his own, which were in a pile near a tree.

The dark-haired witch glared at Dom as she stood

neck-deep in the pool. "Roark, make me something to wear." She still called him Roark, even though she knew his real name. It had been his alias when she'd first met him.

"They'll be wet," he growled, his pissed-off gaze fixed on Dom.

"Then how about a swimsuit?" she shouted.

When she exited the water, Indigo was dressed in a vintage bathing outfit, navy blue, a blousy top, a bow at the neckline, and pantaloons below her knees. She glanced down and rolled her eyes. "Really?"

Ohngel shrugged.

She joined the males to sit on the grassy bank. "Welcome, O frowning one," she said.

Settling his onyx-tipped wings into his spine, Dom stretched his legs straight. "We have a problem, Ohngel. Praevus the Mind Rat has a human in Angor. We had a lead, but he'd already vacated with her. Whereabouts unknown."

"An Earther in Angor?" Ohngel's brows arched.

"A female," Dom emphasized.

The mated couple exchanged glances and nods. Indigo slapped her thigh and said, "Knights in shining armor to the rescue."

"What do you need me to do?" Ohngel looked at his Feard brother, still grinning at his mate's comment.

"Flyovers."

"How can I help?" asked Indigo.

"You can't," blurted Dom.

"Don't make me witch bolt you, O dark, misogynistic one." Indigo crossed her bare feet at her ankles. "I'll be joining Hotness for the task."

Though Ohngel laughed, Dom still didn't understand this warrior's attraction to the sassy but powerful mage from Scath. The fire-winged assassin, who lived for the hunt, needed to get her under control. "You can't fly."

"True. But I have my loyal Oskar."

She summoned a modified gryphon she'd once claimed to have "bedazzled" with scales. He was unique, having the head and wings of an eagle, the neck and torso of a dragon, and the haunches and feet of a lion.

He plopped onto his fat rump and snorted, sending out sparks of fire that landed on Dom. The black-winged assassin brushed off the hot spots. "Do that again and you're toast."

Indigo patted her gryphon's haunch. "There. There. He didn't mean it."

Dom snapped, "You can't take the gryphon into Angor or Vast.

"Hmm." Indigo scratched her chin. "A problem in need of a resolution."

Ohngel didn't look happy, probably because Indigo sounded as if she had a scheme in mind.

T.M. SMITH

Chapter Four

Madeline awakened, bouncing on Praevus's shoulder as he scurried through a door into a deserted alley. Once clear of the narrow passage, the monster took to the air, bat wings shooting from his spine, pounding up and down to lift off the ground. Maddy screamed, unable to hold back her shock and fear.

Holy shit. I'm gonna die.

When he shifted her in his arms, cradling her like a baby, she watched buildings get smaller and smaller until he leveled out and zoomed forward. They soared above a crumbling, shabby urban area, the air filthy, factories belching noxious exhaust through chimneys.

Abruptly, Praevus changed the angle of flight, eliciting a gasp from Maddy. He straightened the slant of his body, his wings pounding up and down. His boots touched the ground near one of the fume-spewing factories.

Setting Madeline on her feet, he maintained a firm grasp on her wrist. Though shaky, she attempted to peel off his fingers, but Praevus was too strong.

He looked both ways, then opened a metal door and shoved her inside. She fell to her knees. Another cavernous warehouse, dark and reeking of mold and mildew. She heard the snick of a switch.

Light.

Madeline fought Praevus as he bound her wrists and ankles with rope. He won easily and would have even if her arms and legs hadn't been so weak.

Her gaze flicked from the monster to her surroundings. The concrete was filthy, with dark blotches of God knew what. But since she trembled from exhaustion, she flopped onto the floor with her back to the wall, her legs straight out in front of her. Maddy refused to think about what was under her, including any bugs or rats in residence.

New digs. Same problem. What did he want with her? What plan could she devise to escape? She couldn't break free from the ropes, though she kept trying. Best thing was to stay alert. Wait for an opportunity. But if she got away, where would she go?

Focus. Don't worry about that now. Devise an escape first.

To calm herself, she ignored Praevus and mentally shelved books in the library, using the Dewey Decimal System while she tugged on the restraints at her wrists. The result was to open fresh wounds on unhealed skin. Able to reach the bindings securing her ankles, she gave them a jerk. Not going anywhere.

When she lost focus, Madeline felt herself slipping into old, destructive patterns—watching someone else, waiting for them to act, being afraid they would, and losing control of her environment. She wanted to run or curl into a ball, duck her head, and hide. She shook off the disabling behavior.

No!

Once, her sisters had returned home to find her cowering in a closet, hiding from their drunken mother. After hugging her and telling her she was safe, they scolded her. Darya made her plan a different way to deal with the problem, one where she would be in control. Life was about control.

That's what she needed now. Madeline drew in a calming breath through her nose, refusing to even blink. That tiny motion might be all it took to dissolve any sense of control, any sense of order and precision she might gain from the breath. Like when she'd been at the mercy of an alcoholic parent.

Interrupting her reminiscences, Praevus pulled a chair on wheels close to her and sat down, elbows on knees. He stared at her.

She held the monster's fixed gaze. "What do you plan to do with me?"

Praevus straightened and smiled, but his grin was far more terrifying than his slumped posture and grim stare. He tilted his chin to one side. Then the other. He scratched his jaw. "I'm beginning now. Pay close attention because I am a master of my craft."

Bending forward, he set a palm to each of her cheeks, squeezing her face between them. Pain shot through Maddy's head, churning her stomach. Instead of barfing, she slammed her eyes shut tight while she concentrated on driving out the agonizing headache.

When the pain lessened, she reorganized her closet, putting the items in alphabetical order. Blouses, pants, t-shirts…

Praevus jumped to his feet and grabbed a fistful of her blonde hair. "Stop it," he screamed. His white eyes blazed with anger.

Stop what?

Maybe it was her concentration on arranging her wardrobe. She chuckled. He didn't like her itty-bitty OCD thoughts.

Screw him.

Though he continued to hold a chunk of her hair, he relaxed his grip. "I can see you will take time."

She grouped the closet items by color. Blue, green, red… Then, by season and, finally, by length, creating a beautiful diagonal line of hanging clothes.

Eventually, Praevus stomped off, leveling her with an evil, melodramatic cackle. "You are so fun."

When darkness swallowed an exhausted

Madeline, her antagonist starred in her nightmares.

When she awoke, Praevus offered her a plate of food. Bound with her wrists in front of her, she fed herself. Madeline pushed the items around, sampling small bites, not trusting the meal he'd set on the floor beside her. It might be drugged. Still, what choice did she have? If she didn't eat, she'd weaken and be unable to escape when an opportunity arose.

With a spoon of something resembling fruit salad hovering near her lips, she stared into Praevus's unnatural, freakish white eyes. She shoved the bite inside her mouth. *Not so bad.* The man was depraved, and whatever he had done to her made her temples pound like the drum solo in a heavy metal band's song. She swallowed a second taste, her arm quivering from fatigue or fear.

Praevus snatched the plate away before she finished. "Time for another session." He pulled his chair close again, reaching out to touch her hair, resting an unwelcome hand on her head.

He was rummaging around in her mind. *Crazy, huh?*

Twisting her head from side to side, she dislodged his palm. With more wiggle room in the rope, she raised her hands to fight the dissolute Scourge.

When she scratched his face, he slapped her so hard her teeth rattled. "Enough," he screamed, his white eyes an imitation of flashing headlights as blood dripped down his cheeks. One point for the prisoner.

While she was recovering from the blow, he fisted her hair. Maddy's eyes rolled up as pain shot through her. "Stop. W-w-what are you doing?" She just wanted relief from the bulleting agony. Praevus was a dentist drilling out a deep cavity, striking nerves without the benefit of Novocain.

She'd recited the Dewey Decimal Classification System. She'd re-organized her closet. Time for famous authors in alpha order while she ignored the throbbing spasms rocketing through her, a dark cloud eclipsing her concentration. But she forged ahead. American. Alcott. Angelou. Baldwin. Faulkner. Fitzgerald. Hemingway. Lee. O'Connor …

Once Praevus removed his hand from her head, she sighed with immediate relief. Still, something was wrong. She'd been … violated. She felt dirty, as if his fingers had been everywhere. She'd been mind-raped.

Madeline struggled to speak. "W-w-what? W-w-why?" Slurred words tumbled from her mouth.

Wiping sweat from his brow, Praevus leaned back in his chair. "I am making you mine." His shoulders slumped and he released an exhausted sigh.

Maddy's chin rolled to her chest, but she jerked up to fix on his crazed, chalky eyes. "D-d-don't understand."

"It's none of your concern. After I rest, I have an errand. Don't miss me too much." He cackled.

Worst movie villain ever.

But Madeline couldn't let go of his words. "I am making you mine."

No. Never. Not happening.

Still, how do you fight someone who can touch your mind? Make it feel dirty, violated?

When he returned, she resisted the next incursion by focusing on alphabetizing canned goods. Darya and Fia had drummed survival into her. They taught her control, that every situation had a way out, that she could protect herself, and that she was self-reliant.

But she collapsed, dreaming. She returned to the house with her drunken mother. Surrounded by empty booze bottles and overflowing ashtrays, the woman hurled insults, blaming Madeline for everything. For the father who had left. For her miserable life. For her addiction. For the steady stream of men who wouldn't stick around.

"No," Maddy shouted, jolting awake.

I am responsible for myself. For every situation, there is a solution. I will get out of here because I'm in control.

But something wasn't right. Her head bobbed forward when the dark cloud swallowed her again.

****

Praevus studied the human from a shadowy corner, eager to continue his sessions with Madeline but content to observe for the moment. He was lucky a Scourge had warned him of Ike's betrayal so he could escape with the female. The hard-won prize he'd found at his employer's cabin in the Razor Mountains.

Serita, the trustee Scourge who was his boss at the restaurant, had called him to her place to give him an assignment. She told him she would be absent from her cafe for a while and asked him to manage it while she was gone.

That's when he heard a sound from the other room. Sheets rustled as someone tossed and turned in their sleep. Curious, he shoved inside to find a human tied to the bed, a delicious female whose mind was ripe for the taking. Praevus lost control of his urges. After nearly beheading his employer with his bare hands, he stole Madeline. After all, he deserved a chance to use his gift. Then he panicked.

Stupid. Stupid. Stupid. But the deed was done. Now he would enjoy the fruits of his rashness.

Stroking a palm across his jaw, he tilted his head to the side. The pretty young thing was unconscious again. Though her blonde, chin-length hair was dirty, the choppy cut gave her an air of innocence. She was a tall female with a trim but lush body. Revealed beneath a torn white blouse, her breasts were full. He closed his eyes to imagine testing their weight. He'd raped her mind. In time, her flesh would be his. His cock stirred, a rarity for him these days.

Not yet.

She was a fighter. Usually, he abhorred strong females, preferring fractured, subservient ones. Still, he loved the prospect of breaking this one, splintering her mind. He would enjoy the look in her eyes once she realized her will was shattered. His mouth watered with anticipation.

She woke.

Her breathing steadied. She appeared calm, pinning him with a glare as she sat with her back against the wall, her bound legs out straight in front of her. Despite her controlled expression, he sensed her mind floundering in chaos, screaming with fear. Yet she refused to show it. *Interesting.* Earlier she had proved a strong subject, fighting his invasion. He would ramp up his efforts.

"Hello, Madeline. Are you happy to see me again?"

Her lips squeezed tight. Her eyes narrowed.

He grabbed the back of his chair and dragged it across the floor, the scritch of metal on concrete echoing through the cavernous warehouse. Sitting near her, he leaned forward and slapped a hand on her head, curling his fingers so she could not escape his grasp.

Once she stopped whipping from side to side, he began.

To Praevus, the mind housed a beautiful, intricate series of underground burrows that turned left, right, up, and down, a maze of interconnected pathways. He always started at the outermost point before working his way inside. The closer he traveled to the center, the greater his control over the being.

Most often he slipped into the first tunnel with ease, the shaft to the mind open, allowing access. Later he might come across a collapsed area—that was how he thought of it—where he had to dig through rubble. If he ran into a wall of debris, he recognized it as damage. Then he backtracked until he could plow forward again.

Madeline required more effort. He realized this from his earlier attempt to breach the exterior of her will. When he could not find an unobstructed shaft, he had left, too exhausted and puzzled to continue. Now he resumed the task with a re-invigorated determination.

He still saw no doorway that led deeper into her mind. Continuing to explore the outer surface, he sought a way inside.

Ah. There it is.

A gigantic metal door. Sturdy. He pulled on the handle. When it didn't budge, he leveraged a phantom foot on the frame and tugged.

No success.

Praevus paused in his failed pursuit so he could study Madeline. She drew her lips into a grim slash. Her facial muscles tensed with the pain of a headache caused by his intrusion. He rose from his chair, stretched his arms overhead, and bent left and then right. Altering a mind and setting triggers was a physical task as well as a mental one. He laced his fingers together and curved them until he heard cracking sounds.

Better.

Back inside her brain again, he sought a way to disrupt her battle against him. At the imaginary doorway, he turned around, pretending to ignore his task. As he suspected, Madeline, weary from the struggle, relaxed.

When she did, he barreled through with a sneak attack.

Success.

He made it into the first tunnel, deception being a marvelous tool.

Praevus, Mind Rat extraordinaire, halted, examining his location and what surrounded him. Hers was unlike any mind he had breached before. Most, even those of Immortals, were open, more easily accessed. But in Madeline's brain, a burrow in front of him had collapsed, requiring him to dig. Metaphorically, dirt, pebbles, and larger rocks filled it.

He clawed through. When he hit a clear patch, he caught his breath and scurried ahead.

Damn. Another collapse.

Praevus dug his way forward.

After hours, sweat dripped into his eyes, his arms quivered from tension, and his own head ached from the labor. Praevus released his hold on the human. To preserve his strength, he would require more than a couple of days for this mission.

He could use brute force, but that would leave Madeline a drooling, useless blob of flesh. Using stealth and finesse, he would be more pleased with the result. She would become a thrall to his desires, his errand girl, his slavish lover, his waitress, his housekeeper, his cook, his admirer, his greatest fan.

Using his skills on the Scourges in Angor was unrewarding. Their brains did not exercise his superior Mind Rat talents. But now, he was free to do what he wished to this human.

When he retreated from her mind, her eyelashes flickered, indicating she was equally tired.

Rising from his chair, Praevus stretched his arms and rolled his shoulders several times. He cracked his knuckles. Shaking out his hands, he planted his ass back in the torn leather seat. He cradled a palm on her head again to hold her in place and because touch was necessary with someone of her will.

"Once more, my dear." He smiled though she did not see him. Still, she fought him, her eyes clamped tight. *Valiant.* Eventually he would win.

To distract her while he invaded, he shared incidents from his life, his eons in Vast, his unfair capture, and his many punishments since his arrival in Angor. Once his words lulled her, he drew a deep breath, traveling to the last point of his intrusion.

Determined, he once again faced collapsed rubble. Larger metaphorical boulders blocked his path. With effort, he heaved them aside until he cleared the way.

Strolling forward, he paused to admire how her mind worked. It was well-shielded. Trauma, perhaps. But he was an expert Mind Rat. With a phantom hand, he touched a thin-membraned wall, planting a command that would activate later.

A trigger.

Several steps ahead, he plunged downward. *Unusual.* The pathway on which he strode had given way, tumbling him into an unexpected shaft. He must be more careful. She was a dangerous subject. He risked getting lost or injured while manipulating her will. Praevus created an imaginary ladder and climbed out of the pit to continue his journey.

Damn. Another mound of debris.

He needed food and rest. Never had he been so challenged. What a delight the human turned out to be. Such a great self-reward.

His boss, Serita, had become involved in something big. After he had worked for her at the restaurant in Angor a long time, she offered him a hush-hush job. On the side. When he consented to be her errand boy, she freed him from the Ordeals and gave him better accommodations. She had powerful friends in high places, but he had blown that deal when he attacked her and stole the Madeline.

Again he planted what he liked to think of as a bomb, or trigger, that would explode at a later date. If Madeline passed from his hands to another's, this would be a pleasant surprise for her new owner. Praevus had no doubt that she'd eventually be taken from him. He chuckled with delight.

Mind Rats came in many varieties. At the low end of the spectrum were those who did nothing but destroy brain matter, leaving their victims catatonic. *Sloppy*. A middling ability allowed the Rat to twist the subject to their will. He possessed that skill. But at the upper end were those few who set triggers to activate later. This prowess made him special.

After planting the second trigger, Praevus released his hold on Madeline and wobbled to his feet.

Yes. Food and rest.

Her chin bobbled to her chest when she fell into unconsciousness. He had to be careful to keep her alive. Despite her strong mind, human flesh was weak. Nonetheless, Praevus had not had so much fun since his capture. Once again, he was somebody, a master of his art. How dare the OneCreator call his gift a malady. It was his genius. His greatness.

If Serita suffered for what he gained, so be it. He owed her nothing.

T.M. SMITH

Chapter Five

Maddy woke curled face down on cold concrete. She licked her lips. Thirsty again. Her cheek scraped the gritty floor. Rolling onto her back, she flung her arms to the side.

Something was different.

Realizing her wrists and ankles were unbound, she wobbled to a sitting position. Her eyes wide, Madeline checked out the warehouse, twisting left. Right. She listened. No sounds. She called out. No answer except an echo.

Maddy scooted until her spine flattened against the wall. With a tentative push, she rose from the floor, brushing off the dust that clung to her soiled skirt, torn white shirt, and face. Her gaze pinged around the room while she crept along, palms to the wall to steady herself.

She was alone.

Praevus was gone, and she wasn't chained like a psycho's prisoner. Why? No time to think about her good fortune. She continued her exploration of the dimly lit warehouse. Being barefoot, she made no noise. At a tall metal door, she paused. Drawing a deep breath, Madeline opened it to eyeball the street outside.

Damn.

It led into a crowded alley where leather-winged beings like Praevus shuffled to and fro. No way was she going out there. After she snapped the door shut, she plastered her back against the warehouse wall and slid to the floor, unconcerned with the dirt. She pulled her knees to her chest and held them tightly.

Maddy willed tears not to fall. Crying useless. Al-Anon and her older sisters had taught her to approach problems with a clear mind. Panic muddled thoughts. Tears drowned them. She was a cautious person who thought situations through, examining the pros and cons of an issue from every side. She weighed the consequences. Only then did she act. Should she buy the blue shirt on the rack in her favorite boutique shop? Pro—it was the latest style and cute. Con—it was expensive, and she already had one in a similar color. So, no. Turmoil was unsettling because sometimes it called for a snap decision.

Order. Control.

The story of Maddy's life. She ironed her jeans, applied her makeup perfectly, and got a weekly mani-pedi. She liked chatting with friends at bars, flipped off bad drivers, booed the umps at Cardinal games, and enjoyed rare sexual relationships. Not being quiet or demure, she defied many librarian stereotypes. Still, her career choice fit her most necessary requirements. In addition to the each-book-in-its-place kind of order, it rarely required an instant decision.

Now, her heart pounded, a hammer against her ribs. Her chest bounced with rapid, shallow breaths.

Relax. Think. What happened to her escape plan?

She breathed in through her nose. Out through her mouth. She dropped her shoulders. What did she control? She could move around in the empty warehouse. She could open the door to leave. She could crawl into a corner, curl into a fetal position, and sob.

What didn't she control? Praevus could return at any moment. Her clothes were dirty and ripped. She didn't know where she was. If she went outside, she would be among people like her captor. Lots of them. Most of all, she couldn't control what they would do to her.

Deep breath. Stand up. Choose. I can control the

choices I make.

Maddy cracked the door again, eying the busy alley. She opened it wider to slip out of the warehouse. Decision made. Part three of talk show host Lizette Lee's strategy was in play. She was escaping. Carrying out her plan.

People bumped her shoulders, jostling her, barely giving her time to glance around at the surroundings before sweeping her along. They seemed too distracted to notice her.

Good.

Outside, the day was cloudy and cold. She clasped the fabric of her torn blouse together, shivering, her teeth chattering. A passerby, showing actual fangs, growled at her when she bumped into him.

With her hand clutching her shirt, she fixed her gaze on the ground while she scurried forward. When she reached a corner, she dared to challenge the crowd by weaving through them to turn right as they continued on their way.

Using her peripheral vision, she observed that most walkers wore tattered, soiled clothes. A few had slightly better attire. Some veered into storefronts which lined the street. Others kept a stuttering pace, heading for destinations further along. They all looked scared. Like her.

Assessment.

She was in a busy city. The neighborhood wasn't upscale. Trash spilled out of knocked-over cans. Windows were grimy or boarded up. Paint peeled from crumbling exterior walls.

A strong wind blew, pushing her faster as she stumbled. As quickly as the gale had started, it stopped.

Swallowing the lump in her throat, Madeline hurried forward, her feet cold, sticky, and cut from shattered glass that littered the sidewalk.

Walking until she nearly collapsed, she finally rested against a graffitied wall. The crowds thinned as people disappeared from the street. An already dim sky darkened. Though a crowded city was scary, an empty one at night would be worse.

When the wind kicked up again as the climate changed, debris churned through the air. Madeline curled her free hand around her eyes as a shield and shoved off. A strong breeze brought hot air, pushing out the cold. With a ragged sleeve, she wiped sweat from her forehead.

Can't the weather make up its mind?

Maddy thought of sleep, would love to sleep, but that was not an option. She stopped in front of a shop with a clean window. Chancing it, she opened the door. Inside, a woman screamed. A lump stuck in Maddy's throat as she spun around, too afraid to investigate.

Nope. Not there.

She hustled on her way, hopping on one foot to pull a shard of glass from the other heel. Tired, she paused again, staring at the graffiti, which was more plentiful than paint on the buildings. The favorites were *HELP* or *EXTINCT THE OC*, whatever that meant.

Madeline stumbled, falling to the concrete, fighting the desire to cry. Sobbing never solved a problem, she reminded herself. But damn, it was getting hard to resist. Brushing a strand of dirty blonde hair out of her eyes, she got onto her scraped knees, pushed to her bare feet, threw back her shoulders, and continued on her way.

She paused in front of a well-lit bar where she considered going inside because a public place should provide safety. When she stared through the open doorway, however, her premise fell apart. Loud music blasted her ears while patrons pounded each other with their fists, and drinks flew across the room. She wrinkled her nose. Stale cigarettes and spilled booze.

When she backed away, three behemoths stopped beating the shit out of each other to snap their faces in her direction. Their hair hung limp on their shoulders while their mouths twisted into a strange pucker as if they prepared to whistle. Their dreamy-like eyes almost drew her to them.

But she shook off their mesmerizing appeal. Horrified by the sight, she limped off. In the weather's ever-fickle manner, rain fell from the dark sky. What little light there was from streetlamps dimmed behind a downpour.

She spied a wrecked, abandoned car on the curb. The rear bumper dangled on the ground, the hood was ajar, and the grill was bent. She peeked inside. Empty.

While ignoring the dirty, torn front seat, Madeline opened the door to slide in. She prayed the locks worked. They did. *Click.* Feeling a bit safer for the moment, she curled onto her side.

As the radio talk show psychologist Lizette Lee had advised, she'd identified the problem, planned an escape, and carried out the plan. Now, she faced round two. She'd analyze the new situation and run it through the steps later. She was so exhausted she closed her eyes for a minute.

Maddy's lids fluttered. Just a short nap. Haunted by her past, she was in limbo, caught in a restless dream-awake state.

Her biological parent, or parents, had abandoned her in front of a Catholic church in St. Louis when she was an infant. She never sought their identity. They hadn't wanted her. She didn't want them. Then shortly after her arrival at the orphanage, the Williamsons had adopted her.

For years, she was the treasured, spoiled only child in a wealthy family. She remembered snippets with her new parents. They showered her with gifts on birthdays or holidays, took her on fun vacations to Disneyland or the beach, and were kind, caring, and devoted to each other as well as to her. She rode on her father's shoulders to watch parades, ran into the kitchen smelling chocolate chip cookies, and learned to bait a hook on a fishing trip. They laughed easily and often.

She attended an exclusive preschool. Her mother enrolled her in every imaginable class—voice, dance, piano. Nothing stuck. She lacked those creative talents, but she was told not to worry. She would find her talent elsewhere. She was a clever child.

All was good. But age eight was a pivotal year. It's when the arguments began. Late at night in her bed, she'd hear her parents' angry, muffled voices, objects being tossed, and doors slamming when her father left the house. Then, her mother's tears flowed.

The fights centered around drinking. Being young, Madeline didn't understand why water, coffee, or soda would matter because they had plenty of money for groceries.

One night, after a horrible, loud fight, her mother came into Maddy's room, still wiping moisture from her eyes. She sat on the edge of the bed, patting the blankets, cocooning her in them. "I know you're awake. I'm sorry about all this mess. Though your dad and I are going through a rough patch, I have a solution. The orphanage called about two girls who need fostering. I think they could take our focus off these ridiculous problems. Would you like sisters?"

Madeline rolled onto her back, shifting her arms on top of the blankets. "Would they be nice?"

"The nun assured me they are."

"Would they sleep in my room?"

"No. This space will always be yours. Only yours. We have two spare rooms for the girls. We'll convert my sewing room to guest quarters."

"Will they play with me?"

"Of course they will, even though they are a bit older. They will be your big sisters, great friends."

Fiamma was eleven when she joined the Williamson family. Darya was a year older. Both girls were everything Maddy's mother had promised. They were nice, and they played with her. Mostly. Sometimes, they ran off and did big girl things, but they always made it up to her later, baking cookies, playing house or school, or drawing pictures.

The mother and father stopped arguing about drinking. The household was far too busy for family fights. Fia excelled at voice lessons, eventually having a private coach. Darya danced and enrolled in the best ballet school. Madeline sometimes accompanied them, amazed at their talents.

Once, when she told them she was jealous, the sisters sat her down for a stern conversation. They explained that Fia was the singer, Darya was the dancer, and Madeline was the smart, scholarly one. Each girl had a gift. And while they were not alike, each would be a star.

Darya, the oldest said, "Revel in what you have, not in what you lack or what others possess."

When her sisters walked her home from school, the other kids crowded around, amazed at their beauty. Fia had red hair as fiery as her personality. Everything about her was vibrant. Darya was trim, long-legged, with light brown skin and tight coils in the dark hair that hung to the middle of her back. Maddy's friends wanted to hang out at her house because her sisters were so kind *and thought up tons of games to play.*

Then it happened again. The nightly arguments. The muffled voices. The slammed doors. The loud sobs. Madeline had just celebrated her eleventh birthday at a local pizza place. When they returned, the mother called the girls into the hall to witness an event. Their father had stashed three bags by the front door. He kissed each girl on the cheek, mumbling how sorry he was and how he would still be in their lives. He grabbed his luggage, one under his arm and the others gripped in a fist. He left the house. Madeline, Fia, and Darya stood frozen, shock on their faces.

When the mother latched onto his shoulder, he struggled out of her clutches, shouldering her away. She tumbled to the floor. Quickly, Darya gathered her wits to drop beside their mother and console her.

Mother clutched the oldest sister like a lifeline. "What will I do? What will I do?"

Madeline and Fia came to life, helping Darya get their mother to bed. They sat with her until she fell asleep. Her eyes red and puffy, she cried herself to sleep.

Afterward, Darya called a meeting in the living room. The three girls agreed to be extra kind and help around the home on the housekeeper's off-time.

The following day, her mother stayed in bed while Fia and Darya fixed breakfast. They took charge of getting Madeline to school on time. The entire week was the same routine. Their mother stayed in bed while Maddy's sisters prepped breakfast, packed school lunches, and cooked dinner. When groceries grew scarce, Fia collected money from their mom's wallet and went to the store.

Weeks passed. Their father never visited and the mother kept to her room. Madeline read, read, read. She read about the world, real and imaginary. Darya made a schedule to keep their lives ordered and, knowing all Mother's passwords, paid bills. Since money was no problem, the housekeeper continued to come three times a week, doing the laundry one of the days. Madeline took responsibility for her share of the breakfasts and simple dinners, doing homework, and getting to school on time.

At night, the girls often fell asleep in the same bed, arms around each other, keeping spirits high and love alive, even if only among themselves.

Something woke Madeline. The car was rocking from side to side. Once she flicked her lids open, she saw a man's large head at the window, his palm above his ethereal, mesmerizing eyes while he peered inside. He was one of the giants from the bar, his face punctuated with whistling-pursed lips.

A stream of fog seemed to spurt from his mouth and travel toward her. It flowed through the glass of the automobile as if the window were open. When the mist reached her, fear gripped Maddy's heart, an invisible hand that squeezed it and tore her apart with panic.

She screamed.

****

Haze was the self-appointed leader of his small group of Soul Suckers in Angor. Two males had accompanied him to the bar, where they had gotten into a trivial disagreement over who would be the first to fuck the female Blood Leech with her boots cocked up on a table so she could watch the testosterone action up close and personal. Her leather skirt was short, and with her legs spread, she shared the view of her pussy with the entire bar. It's not like he cared if everyone saw her goods. Haze just wanted the first crack at her before the line got too long.

He blocked a fist from his older buddy, but the younger one grabbed around his neck at the same time.

Haze tossed him overhead into a row of empty stools. Before landing a right cross, he caught a view in the doorway. "Fresh meat!" he shouted.

A blonde with rumpled, torn clothes peeked inside. Her need of a good bath did nothing to hide her curves or innocent face.

His older buddy dropped his arms to the side to stare, no longer interested in exchanging fists to get first dibs on the Leech barfly who'd inspired the fight. Haze kicked the ribs of the younger, now moaning, Soul Sucker. "Getchur ass off the floor."

The guy rose, stumbled upright, unsteady, and held his side where Haze had planted his boot. "Wassup?"

"Action." Haze signaled his guys to follow him outside after they paid their bar bill with the OneWorld's exchange—creats. On the street, he glanced left. Right. She was gone. They split up, their heavy footfalls thundering on the concrete while they searched for her. Unsuccessful, they reconnected in front of the bar.

Haze spied the empty car. Rubbing his fist in a circle to clean a spot on the side window, he peeked inside. Putting a thumb and finger to his mouth, he whistled. "Here." He laughed when the female opened her eyes and scrambled into the backseat, yanking her knees to her chest as if making herself small would help.

Being a Soul Sucker, he could draw her to him with his hypnotizing gaze.

But the blonde bitch dropped her head onto her knees, refusing to look at him. Haze and his guys could bust through a window, but where was the fun in that? Since their malady let them eat emotions or feed them to others, he drew a deep breath and released fear. Not that she needed it, but more was always better.

Her shoulders jumped up and down as she

trembled. Haze inhaled her emotions through his nostrils. "Aah," he moaned. "Love the taste of fear at dusk."

He bent toward his boots and curled his meaty hand around the car's frame. He rocked it up and down, giving her an earthquake ride. When his followers got with the plan, they gave him an assist, one on the other side and the young Soul Sucker at the trunk. Up. Down. Side to side.

The female scrunched her body tighter, lifted her head, and screamed. Music to Haze's ears. "Keep at it, baby. Maybe more Scourges will hear you and come running."

That shut her up. For a few. Then she started in again.

Rock up. Rock down. Rock to the side. Scream. Scream. Feed from the female's emotions.

T.M. SMITH

Chapter Six

On a street in Stupool, Dom passed three muscled Soul Suckers bouncing an abandoned car. The Scourges' fascination with automobiles puzzled him. They had fucking wings. Why did they need a machine? But these cages on wheels were becoming popular in Vast, too. Go figure. Inside the auto, a female screamed, but he didn't give a shit about some Scourge.

He caught a faint, familiar scent. Old books. The crisp, pure air between Angor and Vast. OneWorld oranges.

The human.

It was time to give a shit. Dom spun around while drawing his sword from the sheath on his back. The special rig had been made to account for wings. It was quite a contraption.

Swoosh.

He waved it in a figure eight. "Hey, Suckers."

They didn't bother to glance his way, but the biggest Scourge, still gripping the car frame, got mouthy. "Fuck off. She's ours."

Goddess. I hate it when they're stupid.

"You're wrong, asshole." For giggles, he sliced an X in the younger Scourge's dirty tee.

The guy glanced down at the pattern caused by the blade and dropped the front bumper. When his gaze slid to Dom, he owl-eyed him. "Haze, it's an assassin."

The biggest pale-skinned idiot released his hold on the car. "Dominion."

"Haze. Nice to see you again. Whatcha got there?"

"A female. She's stuck in the vehicle. We're

helping her out."

Since he knew Haze was more bluster than muscle, Dom re-sheathed his sword. If he had to, he could take the guy out barehanded. "When did you get to be such a kind Scourge?"

Haze leaned against the auto, folded his arms, and kicked one foot over an ankle. "Oh, I thought maybe the OC would count my good deeds against time served."

"If only," said Dom, his lip curling into a sneer. "Back away. And stop feeding me emotions. Won't work."

The problem with Soul Suckers was they had to try. So, they bombarded you with emotions, hoping to break you. Or they extracted those you had to make you zombie-like. Right now, the three were struggling to give Dom an overload. Their efforts wouldn't affect him since his receptors were locked down tighter than a celibate goddess's snatch.

He'd know about abstinent goddesses, too. Once in Vast, when he'd been particularly horny, he flew over the Temple of Virtue. Backtracking, he dropped into the courtyard and tried to talk a chaste Immortal into having a go at him. She'd smacked his face and sent him on his way after giggling behind her palm for a sec. It had been worth a shot, though.

Sorry, bastards. Wrong guy.

The young, stupid Scourge said, "She's ours. We saw her first."

Wisely, Haze cautioned him, "Shut up."

"This can go a few ways." Dom raised his index finger. "One, I can walk away, leaving her to you. Let's count that out. Not happening." He lifted his middle finger. "Two, I can start lopping off body parts. My fave and likely to happen, or…"

He didn't get any further because the oldest Soul

Sucker in the trio, who still had a modicum of brain power, interrupted. "We get it." He glanced at his buddies. "Let's go back to finish what we started. The female Blood Leech in the bar's a sure bet even if we have to stand in line."

Dom wagged a thumb at the guy. "I like him. Now, hustle along. Live to be punished another day."

After he watched the Soul Suckers march into the bar down the street, he peeked into the car. The female was in the center of the backseat, tucked forward, hugging her knees to her chest. A soiled, ripped blouse stuck to her body, damp from the hot, moist heat. She twisted her neck to stare at him.

She was human. Dom didn't hold the species against her. It was what it was. He hadn't had contact with her kind for centuries. Like many Immortals at that time, he'd been curious about the Immortal Gabriel's *Homo sapiens* creations. So, he traveled to Earth to walk among them, finding them interesting. But the brief experience was enough. He'd returned to OneWorld, his curiosity satisfied. He did admit to a fascination with American TV shows, as did most Immortals. They imported the stuff, though he wasn't sure how. Some things required more than a snap of the fingers. Of course, no one watched as much film or tube as Remi.

Dom motioned with curled fingers. "Get outta the car."

She neither moved nor opened the door. Dom jiggled the handle. Locked. In case she hadn't heard him, he raised his voice. "Now!"

She winced, curling into a tighter ball.

Maybe he was too gruff. He opted for the pleasant approach. "Human female, I'm a winged assassin for the OneCreator. Here to help you. Get the fuck out of the car."

Much better. Almost caring.

She jerked her head up, glaring at him. With a patch over one eye, blades at his hips, the sword on his back, and a frown on his face, he didn't think he'd get a Mr. Congeniality award. He'd try to smile, but his skin might crack since he was out of practice.

Her fascinating blue eyes lit with a slight spark of understanding as she responded to his winged-assassin comment. "Like Ohngel?" she questioned, her voice strong even though she trembled.

So she'd heard of Ohngel. Likely from all his press on Earth. He was the strategist, the planner, the savior, the male as hot-blooded as his fiery feathers. Remi was the playboy, a master manipulator, while Ely was the thinker. Gareth had been the social one turned deceiver. That left Dom proud to be the blunt tool, the hard, unemotional blade of justice with a heart as dark as his black wings.

In character, he growled, admitting to himself he was tired of Ohngel-the-publicity-hound's notoriety. "Exactly. Like your hero, I work for the good guys. Open the fucking door."

Her mouth dropped wide, and she shook her head. *Now what was wrong?*

He blew out an exasperated breath. When he popped the handle off the back door, she scrambled to the far side, shrinking away from his caring, outstretched hand.

Dom changed his approach. It was either that or he'd strong-arm the Earther. Since the OC had a soft spot for humans, negotiation was the wise move. He slid into the car to sit but avoided touching the female. "What's the holdup? Let's get outta here." With his patience on empty, he wanted this search-and-rescue to end. There were Immortals out there who needed capture or extinction. He lacked the time and tolerance to care for the weak species.

Instead of obeying his kind offer, she shook her head.

Again.

He relaxed into the seat. "The name's Dominion. Dom. My ... um ... associates and I have been looking for you. We heard about a human in Angor. You don't belong here."

"No shit," she mumbled into her knees.

"I can get you home," he offered, stifling an impatient growl.

"Home?" She jerked her head up and twisted her body toward him. She cleared her throat. "Praevus?"

"What about him?"

"You said you're Dominion. He mentioned your name. Did he send you?"

"Fuck no."

Tears streamed from her eyes, leaving rivulets through the dirt on her face.

Damn. I hate crying females.

She asked, "How do I know I can trust you?"

Dom sighed. "You don't. This is one of those go-with-your-gut moments."

Her gaze fixed on his eye patch as she sniffled back the boo-hoo-hoos, her legs still tucked in tight.

Best to throw the obvious out there. "Yeah. I'm scary."

She nodded. "And really big."

"That too. Look, female, this can go several ways." He raised his forefinger. "One, I can walk away and let Haze and his band of pale-skinned bastards have you." He lifted another digit. "Two, I can drag you out of the car." A third joined the pair. "Or, three, you can keep your dignity, slide across the seat, and come out under your own power."

Options were good. Of course, the first one was a no-go, even if she chose it. Dom didn't mind lying for expediency's sake. Her only real choices were the last two. She was coming with him. The how of it was up for grabs.

She glared his way, chewing her lower lip, thinking.

Great. A slow-witted human female who requires special handling and time to cogitate.

Dom stretched out a hand to give her an assist. She waved it off. "No. Don't touch me. I'll follow you."

He unfolded from the backseat, stepped away from the car door, and leaned a hip against the fender. By crossing his arms over his chest, Dom believed it made him look patient.

Snowflakes landed on his black tee. Terrific. The human's skin was damp from the sweltering heat of a moment ago. Now, she'd be freezing. She'd probably die from a cold or frostbite on his watch. Her species were known to be susceptible to illnesses.

Dirty, bleeding bare feet poked out first. Bruised legs exited next, her skirt bunching higher. He was disappointed when she tugged it down, figuring he deserved to be rewarded with a panty shot given all the trouble he was going through. Her head, crowned with tangled, grimy hair, swung forward as she heaved herself out of the car, holding her blouse together. Dom let her steady herself.

Though frightened, the female raised her chin and fixed on his good eye. "Now what?"

He faced her, his hip still propped on the fender. "Just a sec."

Dom telepathed the OC. *Busy* was his answer, followed by, *Later.*

Next, Dom pathed the Feard. *Got her. Going to my place. Keep looking for Praevus.*

He snarled, glancing up at the sky. "We'll be flying. How are you with heights?"

All he needed was a smelly, dirty human passenger who'd scream all the way to his house in the White Mountains.

She continued to strive for modesty by gripping her torn shirt. "Heights don't bother me."

"I'll be touching you," he warned.

She glanced at the cloudy skies. Then back to him. "Don't you dare drop me."

"Didn't cross my mind until you mentioned it." Her squint-eyed glare caused him to revise his response. "I'm very strong. I don't drop hitchhikers."

When her blue gaze crawled up his body, it missed nothing. "Good to know."

He flexed his biceps while she examined him. *Show off. Stupid.* "What's your name? I can't keep calling you the human female." He tried out a grin to make her more comfortable. Since he was pretty rusty at it, he was surprised his lips didn't creak.

She seemed more startled than comforted. "Friends call me Maddy. You may address me as Madeline." In the low temp, her breath came out as puffs of smoke. She shivered.

"Okay, Madeline." He smirked, emphasizing her name. "Here we go."

"Here we go where?"

"My place. Now, I'm gonna lift you before I take off from the ground. If you want, close your eyes. If you're brave, open them. We'll be in the air about fifteen minutes."

She stiffened. "I don't trust you."

"Smart." When she flinched, he tried again.

"We've been over this, though. It's me or Haze."

"You're not very reassuring."

"Not my gig."

"I can see that." Her gaze remained wary.

"I'd be insulted, but I don't really give a shit." He wondered if that was true since he kept trying to gentle his approach with her. *Nah*. He just wanted to finish the job.

She tilted her chin, arching her brows. "You're rude."

"Yeah. I've been told." He sighed, the convo going nowhere. "You're gonna have to trust me. I'm your only bet."

Dom stretched out his arms.

Madeline nodded at the invitation, faltering toward him as if on her way to the guillotine. Dom curved one hand around her back and the other under her knees.

When he cradled her against his chest, she squeaked. "Sorry. A bit nervous."

"No problem. I make everybody nervous."

"I bet."

His lips twisted into a slight curve. When he shushed out his black wings, she drew a deep breath and crammed herself closer. He rose off the street, heading toward his abode on the western edge of Angor.

With her in his arms, his cock twitched, and his heart beat faster. As with all Immortals, he was a highly sexual being. But sex for Dom was about release not emotional ties. Suddenly, this smelly, dirty human was doing an unexpected number on his libido. He didn't like it, and he didn't understand it.

When she shivered, Dom squeezed her tighter to keep her warm. She moaned, snuggling deeper. He inhaled. What was it about her? She hadn't bathed in a while, but beneath that odor was a pleasant scent. Old books. Fresh, crisp air. Oranges. Not top-shelf booze, a great cigar, or a juicy steak. Right now, though, it was an aroma that surged through his veins and pooled in his groin. Not good. Besides, humans were weak. He'd break the female if he attempted her.

Dom glanced down at his cargo, tempted to dip his head and press his lips to hers. Her eyes were closed, her thick lashes fanning out on her cheeks.

But once she stopped shivering, they slid open. When she caught him staring, she grinned and stretched her neck to peer over his arms. At first, she tensed. Then she surprised him by relaxing, angling for a better look-see.

He sniffed.

"What? Why do you keep smelling me?"

"Reflex. You smell bad." He paused. He wasn't about to share the effect her underlying scent had on him.

"Excuse me for not bathing and shampooing my hair while in captivity with an asshole. Get used to the stink until I'm near water and soap. Clean clothes would be a bonus."

He grunted. She was a bit snarly for someone he'd just saved. But since she was probably traumatized … he'd heard that expression on some TV show … she deserved a pass.

A bright double moon hung on the horizon, illuminating the ground. Madeline gasped. Below, patches of fog crept across the meadow.

"How beautiful," she said.

"The fog is likely toxic. It keeps the Scourges from wandering this way."

"But it's pretty from here."

"Most everything looks better from the air, but it's an illusion."

She swung those blue eyes toward him. "You're a glass-half-empty guy, aren't you?"

"Life lessons have taught me that nothing's in the glass unless you fill it yourself."

"We musta had the same teachers." She changed the subject. "How much farther?"

"Are you anxious to escape me?"

Her soft hand stroked his chest, eliciting a quiet groan from Dom. Seeming to realize where her palm was, she snapped it back. "No. I'm enjoying the ride."

"Then we'll take the scenic route." He dipped a wing and curved left, evoking a shriek from Madeline. "Sorry. Didn't mean to scare you," said Dom.

"I wasn't frightened. Just surprised."

"Warning. We're gonna drop a bit, but I'll slow it down." *Damn.* He was acting like a fucking Angor tour guide. When did he get to be such a nice guy? He was almost chatty, a trait he never suffered from. Of course, his kindness had nothing to do with trying to impress the curvaceous blue-eyed female snuggled against his chest.

Obviously, Dom needed a shot of sex. Otherwise, the dirty, smelly human would not have kicked his libido into overdrive.

She twisted her neck to stare at the scenery as he arched his wings to decelerate. Flying above a snow-capped peak, he treated her to a great view of the mountain range near his home.

When she looked, the corners of her mouth tilted up, her smile pleasing him.

So Dom climbed and roller-coasted through the mountains, eliciting the female's prolonged, joyous screech each time he dipped. He was sorry when he had to end the tour. If not, she'd turn into an icicle. Circling his abode and the bay it overlooked, he held his body upright, pounding his midnight wings against the air and preparing to drift through the open roof into his salon.

T.M. SMITH

Chapter Seven

Madeline clung to Dom, her blanket on a frosty night. She wasn't on Earth, a madman had abused her, and now she was in the arms of a self-proclaimed warrior good-guy.

Through a cloud break, she wide-eyed a structure below. Part of its foundation was embedded in a craggy mountainside. The rest of it dangled over the sea below. Its shape was rectangular with glass exterior walls held up by steel supports. Two side wood decks spilled onto green lawns with a third hanging out over the water. There was no roof. Nearer, she realized her mistake. There were no glass exterior walls either. The building was open to the air. Yet she could see interior walls that divided the home into rooms.

She squeezed her eyes tight, biting back a screech when they magically dropped through what should have been a roof and onto a stone-tile floor.

The room where they landed could have been a cold shrine, but scattered, colorful pillows and other decor saved it. In the middle was a fireplace, a marble giant rising from the floor to what should have been a ceiling. Rugs hung like artwork, decorating interior walls. Sculptures and pottery perched on stands and shelves. If this was Dominion's place, it was incredible— magnificent. The feel was airy, modern, and elegant—a homey museum.

Her gaze continued its journey, interrupted when a figure landed near them in a rush of leathery bat wings.

Dom's eyes flicked from Maddy to the new arrival and back again.

The woman cocked a fist on a hip and jutted out a

fishnet-stockinged leg that ended in a short stiletto boot. A red bustier struggled to hold up her big boobs. She arched a brow as if Madeline were a surprise.

For some reason, Maddy felt a bit snippy. "Cleaning lady?"

"In a way," said Dom.

Maddy studied the arrival, feeling a bit judgmental. In a comparison taste test, the woman won hands down. She had long, dark tresses, racetrack curves, and pouty lips. *Yep.* All in all, a *femme fatale,* most likely here to bag Dom for the evening. Instant dislike bloomed in every fiber of Maddy's being.

Unsettling.

Strutting across the tiled floor, the woman loose-hipped her way toward Dom and Maddy. "You got us a threesome. How marvelous, love."

"Not a good time, Mora." Dom snarled as the *femmes'* long, deep-red fingernails slithered down his arm. A possessive move.

Once he shook off his visitor's touch, he set Madeline on the stone tiles. She winced from the painful cuts on the soles of her feet. Lifting one foot, she saw a bloody print on the floor.

So did the visitor. She licked her lips and smiled, flashing very sharp, bright white canines. "Yum," she said, zeroing in on the blood. "Fresh."

Maddy's mouth slackened. Without thinking, she backed into Dom for protection from … what? … a vampire.

"Knock it off, Mora," said Dom with a bit of force behind his warning.

The woman's eyes swallowed Madeline, dirty toes to head. She blurted, "She's breakable. A human. Couldn't you find us a sturdier partner?"

Dom sighed. Holding up a palm, he gestured for

his visitor in the red bustier to stay put. He scooped Madeline into his arms again, beelining through a door and into a bedroom. He continued to a connecting bathroom, where he set her on the counter, her legs dangling off the edge.

Still peeved, Maddy asked, "What about your guest?"

Dom rummaged through drawers. "Mora will wait." Her winged savior whisked out a washcloth. Turning on the sink faucets, he wet it. While she stared at him, he cradled one of her heels in a palm, patting the dirty, bleeding sole until it was clean. When he blew on the cuts, she watched them knit together.

Madeline grabbed a foot, twisting it up to have a look-see, her irrational green-eyed monster forgetting about Mora. "Amazing."

Dom dried off her feet and then grabbed her waist to help her stand.

Prying her gaze off the powerful assassin with the god-like body of ripped muscles not even a t-shirt could hide, she took in his lavish bathroom. A giant tub and an open shower with multiple shower heads on the ceiling and sides. "Nice." A sumptuous modern spa.

When she spun toward the mirror, Madeline gasped. Still clutching her torn blouse, she combed the fingers of her free hand through her hair, getting them stuck in the snarls. She tried to wipe dirt off her cheek. Not happening. "What a mess! I need to clean up."

"I'll have clothes waiting for you."

"You keep a supply of women's clothing around your house?"

He drew his brows down as if her question was absurd. "No."

When no other information was forthcoming, Madeline shrugged and asked, "A towel?"

Her rescuer pointed to a cabinet in the corner.

With two towels in hand, Madeline heated under Dom's intense stare. Recovering, she bobbed her head toward the door.

He continued to thoroughly assess her body until he caught on to her gesture. "Oh. I need to leave."

"Uh-huh. Tend to your company instead of ogling me."

"I was sizing you up for a t-shirt and warm sweatpants."

"That's comforting because I don't want what Ms. My-bustier's-too-snug is wearing. You better get out there to her. She probably charges by the hour."

Dom's chin dropped to his chest, but when he lifted his head, he shot her a grin as if he knew she was neon-green with envy. He ambled toward the bathroom door, leaving her alone.

Maddy's heart thumped against her ribs as she surveyed his firm retreating ass. He was over six-and-a-half feet of toned muscle with biceps and shoulders that threatened to rip his tee. Ebony hair trailed to his mid-back. And goddam wings. Beautiful black wings. Not bat ones. His front wasn't bad, either. A spectacular chest. High, sculpted cheekbones. A single, vivid though cold, green eye. An ominous-looking patch over the other.

She cleared her throat. Why was she ogling the man? Praevus must have done something to lower her resistance when he rummaged around in her head. She didn't normally pant like a dog in heat when she saw the bulky types. And she didn't normally get jealous of other women.

For now, she'd ignore the unexpected fascination with her rescuer. Clean up. Deal with one problem at a time.

Loud voices from the other room faded when she

turned on the shower faucets. A lover's quarrel? She hoped she was the cause.

Oops. Another libidinous lapse.

Why the hell would she be jealous with a man she'd just met? An inhuman man with wings. Madeline sighed. Everything was unsettling. She couldn't deal with these feelings now. So, she shoved them to the side to be examined later.

When she removed her dirty, torn clothes and stepped under the warm water, a long sigh escaped her lips. Pouring a large dollop of shampoo into her hand, she raised it to her nose.

Outside, Dom's natural, delectable scent had woven itself around Madeline like fog. He was a hint of ocean spray, the aftermath of a storm, a mellow bourbon. But his bath product was odorless. It figured he would not use coconut-scented bath products.

She lathered twice.

Glancing at the shelf, she saw no conditioner. *Oh, well.* Soaping her palms, Madeline rubbed her hands over her body, watching dirt swirl down the drain. She still felt unclean. Eying a loofah, she chuckled. Even Immortals sloughed. Would he mind her using it?

Don't care.

She soaped again and scrubbed off the lather.

Refreshed, Maddy turned off the faucets and stepped onto the rug outside the shower. Wrapping one towel around her, she used the other to dry her hair. Flinging her head forward, she shook out her clean locks. In the mirror, she finger-combed them, the shaggy chin-length cut falling into place.

No competition for Ms. Fishnet Stockings but presentable.

Damn. There it was again. The unexplainable smoldering heat of jealousy.

Maddy's gaze scanned the bathroom. Body lotion? None on the counter. Opening the cabinets, she rearranged a few items that weren't in order but found no moisturizer.

Then, because she was a neat freak, she folded her torn, filthy clothes and set them on a stool.

With the towel tucked above her breasts, she tiptoed to the door. Peeking out, she sprinted to the bed, which was large, fit for an orgy with Ms. Dangerous Curves and Friends. Dom had left a black t-shirt on the coverlet. No bra. She slipped the snug tee over her head, glancing down at her jiggling boobs. Next. No panties. She stepped into matching sweatpants. Since she refused to re-don dirty underwear, she'd have to endure the bounce. No shoes.

Madeline padded through the door toward the central room of Dom's home, hoping she wouldn't interrupt him entertaining his guest. She prepared to retreat if necessary.

Nope. Empty.

While she waited for Dom, she strolled to the far side of the house beyond the fireplace and onto the rear deck. No rails. Leaning forward, she peeked over a steep, craggy cliff that dropped to the water below. It was a long fall, but winged beings probably didn't mind. Double moons still lit the sky until a thick mist crept in, obscuring the view.

Madeline pivoted. Dom, his bulky thighs encased in leather pants and his chest bulging in a tight black tee, stood frozen with two glasses of what looked like wine in his clutches. He cleared his throat, staring at her. His steps stuttered as he moved forward.

She tugged on the hem of her shirt. "Bigger would be better. And a bra."

Setting the drinks on a low table, he snapped his

fingers. Her shirt was a size larger. Fingering the neckline, she peeked down. A bra. "How did you do that?"

She lost any train of thought when a grin lit his face. "Practice."

Nothing about this gorgeous man said he was safe. If she saw him skulking down a sidewalk in St. Louis, she'd cross to the other side. So why this heart-pounding reaction to a beefed-up thug?

She reminded herself that Mora had been comfortable dropping into his home. But the fanged woman had vanished. Unless he had her cuffed to a bedpost elsewhere. Perhaps Madeline had been too quick to judge. She could have been here to talk about an upcoming church social.

Yeah. No.

Dom was a category five hurricane in her otherwise orderly life, the poster boy for a dark fantasy, a hot Greek hero with strokable midnight hair and olive skin. A marble statue, tall with chiseled granite muscles. The total package screamed he could kiss or kill with no thought of consequences.

So why wasn't she scared out of her mind? He had saved her, but for what? Would he return her to Earth? Or would she end up worshipping at his feet in her own fishnets and bustiers? *Get a grip, girl.* She finally asked, "Your visitor?"

He motioned Maddy to one of the pillows beside the table with the glasses. "Gone."

"That was fast."

"I'm quick."

When Madeline laughed, he growled, "I didn't mean it that way."

"Hmm," Madeline mumbled while she strolled around the room. Instead of settling on a pillow, she fingered a few sculptures and rearranged what looked like priceless items when their placement didn't suit her.

"I didn't … entertain … her." Dom's gruff voice faltered.

His gaze tracked her borderline rude behavior. Rather than react to her re-decorating, he snapped his fingers, causing flames in the fireplace to come alive, crackling and flickering. In an instant, she warmed.

Still not hurrying to sit, Madeline touched a smooth, white marble statue of a warrior holding a sword. Where would she shelve Dom if he were a book? In the 800s? Homer's *Iliad*. The superhero Achilles, who had a flawed heel. What was Dom's flaw?

Madeline paused her rearranging efforts to shake her head. *Nope.* Seeing him as a mythic hero was dangerous because Dom was bottled raw power, ready to explode. She could see that in his tense muscles. He was a train under full steam coming down a mountain. And given her unpredictable reaction to him, she was the damsel tied to the track.

But she'd learned she was an excellent judge of character. If you grew up around an alcoholic with vicious mood swings and unpredictable male drinking buddies, you learned to assess others with unerring accuracy. Dom may be dangerous, but not to her.

On Maddy's trip to the pillows, the fireplace mantel distracted her. *Disarray.* Unable to stop, she re-grouped the vase, book, and candleholder on the right.

When she turned around, Dom arched a brow. "Better?"

Madeline stared at his luscious, full lips. His voice was deep but soothing, flowing across her skin like a breeze. She shook her head, unsure whether to clear it or answer the question.

Despite her odd desire for order or the many

stereotypes about librarians, she wasn't shy or quiet. In fact, her sisters often accused her of needing a plug for her mouth. "No, but I'm too tired for more. Nice artwork."

"A friend collects this shit. When he gets overrun, he farms out his stuff. I have more stashed around the place. Shuffle what you want."

Wow.

Free rein to feed her OCD. Madeline finally sank into a bright blue, silk-covered cushion, hoping she wouldn't be in Angor long enough to take him up on the offer. But for now, she was practical. She'd evaluate the situation. Once she had the facts, she'd act. She had earned her safe, cautious, orderly life in St. Louis. She'd be damned if Praevus, Angor, or a dangerously gorgeous rescuer would steal it from her.

Fixing on Dom's good eye and needing a distraction, she asked, "So, how do wings work with your shirt? Do you have holes in it?" Madeline patted her back.

T.M. SMITH

Chapter Eight

"That's the great mystery you want to solve about OneWorld?" Dom raised a wineglass to his lips. When he should be pondering how Praevus had kidnapped a human, his attention bullseyed on Madeline.

Could bringing the female to his home get any more fucky? Mora had dropped by for their weekly hook-up. She had been pissed about Madeline. Unless they could do a threesome. Hard no. The human seemed equally peeved about Mora. He'd had to use tact to shoo off the Scourge while not issuing a permanent goodbye since he looked forward to her topping him off on Fridays. Disaster averted. Physical conflict was okay. Even exciting. But Dom hated personal conflict.

Madeline picked up the conversation again. "It's a starting point. Well? How do wings work with your shirts?" she persisted.

"Wings are not concerned with clothes." He studied her, puzzled by his fascination with the human. When he saw her showered, his breath had caught in his throat as if he'd slammed into a brick wall at high velocity. And his heart stuttered each time her sky blues peeked at him through thick lashes.

"Not very informative," she said.

Dom struggled to maintain the thread of conversation. "It is what it is."

"Let's back up for a sec. What's OneWorld?"

"Angor..."

"Where we are."

He nodded, growling low because he hated to be interrupted. "Vast and Null."

"Vast I've heard of. What's Null?"

"A boring dimension. No plants. Desert terrain. No weather to speak of unless you count sandstorms. Aren't you curious about how I can make clothes for you with a snap of my fingers? I don't even need the hand action. A thought works."

She shrugged. "That's pretty great."

He almost smiled. "Happy to impress you."

Damn. He was screwed up.

Madeline sniffed the mulled wine before taking a sip. "So, Anger…"

"Angor. With an *or*."

Cradling her glass, she swirled the liquid, creating sheets of undulating crimson.

On a physical level, he understood his fascination with the human. She was pretty and had an interesting face showcased by chin-length, choppy blonde hair. The cut made her look tussled after a bout of wild sex but still innocent. His cock stirred, necessitating a shift in his position on the pillow.

Finished studying her wine, she said, "On Earth, I watched news stories about Scath, Darque, and Aeternals. Are they part of this OneWorld? What's the difference between Immortals and Aeternals?" She tilted her glass to sip. With each swallow, her long neck muscles bobbled.

Dom sighed. "So many questions. First, Aeternals, those beings created by the Immortal goddess Gahya, do not live for an eternity, despite their name. Though once they did, their violence eventually led the OneCreator to infect them with an aging virus. They die from it. And to answer your second question, no. Their realms are on your planet, hidden from your senses, while the Siblings created OneWorld elsewhere."

"The Siblings? I don't know about them." She inched forward on her pillow, attentive.

Dom wasn't into prolonged conversations with

enticing females. They had other uses that didn't involve so much talking. And yet, with Madeline, he'd been downright chatty. But he had reached his limit. "Too many questions."

Madeline frowned. "Excuse me. I'm not used to being kidnapped, tortured, and cut loose in a place I know nothing about."

Damn. He actually saw her point.

"Fair enough." Not an expert at empathy, he shrugged and tried to imagine what the human had faced, her first encounter with their kind being Praevus. The fear of not knowing where she was. Wandering the streets of Stupool with Scourges. Likely traumatized. Actually, she was handling things well. No crying. No screaming. A tight jaw but not much more on the surface.

He decided to answer her. "The Siblings are the OneCreator, his brother Chaos, and their sisters. Only the OC exists now. The five helped to form the galaxy shared by your planet and the dimensions of OneWorld."

"Interesting." After a taste of her wine, she licked her lips, wiggling and settling comfortably in her pillow again. "Praevus said he was a Scourge, but he'd been an Immortal. You're an Immortal?"

Dom nodded. Overhead, the clouds turned an ominous black. He snapped his fingers, shrouding his home in an invisible shield. When the rain poured from the sky, they were protected.

Madeline cast her gaze upward, smiling. "Handy." She returned her attention to him. "Go on."

"A Scourge is..." How to explain? "...my kind gone bad." Dom followed the path of her tongue across her kissable mouth.

"Does Immortal mean you never die? Unlike Aeternals who do?"

"Yes. Though six of us can extinct others."

"Extinct?"

Dom chuffed. So much talk. "Send them into non-existence." It sounded better than *kill*.

"You kill them?"

Fuck.

She saw through his euphemism. Smart. "In a way, but I also give them peace."

Madeline squinted, her gaze penetrating. "Otherwise, your kind can't be killed."

He nodded, though it wasn't a question.

"What if you're chopped into tiny pieces?"

Dom canted his neck, speaking matter-of-factly. "The parts rejoin."

"Hmm. What if you're blown to smithereens?"

"From a surviving particle, we will regenerate, but it could take millennia and be quite painful. Unfortunately, sentience regenerates first. If recovery will be too long or too unbearable, the OneCreator gives the Immortal the choice of extinction."

Dom sank further into his cushion, relaxing. This talking shit wasn't as hard as he'd thought.

"Do you all have wings?" she asked.

"Yes."

"Parents?"

"Not as you think of them. The OneCreator gives us life. Afterward, we hang out in a haven until we are mature. Then we go forth." Talk of havens always brought unwanted memories of Gareth. He shoved them aside.

"What's a haven?"

"A nursery. A group home. A nurturing environment until maturity. Don't you want to rest quietly for a while?"

"Not really. The news said the man who saved Earth, Ohngel, was an Immortal."

Ohngel again. "He is. He's like me. A winged assassin of the OneCreator. We're also called the Feard." They had been five, but after Gareth, they were now four.

"And you extinct bad guys like Praevus?"

"Yes."

"He isn't dead. Did you screw up?"

"The OC deems some Scourges can get back onto the straight and narrow."

"Big mistake in Praevus's case. When are you taking me home?"

Dom scrubbed a fist across his jaw. "If you keep asking so many questions, never. I'll be too tired."

"Funny."

He grinned. "I'm rarely accused of having a sense of humor."

She studied him, tilting her head to the side as if trying to understand what made him tick. "Perhaps your friends can't see behind your frown. Will you return me to St. Louis soon?"

"When I'm certain you're okay."

"How will you know?"

"I'll observe and ask certain questions."

"Start quizzing. Let's get this over with." She held out her glass for a refill.

Dom rose to fetch the bottle. He tipped it, poured from it, and set it on the table. After kicking off his boots, he stripped his socks from his feet. Flopping into a cushion, he twisted onto his side and rested his cheek in his palm, elbows deep in the pillow. "What do you remember about how you got here?"

She fluffed the pillow at her back. "I'm a librarian in St. Louis, where I specialize in research." She paused. "I help find answers to questions."

Dom grinned, getting more comfortable with his lips curling. "Fitting labor. You're good at asking them."

"Occupational hazard. Anyway, it was quitting time. I exchanged my heels for winter boots and grabbed my purse. My purse." She glanced around as if it would pop up beside her. "Somebody probably picked it up. My credit cards and driver's license are in it. A thief could be charging stuff right now."

She waved a dismissive hand through the air. "Oh, well. After I closed up, I walked home. Since it was freezing cold, I wore a long, heavy coat. Because I scrunched into it to stay warm, I didn't see where I was going. A man bumped into me when I crossed the street. He grabbed me." She swallowed a large gulp of wine. "Then nothing until I woke up in the warehouse tied to a wall. No. That's not true. I think I was somewhere else first. I remember a woman." She pressed a palm to her head. "I don't know. Maybe not."

Dom leaned toward the human, his nostrils quivering with her scent. "Describe the female."

"I can't. I'm not even sure it happened."

"Okay. We'll skip that for now. What did Praevus do to you?"

"I recall little about the first warehouse where I woke up other than it smelled bad. Later, Praevus cut the ropes and flew me to another place. Then things got weird." She snorted and slapped a hand over her mouth before continuing. "I mean, weirder."

"How so?"

"He sat close to me, touching my cheek or forehead. When he did, I'd get these horrible headaches. They lasted until he stopped. Afterward, he seemed tired, but he kept coming back."

"How many times?"

"Maybe four. I know this is crazy, but I could swear he was fiddling inside my mind."

Dom studied Madeline. Other than clenching her

jaw, she looked normal. What was normal for a human, though? The little experience he had with the species was millennia ago. "He's a Mind Rat. He can get into your head."

Madeline pressed a hand to her heart, her breaths short, choppy. "Why would he want to?"

"It's his sickness. He gets perverse pleasure from rummaging around in your brain."

Her shoulders sagged. "That doesn't sound good."

"You aren't showing symptoms, though."

"Symptoms of what?"

Dom shrugged. "Of any permanent damage."

Madeline set her empty glass on the table. "Silver lining."

"How did you escape?" Dom threw back his wine.

"The last time I woke, I was untied. Once I talked myself into doing something other than sitting on my ass or bawling in the corner, I risked going outside."

"Brave."

"What choice did I have? If I'd stayed, Praevus could have returned. Why did he want me? Was I a random victim on National Grab-a-human Day?"

"I don't know. How he got you is also puzzling." Dom swiped a hand across his chin. "Scourges can't leave Angor. Means he had a partner. Maybe the female you kinda remember. Someone capable of traveling to Earth and back here."

"Can just any Immortal fly to Earth and then here?"

"Most. Is there anything else you recall?"

When she shook her head, her stomach growled.

"Are you hungry?"

"Starving."

"Good. Maybe you won't talk so much when your

mouth's full."

"Rude."

"Truthful." Even though he was getting the hang of chatting, talking was not how he wanted to pass the time with the female. He'd never heard of an Immortal fucking a human. Could the experience kill them? Was he willing to take a chance? Probably. He'd sent Mora on her way, but he needed a fix. Sex would settle his mind. It always did. Dom didn't like to overthink situations. Yet here he was.

Trying to erase thoughts of the alluring female, he ignored her to reach out to the OC. Again. His reply? *Busy,* adding, *Shut the fuck up for a while.* Ohngel, Remi, and Ely had nothing valuable to report.

"The kitchen," Dom snapped to Madeline. *Damn.* First Angor tour guide. Now chef. The human was disquieting. Immortals didn't fuck Gabriel's *Homo sapiens*. Yet, he had a troubling desire to strip off Madeline's t-shirt and trap her under his body.

Not happening.

She followed him, her footfalls soft on the stone flooring.

With his head in the fridge, he grabbed a Bolognese from the other day. After slamming two pans onto the stovetop, he poured the sauce into one. In the other, he put water on to boil for pasta. Television cooking shows were popular with Immortals. They were Dom's favorite, along with crime dramas.

Lucky for Madeline, this dish was his specialty. Since comforting words weren't his thing, he hoped a typical home-cooked meal would soothe her. Opening the bread drawer, he chose a baguette bought from a *boulangerie* in Vast. Sliced it. Buttered it. Sprinkled on garlic salt. Sprinkled on extra. Maybe bad breath would keep him from ravaging the human temptation.

He shoved the bread in the oven and opened a package of fresh spaghetti. Under her watchful eyes, he set out plates. *Wine.* He grabbed another red. Uncorking it, he filled glasses. For some reason, he was nervous. He never felt this way when his Feard brothers dropped by for dinner, which they did since he was the best cook of the lot. Why was he on edge with the human female?

Seeing a clean Madeline perched on a stool did nothing to temper his desires or deflate his dick. She continued to pose while he served the pasta on plates, placing one in front of her. Finally, he opened the oven to remove the garlic bread.

She stared at her food. "You cook? Can't you just … I don't know … snap up some dinner?"

He nodded, taking the stool beside her and picking up his fork. "I can, but the experience lacks joy."

When he saw her hesitate, he said, "The food's safe." He twirled his utensil in the spaghetti and shoved it into his mouth. "See? No poison. No drugs. No foaming."

She rearranged her silverware—knife and spoon on the right, fork on the left—before sampling a bite. Then, apparently convinced he was truthful, Madeline shoveled spaghetti through her open lips. Fast, her utensil whipping back and forth while she studied him.

Dom held her gaze. Finally, she set her fork on an empty plate. "Sorry. I was hungry. I didn't eat much of what Praevus gave me. I didn't trust it."

"How long do you think you were alone before you woke up and escaped?"

"It's all foggy. Maybe a day. Maybe more." She fiddled with the napkin on her lap.

They fell into a companionable silence as he continued to eat. She watched each bite he took. Dom finished off his spaghetti and dragged large chunks of garlic bread through the sauce.

She eyed the empty bread plate.

"I can make more," he said.

Madeline pressed a hand to her stomach. "Thanks, but no. I've had too much."

"Let's go back to the salon. We'll finish off the wine there." Dom pushed off his stool.

Madeline's gaze swung around the kitchen. "The dishes."

"Later."

She wrinkled her nose. "We should do them now."

"You almost face-planted in your dinner. Would have if you hadn't been giving your fork so much action. You need to rest. The dishes will wait."

She glanced back at the messy kitchen.

"Okay." He snapped his fingers. Dishes clean. Stacked in the cabinet. Utensils, the same. Pots and pans done.

She smiled. "Now, don't you feel better?"

He didn't care but nodded to make her happy as they returned to the salon. Dom flopped onto several pillows, lazing, one knee bent as he sipped his wine, enjoying the hissing, sparking fire. From here, he could see the first light of dawn creeping over the horizon. Maybe it would be sunnier and warmer today, the weather less changeable. Probably not.

Madeline angled forward, blurting, "I've decided to trust you."

Dom faced her, a slight smile curling his lips. "I'm ecstatic. Can't tell you how relieved that makes me."

"I've also decided you're a bit of an ass."

"Good judge of character."

He stared into the fire for some time until he heard soft snuffling sounds from Madeline, a very female-like snore. She was sprawled across two plush pillows, one leg collapsed to the side and her shirt riding up her abdomen. His breath hitched. Her skin was pale and smooth. Leaning toward her, he stretched out an arm to touch her but pulled back. *No*. He wouldn't do that.

Distance.

The human lacked the artifice of females in Vast or the overt sexuality of those in Angor. Dom enjoyed the gender. Hence, Mora. They scratched an itch, but he didn't allow their claws to sink into his flesh. He didn't even spend the night, and neither did they. No kissing. No cuddling. No talking about the future. No getting to know each other. Get serviced. Get the hell away.

Lost in the blazing light of the fire, he thought through everything Madeline had told him. Who wanted a human librarian in this dimension? Who was capable of traveling to Earth and returning to Angor? Who was the female in cahoots with Praevus?

Using telepathy, he reached out to Ely. *Got anything on our Mind Rat?*

Rumor says he's been excused from the Ordeals.

Dom propped his feet on a pillow, still eying Madeline. *Do ya know why that would be?*

Not at all.

After a mental hang-up, he contacted Remi. *Any news on Praevus?*

Just a source saying he was exempt from Ordeals.

Heard that from Ely. The OC is not taking my calls. I'm gonna visit in the flesh.

After touching all the bases, he rose from the floor and scooped Madeline off the pillows, cradling her in his arms.

She mumbled something incoherent as her head rolled onto his chest, where her small hand stroked him.

He strode into his bedroom, pulling back the

covers on his bed. He could have taken her to the guest room but didn't. Instead, he gentled her onto his silky sheets and spread a light blanket over her legs.

Despite his caution, she awoke. She jerked upright, her eyes wide with fear. "Dom, what are you doing?"

"Nothing. I have a task, but I won't be long. You can walk around the house, though I advise sleep. If you do wake up, stay inside. You're safe here because my home is warded against intruders. No one will get in. Do I have your word?"

"You're certain nobody can enter?"

He nodded.

"Not even Mora?"

"Correct. Will you stay inside?"

"Yes."

"Okay. Now, sleep. If you wake, the house or anything in it is yours."

She grinned. "Including you?"

His heart beat faster. "Why would you want a hardened asshole like me?"

Madeline blushed. "Ignore me. I must be exhausted. When I'm sleepy, my mouth crosses the finish line before my good sense. My sisters always said I was smart but needed to slow my words until my brain caught up."

Dom ignored her explanation. "I won't be long."

She yawned. "I'll probably still be snoozing by the time you return."

He almost threaded his fingers through her silky hair.

What the fuck am I doing?

Instead of leaving the room, he leaned against the bedroom door jamb to stare at Madeline. She had rolled over and curled into a ball, nodding off to sleep once more. Emotions bubbled up inside him. He didn't like them. He'd suppressed feelings for so long. Detachment was his comfort zone.

While he watched, his dispassionate self retreated. That's how he thought of it. His alter ego. The him-but-not-him.

He'd allowed this indifferent alter ego to run his life after Gareth. It refused to make new friends, even keeping his brother Feard at arms' length. He figured the farther away they were, the less likely he would suffer if they turned Scourge and he had to extinct them. The him-but-not-him was the better killer. It wasn't the prankster. It didn't laugh much, and it followed orders without question.

Now, this human female threatened his detachment. She was a light in his dark world, but he craved the stormy night skies, the shadows, and the dim corridors. They protected his heart. Never again would he leave it unguarded.

Dom turned from the doorway to trudge into the salon, where he jammed on his boots and shrugged into the him-but-not-him persona. Snapping his fingers, he extinguished the flames in the fireplace. Then, fully dressed, his sword in its sheath, two knives strapped to hip holsters, his alter ego in control, he soared out the roof and sped toward his destination. Best to keep things real.

T.M. SMITH

Chapter Nine

Vast, OneWorld

Indigo sat a step below the OneCreator's throne, one leg extended straight, the other bent and an arm wrapped around it. Her long, flowered skirt pooled around her. She had tamed her black curly hair by twisting it into a braid which reached her ass. Around her neck, resting between her breasts, was an amethyst necklace.

She rocked back and forth. She was on a mission.

Roark waited at the bottom of the steps, his hands clasped behind his back. A proper assassin with good posture and a respect for the distance between himself and the OC.

The OneCreator, ruler of OneWorld, preened bare-chested on his ornate throne decorated with rubies, emeralds, and diamonds. At six feet nine inches, the delicious hunk of male outshone the embedded gems. His golden hair flowed like a waterfall beyond his shoulders, and his nose was as regal as his stone-chiseled jaw. His purple eyes reflected the mysteries of the universe. Not as handsome as Roark, but a head-turner nonetheless. He propped elbow on his leather-panted thigh, resting his chin in his palm.

Indigo aimed for flattery. After all, he was male. "You look good in blue, OC."

He straightened and smiled, fingering the sleeve of his silky shirt. "I do indeed." His brow-scrunched gaze said he questioned Indigo's choice of places to sit.

Since she didn't work for him, she didn't care. Besides, she saw her job as ruffling his royal feathers.

"Why exactly are you bothering me?" he asked.

Indigo glanced at Roark. It was clear her mate was letting her roast alone. The trip here had been her idea. Not his.

"My Roark…"

"Who's Roark?" asked throne-guy.

She crinkled her forehead. "Ohngel. Roark. Samey-same. You know who I mean. Don't play dumb."

The OC leaned forward. "Why do you insist on calling him by the wrong name?"

"Why do you insist on pretending you don't know who I'm talking about?" When he glared, she said, "You win. He was Roark when I met him and Roark when I fell in love with him. Okay?"

"So, your Ohngel…"

She sighed. "…Has wings. You have wings." She waved her hand through the air. "Right now, my mate has to carry me like a baby in his arms whenever we come to Vast or Angor. It's humiliating." She glanced at the OneCreator to see if she had his attention. He could be a bit distracted at times. So far, she had him in the palm of her hand.

"And this concerns me how?" he asked, shifting his position, slouching into his throne, one leg thrown over the arm.

Roark widened his stance, typical warrior position. Bored. Or possibly prepping to avoid bolts of lightning from his royal-Immortal-pain-in-the-ass boss.

"Now that I'm one of you guys…"

"You are not an Immortal." The OneCreator shook his head, his expression saying "tsk, tsk, tsk."

"Kinda-sorta." Indigo flipped her hand from side to side. Should she be insulted not being lumped in with the big folks? *Nah.* She was comfortable being an Aeternal witch with a lifespan the OC had set to match

Roark's. Her business card said it all. She was the reader of the river, the incomparable finder of lost objects, witch extraordinaire, sister of Alarik, blah, blah, blah. She was an entrepreneur, proud of her accomplishments.

"Are not," he quipped.

"Am so."

"I can change access to my dimensions." He drew his regal brows into a frown.

"Now you're just being mean. Did you get up on the wrong side of the bed, Oney? Cause you seem a bit grumpy. I can come back another time if it would be better." She hoped he didn't take her up on the offer because she had finally puffed up the courage to ask the big guy for a favor. Something Roark said was always a bad idea. A favor meant you owed the OC, and indebtedness to an all-powerful being was dicey.

Both her mate and the OneCreator exchanged glances and shouted, "No."

"Good. I was thinking I might be in line for some snazzy wings. Something colorful. A little magenta. A few blue feathers. A touch of lilac."

The OneCreator stared at her, a slight spark in his eyes.

"I see you're interested in the idea." No harm in being positive.

"I'm not."

"Does that mean I'll get my very own fabulous wings?" Again, looking on the bright side, namely ignoring his words, might change his mind.

"It does not."

"After all I do for you?"

"Can you give me a list? Because I cannot think of a single thing you have done for me." The OneCreator's eyes narrowed as if he were stumped.

"Sure. I figured out your damn puzzle when

Roark broke that teeny-tiny rule of yours. I woke him up even though you'd planned to let him sleep for a millennium as punishment. As an aside, I know you didn't really want him to nap that long. And I'm a breath of fresh air in your musty ol' court."

The OneCreator growled.

Hmm. He didn't seem pleased. Time to backtrack. "Okay, the last thing may have been a tad snippy. Anyway, I deserve wings."

"You don't."

The OneCreator waggled his pointer finger at a placard above his throne. According to Roark, it read, "I giveth. I taketh away." Who knew? It was written in some dusty language nobody else understood. Her mate said the next line should read, "So don't fuck with me." Indigo, however, was undeterred even when he called attention to the memory aide.

"If not wings, I should be able to conjure Oskar while I'm in OneWorld," she persevered.

"Who's Oskar?" There went the big guy's brows again. For an all-knowing, all-seeing dictator, he sure was dense at times. She was wise enough not to verbalize the observation.

"He's my best bud," she whispered, a hand cupping her mouth, hoping Roark didn't hear. Jealousy was a bitch. Of course, with his super-duper Immortal senses, he probably had. "He's a gryphon with an upgrade. Eagle, lion, and an added bit of neon dragon scales. Nifty, huh?"

"And how will he help you fly?"

"I'll have a saddle and reins."

"Ohngel?" Was the OneCreator consulting Roark? Going to the hubby as if the wifey needed permission? What was she? A throw-back character on *Happy Days*? Indigo shot her mate a squint-eyed glare.

"Yes?" He snapped upright. Roark was cautious because he'd previously interfered in events concerning Aeternals and humans. A big no-no. Of course, he'd saved two species, but did he get credit for that? *No.*

"What do you think?" the OneCreator asked his fire-winged assassin.

Roark grinned. "She won't give up until she gets her way."

The OneCreator stroked his chin. "She strikes me as obstinate."

Was that a negative?

"That's why we both love her," said Roark.

So, no, it wasn't. Good thing 'cause she didn't think it was a character trait she could change.

"Look, Oney." Indigo pursed her lips, getting serious. "You have only yourself to blame."

"How's that, witch?" The brows again. Did he possess an alternate expression? The male needed lessons in reading females.

"I know you want me happy because I'm your favorite." She pulled out the big guns, batting her lashes at his royal peacockyness.

The OneCreator and Roark exchanged looks. They both shrugged.

"True. And I fail to understand why. Okay. Oskar may accompany you."

"Thanks. So kind. How about his cousins?"

He sighed. "Yes."

"Thanks revisited. Another tiny request. May I tootle around OneWorld even when Roark isn't with me?"

Both males again shouted, "No!"

Indigo frowned. "I don't like how you're teaming up against me."

Three pairs of eyes flipped up to gaze overhead.

An Immortal was coming in for a fast landing. Dom. Indigo didn't figure the black-winged assassin would take her side on any issue. He was a cranky bastard.

A while back, Roark had put plans into action which saved both Aeternals and humans from destruction. Since the OC wasn't happy with the interference, he put her lover into stasis. During that time, Indigo met Dom. Mr. Grumpy wasn't the most helpful male around, and they still hadn't made nice-nice with each other. So, she wasn't happy to see him.

Before he dropped into the throne room, Roark whispered in Indigo's ear, "He didn't ask how many cousins your fat-assed gryphon has."

"His mistake."

Landing, Dom touched a knee on the stone tiles to steady himself. His one eye took in the crowd. "OneCreator. Indigo. Ohngel. Glad you're here."

"How's the human female doing?" asked Roark.

"Great, given the circumstances." He twisted toward Indigo. "I could use some ideas for clothes, not being up on female fashion."

Indigo stroked Roark's arm. "My sweetie will drop off some fashion mags."

The OneCreator leaned forward on his throne again. "Human female? Would anyone care to enlighten me and explain why I'm the last to know?"

Dom stood his ground, spine stiff. "I called multiple times. You refused my paths. So the Feard decided to look into it until we had a better handle on the sitch, but things have happened that require answers."

"Things? Could you be more precise?" His leg popped off the arm of his throne, and he shot upright.

Indigo hoped he wasn't about to zap Dom out of existence. The OneCreator was moody that way.

****

Dom stared at the couple. Indigo and Ohngel. They still puzzled him. The witch was sprawled a step below the OneCreator, chatting him up as if they were friends, equals. Why did he allow her such freedom? Ohngel stood off to the side, his gaze pinned on his mate, clearly taken with every word she uttered.

The Aeternal female was frivolous on the outside, but Dom suspected that inside was pure substance. She had not given up on Ohngel when he had been in a millennium-long stasis. She had awakened him early. For that, Dom respected her, though he continued to study the unlikely pair, wanting to figure out what attracted them to each other.

The OneCreator cleared his throat. "I'm waiting to hear about this human in OneWorld."

Dom flipped his attention from the mated couple. "Yes. She's a librarian from St. Louis, a city in America. She was grabbed off a street, and the next thing she remembers is coming to as a prisoner of the Scourge Praevus, though she has a vague recollection of a female accomplice."

The OneCreator stroked his chin. "Praevus, the Mind Rat. A particularly cruel male. I was conflicted with him, wondering whether I should issue a capture or extinct order. And a female. Go on."

In typical OC fashion, he didn't fess up to making the wrong decision about Praevus. Always right even when he was wrong. "The Rat discovered we were on to him, released her, and went into hiding. He likely thought she would cause enough of a stir to buy him some time. I found her surrounded by Soul Suckers. Once I sent them on their way, I stashed her at my place. It's warded."

The OneCreator resumed a slouch on his throne. "The solutions are simple. Find Praevus and anyone else involved. Show the female home. Leave me alone. I am beset with pressing problems."

"We've divided up for the search, but he is illusive." Dom crossed his arms over his chest.

Ohngel nodded. "I've been conducting flyovers. No sign of him."

The OC smoothed his fingers through his hair. "Unusual. Scourges are not so clever or lucky."

Dom said, "Rumor has it that Praevus wasn't doing his Ordeals. He was excused from them. Your decision?"

"Nope."

"Here's a bigger question. How did he obtain a human when he can't leave Angor? Obviously, he has a friend who can. Could be the female accomplice. Maybe someone else. We haven't extracted names from anyone."

"Have you talked to Michael?"

"We haven't questioned Michael." Why should they? "Could Harmony, your manager on Angor, have conspired with Praevus?" Dom knew the OC favored her, but he wasn't so sure of her loyalty. She'd fucked up once and could again.

"I trust Harmony, but feel free to talk to her. She may have some ideas."

Once a Scourge herself, Harmony had opted to remain in Angor after her rehabilitation. She cited the need for more penitence, and the OC appointed her to manage the dimension in his absence. Over the millennia, she'd become his confidant and someone he leaned on heavily.

The OC stroked his chin. "Another rebellion?" The OneCreator's eyes wandered far away as if he were lost in thought.

Indigo shook her head, her braid whipping back and forth. "Fill me in. I'm in the dark."

Ohngel took on the task. "Three millennia or so ago, an Immortal in Vast led an uprising. His name was Lucian. There is some question whether he suffered a malady, but it seemed likely. Regardless, he gathered others to his cause. Once he had enough ass-kissers, he hacked his way to the throne room, leaving blood and body parts in his path. He challenged the OC. A monumentally stupid move."

Indigo arched her brows. "And?"

Dom sighed. "The OC lopped off his head. Luce's followers turned tail and flew off."

"And?" she repeated.

"I condemned him to Angor. It took about one-and-a-half millennia for his head to grow back. Painful, I hear, but tough love. He was on a destructive path." The OC's eyelids drooped, sad. "What's Luce up to now?"

Ohngel shifted from foot to foot, his wings flicking out and snapping back in. "Word is he's the perfect Scourge. Takes his punishment. Lays low. Quiet. But Luce isn't capable of traveling to Earth to kidnap a human and returning. Is he?"

When Dom looked to the OC for confirmation, he was met with a passive, non-committal expression.

"Are you going to answer?" asked Indigo.

His lack of expression remained intact.

The closed-mouthed OC made Dom's head ache. He rubbed a temple with the palm of his hand.

The OC wagged a finger at him. "Investigate this shit. Leave me out of it until you know what is what."

Dom swallowed his grumble. The Feard didn't investigate crimes. They tracked Scourges and captured or extincted them.

The OneCreator swiped a hand across his brow.

Then, the impossible happened.

The floor quaked beneath Dom's boots. He spread

his stance, shooting the OC a bewildered look. Ohngel lunged to steady Indigo.

The OneCreator jumped to his feet, his palms pressed to his temples, his eyes barely a squint. When the ground settled, he recovered and shrugged. "An oddity. A rare disturbance in OneWorld."

But Dom had seen the pained expression and the indications of a headache. As he pivoted to stride out of the throne room, the OC coughed. The black-winged assassin snapped around to see him bending forward to hack over and over again.

"Out, I said." The OC recovered, swiping the sleeve of his robe across his nose.

Fuck! The boss doesn't get colds, seasonal hay fever, or headaches. He only suffers from catastrophic mood swings, which don't lead to coughing or earthquakes.

On the steps outside the OneCreator's palace, Indigo conjured Oskar, her golden fur-rumped gryphon who nuzzled her neck. He flared his nostrils at Ohngel and Dom, which was all the greeting the assassins would get. The damn beast was a jealous creature.

Indigo stroked Oskar's scales. "Aw, buddy. You get to be my transport wherever I go in OneWorld."

The gryphon smiled. At least, he opened his beak and snorted a puff of smoke.

The witch conjured a saddle along with reins. When Oskar crouched, she crawled onto his hind leg, heaving herself onto his back. He flicked out his wings, stroked downward, and took to the air.

Ohngel spread his fiery wings and followed his mate, calling out to Dom that he would continue his search for Praevus. With the sun rising, the black-winged assassin wanted to fly home, strangely anxious to see the human again. Instead, he headed for Stupool and answers.

****

The OneCreator slumped back into his throne. He had a headache and post-nasal drip. *What the fuck?* He rested against the chair, his eyes gazing at the ceiling. Then like an old human in a nursing home at the end of his life, he revisited the past. The time before the problems began.

Along with his brother and three sisters, he awoke before the first dawn. Afterward, an explosion followed the march of eons. Fully formed and sentient, the five Siblings drifted amid the galaxy they would call the Milky Way.

An immense spherical gas cloud collapsed and began to rotate. With wreckage coalescing everywhere, the Siblings dodged collisions of matter. In this volatile setting, the OneCreator was the first to recognize his power. With his hands, he clumped together particles, forming larger and larger masses he called planets. Pleased with the outcome, he created four dimensions where he, his brother, and the sisters would eventually dwell, naming them OneWorld—Null, Angor, Vast, and Evermore. He situated the planets and the dimensions in a spiral arm known thereafter as the Orion Spur. Locked in the fiery orb's gravitational pull, they rotated around the sun.

As the grimmest of the Siblings, his brother Chaos observed the accomplishments with awe but held himself in check, acknowledging his own power was in destruction. Marveling at the incipient galaxy, he had not wished to lay waste to it with an errant thought.

His sisters were elemental. Their gifts brought beauty to his creations and the surrounding skies.

When Melodia sang, her breath swept across lands as a gentle rolling breeze, infusing spirit into quiet places, freshening the air with scents redolent of life. Delighted, Lumia clapped her hands and laughed. Focusing her brilliant mind on her own power, she radiated light, making the sky brighter, painting stars on the canvas. Prima cried upon seeing the beauty of her brother's miraculous creations and her sisters' contributions. When she did, the water of her tears fell as rain, giving rise to rivers, lakes, and oceans. Flora covered the terrains.

The exception to their powers was Null, which unexpectedly resisted their efforts, remaining forever a dull, lifeless dimension. The environment was mostly flat and barren. Bushes, if they existed, were small and scraggly. Though some plants flowered, the blooms were not vibrant colors.

The five had such hope. Everything was fresh, uncomplicated, and awe-inspiring. They were enough.

The OneCreator brushed aside his memories to listen to petitions from his Immortals. Finished listening to their sometimes petty, sometimes important concerns, he shuffled off to his private chambers. Alone.

Chapter Ten

Angor, OneWorld

With the dawning sun, Dom continued his search for Praevus. He tightened his onyx-tipped wings against his spine to keep the feathers from dragging on the city sidewalks. Stupool was a pit. Industrial waste and fecal matter from Scourges. Probably other sorts of shit littered the ground, too.

With a city map in his head, he began at the vacant warehouse where Praevus had last kept Madeline, exploring street by street, alley by alley. He banged on doors, routed Scourges out of hiding, and interrupted a shit ton of activities as depraved as the ex-Immortals living here.

Of course, not everything in Angor was doom and gloom. Some Scourges worked hard, saw the light, and redeemed themselves. When that happened, they met with Harmony and, in consultation with the OC, their Immortal appearance kicked back in and they returned to Vast, their rehabilitation complete. Though some made it out, most didn't.

Dom pounded on a door facing the street. No answer. He slammed a shoulder against it until it splintered. He drew air into his nostrils. *Terror.* "Get the fuck out here now," he said, "unless you want to taste my blade." Dom popped his sword from the sheath at his back.

When it swooshed into view, two Blood Leeches crept from behind massive cardboard boxes. "We're in hiding," whispered the taller male, large fangs protruding from his gums.

"From whom?"

The same guy answered. "We don't wanna go to the Fountain of Blood. The fucking poison makes me puke my guts out."

The punishments in Angor fit the malady. The Leeches drank tainted blood from a fountain, drowned in the Rushing River of Blood, or dodged sharp steel in Blades Forest. Flesh Eaters were boiled in pots of acid or exposed to skin-eating vermin. Mind Rats faced the horrors of Fear Mines and Hallucination Woods. Soul Suckers spent time at the Slough of Despair or on Frustration Mountain. And there were many more Ordeals.

"Sad. But if you do the crime, you do the time. I'm not here to bust your chops about absences. Someone else will have that fun. Have you seen Praevus?" Dom wasn't interested in the Ordeal dodgers.

The shorter male shook his head while the talker tapped an ear. "Rumor tells me he got a sweet deal."

Dom was about to exit the same way he'd entered, but the shout-out pulled him back. "What do you mean?"

"Don't know much. Just talk around Angor. Rumor has it he earned a new place to live and an absence from the Ordeals. You know. Sweet deal."

The quiet Scourge pursed his lips and nodded.

"Gotcha. So where is Praevus's new palatial estate?"

Dom left with an addy for the Mind Rat's digs. Turning right at the corner, he stared up at a building. His gaze crawled from ground level to the eighth story. The place was cleaner than its surroundings. Though the white stone was grayed from smog, it wasn't crumbling.

Nice.

Applying muscle, Dom broke through the outside door. Most Scourges didn't live in locked buildings.

What's next? A security desk?

Nope.

Empty lobby. Dom's boots echoed as he strode across the floor to an elevator. He punched a button. Damn thing worked. The door swooshed open, and he stepped inside, riding it to the fifth floor, where he exited into a red-carpeted hallway.

Dom shook his head. None of this made sense. Only trustees earned these lodgings. Praevus didn't fit the bill.

After a pause in front of the correct apartment, Dom kicked in the door. He flicked on a light switch. The view made him puzzle his chin.

He smelled fresh paint and newly laid carpet. The furniture in the large great room wasn't new, but it was in good shape and clean. Off to the left was a kitchen with shiny stainless-steel appliances. Nothing was measuring up to reality as Dom knew it.

Off the kitchen was a single bedroom. It had been tossed. The closet door hung wide. Discarded clothes littered the floor and bed. The dresser drawers had been pulled out and emptied. He glanced into the adjoining bathroom. Same treatment.

Praevus had boogied. Dom investigated but turned up nothing useful. So far, all he had was a shitload of questions, a vacated too-nice apartment, and no answers. He searched for signs of a female companion. None.

Dom was used to capturing Immortals-turned-Scourges or extincting the hell out of them. Investigating a crime was not his thing. It made his fucking head hurt.

He exited the same way he had entered the building, this time taking the stairs. Out on the street again, he prowled the alleys, checking behind closed doors for any sign of Praevus.

Near a toppled trash bin, he kicked at a bundle on the ground, obviously a Scourge who hadn't secured a home yet. Meant he was a newbie, lazy, or stupid. Dom's boot connected, but the body felt strange. The black-winged assassin bent forward, pulling back a raggedy, soiled blanket. He toed the guy over.

What the fuck?

It was Ike. Their informant had been extincted.

Finding a Scourge under a blanket on the street or in an alley was not unusual. Finding a dead one was ... what? Impossible.

Immortals didn't just croak. They had to be extincted. And only a few could do that job. Him. His Feard brothers. Michael. The OneCreator. Short list.

Dom crouched beside what had been their informant. When he touched an arm, it ashed. *Yep*. The body was nothing more than a husk. Any good wind through the alley would turn the remains to dust. Immortals and Scourges disintegrated at different rates. He never knew who would instantly poof and who would slowly crumble. This one suffered a slow death.

Join me now. Dom broadcast his message to the other winged assassins, his thoughts a loud GPS beacon.

It didn't take long before Ohngel, his wings blazing fire, landed with his crazy witch riding her gryphon. Ely came next. And finally, Remi arrived, his bronze-spiked wings pounding against the air as his feet touched the ground.

Ohngel glanced at the remains of the body first, lines forming above the bridge of his nose when he squeezed his brows together. "Get a little carried away, Dominion?"

Dom glared.

Ely's expression remained disinterested. "Shouldn't we have talked about this before you took it on yourself to off him?"

"I didn't do it." Dom studied each of his brothers for a sign of deception.

Ely shook his head. "Not me. I'm a good do-bee."

Since Remi hadn't answered yet, all gazes tennis-balled to him. "Don't look at me. I got no reason to waste the Scourge." He winked at Indigo, who flashed a grin.

Apparently, Ohngel didn't appreciate Remi flirting with his mate. He glared, a growl rumbling from his chest, before he asked, "Did the OneCreator put out a hit on the asshole?"

"None I've heard of." Remi avoided the snarly fire-winged assassin's displeasure by leaning over the partially ashed body.

Ohngel's quirky witch clapped her hands. "A mystery. I love a good mystery." She reached into a pocket, extracting business cards. She passed them around to everyone except her mate. "I'm for hire."

Indigo tapped on the one in Dom's grasp, pointing out her description. *Reader of the river, the incomparable finder of lost objects, witch extraordinaire, sister of Alarik, aunt of Rein, daughter of Tor and Adriana, madwoman, quirky bitch...* "Notice, I've added *mate of Roark, and crime solver.*"

Ohngel grinned, rolling his eyes while he looped an arm over her shoulder.

After he shook his head, Dom pocketed the card.

Joining Remi, Ely studied the body. "Michael may have accepted an extinction order."

Dom agreed. "It has to have been Bright Boy." He nodded at Indigo, who had come up with the perfect handle for the asshole Immortal Michael whose skin often radiated with light. "But why would the OneCreator issue a command to take out Ike, the male who turned us on to Praevus's activities? He certainly didn't mention it in my meeting."

All heads shook.

Indigo asked, "Are you sure you know everyone capable of extincting Immortals."

Gazes ping-ponged around the group.

"Hmm. Thought we did," grunted Ohngel.

Dom went on to share his intel from the two Leeches, telling everyone that Praevus's deal had not only exempted him from the Ordeals but had earned him better housing.

With the same division of labor, the Feard and the witch took off to find Praevus or info on whatever the fuck was happening.

Before Dom continued his search through Stupool's streets, he pathed the OC. *Ike, our informant, is dead.* He waited for the bomb to explode.

What do you mean dead?

Extincted. Ashed, Dom explained.

May I assume it was not you?

Yep. Did you order it?

I did not. Nor did I perform the deed myself. That leaves Michael, Ohngel, Ely, or Remi.

Not the Feard.

After a pause, the OC pathed, *Check out Lucian.*

Lucian? Him again? Dom wondered if he could believe the OC. The male was enigmatic at best. A downright deceiver at worst. He wouldn't put it past him to be playing a game, a court diversion. Lay a mystery at the feet of the Feard. Scatter puzzle pieces, such as an extincted Scourge. Watch his assassins hustle to find an answer. Very entertaining for the court. On the other hand, he doubted the OC would kidnap a human as part of the game. He had always been protective of the weak species, guarding their independence and self-determination. Also, the guy seemed surprised by the news of Ike's extinction.

****

Praevus watched the winged assassins from a rooftop. What he saw was not good. Dom, Ely, Remi, Ohngel and some female riding a winged beast. Though they were targeting him, that's not what caught his attention. Somebody had extincted Ike.

He was certain Dom hadn't done the deed because Praevus had been here when the body was found. The others who landed after the onyx-winged assassin claimed innocence. Somebody else had offed Ike. Not that Praevus cared. Served the guy right for ratting him out. But who, if not the Feard? And who had his back and showed it by extincting the snitch for his betrayal? Couldn't be Serita. *No*. She was too busy regenerating since he had taken the human from her.

Praevus flattened himself to the roof when Ely and Remi took to the skies. With his dark clothes and wings pulled over him like a blanket, they wouldn't spot him.

He believed what he'd overheard. None of the Feard had done the deed. Hence, Praevus concluded that Serita's fellow rebels were powerful. Did he want to be aligned with Immortals and Scourges who had access to such abilities? While he thought he was spectacular, he harbored no belief he ran in those circles. *No*. Friends like that were to be feared, not joined.

Praevus had agreed to be Serita's go-to guy, but by stealing Madeline from her, he was in deep shit. And he had no desire to stick around waiting for an assassin's blade. He believed in saving his own skin above all else.

He swallowed, his throat dry, gritty. Snapping out his leathery wings, he jumped off the backside of the roof and soared into the air.

He flew for hours, thinking. Serita had

approached him with a deal. *I and my compatriot need someone to run errands. You can skip your punishments. You'll get a plush apartment.* Only an idiot would pass on the deal. He was no idiot. For the perks he only had to carry messages between certain Scourges or trustees. Even trustees in Angor were unable to use telepathy and few had access to cellphones.

Then shit turned to dung. Praevus saw Madeline and his urges took hold. Now, the winged assassins were on his tail, thanks to Ike, who was an empty, dry shell about to be scattered in a stiff breeze.

Had Serita been in cahoots with beings so dangerous they could extinct an Immortal? Impossible. Only an elite few had that skill.

Yeah. Yeah. He'd already told himself that.

He pounded his head.

Stupid. Stupid. Stupid.

Praevus was between two oncoming hurricanes barreling toward him at high speed. He had one goal. To save his neck. If the Feard found him, and they would, he'd end up like Ike, nothing more than a husk lying in some dirty street under a blanket.

He hadn't taken the deal offered by Serita to end up extincted. He'd just wanted a reprieve from punishment. The new apartment was a bonus. He figured he'd have fun for a while before he was hauled back to do penance at the Ordeals.

Then he'd screwed up by taking the female.

His wings tired and his thoughts muddled, Praevus landed on a remote mountain where he extracted a cell phone from his pocket. Serita had given it to him for emergencies. This fit the bill. He had two numbers stored. Serita's and her co-conspirator's, a number he was to call only in an emergency. He hit it now. "What the fuck have you gotten me into?" he asked.

The accomplice sighed. "Who is this?"

"Praevus."

"Where is Serita? I can't reach her?"

"I don't know." What story could he use? "She seemed nervous. Asked me to take the human. I did. Now I've got assassins breathing up my ass."

A long pause had Praevus twitchy.

"Explain." The voice was a low grumble.

"I had to change locations with the female since the Scourge Ike sicced the Feard onto me."

"Yeah. Yeah. I know." Praevus heard music fade and a door snick shut. Must be on the speaker's end.

"How'd you find out?" The Mind Rat's heart pounded against his ribs.

"Ely's making the rounds. The one with ice in his veins. He's looking for you."

"They're all mean fuckers. Is he on to you?" Praevus's voice rose in proportion to his fear.

Papers were shuffled around as if the speaker were in an office at a desk. "Nah. When did you last see Serita?"

Praevus scratched his head. "A few days ago. That's when she gave me the human for safekeeping. Anyway, Dom's scouring the city."

The silence from the other end of the conversation had his hand shaking. Did the conspirator believe Praevus? Surely he did.

After a while, the conspirator said, "Run to Serita's cabin. It's crappy, but it has four walls, a door, and a bed. Best of all, I have allies who will take to the air to guard its whereabouts. Take the human with you. You haven't harmed her, have you?"

Praevus already knew about the isolated place because that's where he took Madeline from Serita. "I'm heading there now, but the human's not with me. I ditched her to save my own skin. And, of course, yours. The Feard would never stop looking for her. So, I turned her loose as a distraction. If they find her, they'll be satisfied for a while."

The speaker paused, a growl floating through the phone. "That's not good. We need her. But I can arrange to snatch her later." The conspirator suddenly sounded dangerous. Cold. "Has she transitioned?"

"Has she what?"

"Never mind. Who has her?"

"I don't know."

Praevus thought on better things. Madeline's mind. Though he hadn't reached the core because of her impressive shields, he had done enough. And, best of all, he had set triggers. *Yes*. His *coup de grace*. His *creme de la creme* of skills. Only a handful of Mind Rats could compete with him. "Jokes on them," he said, hoping one of the Feard located the human.

"What do you mean?"

"The female will surprise whoever has her."

"What the fuck does that mean?"

"Nothing. It's time to run. You'd be wise to do the same. Ike's dead. Whoever is setting up this shit is capable of extinction. Is it because he squealed on me?"

The speaker met Praevus's question with another long silence. "I don't know. The leaders of the rebellion are powerful."

"I'm not gonna waste my time figuring everything out. Can you get me out of Angor?"

The speaker laughed. "I can't even get myself out of this cesspool."

Praevus clutched his chest, his breath hitching. "Okay. I'll take care of myself and go to the cabin."

"Destroy the phone once you disconnect." The speaker sounded a bit more nervous, his voice quivering, unsure. "If you are captured and you mention my name, Ike's fate will await you."

Praevus had no intention of getting rid of the cellphone. It was his only link to the conspirator. Already planning to fly to the Razor Mountains, he disconnected, flicking out his leathery wings, not as handsome as the ones he'd had when he was an Immortal. With a powerful downward stroke, he rose from the ground.

For a short time in Vast before his capture, he had enjoyed his Mind Rat gift, tunneling into the minds of ignorant Immortals. Getting inside their brains, he had twisted them to suit his desires. Praevus had been good at disguising his malady until he took things too far, opening himself for discovery.

Scourges developed their physical changes at different rates. Some slowly. Some faster. Praevus's eyes did not turn pure white until late in his transition from Immortal to Rat.

Thus, it was easy for him to fool the OneCreator's court favorite, Elise. She was a buxom blonde, not dissimilar from the human he'd had in his warehouse. Flaunting her beauty in front of him, she teased until he had no choice. He caught the minor goddess who was so proud of her status. Then he got to work. It was glorious to delve into her mind. So pure. So innocent. So simple. He wound his way through her brain matter. A twist here. A suggestion there.

Though delicious, Elise was weak. Nothing like the human female who was surprisingly strong-willed. The goddess's brain had been easy to invade. No blocked access. No fallen rock in the tunnels. No surprises.

Of course, Praevus deserved none of the ill-treatment that had followed his fun with Elise. His only crime had been to assuage his urges.

Then after centuries of punishment in Angor, he

had been offered a way out. He'd grabbed it, also gaining new lodgings and time away from the silly Ordeals. It had been sweet. Praevus just wasn't lucky.

And once again his uncontrollable urges had gotten him in trouble.

Chapter Eleven

Dom peeked in on Madeline when he returned. The sheets and blankets were rumpled, but she wasn't tucked into them. The bathroom was empty. No human.

As he strode into the salon, his boots thumped on the stone tiles. Fashion magazines meant to give Dom ideas for Madeline's clothes floated through his open roof and into his arms. *Thanks, Ohngel*, he pathed.

You're welcome.

He smiled, something he was getting the hang of, and set the magazines on a nearby table. Sounds drifted in from the kitchen. The human was singing a tune, off-key but with enthusiasm. Dom found her at the stove, her back to him, her hips swaying to the rhythm. He didn't recognize the song, not surprising since he wasn't into music. Or books. Or...? Much of anything except corralling or killing Scourges.

Pausing in the doorway, he enjoyed the sight of Madeline.

She twirled around. After winking at him, she returned to her task. Over her shoulder, she said, "Eggs, bacon, hashbrowns. I think that's what this stuff is. Okay by you?"

Dom nodded but guessed she couldn't see him. "Sure."

She chatted while shutting off the burner and searching the cabinets for plates. Finding them, she piled food high. Pulling out drawers, she located forks. After laying those out, she poured two cups of coffee.

Joining him to eat, she went on about something. "...since I got up so early and couldn't find you. Anyway, I came into the kitchen to explore. I thought a breakfast might help both of us. I know it would me." She paused, ruffling a hand through her choppy blonde hair. "I also re-organized a few things. Your flatware and plates should be closer to your dishwasher. Stuff like that. You don't mind, do you?"

"No." Dom dug into the food. Good. Great. The eggs were sunny side up, as he liked. The bacon was crisp. He'd never had hashbrowns, but now they might be his favorite potato recipe. Between mouthfuls, he asked, "What got you up so early?"

She didn't answer. Instead, she asked, "Can you snap your fingers and have any shit happen?"

"Pretty much."

"Why do you bother to cook or clean house? I mean, I've seen you light a fire or drop an invisible covering around the house. You claimed joy of the experience, but there must be more." She reached across the table and rested her free hand on top of his. It was warm, soft. He liked the tender gesture more than he should.

"When you live an eternity, it's good to slow the roll," he said.

She nodded, drawing away to eat.

"Besides, if I snap my fingers too much … and by the way, I don't need the gesture … my body weakens." When she turned shocked eyes to him, he added, "Not literally. Figuratively. I like to stretch my real muscles. You didn't answer my question. Why did you get up so early?"

"Too much swirling around in my head. Why I'm here. What I'm gonna do. Everything. I'm very unsettled and don't like the feeling. My solution is to re-organize stuff or take some action to control my environment. Lucky for me, your place needs a lot of work."

"Glad to be of help." He glanced around. His

place looked good to him.

She stopped eating, propped an elbow on the table, and tucked her chin into her palm, staring. "You're quite handsome. In a raw, scary kind of way."

Dom set his fork beside his plate. He grunted, finding the direction of the conversation strange. Sudden. But welcome. Her eyes radiated a touch of lust. That was also welcome, but a reason for caution.

Madeline shoved her plate and coffee across the table, rose, and walked to Dom. Snagging a chair, she sat beside him. Close. He caught her scent. It was fresh, female, and interested in him. He scraped his fingers through his long, black hair.

He wanted to flick out his wings and show off, but he resisted.

Madeline dragged a fork through her potatoes, eventually shoving a bite into her mouth. When she finished chewing, she broke off a piece of crisp bacon and popped it in, licking her lips. "I was thinking about going home, but when you came into the kitchen, I realized how much help you need around here. You probably don't pay enough attention to yourself. Like eating regularly. Your laundry. Cleaning house. I could organize stuff. Take care of your place." She winked again. "And you."

She tilted her chin, a strand of hair feathering across her cheek as she slipped him an irresistible smile. He followed the sweep of her tongue across her lower lip again.

Damn. Things were taking a definite turn toward strange.

Finished, Dom pushed his plate away. He gripped the handle of his coffee mug, taking a sip. *Good.* Brewed just right. He cleared his throat, searching for something to say. Conversation wasn't part of his skill set.

Madeline scooted closer, thigh to thigh, a hand caressing his shoulder, floating down to clasp his bicep. "Don't you like having me here? I could be very convenient to have around."

When her breast brushed his arm, his heart pounded against his ribs. She was coming on to him.

Dom escaped her grip and moved out of boob range. "Be careful, little female."

As she leaned close, her whispery breath puffed across his ear. "I'm not so little."

"Uh-huh." He swallowed hard. What the hell was she doing? She'd gone from scared to distrusting to cautious acceptance. Now this? Was this typical human behavior?

She inched nearer again, heat radiating off her body. He never turned down an offer from a female, and this one was cooking more than breakfast. But Dom was cautious. He didn't like not knowing the game.

Madeline tilted into his chest and crushed her lips to his.

To hell with caution.

Not about to allow her to control the situation, Dom yanked her onto his lap, her legs straddling him. He took over, forcing her mouth open and caressing her tongue with his. As she melted against him, his cock got with the game.

Dom shoved his hand under her t-shirt. As he fingered her nipple through fabric, it tightened into a hard bud. Pausing the kiss, he tore off her shirt and bra. For such a slight female, her breasts were heavy, spilling over his hands.

She ripped his shirt from neck to hem as her ass ground against his aching erection.

Grind. Grind.

Dom kissed her again, the points of her breasts

scraping his chest. When he rocked his hips forward, she moaned. He was hard and ready. He'd never fucked a human before and hoped she wasn't fragile.

He thrust his tongue in and out of her mouth, succumbing to her keening moans. Grabbing her ass, he lifted them both from the chair.

Madeline's feet dropped to the floor, her fingers seizing the snap on his pants.

Hell, yes.

Despite her unexplainable, sudden-onset desire for him, Dom was on board with the action. He wasn't a damn choir boy, singing the praises of the goddesses in Vast and abstaining from sex.

She unzipped him, shoved his pants down, and curled a hand around his swollen erection while he lowered his head to draw a nipple into his mouth. Responding aggressively to his sucking and licking, she demanded, "Harder." She arched into Dom, continuing to stroke him.

Maybe humans were not so breakable. Madeline was a greedy participant. Lusty.

He obliged. When she dropped to her knees, fixed on his gaze, and squeezed his cock, he nearly spilled. Dom pressed his palms to each side of her face.

She sighed, saying, "You're bigger than I thought." Madeline's tongue flicked out to lick the crown of his dick as she angled her chin up to watch him.

A warning wormed its way into Dom's mind. Something was very wrong. Her eyes, usually as incredibly blue as the sky of Vast, were vacant. He saw only ash where there should have been fire.

He released Madeline's head. The whole *let me take care of you, organize your place, and suck you off* was disquieting. He checked out her eyes again.

Yep. Hazy.

Holding her at arm's length, he yanked up his pants.

Damn. Damn. Damn. Fucking choir boy time.

"Don't you want this?" She squeezed her breasts, plucking at her nipples. Suddenly, she blinked and glanced down. As if seeing she was bare for the first time, she blushed.

He removed her cup from the table, shoving it into her hand. "Madeline, sit down and drink your coffee."

"Okay." After she returned to the chair, she scooped a level teaspoon of sugar into her mug and stirred. She raised the cup to her lips and drank.

He shoved his empty at her. "Get me another coffee."

She jumped out of her chair to do as ordered while he ignored her gorgeous bouncing breasts.

After she set it in front of him, he said, "Madeline, sing for me."

Like a diva, she belted out a tune. Off-key again.

Dom interrupted her performance. "Go into the salon and put on some clothes. They're on a pillow."

She glanced down at her perfect breasts with the pointed nipples. "Don't you want to fuck me?" She slapped a hand over her mouth and tried to cover herself with the other.

"No. I don't." He lied. His body was so primed that he had to adjust his pants.

The blushing female raced from the kitchen, returning dressed in a new bra, top, and shorts. "Is this better?"

He nodded. "Much." Not really, but safer. "Sit across the table from me."

"Of course." She did as ordered.

Dom rubbed the patch over his blind eye, which

constantly ached when he was troubled. "Damn. Clean up the kitchen while I take care of something."

Did he feel guilty about nearly going through with the blowjob? Not entirely. At the time, he had been unaware Madeline wasn't quite right. Maybe he'd suspected something, but not this. Besides, a little action from the human was ... welcome. In his defense, she'd driven off Mora, and he'd needed big-time relief.

Fuck.

He should kick his own ass.

Dom telepathed the OneCreator, who responded, *Busy. I'll take your calls when I'm ready.*

This is a new development, pathed Dom.

No response.

In the salon, he walked to the edge of the room and onto the deck, looking over the cliffs onto the shoals below. The sky was gloomy, but he could see a bit of Remi's house across the bay. He aimed his thoughts at all his Feard brothers.

I think we've got a problem.

Across the sea, a bird of prey swooped out of the sky, snagging some critter on a rock. He waited for an answer.

Yeah? What? asked Remi.

I'm getting strange vibes from the human female. She came on to me. Get over here and bring your ideas?

Remi responded immediately. *Already got one. Get laid before she changes her mind?*

Dom snapped, *Be serious.*

I am. I volunteer for the job if you don't want to get your rocks off.

When Dom didn't respond, Remi pathed, with a mental chuckle, *"Dawg, you already got some."*

Dom refused to answer.

Wish I'd found the human first, said Ely.

Ohngel, who had a mate, seemed disinclined to join in on irritating Dom. *On my way with Indy,* he pathed.

Chapter Twelve

Dom thought he'd identified the problem, but there were some twists he didn't understand. He needed other opinions. And a solution.

The happy couple was the first to drop into his salon. Ohngel landed, his feathers blazing. Indigo rode in on the back of her gryphon. Stumbling to his knees when he tried to set his taloned feet to the tile, Oskar eventually righted himself. He tucked his wings in as the witch slid down his flank.

Madeline, resting on floor pillows with her hands twisting in her lap, wide-eyed the spectacular arrival.

Dom pointed at the beast. "Is he housebroken? I don't want him shitting in here." Before she could answer, he added, "And there's a wolver who comes around on occasion. He wouldn't enjoy being gryphon chow."

When Indigo stroked Oskar's scaly neck, he purred, a sound that didn't fit the eagle-lion-dragon mix. "Aw. Dom, you have a pet."

"No. I do not," he snapped. "The critter's not mine. He just stops by for food now and then."

Indigo jerked her hands to her hips. "Well, Oskar would not be so crude. He's a terrific houseguest. You hear that, buddy? No tasty wolver for you. And no pooping on the floor."

The gryphon blinked.

Madeline had rocketed off her pillow. She'd likely never encountered a gryphon before. Or even someone like the witch. Maybe it was Ohngel who made her googly-eyed.

Once Dom made the intros and Madeline insisted

on being called Maddy, Indigo flashed a smile, shook out her skirt, and rushed toward the human, her shitload of bracelets jingling. She gathered the female in for a big hug.

Watching the exchange carefully, Dom prepared to intervene in case Indigo cast a spell or some such shit.

When Madeline broke from the embrace, her eyes bounced from Indigo to Oskar. "What's that?"

Indigo said, "A gryphon. Pretty much."

Oskar plopped his large ass down, occupying an unfair portion of Dom's salon.

Madeline was slack-jawed. "A live gryphon? They're real? I've seen pictures of the mythical beasts, but they didn't have scales."

Ohngel's mate sported a proud smile. "Indeed, they are real. Mine's a dragon upgrade, though. He was a little despondent, feeling unattractive. We agreed some scales were just the bling he needed."

"May I touch him?"

"I don't know. Ask."

Madeline smiled. "He talks?"

Indigo shook her head. "No, but he understands."

"Oskar, may I pet you?"

His neck whipped up and down.

Once he'd consented, the mesmerized human stroked the fur on his haunches. Oskar twitched, swung his head around, and licked her hand with a long tongue. She jerked back, laughed, and resumed petting the creature.

Ohngel stopped the lovefest. "You called us to talk, Dom."

Continuing to stroke Oskar, Madeline said, "You're Ohngel. The Immortal who saved Earth. I saw you on the news."

Seeing her star-struck by his fire-winged brethren,

Dom contained the unexpected jealousy that bubbled up inside him. It was irrational. This female brought out emotions he chose to bury, and he didn't like them. He'd avoided messy connections for centuries. Yet now, a human threatened his stability.

What the fuck?

Dom signaled Madeline to return to her pillows near the fireplace, which she did immediately upon his command.

He studied the human and Indigo as they settled close to the warmth and each other, chatting like old friends, their heads together while they whispered.

Ohngel chose nearby cushions, his gaze also on the females. The fire-winged assassin stretched his legs out, his ankles crossed and his arms behind his head. As always, when he stared at his mate, his gray eyes, normally razored chips of glass, warmed. The consummate warrior morphed into a lovesick wolver pup.

The two assassins remained quiet, talk not interfering with their concentration on the females.

Dom glanced outside. The temperature had dropped. When the wind picked up, he cast the invisible wall around his house. The Feard would be able to enter despite the undetectable shield. Beyond the deck, a blizzard raged, the snow so thick it was a white drape that obscured the craggy edge and the water below.

Remi arrived, floating into the salon, brushing flakes from his long-sleeved black t-shirt. After a few moments, Ely followed. Like a wolver, he shook his entire body, the wet droplets on his icy-white hair scattering across the room.

Dom made the intros and provided his guests with mulled wine to drive away the cold.

Once everyone settled in with a drink, Dom began with the easy shit. He recounted his convos with the

OneCreator. "The boss denied knowing about a human in Angor, denied ordering the extinction of the Scourge Ike, seemed to accept we had nothing to do with it, offered up Michael, and defended Harmony. And here's a good one. He said we should check out Lucian. We need to find Luce, get together with Michael, and reach out to Harmony."

Ohngel said, "I'm the only member of this friendly group Michael might talk to. So setting up the meet with him falls on me. And since I'm doing the flyovers, I'll likely be the one to spot Luce."

The Feard nodded.

"I'll get with Harmony. Is the OC playing a game?" asked Ely. "He loves games. He could be entertaining court with a mystery to solve."

Indigo relocated, flopping onto a pillow beside Ohngel after giving Maddy a reassuring shoulder pat.

He lifted his free arm to wrap it around his mate. "Indigo and I were in on the face-to-face with the OC. I don't think he's involved in any deceit, but he's a master manipulator. You left out a few deets from our visit, Dom. A minor earthquake shook Vast while we were there."

Remi nearly choked on a mouthful of mulled wine. "What? Vast doesn't have earthquakes."

Dom sighed. "It did then. To pile onto the mystery, the OC had a headache and a coughing fit."

Ely cocked his head. "Dust."

"Not a whisper of it," said Ohngel.

After they tossed about the incidents some more, Dom got down to the real reason for the confab. He called on Madeline to tell the story of her captivity. Rising from her place by the fire, she arranged herself in Dominion's lap.

Eyes tennis-balled between them. But nobody

said a thing. They just observed Maddy's interaction with Dom.

With an arm looped around his neck, she recounted her kidnapping. At the end of the story, she said, "I think I was drugged, but before Praevus had me, another woman was around. She fussed over me and fed me. I'm sure of it, even though my memory is a bit foggy."

Remaining passive despite Maddy's constant caresses, Dom asked her to elaborate on her time with Praevus.

She jerked upright, acting excited to talk about her captor. Her hands painted events as if she were reading aloud from a book, infusing life into the characters, giving them voice, emphasizing the exciting parts of the plot, pausing before the climax to build tension, and unraveling the tale at the end. She was a great storyteller. Librarian fit her.

When she finished her yarn, she snuggled against Dom, who couldn't help but smile down at her. He quickly altered his expression into a frown.

Indigo surged to the edge of her seat. "Did the surly black-winged warrior just grin?" she asked Ohngel.

Dom feared his attraction to Maddy was showing. But he hadn't invited them here to analyze his behavior.

Brushing aside her own question, Indigo continued, "Anyway, why did this Praevus let you go?"

"I don't know." She paused, stroking Dom's chest with her palm. "I'm not sure I've been clear. On occasion, he was kind to me, giving me food and seeing to my injuries. Maybe he felt guilty."

Dom remained silent, wanting his friends to draw their own conclusions.

Ohngel pretended to ignore Maddy's hands-on adoration of Dom. "We know Praevus couldn't have kidnapped Madeline. Since he can't leave Angor, someone else did that honor and passed her off to him."

"I guess that was lucky, huh? He was a thoughtful jailer," said Madeline.

A proverbial pin dropped in the room. And Dom heard it ping on the tile floor.

He arched his dark brows, watching the others for their reactions to her kind words about the Rat.

Their gazes flicked around the room as if they were trying to figure out what was going on.

Madeline slammed a hand over her mouth, wrinkling her forehead. "What am I saying? Praevus was a bastard. A monster who scared the bejesus out of me. He shackled me. He rummaged through my head. Even though he released me, he didn't leave behind shoes, food, or water. He abandoned me to wander Angor alone, leaving me at the mercy of terrifying Scourges."

Dom nodded, untangling her arm from around his neck.

Then, like a pancake flipping on the griddle, she changed direction again. "Of course, if Praevus isn't the one who kidnapped me from St. Louis, perhaps he rescued me from a predator in Angor. Maybe the woman. After all, he provided me with shelter." She blinked.

Indigo blurted out, "I think the hemisphere that controls her speech is disconnected from the rational part of her brain. In other words, she's Loonie Tunes. No offense, dear."

Maddy smiled. "None taken."

After Dom scooted Madeline from his lap to a pillow beside him, she scurried back again, explaining, "Praevus told me stories about what a wonderful Immortal he'd been in Vast. He worried that his friends must miss him. He talked about his important job, its stresses, and how he was underrated. We were both librarians, you know." She paused, glancing at her audience. "So, I understand that his career was vital—cataloging the accomplishments of a culture and managing a place that holds all the knowledge of his people. An honor. He touched upon how being looked over for promotions had affected him, leading him to do things he now regretted."

Madeline's hands collapsed into her lap. "Before he could confess his sins and seek absolution, though, the OneCreator passed judgment on him. When he was captured, Praevus tried to explain his situation and ask for forgiveness. Instead of listening, Dom clipped his feathers and dropped him here. Perhaps you should all go easy on him." She twisted her head toward Dom. "I don't blame you, of course. You were doing your job." She started the chest pats and strokes again.

Dom glanced at the others.

On a roll, Madeline continued her defense of Praevus. "He described how he'd been tormented in Angor. To me, his punishment sounds unfair and excessive. Brain-eating insects and worse. I don't forgive him, but I understand."

She tapped a finger on her chin while everyone stared, cleared their throats, or squirmed. "Now that I think of it, he may not have restrained me at all."

Indigo frowned. "You weren't pinned to his wall."

"Yes. I was, but perhaps he didn't put me there." She chewed her lower lip.

Ohngel waded into the twisted convo. "Who did?"

"I don't remember. I'm just saying it's possible."

Indigo chuckled. "It's also possible questing beasts fly." When Madeline wrinkled her forehead, the witch explained, "Questing beasts don't have wings."

Dom lifted Madeline's arm, showing her and

everyone else a raw, scabby wrist. He dropped it, letting it flop back onto her lap. "Praevus did this to you."

Madeline rubbed the healing scars. "Maybe he didn't want me to go outside where it was dangerous. He could have been protecting me from other Scourges. It's worth considering." Studying him over her shoulder, she said, "Don't be angry with me. The ordeal with Praevus is over. I forgive you for bringing him to this awful place for punishment. You're my savior, and I'll do whatever you want." She fluttered her eyelashes and fixed her adoring but hazy baby blues on him. "Whatever you want." She caressed his arm.

Pat. Pat. Stroke. Stroke.

Ely and Remi's scrutiny flipped from her to Dom, to Ohngel, and to Indigo.

Dom cleared his throat. "The praise for Praevus is a new development, but she seems," he paused to find the words, "unnaturally attached to me. Thoughts?"

Remi blurted out, "She's a Sycophant. The asshole Mind Rat made her a Syc. And without him, she's latched onto you. You can tell by the eyes. They're as foggy as her brain when she talks about him. Or, for that matter, you."

Madeline asked, "What's a Sycophant?"

When Indigo seemed equally confused, Ohngel jumped in. "Skilled Mind Rats enslave Immortals, in a way. By burrowing into their heads, they can wipe memories, re-shape thoughts, and take away willpower, making their victims obedient, subservient, and adoring. Willing to do anything for their ... uh ... obsession."

"No." Madeline trembled. Whether from outrage or simple denial, Dom had no idea.

Everyone turned sympathetic eyes her way.

"I am not a Sycophant. He doesn't have control of my mind." Madeline drew up straight, her jaw locked tight.

"You've been defending him. It's strange behavior toward a captor." Dom refused to lie to her. "And you've been throwing yourself at me. A sort-of transference."

She blushed, probably remembering this morning. "Stockholm Syndrome." Madeline scooted onto her own pillow, isolating herself from Dom.

"What's that?" asked Ely.

Madeline cleared her throat. When she reached out a hand for Dom, she jerked it back. "It's a psychological connection a captor develops with her abuser." She settled her gaze on Dom. "Or her savior, I suppose."

He wanted to touch her, to comfort her. *Fuck*. The feelings were unexpected and unwanted. *Damn*. If he were honest, Maddy tempted him in a way no other females ever had. But this seemed like a good time to keep his hands to himself. "Sycophancy must be similar, but Stockholm Syndrome sounds much milder. A Mind Rat creates a physical link rather than a psychological one. It obliterates the will of the Syc."

"Can the link be broken?" Madeline wiped tears from her cheeks, turning away from Dom. Likely trying to control her urges to jump him. Given what Praevus had done to her mind, he thought she showed remarkable restraint.

Dom answered, "Yes. But it depends on how much time passes, how fast the scar tissue in the brain heals, the victim's willpower, and finally, the Rat's skill level. Of course, that's with Immortals."

Madeline's hands twisted together, her knuckles white. "Can I still go home?"

Dom gave a slow shake of his head. "We don't know how Sycophancy affects humans. You could be dangerous to others."

Maddy slapped a hand to her chest. "Dangerous? Me?"

Everyone nodded.

Ohngel's brows pulled down tight. "How long has Madeline been … uh … taken with you? Since you found her?"

Dom rubbed the patch over his eye. "No. That's the strange thing. Not until this morning. Why? What are you thinking, Ohngel?"

"A consideration. Sycophancy is usually not delayed. Once the Mind Rat burrows deep enough and lays the suggestions, the victim's helplessness is immediate."

"Why was Madeline's response postponed, then?" asked Dom. "And transferred to me."

"I think we need a better understanding of Sycophancy," said Ely.

Dom slid his eye shut to focus on telepathing the OC again.

The boss answered. *Your voice in my head is unwelcome.*

Madeline's a human in a Syc suit.

Not a shocker since the Scourge is a Mind Rat. Have you talked to Michael and Luce? How about Harmony, our Scourge expert? I have more important matters that need my attention.

More important than an Earther in Angor?

The OC disconnected without a goodbye or an answer.

Mutherfucker.

Dom rubbed a palm across his jaw. Maddy's lids were closed, and her head was shaking as if she were having a serious discussion with herself. Likely struggling to understand how she could defend a despicable Scourge or come on so strongly to her self-described savior.

For now, Dom left Madeline with her thoughts as his guests departed. Indigo waved goodbye. "Good luck."

Madeline barely nodded.

With the visitors gone, Maddy took a pillow closer to the fireplace, staring into it, looking more defeated than she had been when he'd found her huddled in the car surrounded by Soul Suckers.

"I'm not sorry. I … uh … came on to you."

"Me neither, Madeline. But I'd rather you'd wanted me rather than needed me." Dom had no idea why he threw that out there.

She didn't respond.

"Maddy?"

"What? I did want you," she mumbled, focusing on the fire again. After a period of silence, she twisted toward Dom. "I need to research Sycophancy. Can you get me some books?"

"Should be a few in my study, but I can obtain more from the library in Outcast Tower." When she crinkled her nose, Dom explained, "The main government building in Angor."

She returned to staring at the flames, but they did not contain answers. He and his brother assassins didn't have answers either. Could Sycophancy be delayed? Could it be transferred? And what about all the other shit hitting the breeze? Who was the unidentified female? The OneCreator claimed to be clueless. Could Michael or Luce be involved? What about Harmony, the OC's stand-in in Angor? She'd gone off the rails before. Or was some unknown game at play? He hated being in the dark, a puppet of master manipulators.

T.M. SMITH

Chapter Thirteen

A few days later, Madeline watched Dom take to the air, his black wings disappearing against a dark cloud. He'd said he needed flight time, soaring into the sky as fast as possible. Missing him already but acknowledging her obsession with the guy, she reminded herself she was a Syc.

How much of what she felt for this too-serious Immortal was real?

Maddy stroked a finger across her lips. She'd kissed Dom before he left. And he'd responded. She hadn't imagined his soft lips, his tongue stroking hers when she opened her mouth to let him in. But suddenly he'd jerked away.

Ouch. Burned.

Dom's friends had defined Sycophancy. Her actions fit the description. Life had not taught her to deny reality. So, what to do?

She struggled with these new impulses. Sometimes she was successful, and sometimes she wasn't. She and Dom had traded furtive glances, warm touches, and flirtatious comments. Yet, he didn't act on any of his obvious urges. And she practiced control of her unnatural response to him.

But as she watched the black-winged assassin turn into a dark dot and disappear in the sky, she clasped a hand over her heart. Her attraction to him was more complicated than Praevus's tangled wires in her head.

None of her relationships with boyfriends in St. Louis had been long-lasting. The guys had never been a perfect fit. They were nice, nerdy types, pencil pushers, well-educated, quiet men. But Dom, who was powerful enough to crush her with a thought, was not human. He possessed an almost cruel masculinity. Oddly, it appealed to her.

Damn. She was way out of her league.

Now, Maddy could almost tell when she slipped into Syc-think. One sure sign was that she would stumble when reciting parts of the Dewey Decimal Classification System. Another was hazy eyes. Dom had told her about that physical characteristic. So, she visited the mirror often.

She'd begun to think of herself as having dual personalities. Syc and Sane. Two women. When Syc, she scrubbed floors, rewashed clothes in Dom's closet, and cooked or baked. She avoided falling to her knees to worship at his feet. And her brain was fuzzy.

When Sane, she was clear-headed.

At this moment she was un-muddled. Wanting Dom was real. Her attempt to give him a blowjob the other day, even though it was because of Praevus's machinations, had triggered feelings for the man—strong desires that manifested whether she was Syc or Sane.

With all the thoughts tumbling through her head, a voice from outside made her jump.

At the bottom of the steps leading to an expansive lawn was a dog. *No.* Too big. A wolf. His thick brown fur was streaked with golden highlights in the fading light. Madeline stared, hoping Dom's wards kept out feral animals.

The animal cocked his head to the side. "Who are you?" he asked, his ears stiff points.

Maddy's mouth dropped. Instead of backing away, she inched closer, wrapping an arm around a marble column. "You're talking. I didn't imagine it."

"Of course I am. Do you think I'm stupid?"

She shook her head. Slowly to the left. Right.

"No." Unlike some zoologists who wrote about the behavior of animals, she believed they exhibited thought. But she never believed they could talk. They didn't have the correct anatomical parts. Yet this wolf was speaking.

"Again. Who are you? I hate repeating myself." His ears flattened to his head.

"Madeline."

"Could you be a bit more forthcoming, Madeline? I am hungry."

As his ears flicked up and down, she said, "Where I come from, wolves don't talk."

"Which is where?" He lowered his head, his bright golden eyes fixed on her.

"Earth."

"That explains your odd behavior." He loped up the steps and into the salon, his long, fluffy tale twitching. A foot away from her, he lowered onto his haunches. "I'm a wolver. A prototype for your wolves. The OneCreator made my kind but left out the good parts when he sprinkled similar beings across your Earth."

Madeline drew a deep breath. She had to think about that later. For now, she worried about the wards. "Dom said nothing could get inside the house."

"Since the black-winged assassin is not too stupid, he likely said 'no one' could get inside. I fall outside the 'no one' label.

"Uh-huh. He said, 'no intruders' also." Was she arguing with a wolf?

"Not an intruder either. I'm a friend. And do not ever call me a pet."

"I wouldn't dream of it. Why did the OneCreator leave out talking when he put wolves on Earth?"

Ignoring her, the creature paced the room, finally stopping near the kitchen entrance. "Hop to it, Earther. A bowl of water and chow."

Madeline nodded, racing into the kitchen. Flinging open cabinets, she withdrew two bowls, filling one with water. For the second, she opened the fridge to peek inside. "Do you have a name?"

"Of course I have a name. Freki."

I don't believe I'm talking to a wolf ... wolver.

"Do you have a favorite food, Freki?"

The creature paused from lapping up water. "Dom usually keeps a package on the third shelf for me."

"Got it." She removed the raw meat, chopping it into what she believed were bite-size pieces. She placed that bowl beside the other on the floor. Pulling out a kitchen chair, she watched him eat. Since he'd avoided her question, she asked again, "Why did the OneCreator omit talking in Earth's wolves?"

Finished, Freki smacked his mouth, returning to stare at her. "He said we were annoying. I can't imagine. If so, it's his problem. Where's Dom?"

"Do other animals in Angor talk?"

"Very few. The OC claims he saw the error of his ways. He can be a smartass. Dom?"

"He's out flying around, clearing his head."

"Ah. When he gets home, ask him what the fuck all those gryphons are doing in my meadow."

"They could belong to the witch Indigo." *Surreal.* She was talking to a wolf. *No.* To a wolver about a witch. Life had thrown her a curve. She hated curve balls. She wanted her predictable life back. No talking wolvers. No Immortals with wings. No OneCreator. Maddy had worked hard to make her life stable and predictable. She'd purchased a condo. Had a rewarding job. Set routines to keep her mentally healthy. Her situation now was far from healthy.

Her shoulders sagged. Was she lying to herself? Did she really want a life with Dom, messy or not?

Maddy drew a deep breath. *No. No.* She needed conventional, humdrum.

Freki pounced down the steps and loped away. She stared until he pranced out of sight.

Where was she? *Yes.* Missing Dom. *No.* Missing her normal life.

Since, for the moment, she was clinging to lucidity, she wanted to read the books on Sycophancy. She was ready to face her problem head on and find a solution so she could go home. Dom said he'd laid out a collection from his study and from Angor's library.

When she opened the door to his office, she gasped. It was a massive room with floor-to-ceiling shelves on three sides. On the fourth wall was a fireplace with two comfy chairs and a small table in front of it. Perfect for reading.

But a mental alarm sounded when she perused the spines of the beautiful, ancient, leather-bound books in the library. They were arranged on the shelves haphazardly, no thought to any order. Maddy knew her future task. Though she itched to begin the job immediately, she wiped the idea from her mind. But how could she concentrate in such a chaotic environment? *Easy.* She gathered the books Dom had placed on the gleaming mahogany desk and raced into the salon.

She stacked the research material near floor pillows in front of the fireplace.

After brewing a pot of coffee, she poured a cup, adding one level teaspoon of sugar. Once she settled into the cushions with her mug beside her, she rested the nearest book in her lap and began her research.

Consulting the table of contents, she scanned for information on Sycophants. The first book had only a few pages, which detailed what she already knew. Grabbing another, she found a longer entry. Madeline read, committing the information to memory. Once she had absorbed chapters in five books, she set them aside to review the facts while she sipped her coffee.

Sycophancy brought on by Mind Rats was not good. Their Immortal prey became mindless creatures who lived only for their obsession. They waited on what they called their masters and followed all wishes or commands, even second-guessing to please them. At best, they were sex objects, enforcers, or maids. At worst, they waited mindlessly in corners for their next command, unable to act without an order.

She'd read about skilled Rats who could plant triggers. These unique commands, as the book had called them, varied. Her delayed response to Sycophancy could be one trigger and the transference of her obsession to Dom could be another.

Without the Mind Rat present to maintain the compulsions, most Sycs healed. Most. Not all. While some took weeks or months to overcome the obsessions, others took years, centuries, or longer.

The books documented only Immortals. None mentioned humans, for whom the symptoms would surely be more devastating, taking longer to heal or never healing.

Sinking deeper into the cushions, Madeline closed her eyes to think, hating that her actions were no longer her own. Instead, her damaged brain controlled them. Her situation was worse than her childhood had been. A psychiatrist had once told her the behaviors she'd learned in her youth had served her well. But no longer, he'd said. She had to develop positive behaviors rather than keep the extreme survival ones. So, rather than accept chaos, she had ordered her life, creating new behaviors.

How did Dom figure into this nightmare? Was he only an obsession planted by Praevus, or was he more?

With absolute certainty, she knew he was more. Maybe it was Syc-think that had made her try to go down on him, but the desire was genuine. And she knew he wanted her, but since he thought she didn't have control over her actions, he nobly rejected her.

Madeline shot upright. Having once fought hard to control her actions and surroundings, she'd beaten the odds. She'd do it again. This shit was not going to take her down. And it wouldn't keep her from having a relationship with Dom.

If she wanted one. If he wanted one.

The silent declaration cleared her head, reinforcing a temporary freedom from Praevus's wiles.

Madeline refused to give up or give in.

Tired of reading, she set aside the books and scrubbed the kitchen floor, fluffed all the pillows in the salon twice, organized Dom's closet, polished his boots, and then sat in a corner with her knees bent and her arms clasped around them as she pined for her assassin. She was having a Syc moment. A very long-lasting moment. Her obsession with Dom drove all other thoughts from her head.

Where was he? What did he want her to do? How could she please him?

She was a ping-pong ball at the mercy of the players.

Ping, I'm Syc. Pong, I'm Sane.

T.M. SMITH

Chapter Fourteen

Light turned to dark as Madeline waited for Dom's return. Again. Was he having an I-gotta-get-out-of-here moment or scouring Vast and Angor for signs of Praevus or the others she'd heard mentioned—Michael, Lucian, Harmony?

On days when she was lucid, she begged Dom to take her home. He always said, "No. Not yet." Of course, when she was Syc, she wanted to stay to serve him. In all ways possible.

Today, tired of shared furtive glances, withheld touches, and long sighs, she had a plan. Certain her re-wired brain was working right, she planted herself in Dom's bed. Resting on her side, she cocked her elbow, put her head in her palm, and bent her knee. Very seductive in the transparent nighty.

Madeline didn't belong in Angor. Her life wasn't here. Nonetheless, she was drawn to the grim Immortal who had saved her. Was it gratitude? *Maybe*. Was it that she was a Sycophant? *Not right now*. Her feelings for him were complicated.

They were real. If not real, at least they were curative. *Yep*. Madeline planned to use sex with the black-winged assassin to soothe her shattered nerves. Then when given the all-clear, she'd be ready to go home. No regrets.

She heard the swoosh of Dom's wings, and her heart beat a staccato rhythm in her chest. Madeline was no shy virgin, but she wasn't promiscuous either. The excitement of the first time with a guy made her nervous. The tentative exploring of bodies. The kissing. The slow build followed by an explosion. Those times were magic.

Yep.

Still, not one date or brief fling had stirred her emotions as Dom did.

Listening closely, she heard his thundering footsteps draw nearer. He shoved into the bedroom, his gaze on the floor until... He froze. Taking her in from bare feet to breasts exposed through the sheer nightie, he stopped at her eyes. "What are you doing, Madeline?"

"Maddy." She batted her eyelashes. Very Barbarella of her. Maybe Sharon Stone in *Basic Instinct*. She'd go with either. "I would think it'd be obvious unless Immortals do things differently. But I believe not."

His voice was rougher than usual. "No."

"No, what? No, Immortals don't do things differently? No, you won't come here? Unconfuse me."

"No, I won't fuck you."

"Yes, you will." She beckoned him closer with a finger. *Oh, that was good.* She felt quite wicked. A temptress.

Dom moved cautiously to the edge of the mattress. She'd surprised him. *Hell.* She surprised herself. "Where did you get the..." His hand waved over her outfit. "I didn't make it."

"Indigo. Do you like it? I think she's playing matchmaker."

For the seduction, Maddy wore a gossamer, red shorty nightgown. The bottom was a barely-there matching thong. The finishing touch was a garter belt with silk stockings. Perfect.

"This is not you."

"You don't know me. See, here's what I hear coming from your mouth. 'Blah. Blah. I don't have the balls. Blah."

He grinned. "You know I've got the balls. You've seen them."

She grabbed onto the waistband of his pants and tugged him closer. "Show them to me again. I may have forgotten with all the shit Praevus did to my head."

"I refuse to take advantage of you." He tried to pull away. Not very hard.

"So sweet. But no worry. Look at my eyes. What do you see?"

"Blue. Bright blue."

"Right. So, I guess I'll take advantage of you. Afterward, you can feel guilty about the whole thing." She rose onto her knees. His pants were no obstacle. She unsnapped them, drawing the zipper down. His gaze followed the drawn-out progress.

She joggled her fingers inside the gap until they reached his thick shaft. He was hard and ready.

When she stroked him, Dom hissed, gripping her hand to stop her. He fixed on her eyes.

She batted her lashes. "See. Sharp, shiny, and lucid. I'm my own woman. Take advantage of me while you can. I'm fair game when I'm clear-headed."

Maddy leaned closer, laying a row of kisses on his golden chest. She trailed her lips down the line of dark hair to the flat expanse of his belly, his ridged abs. She shoved his pants down his hips and freed his erection. "Now I recall your big balls." She grinned. "I like them."

Dom yanked his shirt overhead and jerked out of his pants. He tumbled Maddy onto her back, threw his heavy body over her, and slid down until he was between her spread thighs. "Just to be sure. Is this the Syc talking or Madeline?"

She tapped her head. "Maddy. Head's as undimmed as a cloudless sky."

"Sycs do have moments of clarity."

"Then let's get going before I'm not me again."

"These have to go." He ripped off the red thong

and tossed it over his shoulder, leaving her in the see-through top, garter belt, and stockings. Running his large hands up the insides of her thighs, he shoved her legs farther apart, baring her sex to his hot gaze.

Under Dom's intense study, she moaned.

When she wiggled her hips, Dom emitted a growl as he bent her knees toward her chest, pushing them wider and opening her further to his scrutiny. He fixed her with a scorching stare.

Without warning, he dipped one thick finger into her sex. Since she was soaked with arousal, he thrust deeper. Withdrawing, he slid his finger up and down, smearing her wetness all around, teasing her clit.

She pushed against his fingers, her hands gripping his forearms. When she cried for more, he obliged by bending his head and licking where his finger had been. Madeline shouted, "Yes. Yes."

He tortured her with his tongue, stroking back and forth as she pleaded for more, plunging inside her again with two digits. Her hips rocked into his hand. "Harder. Faster."

Dom picked up the pace until she screamed his name, the orgasm rocketing through her.

She'd been right. He was the perfect balm for shattered nerves.

****

Dom's gaze feasted on Maddy, her head resting on a pillow, her body loose, sated. No panties. He'd seen to that. A garter belt with stockings. Sexy. His dick ached at the sight. But the top was in his way. He paused a moment to analyze whether he was taking advantage of her.

Nope.

She'd said she was clear-headed, and he believed her. No hazy eyes.

Madeline sighed and flung her arms to the side. She blinked, and a satisfied smile curled her lips. "That was great."

He thought so, too. He'd spent days restraining himself, not acting on his desire for Maddy because she was sick. But the female in his bed was not a Syc. She was as lucid as he was. "I'm not through. Are you okay?"

"Perfect. What's next?" She rose onto her elbows.

"Are you sure you want this, Maddy? It's not too late. We'll stop right here if that's what you want." Wasn't he all considerate, but he meant the words even if his cock was pissed at him. It was hard and demanding.

Dom wanted this human more than anyone or anything for centuries. He would allow himself—this one time—to care. Then he'd lock down his emotions. He'd done it before. He could again.

"I'm sure, Dom." Her hand moved to caress a breast, her fingers pinching a nipple. "Positive."

Damn.

Her robin-egg blues were vibrant, lacking a Syc's mindless gaze. He crawled atop her. "Keep your eyes open. If they glaze over, we're stopping. No matter what." He'd keep his promise even if it killed him.

His mouth crushed her warm, eager lips, laying claim to her body.

Madeline clung to him, her fingers digging into his shoulders.

Dom drew away from her mouth and rose onto flexed arms, his stiff cock cradled between her thighs.

"Kiss me again," she demanded.

Aiming to please, he lowered himself slowly, his weight crushing her into the mattress, her heat sparking his desires. He kissed her neck, the tender skin near her ear, her jaw. When she shivered, he moved to her mouth. His tongue slipped between her lips, tangling with hers.

He licked, savoring Madeline's taste, sweeter than the nectar in Vast, spicier than a Farfield curry.

Despite her objections, he retreated, balancing on a stiffened arm. "This has to go."

He ripped the sheer red nightie, letting it fall to each side of her. Afterward, he hummed at the bared sight of her breasts, full mounds, and the tawny pebbled nipples aching for his touch.

Madeline groaned when he captured one in his mouth, a perfect, peaked nub. He licked. He sucked. He enjoyed. Then he moved to the other, his teeth grazing her, his tongue laving her skin.

She arched into his advances, pressing firmly against him, encouraging him to suckle her. "Harder," she whimpered, arching her back.

He opened his mouth wider to take more of her flesh. Blissful, Dom curved one hand around her hip and pulled her tighter into his body, letting her feel the hard jut of his arousal.

"Dom," she whispered, undulating against him, her fingers tangling in his hair.

He flexed his hips and nudged the tip of his cock inside. Shuddering from the pleasure, he took another inch. As she moaned, he slid deeper. Deeper, not stopping until his balls slapped against her.

Maddy's tight sheath squeezed him. "Fuck." Dom growled, the fit perfect. He stilled for a moment, feeling her tremble around him as she adjusted to his thickness, to the hard length of him.

She blew out a shuddering breath.

Dom tilted his head down, spearing his tongue into her mouth. Slowly, he began to move, mimicking the action of the kiss. Withdrawing. Pushing back inside. Doing this repeatedly until her snug sheath relaxed its hold on him.

She moaned, the sounds soft, muffled. When desire overwhelmed him, he lifted himself onto his flexed arms, pulling his cock nearly out until only the crown was drenched in the wet heat of her body. He plunged deep again with a powerful thrust.

Maddy locked her heels around his waist, her hips lifting to meet his downward strokes. Reveling in her slick heat, Dom pounded in and out, driven by a lust he'd never felt before, driven to claim her as his own.

But Immortals did not claim lovers, though some were monogamous. So, he expelled those crazy thoughts, allowing desire to swamp him. Increasing the rhythm, he rocked forward. Backward. Faster.

"Yes. Yes. Don't stop," she shouted, her eyes still blue and unclouded.

As if he would. As if he could stop. "Come for me, Maddy." He pulled nearly out and slammed back inside.

She froze, crying out his name. Once she began to orgasm, Dom surged into her, the stroke of her sheath against him an erotic friction. A sensual haze fogged his mind, whipping him into a frenzy. He hammered into Madeline until his balls tightened. His dark wings shot from his spine when his seed spewed into her, flowing on and on until he was drained, wrung dry by this human female.

Barely conscious, Dom pushed onto his arms, his groin still pressed tight to Maddy. Once his wings returned to where they belonged, he rolled to the side, taking her with him. She cuddled into his chest, her lips against his skin.

"Hmm," she moaned, relaxing in his grasp.

Dom sighed. *Fuck.* He had to give her up soon. He had to return her to Earth. She'd made him feel, but he couldn't keep her.

It was for the best.

He had to be honest. "Maddy, we can never be. Once you are cured, I'll be taking you home where you belong."

Her soft fingers stroked his chest. "I know, Dom. But let's pretend until that time comes."

"I'm not good at pretending." He gripped the back of her head and held her tight to him, loving the feel of Maddy.

Damn. What was he doing breaking his rules? Never get close to anyone.

Chapter Fifteen

Inside the cabin hidden in the Razor Mountains, Praevus closed all the curtains and flopped onto an old, dirty sofa.

When he'd arrived, Serita's nearly decapitated body lay on the floor where he had attacked her when he'd stolen the human. But the cells had begun to regenerate. Soft, pained moans rose from her throat. Her recovery would be a very long, very painful process. Centuries. Millennia. Perhaps longer. He preferred not to listen to her strangled, endless cries of agony. Instead, he'd thrown the female out the door by a bush.

Afterward, he kicked his booted feet on the coffee table, thinking of anything except the hunger pangs brought on by his urges. He wanted another taste of Madeline's mind. If not her, he wanted to tunnel into any Immortal and explore until he turned their brains to ground meat. A Mind Rat wasn't meant to stay isolated from potential victims.

Though some would say it was his malady talking, Praevus didn't care. His desires were the natural outgrowth of his personal evolution. He was superior. As an Immortal in Vast, he had been common, ordinary. Nothing set him apart, neither his job nor his personality nor his looks.

Since arriving at the cabin, he had tried to rein in his wandering thoughts but found doing so difficult. For days now, he lacked focus, disappearing into black holes on occasion. He was restless, jittery.

When he leaned his head back on the sofa cushion, he struggled to remember how he had gotten into such a mess.

Praevus was handsome. But so was every Immortal. Though not timid, he lacked the charisma to win over others with clever conversation or amusing antics. He supposed some thought him boring.

He was one of many assistant librarians in Vast's Hall of Time, where the great histories were kept. His job in the acquisitions section was to gather new records of their people, cataloging and shelving them. Once Immortals invented new techniques for storing millennia of documents, his task was to convert ancient and new chronicles to digital format. Though Praevus enjoyed the undertakings, they did not contribute to his individual growth.

When he felt himself withering away, he applied to be the documentarian. The position was one of status. The Immortal who held it was important, an attendee at all court functions and the recorder of significant occurrences in Vast. Though he interviewed with the OC, the job went to someone else. The re-named Scribe was a preening, insufferable male with few literary skills. His writing was flowery and effusive. Adjectives were Scribe's preferred parts of speech, sprinkled liberally throughout his compositions and lacking merit. But the OneCreator favored the Immortal. It was the only reason for his appointment. Praevus was a superior writer, as shown by his journals.

Of course, since his journals recorded his evolving thoughts and desires, he had not shown them to the OC during the interview. Thus, the ruler of Vast was unaware of his expert writing skills.

The slight ate away at Praevus for centuries. His daily duties at the Hall of Time continued to be completed with his usual skill, but gnawing envy took its toll. Whenever he cataloged a current document from Scribe, his anger roared to the surface.

His growing interests dominated his thoughts. At first, they seemed touched with genius. Later, they appeared deliciously wicked. At night, he lay abed, searching through his mind, examining his new-found abilities, wondering what he might do with them. He pictured a female laughing at his quips. After she flirted with him over a meal, he would take her to his bed, where he would continue to invade her brain, to crush her will.

He began testing his newly acquired skills on fellow assistant librarians or patrons. Nothing they could detect. He entered their heads, buried a thought, and scampered out. He planted small commands. Get lunch early. Leave for the bathroom now. Take out such-and-such book from the shelf. *With these successes, he moved to more delicate commands.* Ask me how my morning is going. Compliment me on my choice of shirts. Offer to pour me another cup of coffee. *The experiments lent excitement to an otherwise tedious day.*

Each week, Praevus extended the boundary of his skills. His mission was to stretch his abilities. With each test, he mined deeper, never using the same Immortals for his investigations. No. He was clever.

Called into Librarian's office on the main floor of the complex, Praevus was advised his work was slipping. He was cautioned to take care.

For a century thereafter, he controlled his urges. But when ennui again enervated him, he returned to what gave him joy. He was, however, not so careful this time. He did forego practicing on Immortals in the library, instead turning to strangers. A passerby on the street. A neighbor. A fellow customer in a coffee shop.

Though Praevus was aware he grew too bold, he could not stop himself. He did not want to stop. He was having too much fun.

Delicious.

Practice became more frequent.

One day, he tangled his invisible fingers in Elise's mind. A court favorite of the OneCreator, she collapsed. She was unconscious, and Praevus realized he had gone too far. She would not recover from his invasion for, perhaps, a century. Her circuitry was fried, her memories stolen, and her ability to think obliterated. Praevus was fatigued, but ... he recounted the ecstasy of digging through her mind.

Mouthwatering. Fulfilling.

While she was unconscious, nearly brain-dead, Praevus swiped his hands over the female's eyes, closing them. Since she had provided him joy, he laid her gently on the ground, tucking her lilac gown around her. He stood, prepared to fly home to enjoy the aftereffects. Then, the black-winged assassin blocked his path. "Dominion, I can explain," he said.

The Feard glared at him with his one frightening eye.

"I found Elise like this and was going for help," he explained.

The assassin drew a sword from a sheath on his back. "You have been judged by the OneCreator who sentences you to Angor."

"No. You misunderstand the situation."

"I think not, Praevus."

He snapped out his wings to take flight. Before he rose, Dominion sped toward him, lobbing off an entire wing.

When he tried to fly using only a single wing, he wobbled, his feet stumbling. An impassive Dom watched Praevus's dilemma, judging him. "Stupid."

The assassin manifested a net, throwing it over Praevus's head. He was caught and lifted into the air.

Dominion carted him off like a trapped bird.

Reaching a particular spot in Angor, the assassin cut the netting, allowing Praevus to fall into Angor. When he hit the ground, his bones fractured. Henchmen scooped him up and dumped him in a filthy alley. He lay there in pain, healing with no assistance.

He was a Scourge, his white eyes those of a Mind Rat. With no escape, he was punished and tormented like others. Though he requested work in Angor's Library of Beginnings and Endings, Harmony denied his request. Instead, he was assigned a menial job, one beneath his status, cleaning up and washing dishes in a cafe managed by the trustee Serita.

His undeserved incarceration continued until Serita offered him a deal. He accepted. Who would not choose her proposal over the repeated assaults on his mind and body at the Ordeals?

But now, he was hiding in a cabin that belonged to his ex-boss, fearing Dom or another of the asshole Feard would hunt him down. Eternity was unfair to Praevus. He deserved better.

He jerked when he heard a sound outside. Springing to his feet, he fingered the curtain, peeking through the slight crack.

Nothing.

What was going on out there? Had the hunt for him stopped? When could he come out of hiding? Surely, he wasn't expected to remain here permanently. He needed a fix. He needed to explore a mind, one as delicious as Madeline's. As challenging.

Praevus palmed the phone that he had kept, regardless of the command from Serita's co-conspirator. But he'd wait.

Once again settling into the stained sofa's cushions, Praevus contented himself with fantasizing about what Madeline might do because of his tampering.

Yes. He rested his head and closed his lids. Retracing every step in his journey through her mind, he swallowed, moisture gathering in his mouth. *Succulent*. He had fought for every inch gained. She was strong-willed. Though he had never reached her core, he had ensured what was done would be effective. Others would understand his power. They would see how he had laid triggers and made the human a Sycophant, a living work of art that carried his signature. And best of all, her Sycophancy was delayed, and her slavish obedience would transfer to a new master.

****

Still searching for some sign of Praevus, Remi took a flight path over the southern range of the Razor Mountains. He banked left, flying low enough to see the jagged peaks. Below him, surefooted, cliff-dwelling goats scrambled up the rocks. Their stubby wings helped them move easily, though their hooves were their greatest advantage. High as they were, few predators could reach them.

He glided above the range, soaring when he caught a wind current. Adjusting a wingtip, he maneuvered left. In a meadow beyond a tree line, a pack of wolvers stalked a dorik, a grass-grazing creature, a tasty meal for the beasts of prey.

Just to the east of the mountains, he set down in Loneliness Desert. The sand was thick with Soul Suckers.

At this Ordeal, emotions flooded some of them. Abandonment. Loneliness. Loss of loved ones. Rejection. Isolation. Pity. They beat their chests, tore their skin and hair, and sobbed nonstop.

For others, the emotions were sucked out of them, leaving them hollow. Those Scourges wandered aimlessly in the desert, their eyes empty, their jowls slack, and their minds as deserted as the wasteland beneath their feet. They stabbed themselves, trying over and over again to commit suicide. Useless since they were once Immortals, incapable of death except at the hands of a few.

Remi hated the Ordeals for the Soul Suckers most of all. This region where the Scourges were tormented with either a surfeit or a lack of emotions was infectious. When his feet hit the sandy soil, he immediately felt sad, an emotion he hated. He persisted despite it, questioning a few prisoners but getting nothing. Most didn't know Praevus. Those who did hadn't seen him. No surprise. Soul Suckers and Mind Rats weren't the closest friends, their maladies seeming to set off the other too easily, one all about feeling and the other about the mind.

Enough of this shit.

He spread his bronze-spiked wings and took off, seeking another Ordeal. Remi circled back to the Razor Mountains, heading north. At least the air up here was fresh, not filled with debilitating emotions. His feathers warmed, catching the sun, which sparkled through a break in the clouds. Before he could enjoy the warmth, he identified four dots in the distance, closing in. As they drew close, he recognized them as Scourges. What were they doing? Coming or going to an Ordeal?

Remi hovered in place. When they neared, he didn't recognize any of the Scourges. Not unusual. One of his fellow assassins could have brought them to Angor.

They were Leeches, their mouths open, fangs protruding from their gums. One male flew in front of the others. Remi figured him as the leader. He spoke first. "You're in our skies, Feard. Leave."

Remi's brows arched as a smile twitched on his lips. A challenge from a bunch of fucking Scourges? The day was looking up. "Your skies?"

"Yep," said the male to the right of the leader.

The remaining two winged over to flank Remi.

Strange encounter. Scourges challenging a winged assassin? Interesting.

Remi snatched his long-bladed knives from the holsters tied to his thighs. He grinned. A big fan of Earth's Dirty Harry movies, he'd been dying to use the line. Here was his chance. It was doubtful these dumbfucks would get it. "Go ahead, make my day."

One Leech chuckled. Remi would go easier on him. The response showed the guy had promise. Obviously, they enjoyed the same movies. The others gave him empty stares. Oblivious to fine film, they sealed their fate.

The leader charged forward. Nothing clever. Brute force. As the other Scourges flew at him, Remi shot up and flipped over, coming behind the four Stooges. *Yep.* They were a favorite, too.

The Scourges nearly crashed into one another. The bronze spike-winged assassin shouted, "You've got to ask yourself one question. 'Do I feel lucky? Well, do you punk?'" Again, the Harry Callahan line would be lost. Maybe the one guy would get it. Remi caught a slight grin on his worried face.

He sighed, performing a few more aerobatics but receiving no applause. Ungrateful audience. When Remi settled, the four spun his way, their expressions puzzled by his antics.

He waved as best he could with a knife in each hand. "You were saying something about this being your skies? Could you be more specific?"

They flew at him again. No strategy. No skill. He figured they hoped to overwhelm him with bulk and numbers.

This time, Remi pulled in his wings, dropping straight down, boots first. When he powered back up toward his stunned spectators, his wings pounding the air, he sliced a tip off one Scourge's wing. The guy wobbled, but the cut wasn't enough to take him out of action. Remi hadn't intended it to be. This was a game, wasn't it? They would make lame attempts to injure a winged assassin, and he would toy with them.

Great fun.

The foursome slowed, whispering, trying to come up with a plan. Remi hovered patiently. Having devised a strategy, they surrounded him and moved in, hoping to smash him between them. *Stupid.* They were slow. He charged between two of them, slicing the tips from their wings. That left only the leader unscathed.

The guy didn't look so sure of himself now. Though why he had before puzzled Remi. Hadn't they seen the Feard in action? Who was filling their heads with grandiose thoughts?

The leader withdrew a heavy sword from a scabbard at his hip. He shot toward Remi, who zipped to the side at the last moment. The Scourge's fast momentum caused him to speed by when he missed. The idiot's compatriots flew at Remi, but the lost bits of wing and cartilage had done damage. They were slow and off-kilter. A winged creature could not win an air battle without speed and balance.

Remi dropped, performed a forward roll, and came up behind them. They turned and waited for their leader to rejoin them, whipping out their blades as if being armed made them more of a threat.

The leader shouted, "Prepare to die."

Cheesy. Not a worthy battle cry. Even Mel Gibson in Braveheart *was better.*

"But it is not this day! This day, we fight!" Remi shouted. "Aragorn in *The Return of the King*. A much better battle cry. But I tire of your antics. To say nothing of your lame verbiage." He spun in the blink of an eye, whisking his knives through the air and striking out with his unsheathed sharp-edged bronze feathers. He sliced a wing from each attacker. The wide-eyed shock as they plummeted toward what would be a rocky, hard landing was priceless.

Re-holstering his blades, Remi scratched his head. *Dimwitted.* What had they hoped to achieve? Had they spotted him heading into the mountains and gotten some random, crazy idea to attack?

Remi dropped low to spot the four bodies. They had smashed to the ground near each other, though the leader had caught the worst of the fall. He was impaled on a jagged peak. *Ouch.* Had to hurt. He'd be out of action for some time. Healing could be a bitch. A long, slow, painful bitch.

After telepathing Harmony's office to send henchmen to pick up the Scourges, he soared high and circled back toward his next stop. On the way, he reported the attack to the Feard while wondering why Scourges would dare challenge him.

Chapter Sixteen

Sultry heat, rain, wind gusts, dark clouds, and sleet—a mish-mash. Maddy watched it all from the deck, protected by the invisible screen erected around the house. Her mood fit the weather. Changeable.

Dom pulled alongside and enveloped her waist with a strong arm. "You're thinking too hard."

"Why was I brought to Angor?"

He shook his head.

Maddy tilted toward him. "Don't use too many words. You could injure yourself."

Dom's smile transformed him from handsome to spectacular.

She glanced up to see two familiar faces braving the weather—both peppered with snow and ice shards.

Ohngel glided inside first. Indigo followed, reining in Oskar before he crashed into the fireplace. Arms akimbo, Dom glared at the witch out of his good eye.

From the back of her gryphon, she shouted and tugged on reins, "So much for a grand entrance. Oskar doesn't have the hang of a soft vertical drop yet. He'll catch on soon."

After jumping to the tiled floor from one of his haunches, she slapped a hand on his rump to send him on his way. "I'll call for you, big guy, when we're gonna leave. Go chill with your buds in the meadow. And don't smoke that wolver's ass."

Oskar loped down the steps into the yard. A snarling Freki met him, the hair on his neck in stiff peaks. The furry beast circled the gryphon, growling and snapping. Oskar's response was to snort fire.

"What'd I say?" yelled Indigo to her ride.

Oskar hung his head. Apparently, wolvers were dangerous while gryphons were deadly.

Madeline waved and raced to the kitchen. She returned, carrying a tray with four mugs on it. "Mulled wine, everyone? Indigo, why don't you go into the bathroom to dry off."

"No need. Roark. Hit me."

Her fire-winged assassin swept out flaming wings. Indigo stepped close. Insta-dry. "Thanks."

"I live to serve." Ohngel grinned.

Because of the blizzard outside, Dom snapped his fingers to light the fireplace.

Seated on floor pillows, the four crowded around the heat. "Dominion, have you ever considered sofas for this room?" asked Indigo.

"No."

Indigo swiped a hand across her lips after she sipped mulled wine. "Clear. Concise. Simple. Hardheaded. Stupid. Moving on. Before I forget, your wolver isn't happy about the gryphons in the meadow."

Dom frowned at the witch but broke it off when Maddy stroked his thigh. Though Ohngel and Indigo didn't miss the action, she didn't care.

Indigo cleared her throat. "The OC said I could get around here on Oskar. His cousins followed. Not my fault. Since big guy gave me a grazing permit in OneWorld, the wolver can just suck it up. Anyhoo. I'm here because of your predicament, Maddy."

Glancing at Dom, her hand still on his leg, Maddy sighed. "I know. I'm doing things I have no control over, but I have longer bouts of sanity. Then later, my actions or words are pure Syc-think. Today's a bad day. I have trouble controlling my desire to fall slavishly at Dom's feet with my tongue lolling out of my mouth while I wait for his orders, tail wagging."

The black-winged assassin smiled as he patted the back of Maddy's hand. Their visitors' gazes tracked the gesture as if they were surprised Dom had a tender side. Maddy knew he could smile without his face cracking.

Her chin angled up as she stared at Dom, open adoration showing through her foggy gaze. Then she shook her head, eyes clear again. Funny how she was more aware of her swings from Syc to Sane. And better able to control them.

Indigo sat yoga style, crossing her legs under her. "My brother, Alarik, is director of the Ministry of Well Being on Scath. In other words, he's big stuff, a warlock mix with specialized skills that make him a super healer. I'm not just touting him because he's my bro. He's that good."

"So?" said Dom.

Despite Dom's grumpy caution, Maddy leaned forward, anxious to hear what Indigo had on her mind.

"Hear me out. I was wondering about this Sycophancy shit. If it behaves like a brain injury, perhaps it can be healed."

He fixed his good eye on Indigo for a moment. "He's an Aeternal, she's a human, and Sycophancy is an Immortal problem." Swinging his gaze toward Maddy, Dom said, "But it's worth a try."

Maddy nodded. "Anything. Are we talking pills or under the knife, Indigo?"

"Uh ... neither. Mage healers have the touch. No meds. No scalpels. It's a hands-on solution."

"What's your take, Ohngel?" asked Dom.

"When Indy and I talked it over with her brother, he said he'd bring along another mage who specializes in brain disorders. As an aside, he said that healer skills wouldn't work on Immortals with a malady. Something about how our brains are wired. But on a human…"

Madeline bristled. "Because our brains are so puny?"

"No," said Indigo. "Touchy. Touchy. It has to do with the whole eternity and DNA thingy for Immortals. Anyway, he thinks he could have success with you."

Dom squeezed Maddy's fingers. "Your mind. Your decision."

Her shoulders relaxed, comforted by the black-winged assassin's touch. "Does it hurt?" she asked.

Indigo bit her lower lip, puzzling the question. "Not usually. When a healer places hands on you to cast a spell, you'll feel a chill, the shivers. Course, that's with normal injuries. No Aeternal has tried to heal a raging case of Sycophancy. If the process hurts too much, shout out. He'll stop."

Madeline shifted on her cushion, curling denim-clad legs under her. She didn't appreciate waiting for the Sycophancy to cure itself. If it ever did. This idea of Indigo's was proactive. On the other hand, could it make the situation worse? Her struggle with indecision was only momentary. Action was better than acceptance. "I'm willing to try. I need to have me back full-time. It's like some stranger takes over my body, making me do things I'd never dream of doing myself." She grinned at Dom. "Except for some things."

Indigo downed what was left of her mulled wine, set her glass on the floor, and sprang to her feet. "Okay. It's a date. Dom can pick up my bro and the healer from Scath."

The witch blinked. Oskar materialized in the middle of the room with a small rodent in his mouth. Startled he dropped the critter on the floor, a puff of smoke snorting from his nostrils.

Indigo took off after the creature with Ohngel on

her six. They zigged. They zagged, but the little beastie was fast. A growling Dom cast a capture net over the rodent. *Overkill*. Scooping up the critter, he released him outside.

The startled wolver on the lawn took advantage of the situation, outrunning the rat, swallowing him whole, and licking his lips. "Thanks," he called out to the gryphon. Freki was the only one pleased by Oskar's catch.

Madeline stifled a laugh. She enjoyed the gryphon with a bling upgrade and the talking wolver. *How ordinary life will seem back in St. Louis.* Still, that was where she belonged.

When Dom jammed his fists onto his hips, the tension in the room made Oskar a bit nervous. Indigo jumped on his back and grabbed the reins. "Time for our exit, bud. Dom, Roark will let you know when Alarik is ready for the pick-up. Until then."

"Can't wait," said the black-winged assassin, his arms folded over his chest, a frown plastered on his face. Smiles for Maddy. Grimaces for Indigo. Situation normal.

Yep. Maddy was having a great time. Now, if she could just get rid of this Syc shit. She deserved a worry-free moment with Dom before she returned home.

She'd settle down again with her job at the library, meet up with her sisters for some fun, and re-acquaint herself with her routine. When that grew boring, she could dream about the dangerous but handsome black-winged assassin who had been hers for a brief time.

****

On bad days, Madeline scrubbed Dom's already-clean floor, dusted the dust-free house, laundered his already-laundered underwear, and fought her compulsion to fuck him nonstop. She prepped dinner and cleaned up.

The hard way. Without the Immortal warrior snapping his fingers.

On good days, she recited the Dewey Decimal Classification System's major categories, read books, relaxed on the sofa with Dom, made love, and played with Freki when he stopped by for a visit.

Now she chewed her thumbnail, worried but determined to go through with this thing. The Aeternal healer, recommended by Indigo, was on his way to cure her with his brand of surgery. If possible.

At the sound of shushing wings, she glanced toward the sky where the roof should be.

Finally.

Dom flew into the salon with a guy under each arm. Since a monsoon was pounding Angor today, all three were soaked. With a waggle of his fingers, Dom dried himself and then the visitors.

Handy.

With the fireplace crackling, the guests took places in front of it, squirming on pillows to get comfortable, trying to figure out what to do with their legs.

Madeline shook her head. Indigo was right. Couches were a must. If she stayed any longer, she'd find some magazines and point out furniture to Dom so that he could snap more comfortable stuff into existence.

Passing around hot mulled wine, Dom said, "Maddy, this is Alarik, Indigo's brother. He brought along Rath, a mage who specializes in diseases of the mind. Uh … neurological disorders." The men nodded when Dom mentioned their names.

While all three stared at Maddy, she busied herself by settling on a pillow. "Okay. What's gonna happen here?"

With all eyes still on her, she said, "Jeez. Stop

looking at me as if I'll explode when you explain the process to me. I'm not that breakable."

At that moment, Freki prowled inside, shaking and splattering the walls and guests with rainwater. He strutted up to Dom. "I'm hungry."

"I'm busy."

"Don't care." The wolver's ears flattened.

Rising with a huff, Dom lumbered into the kitchen, the creature following.

He returned without Freki while Alarik was acquainting her with his associate. "Rath is the healer who will examine you. If he deems he can help, he will begin the procedure."

Maddy clasped a palm to her chest where her heart thumped wildly. "You haven't worked on Sycophants before, have you, Rath?"

"No. Where we're from—Scath—we don't have Mind Rats who can create the injury. If that's what it is."

Madeline trembled until a cool breeze blew across her skin. When it did, she calmed.

After flicking his wrist, Alarik smiled. "A slight spell to settle your nerves, dear."

Nice. Better than anxiety drugs.

Relaxed, she faced Rath again. "Tell me exactly what you plan to do." The man was an unlikely-looking medical professional. He was muscled, with huge hands, almost clumsy in size.

"I won't know until I examine you. After that, I will give you a step-by-step."

Madeline glanced at Dom, who supported her with a nod. "Okay. Where do you want me?"

"Where you are is fine for now." He unfolded from the floor with more grace than Madeline expected from such a bulky man and stepped toward her.

Dom shot up but didn't confront Rath. He held

himself in check, his hands fisted at his sides.

The healer, though glancing at Dom with uncertainty, crouched beside Madeline. "When I touch you to cast a spell, you may feel a chill." He set a palm on her forehead, closing his eyes.

Maddy didn't know if she should breathe. So she held her breath as long as she could. Finally, she gasped for air. She crossed her ankles. She uncrossed her ankles. And he was right. She shivered from a chill.

Apparently finished after a long ten minutes, Rath shoved onto his feet and paced the salon, having a chat with himself. His lips moved, but Madeline couldn't hear what he was saying.

When the mage resumed sitting on his pillow beside the fire, he latched onto his mug of wine and took a pull. Setting it down, he leaned back, his arms locked around a knee. "Someone has messed with her mind. No question about it. And the problem acts like a brain injury, but her body is fighting it. Quite successfully. Unfortunately, there are patches of … um … resistance. I'm assuming these spots may be what you called triggers."

"Interesting," said Alarik.

Freki joined them by the fire, curling up near its warmth. He raised his head. "Sounds dangerous to me. You got this guy's *bona fides*?"

"Nobody asked you," said Dom. "But Alarik says he's good."

Freki snarled, his snout resting on top of his paws.

Madeline crossed her arms, listening closely as everyone talked around her. "If untreated what will these triggers do?"

Rath shrugged. "First, I need to ask a question. What are the symptoms of this injury?"

Maddy blushed, biting her lower lip while she

wondered how to explain the whole mess. "I guess you could say they make me very compliant. I have a strong need to please." She glanced at Dom whose frowning lips curved into a smile.

"Everyone?" asked Rath.

"No. Only him." She pointed at the black-winged assassin.

"Okay. Here's my guess. They could keep reinforcing original commands. Or I could be wrong. They could be new commands, lying in wait until your body no longer fights them. Then, they could go kablooey. Whatever they are, they appear rather stubborn. But the truth is, I have no idea."

Dom said, "She showed no signs of being a Syc at the beginning."

"Probably means a trigger kicked in," the healer suggested.

"That's what the Feard thought." Madeline chewed on her thumbnail. "Rath, I want all things Praevus wiped out of me. Obliterated. Disinfected. Untangled. Whatever you have to do."

Rath glanced at Dom.

"Don't look at him. It's my mind. My decision." She glanced at Dom but held firm.

"How much latitude am I given?" asked the Aeternal healer.

Madeline shifted her position on the pillow and sipped her heated wine. "Enough to fix me. Not enough to leave me a blathering idiot."

"That's a wide range," said Rath.

Maddy closed her eyes. She fought running to Dom, worshipping at his feet, cuddling in his lap, and pleasing him. Shaking her head, she dislodged the Syc-think. "Do what you can."

The healer stroked a hand along his jaw. "Do you

want to hear about possible side effects?"

"No." Madeline clenched her hands, digging her nails into her palms.

Dom rotated toward her. "Maddy…"

"No, and hell no. Proceed, doc. Where do you want me?"

"I'd like you on your back with your feet slightly higher than your head."

A cautious Dom helped Madeline scoot to the floor and kick her feet onto a pillow. The healer sat near her head, a leg on each side of him.

Crouching beside her, Dom rested a palm on her thigh.

The contact comforted her, and she slid her lids closed.

Rath said to her black-winged assassin, "No one can touch her except me."

She instantly missed the solace his hand offered.

Rath pressed his palms to her temples.

Madeline swallowed a scream, the sensation too similar to what Praevus had done. An invasion. But then, a cool breeze wafted across her skin, which she now realized was thanks to Alarik. She relaxed.

An hour passed. If occasional sharp pains shot through Madeline, she ignored them. Then the healer's invisible fingers retreated from her mind. Her eyes snapped open.

Rath withdrew his palms from her temples, his arms crashing to his sides. Alarik helped him stand and stumble to his place, where he flopped onto a floor pillow. He inhaled and exhaled until his breathing steadied. "I cleared the pathways of residual Sycophancy and removed one trigger, or spot of resistance. Another remains. It has burrowed so deep that excising it may cause damage."

"What is it for?" asked Madeline.

Rath shook his head. "No way to tell."

"Where does it fit on my spectrum between fixed and blathering idiot?"

He inhaled deeply. "I don't think removing it will make you a vegetable. That is an Earther's saying, correct? But you could have holes in your memory."

"That is what we say." Maddy's chin dropped to her chest. Like the healer, she was exhausted. "Get it out." Before Dom could question her resolution, she repeated, "Get it out now."

Dom's mouth was a grim slash. She recognized he had feelings for her and how hard this was on him. Still, her body. Her decision. She mustered enough courage to give him a warm, reassuring, though weak, smile.

He nodded, his stern expression unchanged.

"I need a moment," said Rath.

Madeline twisted her head so she could see the healer. "Sure. Take your time. I'll just lie here stewing." After a sec, she said, "Sorry. I don't mean to be snippy."

Rath stretched his arms overhead. "I understand."

Freki snuggled up to Madeline. When he growled, she patted his fur.

Dom surged to his boots, snapping out his black wings and knocking a sculpture off a shelf.

Maddy lifted her head from the floor. "Don't be a wuss. Get back here. You're my good luck charm."

Dom snorted but once again took up his spot at her side. He would be the last vision before she closed her eyes, prepared for the removal of a stubborn trigger.

Because this incursion was more painful, she blacked out. But when the healer's palms left her temples, she snapped out of the coma with a start. Other than a slight headache, she felt fine.

"What?" asked Dom when she mumbled.

Maddy grinned. "Just reciting the Dewey Decimal Classification System."

"The what?" he asked.

"It doesn't matter. It's only important that I can."

Rath's shoulders slumped, and he twisted his neck from side to side. "Only time will tell if you suffer from memory loss and if your ..." he looked as though he searched for the right words "desire to please has abated. For now, rest."

She curled onto her side, adjusting her arm until it was a pillow under her head. Maddy watched Dom tuck Alarik under one arm and Rath under the other. With his cargo safe, he soared into the sky. Petting Freki, she fell asleep, feeling as if a weight had been lifted from her mind.

Then an arm slid under her legs and curled around her back. Her black-winged hero carried her to bed, throwing a cover over her and crawling in to snuggle against her. "You're an addictive female, Maddy."

She bit her lower lip to staunch tears, unsure if she was happy to be going home soon or sad to leave Dom. He was addictive, too.

Chapter Seventeen

Ely heard the good news about Madeline. She was cured and would be on her way to Earth soon. No danger to herself or other humans. But other aspects of his hunt were frustrating. Harmony was busy. Very busy. Unable to schedule a meet now.

While he waited for her "to find the time," he again took up the search for Praevus in Stupool's hot spots. The rowdiest bar in the large city was crowded. To get through the door, he gripped two inmates by the necks, tossing them aside.

After plowing inside, Ely halted, his gaze circling the dark environment. *Mayhem.* Males were beating the shit out of one another. The reason? Who knew? Maybe the three female Scourges perched on a table, skimpy tops, pushed-up tits, short skirts, legs crossed. Creats, the money in OneWorld, changed hands among them. Likely, they were betting on which fighters got to fuck them first.

Ely spied the bartender, who leaned against the rack of bottles, his arms flung wide to protect the merch. The guy didn't hear or see the assassin move up beside him. Ely snapped fingers in front of his face to get his attention.

The barkeep jumped. He eyed the ice-winged warrior from boot to white hair, his fangs giving him away as a Leech. "Yeah? Whatcha want, Feard?"

"Intel." Ely stifled a yawn as he strong-armed an intrusive Scourge, shoving him across the bar top and into the fray.

"This is a bad time," said the bartender. "And I'm not predicting much improvement in the near future."

Same ol' same ol', Ely thought. *I ask for intel*

from a Scourge. Scourge withholds. I explain why that won't work. Scourge still acts as if he has the upper hand. I ratchet up the query with a little violence. Scourge gives in. Ho-hum.

"I can be bought. How many creats is it worth?" asked the barkeep as expected.

"Zero is fair." Ely relaxed his hands on the hilts of the two short-bladed knives in hip holsters.

The guy shrugged. "Then I won't know anything."

Ely moved, touching his boots to the barkeep's ratty shoes, jabbing a fist to the guy's solar plexus and then to his throat.

The Blood Leech fell against the racked bottles he'd been protecting. When some broke, the Scourge cried like a baby. He barely squeezed out, "I'm gonna be punished for that."

"I'm sad. Now about our convo. Are you feeling chattier?"

He sniffed. "Whatever."

Ely took that as a *yes*. "Have you seen Praevus?"

With a palm on his throat, the barkeep scrunched his brows. "The Mind Rat?"

"The very same."

"His kind don't hang out here much. We get mostly Soul Suckers." He waved his hand around the bar. "As you can see, emotions run high."

Ely nodded. *Yeah*. The fighters were Suckers. They were pounding each other with fists and throwing out a shit ton of touchy-feelies. Lust. Anger. Fear. A damn stew, allowing them to feed on the emotions.

"For a few creats, I'll share a rumor." The barkeeper sniffed back tears.

Ely laughed. Then he glanced at the guy. "You're serious. Fuck off and spit up the intel."

"I hear he's excused from the Ordeals."

"I already know that."

Without a new lead, Ely left the joint, an arm thrust out straight like a bulldozer to shove fighters out of his path. Outside again, he thought maybe he should have stuck around. He wondered whether he could pay the Soul Suckers to make him feel something other than the ennui of eternity.

Fuck the world-weariness routine. Ely was beginning to bore himself.

At the next rundown Scourge tavern a few blocks down the street, he pushed through the door.

Leaning onto his elbows, propped behind him on the bar, Ely faced the crowd. The place was one step up from a sewer, but the drinks were okay. Not watered down. Recognizable brands. Large portions.

Someone pulled up alongside. Malacour, the bar manager. "How about a free ale, assassin?" He held up two fingers. Nodding, the bartender filled mugs and set one in front of his boss and the other in front of Ely.

You'd think Malacour would want him gone as soon as possible. Having the Feard in your bar was bad for business. But the guy seemed almost cordial. For a Scourge. Course, he was one level up—a trustee, about to return to Vast cured of what ailed him.

Oozing a friendly vibe, Malacour asked, "What brings you around?" When he smiled, the tips of his fangs showed.

"Praevus. Seen him?" Ely swiped a hand across his mouth, wiping off foam.

"The Rat? Let me think." He swallowed a large gulp of brew, set the mug on the bar, and shook his head. "Not for a long time. Maybe a month. Whaddya want with him?"

"Ask a few questions. You happen to know where

he is?"

Malacour chuckled. "Being a trustee takes me out of the gossip circles. Since I'm almost on my way back to Vast, my clientele see me as untrustworthy."

Harmony had set the guy up in this bar biz since he was on the road to rehab. Great deal. Before succumbing to a malady, Malacour had flown in one of the elite winged squadrons, and the OC could use him again on side good. He'd been a real hero until he wasn't.

After a little more convivial chit-chat, Malacour said, "Got unfinished paperwork. A boss's job is never done. See you next time, and I hope you catch up with this Praevus."

As the guy strolled toward the back room, Ely noticed the patrons had moved their seats far away. It should please him to have such an effect on Scourges. He was, however, neither pleased nor displeased. It was what it was. They were wise to give him a wide berth.

Was it the ice in his veins? The vacant, uncaring look in eyes? *Nah*. It was probably the fact he could smite their asses if they pissed him off. Still, runaways couldn't answer questions. He picked up his frosty ale and prepped to socialize.

The first table he approached vacated before he arrived. This wasn't gonna work. Despite the loud rap playing through the speakers, he shouted. "Keep your asses in your seats. I've got questions."

The audience froze.

Ely dragged a chair over to a round, wobbly-legged table which was about to fall to the floor. "Gents." Four Scourges nodded, their eyes wide with terror. "May I join you?"

They nodded again, dropping their gazes to their glass mugs. A brave soul spoke aloud. "Could we stop you?"

"Good point. No." Ely slammed his drink onto the table, hauling out a chair. He chatted them up with questions about Praevus, but they were low-level Flesh Eaters who knew nothing. He needed to quiz Mind Rats.

Ely glanced around the dirty bar with its gummy floor, stained walls, rickety furniture, dim lighting, and desperate patrons. If he could feel sorry for Scourges, he would. Had he ever? He couldn't recall. As the oldest of the assassins, Ely found himself having trouble recalling bits of his past. He supposed the faulty recall was normal after eons of time. His brain had to search through mountains of material to grasp a small detail. He had even slept for a century, hoping to awaken from stasis recharged. Then some bad shit had happened—he didn't remember what it was—and the OneCreator called him back to work.

He didn't say, "Hey, OC, buddy, fuck off. I need more time to get my shit together." No. What he said was "Yes, sir. Right away, sir."

Though Ely had awakened refreshed, his good vibrations didn't last more than a few centuries. Now, here he was again with a major case of the blahs. Immortality was a bitch. Each of his fellow assassins handled it differently. Ohngel chose to scheme and plan for millennia. All to keep Aeternals and humans from wiping each other out. Remi dived into sadistic shit. Chains. Whips. Sex. Who knew what else. Gareth eventually lost the battle. He turned Scourge and had to be put down. Dom ... Dom just plowed forward. If eternity got too heavy for him, the black-winged assassin crashed into it head-on, slamming it out of the way. He overpowered it as he did everything in life.

Ely spotted a bunch of Rats at three o'clock. Dragging his chair along with him, the feet leaving marks in the floor grit, he joined the group. "Assholes." It was a good greeting as greetings go. "What do you hear about Praevus?" He might as well throw it out there.

Glances pinged from one depraved Scourge to another.

Ely extracted a short-bladed knife from his holster. He jammed it point first into the table. The males fell all over each other to see who could talk first. Bunch of white-eyed Nancies. He pointed. "You first."

The selected Mind Rat glanced at his companions. "We're not in Praevus's circle. He's … beyond our skills. But I know where he lives. Saw him coming out one night."

"Already found his elegant digs. I need new news." Ely pointed again. "Next."

"I hear he's exempt from the Ordeals. Has a backer."

"Yeah? Who is it?"

"Some valued Scourge."

"Yeah? Who?"

They shrugged in unison. The first talker said, "A trustee, I hear."

Out of the corner of his eye, Ely saw Malacour come out of the back room and signal two stagehands.

Suddenly, the bar quieted. All gazes flipped to the front. A cage, the bars wrapped in black velvet, was wheeled onto the stage. Inside was a female, sitting on a swing. Her back, where long red hair flowed in curls, was to the audience.

One of the Scourges at the table shushed Ely, who jerked up his brows. Now the guy gets a spine?

The two Leech stagehands, their fangs pressing into their bottom lips, twirled the cage around. The female faced her admirers. Ely took notice, an oddity for him. In his current state, he eschewed most pleasures, including sex, but she stirred his groin, until he spied her eyes. They were white. Fucking Mind Rat. He hated Mind Rats.

Strange, though? When he looked more closely, he saw her eyes were translucent, more pale green than white, almost pretty.

When she drew a deep breath, her chest expanded. She opened her mouth. A plaintive song poured out, its melody and lyrics sad. Sadder even than the run-down, dirty bar. Ely glanced around. All the patrons perched at the edge of their seats, enthralled by the sound, by the words, by the female who was messing with their minds.

Ely rose from his chair, her voice getting to him a bit, though the Feard and Michael were mostly immune to Scourge tricks. He wasn't gonna get anything else from this audience. They were about to be knocked out by the song. Literally. Then the fun and games would commence. He left the club before the floor was littered with writhing Scourges, holding their heads, screaming from pain.

Her voice was a weapon to paralyze the patrons. Once they collapsed, frozen in their own bodies and unable to fight back, the play would begin. Maybe a certain note she'd hit would fry their brains. Fun times for all.

The hypnotic voice followed him out the door. "I wanna be loved by you, just you." It was sultry, soul-deep. He shivered.

Ely pathed Dom. *News. Praevus has a high-placed Scourge friend. Possibly a trustee. Don't know who.*

Doesn't tell us the Immortal who kidnapped and handed Maddy off to him.

No. But it's a baby step closer.

T.M. SMITH

Chapter Eighteen

Maddy's mind was clear, no holes in her memory, and she didn't have uncontrollable urges to worship slavishly at Dom's feet. She still wanted the Immortal's arms around her and his lips pressed to hers, but Rath had cured her Sycophancy.

Since Dom had promised she'd return to Earth tomorrow, Maddy expected to sleep better. But she didn't. Hoping not to wake him, she rolled onto her back, disentangling herself from his arm. With the past haunting her, she lay awake for hours.

A week after the father had deserted the family, the mother shuffled out of her bedroom, her hair ragged, her face swollen, a dirty bathrobe tied at the waist, and slippers on her feet. The girls were watching television. She opened the liquor cabinet and snatched a bottle. Afterward, she shuffled back to her bedroom, the booze tight in her grip. Maddy followed her with her eyes, while her sisters exchanged glances.

Eventually, the mother stopped drinking in her room and brazenly set her bottle onto the kitchen table. She took up smoking as well. In all this time, the father never visited as he had promised.

Fia and Darya came into Maddy's bedroom one night for a chat. It was a warm summer night and the window was open.

"Let's face it," said Darya. "Mother will never be able to take care of us. Our situation is permanent."

Maddy was excited to go to the middle school next year. Fia would begin her freshman year in high school and Darya her sophomore.

"She'll get better," said Madeline.

"No. She won't," said Fia. "If she does, it's a plus. If she doesn't, so be it. Don't hope for things that may never happen, Mads."

"I want Daddy back. Call him. Tell him Mama needs him."

"We don't know his number or where he is," said Darya. "Mother has money, though. Lots of it, but the cash has run out. Since I have access to her checking and savings, I've been paying the bills, seeing to all the financial matters."

Fia said, "I'll shop for groceries as I've been doing. We'll continue to share fixing breakfast, lunches, and dinners, each of us taking a day."

Maddy said, "I don't like to cook."

"You'll have to do it anyway," said Darya, more kind than she should have been.

"I don't want to." She was still a child, digging her feet in, hoping that all this would go away if she fought against it hard enough.

"Mads, none of us want this. But this is where we are. Fia and I have had to survive before. It's all new to you. You'll learn. You're smart."

Fia asked, "Can I still take voice lessons? Can you still dance?"

Darya took charge. "Yes. There's plenty of money for those things."

When Madeline began to cry, Fia drew her into a fierce hug. "Tears do no good. They change nothing. Only our actions will change our situation."

"We'll have to take care of Mother too. Make sure she eats. Clean her up. Keep her room straightened. I don't think the housekeeper should go in there," said Darya.

"I won't buy her booze or ciggies." Fia pounded her palm on the bed.

Madeline pushed up to lean against the headboard. "We should talk to her. Tell her we need her to take care of us."

Darya sighed. "We've tried, Mads. She doesn't care. We are all we have now."

They hugged each other, something they did often in the ensuing years.

Restless, Madeline slid out of bed. In the kitchen, she turned on the faucet to get a glass of water. Carrying it back to the bedroom, she set it on the nightstand. With her arms folded under her head, she picked up the sad memory-lane trip where she'd left off.

The girls survived for years, eating, wearing clean clothes to school, doing homework, taking lessons, going to movies, buying books, and finding fun things to do. They also listened to Mother's drunken rants, mopped up her messes, and picked her up off the floor at night to go to bed. Fia and Darya bailed her out of jail for DUIs several times. They hid from her crappy, abusive boyfriends when necessary.

The girls had a few hard-fast rules—they did not invite friends to their house, they were never alone with the visiting men, and they kept their home life secret.

One memorable night, Maddy woke up and went into the kitchen for a drink of water. Mother was there, a bottle on the table, a glass in her hand. Her hair was tangled, her robe mis-buttoned, and her sagging face bore all the signs of alcoholism.

She glanced up from her booze, glaring. Rising from the chair, she stumbled across the room and grabbed Maddy's shoulders. "It's your fault he left." Mother drew back an arm and slapped her across the face.

Maddy crumpled to the floor. Mother kicked and kicked until she lost her balance and fell.

Fia and Darya, hearing the ruckus, raced into the kitchen to find Maddy holding her stomach and Mother passed out. The next day, the girls enrolled in martial arts classes.

They also played out scenarios. What ifs. What if Mother tries to hit one of us again? What if some guy tries to lay hands on us?

Exhaling a puff of breath, Madeline rolled to her side. Her sisters were everything to her, her north stars. What would they say about Dominion? She closed her eyes, but sleep remained evasive because she couldn't keep the past out of her head.

At the end of the summer before Maddy was to begin her sophomore year in high school, Fia and Darya came into her room. They looked serious enough to scare her.

Sitting on the edge of her bed, Darya blurted out, "I'm leaving, Maddy. I was offered an audition for a ballet troupe in New York. I have to take it."

Madeline shot up straight. "But…"

"I'm leaving, too." Fia started to cry, hugging Maddy.

Her mouth hung open. "You haven't graduated."

"I took classes in summer school. I'm finished. I just won't go through a ceremony, but I'll have my diploma."

Maddy swung her feet onto the floor.

Darya looped an arm over her shoulders, swiping at tears on her sister's cheeks. "I feel bad, but I have to take this chance, and Fia must make her way in the world. You'll need to decide which of us you'll come with. The choice is yours."

"But why now?" asked Madeline.

"It may be the only chance I get," said Fia. "We won't be upset no matter who you choose."

Madeline chewed her lip. "I want to stay."

"What?" Darya blinked.

"Until I graduate from high school. Then, I'll move in with one of you for college."

"I don't like it. I won't go to New York," said Darya.

"Yes. You will. I'll do fine until I'm old enough to leave for college. I know the routine."

"When Mother invites over her drunken visitors, barricade your bedroom door," said Fia, brushing a tear from her cheek.

Maddy's chest heaved with short, panicked breaths. "I can do it. What about the money?"

"I'll put your name on the checking, savings, and other financial accounts. My name's still there, too. I'll continue to manage some accounts and answer all your questions. We also hired advisors. Stock the fridge and have the housekeeper fix a bunch of dinners each week. We'll raise her pay. There are plenty of bucks. Enough for college later. Mama comes from a long line of money."

Madeline sucked back the tears. If she lost it now, she'd never stop.

Fia hugged her again. Tighter. "You're never alone, Mads. We are only a phone call away. I'm heading for LA to start a singing career. If you need me, I'll be here on the next plane out."

Darya gave her the same speech.

And they were. When Madeline called either sister with a problem or just needed to see them, they came. Each night they talked on the phone. And they were right. She knew the routine.

Since the sisters had kept in touch regularly, they must be worried about her. But how could she reach them from here? And how would that call go? "Hey, Fia, I'm in another dimension." "Really, Madeline, you have to get your head out of all those books." "Hi, Darya. My date took me flying." "Madeline, I never thought you'd go out with a pilot. A college English professor, maybe." She flopped to her other side, punched her pillow, and yawned.

What was hard was taking care of her mother who grew more dependent each year. She'd even lost interest in bringing losers home.

Madeline joined Al-Anon. At first, for the company. After all, she couldn't invite friends to the house. The meetings did provide a social outlet, but they were so much more. They gave her a basis for understanding why she was a mess.

Her life revolved around an alcoholic mother. She had been abandoned as an infant, then by the only father she knew, and finally by the mother who chose alcohol over care.

The group taught her strategies. They taught her to detach herself from her mother. They taught her to admit she'd been hurt. They tried to teach her not to overreact to situations she could not control. Mostly, they allowed her to talk about her life rather than hide it.

When she was eighteen, Mother died. Her last words stabbed into Maddy's heart. "I have loved you. Not as much as you deserved but as much as I could." The young woman cried for the life she might have had if the mother had been stronger. If the father had not left.

After she wiped away the tears, she felt guilt for the relief. She and her sisters arranged the funeral, but they were the only mourners. Eliza Williamson left her life as a downtrodden drunk, surrounded by adopted daughters who struggled to care. Madeline tried to remember happier times, but it was hard. For her sisters, it was worse because they had known only a few years of the good mother.

Maddy enrolled in college, enjoying her classes and making a few friends. Then her life spun out of control. She broke down. It was all over a test she'd studied hard for but failed. Her sisters came to her rescue, insisting she seek professional help as they had.

That saved her life. Al-Anon had been a start, but she had needed more. She found it in Dr. Marrick. Maddy understood she had a touch of OCD. It was okay. She was okay. She learned to control some situations but not to overreact when she could not control everything.

Her psychologist taught her to manage the fear. How to self-calm. She was neither the cause of her mother's drinking nor the solution to it. She no longer had to hide from friends, worrying they would discover her secrets. She worked on trust issues, trying to form positive relationships. A hard one, but she had finally gone on dates and had a few serious, though brief, relationships.

After each breakup, she fought a sense of loneliness, of fear nothing in life would work out for her. And she fought to maintain the right balance of control—not so much that she was rigid, but not so little she'd spin.

Her go-to comforts had been to keep secrets or to fix things. In psych talk that was called controlling behavior. So, she relaxed, shared parts of her life with friends, and accepted she could not fix all problems.

She finally got a job she loved and was climbing out of the pit of her childhood and teens.

Madeline stretched her arms overhead. She'd fallen asleep but awakened with a start. When she patted the bed beside her, it was empty. Dom was already up, maybe happy she was going home today. He'd be rid of her and all her baggage. Mora could return.

Sitting up, Maddy leaned against the headboard. *No.* Dom wasn't happy to have her go. He didn't always show his affection, but his actions toward her said it all. He was practical, like her. Humans and Immortals weren't a good fit. Oil and vinegar. Spider-Man and Doc Ock. Britney Spears and Justin Timberlake. She'd never forget him. Though she should be mumbling the Dewey Decimal Classification System like a mad woman or having a full-blown panic attack, she wasn't.

She'd changed in ways she hardly believed. Maddy fell for a man who wasn't human, who had goddamn wings, and who killed people for a living. Bad people. But instead of marrying the man, buying a little house with a white picket fence around it, and having a few spoiled brats, she was leaving him. She had to, no matter what. Humans belonged on Earth. They didn't belong in OneWorld with a gorgeous, grim-but-kind winged assassin of the OneCreator.

Chapter Nineteen

Dom had slept with Madeline in his arms most of the night. Her restlessness was understandable since she was eager to return to her home in St. Louis. Though his sleep was troubled also, he didn't disturb her. He left her to her dreams as he pressed against her naked back, enjoying the caress of silky skin for the last time.

Ever since Gareth, Dom had avoided deep connections. Somehow, Madeline had slipped beneath his barriers. He'd miss her. As he stroked fingers through her soft hair, his heart ached. Taking her home was the right thing to do, but for a brief time, he'd had someone who cared for him as much as he'd cared for her. He'd had someone who hadn't betrayed him.

Shaking off his regrets, Dom slipped silently out of bed. He stepped into his pants and headed for the kitchen. After he'd been working on breakfast for a while, Maddy stumbled in, sleep rumpled and knuckling her eyes. She wore his t-shirt, reminding him he'd miss the sight of her long legs, her wit, and her hesitant smile.

Freki prowled alongside, her hand tangled in his fur. She patted his head. "The mutt's famished." She yawned.

Growling, the beast said, "Damn straight. How about some gently seared steak?"

Dom sneered at the wolver but asked Maddy, "How about you?"

"Always hungry." She snagged orange juice from the fridge and poured two glasses. Afterward, she filled the wolver's bowl with water.

Freki lapped it up.

Dom set a plate of chopped beef on the floor next

to the furry creature's other bowl. He returned to the stove, piling scrambled eggs, potatoes, and bacon onto plates. Putting one in front of Madeline, he saved the larger portions for himself. He lugged a stool alongside her.

As they ate in silence, Maddy's hand lingered on his thigh. Dom smothered a groan.

After a bite of bacon, she slapped a hand to her mouth, pushing her plate away. "Ouch." With an elbow resting on the counter, she braced her chin on her palm.

"Problem?"

"Toothache. Just a twinge. Nothing serious. I guess I'll go to the dentist when I get home." She paused, her hand continuing to stroke up and down his leg. "Before I forget to say it, Dom, thank you for saving me."

"No need to thank me for doing my job."

"You do it well." Patting his leg, she rose, gathered her plate, and reached for his.

Dom let the subject hang. He wanted Maddy to stay, but a mortal human didn't belong in OneWorld. Wishing things were different changed nothing. "Leave the dishes."

"Okay." She spun around, calling over her shoulder as she sprinted from the room, "I'll get dressed."

Dom shoved the plates and flatware into the dishwasher, ignoring the crumbs on the counter. Maddy would gasp at his lack of perfection.

Aw, damn.

He swiped a sponge over the countertop.

There.

"What's going on?" asked Freki, his bowl licked clean.

"I'm returning the human to Earth."

"Who's gonna feed me when she's gone?" His ears flattened.

"Why don't you catch your prey like other wolvers?"

"Shouldn't have to. I'm special. The prototype. The first of my kind."

"I guess you'll have to rely on me. Besides, as I recall, I feed you all the time." Dom leaned against the kitchen counter, one ankle crossed over the other.

"I like Madeline better than I do you. She's softer. She smiles more. You're mostly grumpy." Freki snarled, flopping to his stomach and stretching onto his forepaws.

Dom glared. "Yeah? Well, adjust. Life isn't always about what you want."

Madeline strolled back in, dressed in a cropped tee and jeans which made her ass look spectacular. She wore sexy ankle boots. "What are you talking about?"

"You," said the wolver. "I don't want you to go, and Mr. Personality doesn't give a shit."

When she looked dejected, Dom blurted out, "Not true."

The beast stalked to Maddy, rubbing against her legs. Her hand caressed his head before he trotted off, tail in the air, grumbling about how if she loved him she wouldn't leave.

Madeline brushed away a tear while watching a proud but downhearted wolver leave the room.

"Weepy for the damn mutt?"

"You and Freki. I'm a sap." She ran into his arms, nuzzling his chest.

Though they stood clutching each other for a long time, he refused to admit aloud that he'd miss Maddy. The words were too painful. He desired the impossible, and the impossible was best left unsaid.

Maddy seemed to sense that as if she knew him too well.

After they strolled wordlessly hand in hand into

the salon, her chest expanded with a deep breath, followed by a sigh. "I'd like to fly over the snowy mountaintops. A little detour on the way home?"

"Sure." He swallowed hard. Their time together would end as it had begun. Maddy would be in his arms flying over Angor. He had let her get close when he'd sworn never to repeat the past.

With a wave of his hand, he clothed her in a down jacket, gloves, and a warm hat. Placing an arm under her knees and the other around her back, he clasped Madeline to him as before.

She smiled and echoed her first demand. "Don't drop me."

In spite of himself, he grinned. "I'm very strong. I don't drop hitchhikers."

Dom's onyx-tipped wings whipped out before pounding down to lift them off the floor and soar out of his home. He skimmed the tops of the snow-capped mountains. The weather honored her farewell trip with clear skies.

She swiped moisture from her cheek. "It's amazing. I'll never forget."

Dom's heart broke with each tear. Not wanting her to remember sadness, he swooped low, skimming the ocean. When he flew close enough that spray from the wind-tossed waves peppered them, Madeline squealed, laughter erupting from her lips. A roller coaster, he shot straight into the sky, dipped, and looped to the sounds of her delight.

With Maddy happy again and a storm on the horizon, he ended the tour. Dom swung toward the rocky-peaked Razor Mountains. North of that range, they'd take the pathway to Vast. From there, he'd travel to Earth.

As they neared the gateway, six Scourges flew at them from behind a low, dark cloud. They encircled Dom and Madeline.

Without thinking, Dom clutched Madeline tighter, pointed his head down, and arrowed toward a canyon below.

When he touched ground, he shoved her behind him, a mountain at their backs. The Scourges landed, spreading out in a line.

Flesh Eaters. All of them.

To secure Maddy, Dom fanned out his massive black wings. He unsheathed feathers tipped with onyx, sharp-honed blades. Then before the attackers were fully in place, he released two, beheading an equal number of Scourges.

Four assholes left.

He'd make this fast. Recognizing the leader, he asked, "What the fuck are you doing, Farce? You don't stand a chance."

The Scourge's skin peeled from his exposed arms, revealing spots of blackened flesh, just like his buddies. This is what he'd saved Gareth from experiencing.

"Have to try, Dominion." Farce had been an Immortal warrior, part of the OneCreator's personal guard. An honor. Then he was caught feasting on a buddy. Off to Angor.

"Why?"

Farce spread his legs, a battle stance, preparing to fight. "To get out of the Ordeals. Can't stand them."

"So reform."

The Scourge cackled. "Don't think that's in my future."

"If you can't do the time, don't do the crime."

Madeline shouted at his back, "Be careful, Dom. They look scary."

"Just give me the female, and we're outta here. No fuss. No muss."

Why would they come for Maddy?

"Not gonna happen. Fuss away."

On Farce's signal, the four came at him, swords swinging.

Dom spun, nothing more than a cloud of dust with projectiles launching from his wings. He ducked and side-stepped the attackers while blocking access to Madeline. He curled his wings forward, hurling onyx-bladed feathers. When they missed the targets, he drew his sword from the spine sheath. He swung, lobbed off a Flesh Eater's head, and pierced another Scourge's heart. Farce's remaining conspirator took to the skies, a deserter.

"Just you and me. What do you think of the odds, Flesh Eater?"

"The creats and missing the Ordeals were worth the risk." Farce figure-eighted his blade.

Cheesy.

"Who sent you? If you tell me, I won't extinct you."

"That's a lie." He lunged at Dom. "I've sealed my fate for a chance at freedom."

Dom struck with sword and feather. The first to the heart. The other lodged in Farce's neck. Clean and mean.

The once-honorable warrior's attack added to the questions piling up. Who wanted the human female and had the power to hire these assholes?

He sliced off the Scourge's head before he spun toward Madeline, muttering the words, "May my blade bring you peace." She peeked around him to check out the bodies while he pathed Harmony to pick up the fallen.

Dom grabbed Maddy, tucking her against him as he streaked toward the pathway to Vast and Earth.

No more tours or aerobatics. He'd promised to

take her home. While he couldn't be killed, she could. And somebody was set on getting her. Though it pained his heart, he forced himself to picture Madeline happy on Earth, shelving books in the library, enjoying her job, eventually married, and surrounded by beloved children. What he could not bear to imagine was her dead or in captivity as a Scourge's plaything.

Yes. Maddy had gotten under his skin. After he returned her to Earth, however, everything would be normal again. He'd be the perfect winged assassin of the OneCreator. He'd have meaningless encounters with females. He'd keep Immortals at a distance so that he wouldn't feel anything if he had to punish them. And if he got lonely, he'd remember the beautiful blonde, blue-eyed human who had cared for him and whose silky skin he had loved to caress.

When he spied the passage ahead, he kicked up his speed. "There it is. You'll soon be home." Dom held his grief in check for Maddy's sake. Besides, what would he do with a human in Angor? She'd be in constant danger. Without wings, she had no transportation. It would rankle her to rely on him.

Yeah.

He was doing what was best, but he'd miss her. So would the damn wolver, Freki. But screw him.

Chapter Twenty

Madeline screamed when they slammed into an invisible wall. Though they tumbled through the air ass over foot, she remained tight in Dom's iron grip, his wings working overtime. Her stomach tossed with each roll until she was again upright.

Finally in control of his flight, Dom leveled off, rose, and headed toward the gateway once more.

"W-w-what's wrong?" she stammered.

Too focused on the mission, he ignored the question. He inched forward, his wings pounding downward.

She held her breath this time while he approached the shimmering pathway shoulder first.

When he struck the invisible barrier, his body bounced away slightly. He frowned. Still determined, Dom tried once more. Same result.

"What's wrong?" asked Madeline, her voice strong despite her concern over the puzzling situation.

"I can't get through." He arrowed toward Angor's surface, nose down, wings angled, aiming for a sandy shore.

With the wind of their descent blowing Maddy's hair, she glanced at Dom's face. His lips were a grim slash. "Can we take a different route?"

"This is the only one. An impenetrable barrier surrounds Angor, and the gateway is the only exit." He slowed, preparing to land.

"Is it broken?" Automatic doors malfunctioned on Earth. Why not here? An Immortal glitch.

Dom shook his head. "The gateway doesn't break, but I'll test it."

Once the sandy floor was close, he curved his wings, parachuting them to the ground. He set Madeline down, her stiletto boots sinking into the soft surface. She wobbled until she found her footing.

Silent, Dom took flight, leaving her behind. She watched as he sped toward the shimmery passageway. Upon reaching the spot where they'd been stopped, he disappeared as if exiting through a magic door.

Cupping a hand above her eyes to minimize the glare, she waited until Dom reappeared. He seemed to pop out of nowhere and zip toward her. At the last moment, he floated down to join Madeline.

"Well?" she asked.

He rubbed the patch on his eye. "I got through."

"Great. It's fixed. Let's try again."

"Yeah." He didn't sound very sure.

Madeline moved closer, waiting for Dom to lift her. When he did, he gripped her ass and heaved her high. Her legs locked around his waist while her fingers cupped his neck. They flew to the pathway once more.

Her gaze flicked between Dom's unsure, grim expression and the shimmer of the gateway over her shoulder. She twisted around to keep an eye on their progress.

He slowed, inching forward. Once he stopped, she felt a wall at her back. No leaving.

When Dom returned them to the shore, Madeline slid down his leg.

The puzzled, winged assassin snarled, one side of his mouth sliding into a frown. It was an expression she'd seen often, probably the one that had earned him the *grumpy* title from his brethren.

Maddy remained silent, allowing Dom to think for a few moments. She patted her arms. They were tender. Removing her gloves and jacket, she looked at them.

They were sunburned. She glanced at the sky. No sun. A thin layer of clouds. Even when there had been sun, she'd been wearing a coat.

That wasn't her only problem. She hesitated to interrupt Dom while he considered the dilemma of the gateway. But scratching at the irritation, she finally said, "My back hurts. Take a look."

"Huh?"

"My back." She turned around, lifting her cropped tee, exposing her skin to the air.

After Dom stared at her sunburned flesh, he rubbed a hand down her spine.

She jerked away from his touch. "Stop. That hurts. Do I have a rash?" Madeline twisted to glance over her shoulder at Dom.

"No." His green eye caught the sun which shone once more as the clouds retreated. His lips were a cruel, thin slash.

"You're making me nervous. What's wrong?"

"Is your mouth still sore?" He spun her toward him, his hands squeezing her arms where she was bright pink.

"Ouch."

Dom relaxed his grip. "Let me see." He motioned for her to open wide.

She did. First, a little. Then more.

"Fuck." He turned from Madeline and began to pace, his boots kicking up sand.

Stomping toward her again, with thumb and index finger, he lifted her upper lip. He released it.

"Fuck what?" Maddy swallowed. Had she caught some horrible disease in Angor?

"You've got tiny fangs."

Stunned, she stared at the Immortal. Once Dom's words sank in, she shook her head. "Impossible." She stuck a digit in her mouth to explore, snagging it on a sharp tooth. Popping the finger out, she sucked on it. Blood. "And my back?" Maddy wanted to know because head-in-sand was not her style.

"Wing nubs. Well, slightly larger than nubs. Growing."

Madeline's breath hitched. Then she embraced Dom, her cheek to his chest, mumbling against him, "Astronomy, Physics, Chemistry..."

Life wasn't fair. Maddy knew that. *Hell.* Her childhood proved it. But really. Kidnapped. Tortured. Made a Sycophant. And now trapped in Angor, a goddam alien dimension. Somehow, all those occurrences were a tad beyond the life-isn't-fair concept. Then fangs and wing nubs? She couldn't even think about those.

Unwanted and useless tears flowed, soaking Dom's shirt. She held on, seeking comfort despite the weirdness of the situation. She noticed his arms hung loosely at his sides. But give the man a prize. He hadn't pushed her away.

Right now, she needed the comforting, supporting Dom. Instead, she got the grim warrior.

Sniffling in tears, she drew back, wiping her cheeks with a palm. The boo-hoo-hoos never solved a problem. And this one ranked as a biggie. "I don't get it. What's going on?"

Dom scrubbed a fist across his jaw. "No idea."

"Have you heard of this happening before? A human getting wings and fangs?"

"No."

The skin above Dom's nose wrinkled, suggesting there was more. Madeline wasn't certain she could handle more. Though she loved flying with Dom and suspected she was falling in love with the assassin, she did not want wings of her own. She wanted to go home, featherless and fangless. She wanted her life back, her dull, predictable, orderly human life. "I'm getting wings like yours."

"Not exactly." He distanced himself, pacing again.

She needed information, tilting her chin in defiance. "Enough with the tight-lipped man-talk. What's wrong with the wings?"

He sighed, his muscled arms at his sides. "They have leathery feathers."

She blinked. "Like a fucking Scourge?"

"Close enough."

Madeline twisted her neck, trying to see what Dom saw. When that didn't help, she patted her back, feeling nothing because she couldn't reach the right spots. "Are you sure?"

Dom nodded, his throat bobbling as though he'd swallowed a boulder.

"No. Not happening. I'm going home. Let's try again."

"It won't work, Maddy."

"Once. More." She faced off against the stubborn Immortal, fists on her hips. "Don't you dare tell me no."

Dom boosted her into his arms before soaring into the air. Again, they were unable to get through the barrier.

When her skin sizzled hotter, she gritted her teeth against the painful burn. "There must be another way."

"There isn't. Only one pathway in and out of Angor." He hovered in place, his black wings thrashing up and down.

"Something's wrong with it then. An electrical glitch. Equipment malfunction. Again."

"No. Your skin is on fire. Besides, I got through without you. And don't forget the fangs and nascent wings. Scourges can enter Angor, but if they try to escape through the passageway, their flesh fries."

No. No. Un-uh.

"I am not a Scourge. Maybe my newly acquired bling will go away once you figure out how to get me to Earth."

Dom remained silent as he floated them to the surface of the shoreline again, letting her slide to her feet.

Madeline crumpled to the sand, her legs folded beneath her ass. "How can this be happening to me? I'm human."

Dom flopped to the ground, snapping his wings into his spine. "You have all the signs of becoming a Scourge."

"That's impossible." Madeline closed her eyes. *Computer Science, Information, and General Works. Philosophy and Psychology. Religion. Social Sciences. Language...*

Dom interrupted her calming recitation. "Yet here you are."

Drawing a deep breath, she slid her lids open. "Your pragmatism is grating on my nerves. I don't want to be a Scourge."

Dom's wings shot out and snapped back into his spine. "Your body doesn't care."

"There it is again. Facts. Facts. Facts." Pausing, she inhaled. Her slight outburst over, she asked, "What kind of Scourge?" She clamped her hand over her mouth. "No. I know the answer. Leech. I've got fucking fangs. I don't like blood. My knees get weak at the sight of it." Dom, not paying attention to her, looked distracted. "Dammit, what are you doing?" she asked.

He raised a digit. Then he answered. "Contacting the Feard. They'll join us at home."

"Give me a few minutes here. I need to clear my

head."

He nodded. They waited in silence.

When Madeline had left the library to walk to her orderly apartment after work, she'd been snatched. Then she'd been thrown into chaos, losing control of her mind, thanks to Praevus. Now, she'd lost control of her body.

She had been safer when her alcoholic mother went on a rampage or invited over unpredictable, handsy visitors. Though she, Fia, and Darya had practiced what-ifs to deal with those perilous situations, they'd never prepared for this kind of event.

Arching her neck, she glanced up at Dom's expressionless face. Would she become his enemy? As an assassin for the OneCreator, he extincted Scourges.

Damn. Just ask.

"What are you thinking about, Dom?"

"My past. How life repeats itself."

Madeline didn't understand his snarly response because she was too focused on her own problems to pursue it.

Dark clouds and fog blew in, followed by pouring rain. Her wet, stringy hair hung limp. "I hate this weather. I hate this place." Water sputtered out of her mouth.

Without a word, Dom cupped a wing above their heads. When she rested her damp cheek on his pectoral muscle, he flinched. She didn't imagine it. She was becoming what he hated. A Scourge.

"You'll extinct me," she mumbled. He scooted away from her, rejecting her, not even wanting to touch.

When he didn't answer, she added, "I'll hurt people."

"I won't let you." He gritted his teeth.

"Swear it."

"I swear it," he said, not looking at her.

"Thank you."

"You're welcome." He spoke the right words but without warmth, this man she had begun to love.

With her eyes closed, she pictured him fighting off the attackers. His midnight wings had launched blades as he spun and dipped. He was a fearsome, deadly sight, a god gone mad. He was beautiful. And he didn't need the problems she'd brought to him.

Under the protection of Dom's extended wing, Madeline sat cross-legged, elbows on her knees. Chin on her chest. "My life ... if it can be called mine ... is shitty. It's unpredictable. It's disordered. It's my worst nightmare. And I'm growing wings. Not the nice ones. Oh, no. Bat wings." She glared at Dom. "Just jump in if you have something to add."

He growled, "Can't think of anything."

"No. I suppose you can't," she snapped.

He nodded, and they returned to silence. After a while, Dom suggested they leave to meet his friends in his salon.

"I need another moment. Maybe longer. I want to scream, to cry, to run across the sand until I drop from exhaustion, too tired to think. I want to hit someone." She gasped. "God. Soon, I'll want to bite somebody. I'll be the worst Dracula ever." Madeline raised her hand, stopping Dom from throwing in his thoughts. "I know. Blood Leeches aren't really vampires."

Chapter Twenty-One

Ely strode through the marble halls of Outcast Tower, the government headquarters in Angor. He'd been trying to meet with Harmony, but either she was busy or he was on the job. Finally his boots pounded the tile leading to her office.

He shoved into a busy, noisy room. Scourges sat in front of computers, likely monitoring the various Ordeals around Angor. A few looked a little too excited by the violence they were seeing.

In the front of the room, at a table on a raised dais, sat his target. Multiple computer screens surrounded Harmony, but instead of watching anything, she leaned back in a desk chair, ankle boots cocked onto the table, filing her nails. She didn't look busy, but maybe she was a multitasker.

When she spied Ely, she tossed the file onto the table, perched upright, and fluffed her long, honey-blonde hair. She batted the thick lashes framing sultry green eyes. "Ely, baby. You need me?"

He grinned. Harmony had that effect on him. *Hell.* She had that effect on everyone. It could be the snug, black leather jumpsuit that showed all her attributes, especially since the zipper was lowered to display the swells of her breasts. *Mouth-watering view.*

Once, when he asked her why she'd stayed on in Angor, she'd said it wasn't as dull as the dimension of eternal sunshine and backstabbing Immortals. Ely suspected that was a half-truth. She was still doing penance. Guilt was a powerful motivator. Look at Dom.

"I need a minute of your time. If you're not too busy," he said.

"I'm not at the moment. Just kicking back after riding herd on asshole Scourges so they don't do anything stupid. Since they're Scourges, eventually, they do. Of course, shit could change in a moment. Drop anchor, Ely." She pointed to a chair. "How's the winged-assassin biz?"

"That's why I'm here. I need your take on Scourges. How do they get assigned to the Ordeals?"

"I assume you mean the formal Ordeals that we run. Not the informal ones they heap on each other in their off-hours for shits and giggles."

"Yep."

"I have watchers and schedulers here. Watchers keep an eye on the Ordeals as they're running. That's the first three rows." She pointed. "The last three rows are my schedulers. Using a list of all Scourges, divided according to their malady, they assign them to their punishments. I monitor the assignments and add newbies or delete the reformed ones from the master list. I have one worker who assigns pit bosses to run the Ordeals. He also monitors the trustees who manage businesses and so on."

"So how does a Scourge get excused from an Ordeal?"

"Two ways. The OC gives me a jingle, and I pass the good news on to the Scourge's scheduler. Or using my own judgment, I take a penitent out of the Ordeals when they are reformed or promoted to trustee."

"This guy wasn't reformed. How about a trustee or a pit boss? Can they excuse Scourges?"

"Nope."

Ely puzzled the situation. The OneCreator had said he hadn't excused Praevus from the Ordeals. "What if the OC didn't, but the Scourge was excused anyway?"

Harmony arched a honey-colored brow. "Who are

we talkin' about?"

"Praevus. And he's on the run."

"Hmm." She consulted a computer, tapping on a few keys. Disbelieving eyes shot up to fix on Ely. "His name's not on the master list, but it should be."

"Could his usual scheduler excuse him?"

"No, and if the Scourge figured out a way, it'd be a violation. Let's have a chat with him."

She grabbed Ely's arm and dragged him to the fifth row. At the end was a Mind Rat tapping furiously on a keyboard.

"Rat, can you tell me why Praevus would be excused from the Ordeals?"

The male paused and glanced up. "No."

Ely rested a palm on a dagger. "Elaborate."

Returning to his computer, the Mind Rat entered Praevus's name almost as if his life depended on it. It did. At first, he looked confused. Then he raised his white eyes. "He's not on the assignment list."

"I know," said Harmony, her hand jerking to her hip, her elbow bent.

The Rat typed some more. "He's been deleted."

"Who deleted his name?" she asked.

The Mind Rat cleared his throat, "You did."

Harmony raced to her computer setup, her fingers flying across the keyboard. "Sure enough. In his records, it looks as though I removed him from the scheduling master list, citing him as a reformed Scourge." She tapped her head. "But I have a terrific memory and can tell you that the OC never cleared Praevus. And I sure as shit didn't. I don't do rebellious crap anymore. What the fuck's going on? My system's been hacked."

She jacked to her feet, yelling at her Scourge workers, "I want the Mind Rat Praevus found and reassigned to his Ordeals. I want to know who erased him

215

from the scheduling list." They stared over the top of their computers, looking panicked, as if they were about to lose their trustee status. "Now!" she shouted.

The workers' gazes shot to their screens, their fingers busy on keyboards.

Ely believed Harmony was innocent. He asked the next question. "Do you have any missing trustees?"

Her eyes widened. "How'd you know?"

"Who's missing?"

"Serita. I put another trustee in her place when she didn't show for work. I've had my henchmen looking for her. So far, nothing." She gasped. "Damn. She's Praevus's boss."

****

With a wing still arched over her head to shield her from the rain, Dom listened to Maddy's rant about her shitty luck. But his mind was in free-fall.

Maddy was stalling, as if leaving this spot near the gateway admitted defeat. He wanted to comfort her but couldn't. So he resisted stroking her burned arm. Instead, he drew parallels between what was happening to her now and his past. The comparison was inevitable. He hadn't protected himself as well as he'd thought. After centuries of distancing himself from others, his life was collapsing around him because of a human female he'd allowed to touch his heart.

Angling his head, Dom studied Maddy. Even drenched, she was beautiful, but it was her spirit that had lured him. He couldn't deny an attraction, not even with the boulder in his gut warning him to remain detached. She was becoming a Scourge, his nightmare relived.

In silence, Dom flew them home. Afterward, he left Maddy to soak in the tub while he waited in the salon for the Feard assassins to arrive, a drink in his hand, his legs stretched out as he slumped into a pillow and stared into the fire.

He was the meanest mutherfucking assassin, safe in his dark cloud, eschewing new friendships with Immortals. Then he allowed a human into his heart, and she was becoming the thing he dreaded most—a Scourge he may have to extinct.

Again. But he wouldn't allow history to repeat itself.

Interrupting Dom's dark thoughts, Remi flew in first, pausing to study Madeline when she stumbled into the salon in a thick, long cotton dressing gown. No shoes.

Others arrived in a flurry of activity—taking spots on pillows, pouring drinks, chatting. Ely flew in last, explaining he'd been busy meeting with Harmony.

Maddy collapsed onto a pillow beside Dom, but he was careful not to touch her. Though she needed comforting, he was unable or unwilling to offer it. And he suspected the others noticed. "Today, I tried to return Maddy to her home on Earth. We ran into problems."

Before Dom could quiet his guests and explain, Indigo's gryphon screeched, drawing everyone's attention to the grassy area on the side of his home. A howl from Freki met Oskar's cry. After each beast had expressed dismay over sharing the yard, they settled down to outstare each other.

Indigo jumped up, charging to the edge of the salon, screaming, "If I have to come out there, somebody's gonna suffer." When she returned, she sank into her cushion. "Ya gotta be tough with a gryphon. They can be hardheaded."

Ely drew everyone back to the conversation. "Continue."

Dom avoided Maddy's loving glances and shook off her hand when she tried to stroke his arm. "I couldn't get her through the gateway out of Angor."

His visitors caught his aloofness because their questioning eyes flitted from one to the other.

"That's big, right?" said Indigo, leaning against Ohngel, her palm idly resting on his thigh.

"She's becoming a Scourge," Dom blurted.

In slow-mo, Ohngel twisted toward Maddy, his eyes narrow slits. "Symptoms?"

"I have these baby fangs." She opened her mouth, swiping her tongue lightly across her sharp canines. Pointing over her shoulder, she added, "Wings are growing, and I almost combusted when Dom tried to take me out of Angor."

Indigo raised her hand. "Are we thinking Alarik's guy Rath missed something? I can call him back."

Ohngel, still staring, said, "This is not Praevus's doing. He made her a Sycophant. He can't make a Scourge."

Ely nodded. "A Scourge is an Immortal who is infected with a malady. We don't know why some are prone to it while others are not. Apparently, some claim they have urges, but when they fight them, the disease goes away. We do know it's not infectious. I think the important question is, how can a human become a Scourge?"

Remi shifted on his cushion. "You're right. Becoming a Scourge is a molecular change laid into our DNA. Immortal DNA. Even the OC claims ignorance on the subject. The burden of eternity or Chaos's fault are the only guesses." He glanced at Ely.

The oldest of the Feard, nodded.

Dom said, "All we have are questions. Who traveled to Earth and brought Maddy here through the gateway? How did Praevus get her? Who set him up in a swanky place and excused him from the Ordeals? Was there a female working with him? Who killed Ike? Who attacked Remi and why? Finally, who set Farce on us?"

"Farce?" asked Ohngel.

Dom explained, "Yeah. On the way to the gateway, six Scourges led by Farce attacked. They wanted Maddy. It was a paid gig."

"Not that rehashing old shit isn't entertaining, but Harmony answered a few questions," said Ely. "The trustee Serita's missing. And surprise, she's Praevus's boss. Anybody know her?"

"I do," said Remi. "I had a capture order and dropped her in Angor. A Soul Sucker. Let's assume Serita's the mysterious female Maddy remembers, and she passed Maddy to Praevus. That answers one small question."

Ohngel stretched his legs out and leaned back on an elbow. "Ely, how about Harmony? She can get through the gateway. Do you suspect she gave Maddy to Serita?"

"No, but she bears watching in case I'm wrong."

Dom tossed back his drink, pushed off the pillow on the floor, and poured another. He remained at the bar, distancing himself from Maddy. "Interesting, but it doesn't explain why Maddy's a Scourge. Or how. Ohngel, did you arrange a meet with Michael yet?"

"He keeps avoiding me. Says soon. He's busy."

"Who isn't? We need to see the OC again even though he laid the problem in our laps," added Dom.

Madeline's hands twisted in her lap. "I'm going with you to meet the OneCreator."

"No," blurted Dom. "You can't. He's in Vast. Besides, it's too dangerous. He's difficult, temperamental."

Ohngel interrupted. "I just pathed him. He's in Angor to visit Harmony and take care of biz."

Dom growled. *Great.* Maddy could go along.

More together time when he needed distance.

Maddy met his glare with no fear. "There. It's settled. I'm going. I'm through allowing shit to happen to me. I want answers. I trust you to get them, but I'll be tagging along. This is my life. Ouch."

"What?" snapped Dom.

She cast a sorrowful expression at him. "Nothing. These damn fangs. I bit my lip. Let's go."

"Got Oskar, and I'm ready to ride," said Indigo, unfolding from the floor pillow. "You really need better seating in here, Dom."

He ignored Indigo. Though he reached out his arms and Madeline jumped onboard, he found no joy in carrying her. When they soared out of the salon, he reminded himself that she was just another Scourge.

Beyond the lake near Fear Mines, Outcast Tower came into view. It was gray, a mosaic of rocks, the colors varying from light to dark like the clouds above. High walls and round turrets stretched for the sky. The windows, small slits, didn't let in much light. The overall effect was sinister. The Tower even had a drawbridge of ancient wood. Since Immortals had wings, he wasn't sure who used it. Maybe merchants carted supplies in and out rather than flying air express.

From the air, they drifted into a central, open courtyard, alive with throngs of Scourges, hawking goods, chatting, hurrying to and fro, and begging. Some were clothed in rags. Some in finer clothing. Even among the punished in Angor there was a stratified society. The ragged poor who had newly arrived or who refused to earn a living. The middle class who got with the Ordeals, did their time, and kept their heads down. The upper class, the trustees who were about to be fully reformed.

Dom and his cohorts footed it from the large, crowded courtyard to the wide marble steps, weathered by time. They climbed to the palace's interior.

The inside did not live up to the woeful out-of-doors. The halls were striking, lit by overhead lights. Probably because of Harmony's touch, the walls were painted vibrant colors. The floor was made of dark, shiny stone slabs, here and there enlivened with rugs. Paintings showed eclectic tastes. Vases and figurines sat in cubby holes designed for them.

With Madeline stumbling as she tried to keep up, Dom stormed across the floors dragging her along, the thud of his boots echoing through the halls. The closer he got to the OC, the darker his mood. Slamming inside the meeting room, he snapped out his wings so fast she jumped forward to avoid them.

Dom had held himself in check as long as possible. Finally face-to-face with the OC, he shouted, "What the fuck did you do to Madeline?"

T.M. SMITH

Chapter Twenty-Two

The OneCreator unfolded from a high-backed chair and shot to his feet, pissed at the interruption and his assassin's tone. "Excuse me?" He waved off the Scourges who had gathered around him with one petition or another.

Harmony escorted them out the door but returned to stand beside him, a palm on his shoulder.

When he'd arrived earlier and seen her, loneliness had shoved into his heart. Briefly, he'd entertained thoughts of bedding her. Instead, with a sigh, he'd said, "The fiery ardor we once had is gone. What is left is enough, a friendship. But it is not what it once was."

She'd faced him, an angelic smile spreading on her lips. "True. We are older. Perhaps wiser. Too many millennia. Too many occurrences. What we have is good and welcome, though."

"It is."

Harmony, though she had chosen to remain here, had been in Angor too long. As always, he'd begged her to return to Vast.

She refused his plea again, sauntering to him, rising onto her toes, and kissing his lips. "You are the most magnificent male in existence, and I always want you. I'm just not what I once was. You are not what you once were."

He had nodded. Lately, the great burden of emptiness weighed on him. He was alone in the galaxy, in OneWorld. Chaos had chosen extinction for both himself and Kalia, the female he and his brother had loved and shared on many occasions.

She had given them much. Those pieces of her

were treasured, though often difficult to manage. Then Kalia became the first Scourge among Immortals. Blaming himself, Chaos released a deadly spark, obliterating them both rather than allow the ailment to exist.

But it had been too late. The malady had spread to other Immortals, not like an infectious disease. *No.* It was as if it had been planted in their collective DNA, seeking life, waiting for an opportunity to attack. Ultimately, Chaos's selfless act was for naught.

And the OneCreator's sisters were gone. He was alone, despondent, and at odds with his existence. He had looked forward to a visit with Harmony to cheer him up. So far it hadn't.

Enough with dwelling on the past. He turned his attention to the Feard and the human who accompanied them.

Interesting.

The OneCreator flopped back onto his chair, frowning at Dom while he rearranged his purple velvet robe, smoothing the wrinkles. Harmony remained at his side, a calming influence, while the human stared at him, star-struck. He realized he was an imposing figure, his purple eyes brightening at her adoration. Aah, vanity.

The human clasped a hand to her heart, which pounded as he radiated energy so intense she fought crashing to her knees in front of him.

Dom interrupted the pleasant moment, the other assassins at his back. "I pathed you."

He folded arms across his chest and slumped into his chair, having decided to let Dom live despite his impertinence. "What'd I say?"

"Busy."

"Seems as if I answered the question. That should be enough. Don't bore me, asshole. And I caution you to watch your tone." His eyes flicked elsewhere. "Indigo, hey, girl."

"Right back at you, O magical one."

Ohngel threw a possessive arm around Indigo. "There is more."

The OneCreator cocked his head to the side. "There certainly is, like this human still in OneWorld. Shouldn't she be on Earth by now?"

Dom answered. "I've told you how I rescued her. Now—wait for it—Madeline's showing signs of being a Scourge."

"Who's Madeline?"

The human raised her hand. "I am."

He angled forward, Harmony's nails digging into his shoulder, cautioning him to tamp down his power. "You don't say." He stroked his chin, studying the human. The glow in his eyes changed from anger at Dom's mouthing off to a bright light. "Come here, child." He beckoned Madeline to approach.

When she did, he took her face between his hands and smiled. "I should have known this."

"No shit," said Dom, Madeline returning to his side. "But you wanted me to handle it."

"Isn't that your job? Handling shit?" He pressed his fingers to his temples. Another headache throbbed, accompanied by a small rumbling ground movement no one else noticed.

"That's not all. Four Scourges attacked me in the air. Strange, huh?" Remi filled in the blanks of the encounter. "Larry, Moe, Curly, and Runt ordered me to vacate their skies."

Almost everyone puzzled their brows while Indigo chuckled. Madeline explained, "It's a reference to the Three Stooges, old Earth slapstick comedians. Runt was not one of them. I assume he made him up."

Dom added, "Farce and a small back-up crew challenged Madeline and me on the way to the gateway. They'd been paid to snatch her. Are you losing control of the Scourges?"

Things were falling apart. His control was slipping. It was impossible. Yet, it was true.

"No," he thundered, his loud voice bouncing off the walls.

****

Dom scrunched his brows, waiting for insight from the OC. The guy played word games like a master circus ringleader, though. Was he dancing around the truth this time?

When there had been five Siblings, they'd had a division of labor. The sisters, being elemental, gave light, water, flora, and fauna to the worlds. The OC concentrated on creating life. Hence, the Immortals. Chaos had focused on controlling them. Now all jobs were in the OC's hands. A big burden.

The OC snapped to the edge of his chair, one brow arched in warning at his assassin.

Dom took a deep breath. "Did you make Madeline a Scourge?"

The OC relaxed again, his legs stretched before him. He patted Harmony's hand. "You may return to your job, dear." When she strolled out the door, he swung his attention back to Dom. "No. I do not create Scourges."

"Can you change her back?"

He squeezed his lids down tight after studying Maddy for a few moments. When his eyes opened, he said, "No. Apparently not."

"Tell us as if we've never heard the story. How does an Immortal become a Scourge, and how do they un-become a Scourge?" said Dom.

Surprisingly, the OC answered. "The malady infects them, alters their DNA, changes their physical features, and creates unnatural urges. The change is different for each. Some decline slowly. Some faster. If the Scourge is too far along, I order an extinction. If I deem them capable of rehabilitation, I order them sent here. Some use their time in Angor to reform, their molecular structure again changing, allowing them to return to Vast, once more an Immortal."

Continuing to assess Madeline, the OC angled his chin to the side. "Have you talked to Michael yet?"

"Been kinda busy ourselves. Apparently, he is, too. But we will. Tell us, if you can't create Scourges, can anyone?" pushed Dom.

The OC stroked his jaw. "Try Gabriel. He created Earthers. I've always wondered if he has a backdoor to their DNA. Maybe he got his rocks off by making this human a Scourge. If so, it's likely he can reverse the process."

Dom nodded. He hadn't thought of the Immortal prick Gabriel, who created *Homo sapiens* after he'd won a bet in one of the OC's famous gambling games. Still, the OC should know. Had Dom given him too much credit for his power in OneWorld? Had he made all this to lose control of it?

"Did you extinct Ike?" asked Dom.

"No." The OC rubbed circles around his temples with his fingertips.

"Do you have a headache?" asked Madeline.

He seemed surprised by the question but continued to massage his head. "A bit of one."

Before the OC waved them on their way, he muttered, "I suggested having a chat with Luce, too."

Again with the rec to visit Lucian. Dom's wings flicked out. "How does he fit the bill?"

"Just do it. Now fuck off." Once more, he rubbed his temples, his chin resting on his chest, his lids sagging.

After leaving the meeting room, the group assembled in the courtyard. Deciding only Dom and Madeline would meet with Gabriel, they flew their separate ways.

With Madeline hoisted in his arms, Dom spread his wings and soared away from Outcast Tower. On his way home, he summoned Gabriel to his place since Maddy couldn't get travel to Vast.

When the Immortal balked, Dom pathed, *Get your ass here now.*

Waiting for Gabriel at the kitchen counter, Madeline dropped her chin in her palms, her eyes closed.

Dom pulled up a stool across from her. Though he wasn't eager to get into the whole feelings thing since thoughts about Maddy being a Scourge grated on him, he listened to her worries.

Her lids slid up, and she fixed on him. "I'm trying to organize my thoughts. Unfortunately, there are so many that they're crashing into each other. No sooner do I analyze one problem than another shoves it out. I'm a mess. Who's Gabriel?"

Dom rose from his stool and paced. Walking in one direction, he said, "The Immortal, Gahya, created Aeternals, like Indigo." Heading back the other way, he explained, "Gabriel created humans after winning a bet in the OC's gaming room. Both species share your Earth. Not OneWorld."

Lifting her chin and letting her arms rest on the counter, Maddy mumbled, "I think I read about that when all hell broke loose on Earth." Her shoulders bobbled when she inhaled and exhaled. "Against my nature, I'm going to let these muddled thoughts float around in my head and shift into their own patterns rather than try to organize them. I suppose chaos is its own design, though that idea isn't very uplifting."

Dom resisted brushing his lips across Madeline's to reassure her things would be okay. "I know this is hard for you. It would kill most humans."

"But I'm barely human now." She paused with a sigh. "Who's Luce?"

Dom dragged his fingers through his hair as he continued the back and forth. *Pace. Pace.* "Lucian. He was a favored Immortal in Vast until he led a rebellion. Now, he's a Scourge in Angor. I'm not sure why we should consult him."

The shush of wings sounded. When Dom looked up, he stopped pacing to face the visitor, a male with mottled gray feathers, arrogance streaming from his eyes and on the twist of his lips.

The guy started to talk. "Why…"

That was as far as he got before Dom shouted, "Shut the fuck up, Gabriel. I'll do the chatting. You do the answering. Clear?"

The arrogance disappeared, replaced by fear. He swallowed and nodded.

"Sit the hell down."

After Gabriel hustled to obey, Dom blurted out, "Can you make humans into Scourges?"

Gabriel's eyes rolled from side to side. "Why would I want to do that?"

"That wasn't the question." Dom snarled.

"No. I cannot. Once I created the species, all connections to them were severed. I cannot feel them, control them, or alter them. Never could. The OC demanded they be independent, and I obeyed." He glanced at Madeline.

In a whisper, Gabriel asked, "Are you a *Homo sapiens*?"

Madeline drummed her fingers on the countertop. "Kinda."

The Immortal nodded as if he understood, which clearly he didn't.

Dom hesitated, thinking. Then, to Gabriel, he said, "Get lost."

The gray mottle-winged Immortal scampered off the stool, flicked out his dull wings, and soared out the roof just as a raincloud burst overhead.

Dom snapped his fingers, setting the protective shield around his home to keep out the elements.

"Do you have any other ideas?" asked Madeline.

"Talk to Michael and find Lucian. Ohngel's working on those contacts." He opened the fridge. "Hungry?"

"Not very."

"Eat anyway. You need to keep up your strength."

"Why? You'll probably have to kill me soon."

Dom closed the refrigerator door, angry that she was voicing his own thoughts. "How can I convince you, Maddy? I won't fucking kill you." The words snapped out of his mouth but were they true?

She seemed to ignore his surly tone. "No matter what terrible things I'll do?"

"No matter what, I'll keep you safe." Again, a promise he might not be able to keep.

"If I go psycho, will you protect others from me so I don't hurt anybody?"

"Yes. I will. I've told you that. I keep my word."

She exhaled. "I need reassurances."

Ohngel interrupted the going-nowhere, difficult exchange. *I found Lucian holed up in a box canyon south of Necrosis Valley. The place was covered with camo nets. Great hide-out. Lots of huts and Scourges. His kind of gig. I didn't land. Not knowing the gen pop, I thought it best if all of the Feard knocked on his virtual door.*

Happy to leave, Dom pathed, *I'll be there.*

****

The OC sent Harmony back to Angor to handle business. Loneliness squeezed into his heart again. A debilitating, powerful emotion that brought forth memories.

He chuckled, remembering his sisters' entrance that day.

Arriving in Vast like synchronized swimmers, his three Siblings floated onto the OneCreator's bedroom floor.

"Oops," Lumia clapped a hand over her mouth, pretending shock.

His pants were at his ankles while his cock pounded in and out of an Immortal, a species he had created along with beasts to give the Siblings entertainment and companionship. They were magnificent beings, but he had advised Lumia to cease experimenting with them to make them more splendid. More clever. More athletic. More talented. All to challenge his sister's quick-witted mind.

Melodia made tsking sounds. "Sorry, brother. We did not know you were occupied. Though may I state your choice is lovely." Fascinated by female as well as male Immortals, she winked at his companion, who blushed.

He growled but ceased his sexual pursuit to yank breeches over his ass. Gentleman that he was, he helped the female straighten her clothes, took her gently by the elbow, and escorted her from the room while whispering an apology and a promise in her ear.

For a moment, the air hung heavy with sorrowful recollections of Chaos, who had extincted himself and Kalia, believing his destructive powers had caused a terrible affliction to befall her.

Aah, Kalia. The female he and his brother adored equally, neither jealous of the other. She had succumbed to the madness, the first Scourge.

Most of the OneCreator's magnificent species never contracted what came to be called a malady. Some claimed to feel its urgings but exhibited the will to fight the mysterious disease. Others, however, were contaminated. They became dangerous Scourges, blights on the Immortals. Unfortunately, Chaos's final act of redemption, destroying himself and Kalia to stop the illness, was useless and too late. The damage was done. The past was set in stone as lifeless as Null.

After Chaos's sacrifice, the sisters had each other, but the OneCreator had no one except his Immortals.

Facing his Siblings with his arms wide, he smiled, waving them in for a hug. "Why the visit, my dears?"

Lumia shook out the soft folds of her pale azure skirt. Bracelets adorned her wrists and ankles while ornate combs held back her treasured, luminescent blonde hair, which she considered her best feature. Peeking beneath her ensemble were strappy sandals. "We are bored in Null. The skies there are neither blue nor gray nor white. Is blah a color?"

"And we miss you. We are in the mood for fun," the other two said in unison.

Prima's thick lashes slid down. Up. "It was my idea to visit. Of course, we shall leave before causing mayhem."

Brushing aside the momentary gloom, Lumia said, "Let us begin our adventures outdoors."

Agreeing, they teleported from the house where he showed off by hopping atop a cloud. He zipped across the sky, performing acrobatics to gasped oohs and aahs. Once he drifted to the ground again, he smoothed the back of his hand along Lumia's cheek. "You are paler than I remember. Null does not sit well with you. I wish it could be otherwise."

"I wish the same, but such is not to be," she said.

The day passed in pleasure. Melodia, flicking her long, red hair dramatically over her shoulder, sang a recently composed aria, her voice sweet enough to draw in low clouds to listen. Prima danced to her sister's song, her moves graceful, her slender hands artful, her cool elegance giving way to emotion. Her feet glided along the ground, leaving it only when she leaped into the air.

He and Lumia applauded their Siblings' talents, laughing. Though she had no artistic flair, with a sweep of her hand, Lumia called forth light and warmth, comforting their souls and spreading joy. That skill and her intellect were her gifts to others.

The four kibitzed, honoring Chaos and rejoicing about the past, the present, and the future. Snapping out her magnificent blue-hued wings, the color deeper near her spine, paler on the tips, Lumia suggested a race. They sprinted above a meadow of bright purple flowers, the OneCreator winning as usual, his wingspan the greatest. When he set down, bowing at the waist in victory, he glanced at his foot. He had cut it on a sharp rock. When it bled, he winced, unaccustomed to pain.

At the same time, Lumia smashed a hand to her chest. "I grow dizzy."

Prima gasped, her lower lip trembling, her bronze wings as dark as her skin fluttering. "It's time to go before we are too great a danger to one another."

The Siblings came in for a hug, his arms tight around the sisters.

Pulling away, Melodia stiffened her spine, but a tear escaped Lumia's eye. She said, "I miss you when we are apart."

The OneCreator brushed the moisture from his sister's wan cheek, his gaze mirroring a tragic reality. "Until we meet again."

Chapter Twenty-Three

Desperate, Praevus stormed out the door of his hideaway. He was restless, worried, and obsessed with the need to dive into a brain. Madeline had offered a challenge. And he'd enjoyed it. Tunneling into minds was addictive, hers more than most.

He craved the experience again. But no. He was stuck in a Razor Mountain cabin. Alone. Fading. No one to practice on. What he needed was leverage. Blackmail.

When buckets of rain fell from the ever-changing Angor sky, he scuttled back to the cabin, drenched, water dripping from his nose. Oblivious of the puddle beneath his feet, he snatched the cell phone from the corner table, connecting with Serita's accomplice. No hello. No friendly greeting, Praevus blurted, "I can't go on this way."

At first, the guy on the other end didn't answer. "What way?"

Praevus combed shaky fingers through his hair. "Hiding from the Feard. Worrying. Hungry to use my talent."

"And what exactly do you intend to do?"

"I want my life back."

"Your life was shit before. Is that what you want again?"

Praevus had trouble focusing. What had he said? Oh, yeah. "No. Of course not. I want a Scourge to feed my appetite. Better yet, get me out of here and return me to Vast. I'll find subjects there."

"Neither will happen. I can't get myself out of Angor. And as far as finding you a victim, I have no intention of doing that."

Praevus clenched and unclenched a fist. "I'll talk."

The co-conspirator's voice dropped to a snarled whisper. "What?"

"I'll negotiate with the Feard. Give them your identity." *Yeah. Yeah.* That should scare the guy.

Though his accomplice laughed, the sound was brittle. "Are you sure you wish to threaten me?"

"It is not a threat. I ... uh ... inspired Serita to give me your name."

Another pause. "Where is she?"

Praevus chuckled, glancing outside where her body struggled to heal. "Don't bother about her. I will find a winged assassin and spill my guts." He strode one length of the cabin, tugging at his hair. "You'll see." He spun around and traveled in the other direction, his gait unsteady.

"You don't want to do that." The voice was thick.

A thread. Tug at the thread. He'll know you are serious.

Praevus shouted into the phone, "I want a subject. I need one." His chest pounded up and down, his breaths ragged.

The voice turned cold. "Calm yourself. Keep your wits about you. You've already made a mistake by calling me twice on this cellphone."

"Couldn't be helped."

"Do you want Ike's fate?"

Ike? Who's he? Now he remembered. The snitch. The fog of Praevus's obsession cleared for a moment. He was toying with a dangerous Scourge who had powerful friends capable of extinction. He continued his frantic pacing. "Threats won't work on me. I'm desperate. Without a subject to practice on, I don't care to exist."

His associate seemed to understand. "I see.

Where's Serita?"

"Stop worrying about her," he shouted.

Another pause. "Give me some time."

"Okay, but not much."

"I get it."

Before the co-conspirator disconnected, Praevus heard a noise in the background. Music, he thought.

He threw himself onto the ratty couch, closed his eyes, settled his nerves, and imagined what he would do with a fresh subject. The images calmed his shattered nerves. Surely he deserved a new dalliance for keeping his mouth shut.

His fun with the OC's favored Immortal, Elise, had ended too soon. But he remembered the last look in her eyes, the moment she realized he owned her. That was when he had fucked the broken female. Unfortunately, unlike his first subjects, who had been disposable nobodies, she had been popular, missed at court. Praevus had been sloppy. Someone who had seen them together squealed to the OneCreator. The uppity ruler of Vast put out the order for the Feard to capture him.

Though Praevus had fled, he was no match for the asshole black-winged assassin who chased him. Hiding, he was flushed out like a covey of birds.

He took to the skies, his glorious lapis-tipped wings pounding against the air to increase his speed. Dominion was faster. The one-eyed assassin dropped from above to block him. Praevus trembled at the sight of the Immortal, his brute size, his long hair whipping behind him, the patch over his eye. He was the most fearsome of the OneCreator's killers.

To avoid capture, Praevus made a sharp turn, zeroing back toward the direction he had come. Swooping beneath him, Dominion once again prevented his escape.

The asshole Feard laughed.

Treading air, Praevus poked at the assassin's mind. No way. The shields were too strong. To prevent his imprisonment, he tucked his wings and arrowed into a steep dive. Looking to his side, he spied the assassin keeping pace.

Dominion unsheathed dangerous feather tips, honed to thin, sharp blades. Angling his body toward Praevus, he used them to lob off chunks of primaries, severely limiting forward thrust.

Praevus wobbled, grappling to maintain steady flight.

The black-winged assassin tossed out a net, capturing him like a fish. Though he struggled, he could not get free. To the backdrop of Dominion's laughter, he plummeted into Angor. Unable to break his fall, he landed hard, his body bruised, his lungs punctured, his ribs and appendages broken.

Standing over him, grins curling their lips, were two henchmen, the greeters on Angor. They wore long black robes, the hems rustling across the dirt. Their hoods hung low, obscuring their faces. "Welcome, Praevus. You're ours now."

Praevus's life changed forever. Taken into an alley, he had no place to heal. He scuttled behind a dumpster, which became his home for some time. With Angor's changeable weather, he froze, sweated from heat, or was drenched with rain. His glorious lapis-tipped wings morphed into a leathery gray. As he scavenged for food, he glanced at his reflection in a cracked window. His eyes were white. He was a Mind Rat.

His first Ordeal was Fear Mines, where he found himself in a dark tunnel with a pickaxe. Even his

Immortal vision could not pierce the blackness. A voice compelled him to swing the implement into the rock to find his way out. When he did, a thick cloud of dust filled the area. Coughing, he clutched his throat, his thirst unbearable. He explored for water, using the stony wall as a guide. Praevus stepped on something. A canteen, but it was empty. Again, he swung the axe, shattering rock. The mine caved in, trapping him under tons of debris.

When he escaped Fear Mines by digging his way out with his broken nails and bloodied fingertips, he awakened in the same alley again, still hungry, cold, and injured. After he healed, he had a brief respite from torment, during which he sought experienced Scourges for answers. Questioning other prisoners, he learned he needed a job if he wanted food or lodging in the hellhole.

"It's not right," he screamed. "I am the Immortal Praevus." Passersby laughed, whispering he was a Scourge like them. Serita hired him for a maintenance position in a restaurant, assigning him to sweep and clean. The job came with a crappy backroom where he could sleep. He had use of a tiny kitchen while he awaited the next Ordeal.

Like other inmates of Angor, Praevus had stretches of rest and work, never knowing when or what punishment would come. The inconsistency. The wait. Others claimed it was the worst abuse. The OC called it "stewing."

Praevus lost more than his physical characteristics. He lost telepathy and telekinesis. But nothing was so horrific as the loss of excellent subjects for his gifts. Sure, he used them on other Scourges, but something about their brains left an unsatisfying taste in his mouth, as it were.

****

Dom hovered above the camouflaged site south of

Necrosis Valley, relieved to be away from Maddy. His thoughts about her bounced around like the ball in a pinball machine.

Pounding his onyx-tipped wings up and down, Dom asked his Feard brethren, "Lucian doesn't know we're coming, right?"

Ohngel treaded air alongside, a fiery display of power. "Nope. Surprise visit. Hope we're in time for tea."

"It's best if we fly in from different sides. I'll go straight down." Dom signaled Ely. "You take the left flank. Remi, the right. Ohngel, you wait until we're on the ground. Then come in."

Ohngel shooed his Feard brothers on their way with a chuckle. "Be safe. I'll be watching."

As quiet as usual, Ely took off, his icy wings carrying him into position.

"This'll be fun," said Remi, veering away.

When Dom touched boots to the ground, he strode toward Lucian, who posed, hands on hips, his long, golden blond hair tied back with a leather strap. The mutherfucker who had challenged the OC was big, and behind him were a dozen Scourges.

One side of Luce's mouth curved into a sneering grin. "Welcome. Tell Ohngel to get his fiery ass down here. You're in no danger from us."

The Blood Leech rebel, who hid his wings and fangs as always, didn't look worried about the drop-in visit.

Once Ohngel settled in the encampment, Luce signaled the Feard to tag along behind him. They did, but their gazes flicked around the place, looking for attackers, signs of danger, the works.

Nothing.

The encampment resembled a peaceful village. Tents. Cooking fires. Male and female Scourges walking to and fro while they gave the assassins grim looks and the evil eye. But they made no threatening moves.

Outside the most opulent tent, a Scourge arranged chairs in a circle. Luce flopped into the largest, flinging a leg over the arm, lazing against the back. He waved at other seats. "Take a load off. Tell me what you want."

"Why the backup, Luce?" asked Dom, sitting between Remi and Ely while Ohngel chose to stand, his arms crossed over his chest.

"They are here in case you pull something wonky, Dominion. Give me the story in short sentences. I've got places to go and shit to do."

Dom leaned forward, chosen as the spokesman. He rested elbows on his knees, ignoring the Scourges standing behind Lucian. "Strange shit's been happening. A human was brought to Angor. Praevus, a Mind Rat, made her a Sycophant and has been in hiding since she escaped. We have her, but she can't go home. Cured of Sycophancy, she is now a Scourge. Wings, fangs, and all. Ike, who put us on to Praevus, was extincted. Nobody knows anything. Serita, the trustee, is thought to be involved, but she's missing."

"As they say, don't know nothin' bout nothin'."

Dom continued, "It's been rumored you can create a Scourge?" He threw the question out fast, hoping to catch Luce off guard with the accusation.

The rebel slumped further into his chair, looking disinterested. "Why should I care about this human or Praevus or Ike or Serita? And no, I don't make Scourges."

"I'm not sure why you should care, but you were on our talk-to list."

"Hmm. Who put me there?"

Ohngel widened his stance. "The OneCreator and Michael. Along the same lines, can you extinct

Immortals?"

"I don't do that either."

"Did you feel the earthquake the other day?" When he asked the question, Dom watched Lucian's reaction closely.

Now the guy looked interested. He sat straighter, both boots on the ground. "Impossible."

"It happened." Dom added, "And the OneCreator coughed like he had allergies or a cold."

Luce shrugged one shoulder. "Dust in the air."

Dom said, "Not a speck. He's had a headache, too."

"Impossible."

"You keep using the *im* word, but these things happened," said Dom.

Luce took his time. He glanced at his backup Scourges. He took in his encampment. His gaze even focused on the sky, which was turning dark, clouds rolling in. "Michael?"

"Meeting him later." Dom cocked an ankle over his opposite knee. "Can you find Praevus? Or Serita?"

Lucian glanced at the Scourges around him. They all shook their heads. He pointed to a Blood Leech. "Ask around camp."

The guy lit out as if his feet were on fire.

"I'm not involved in any of these matters. I'm keeping a low profile so I can return to Vast."

"Do you still have ambitions for the OC's job?" asked Remi.

Luce grinned, resuming his slouch in the chair. "I have no ambition. I want to fuck goddesses in Vast, fish in the Lakelands there, and watch the sunset."

A female Scourge, who was leaning against his arm, said, "What?"

"Sorry, love. And fuck Scourges. No slight

intended."

"Why set up an encampment surrounded by the malady-stricken?" asked Ely.

"These people were all looking for a peaceful, safe place to lay their heads between trips to the Ordeals. They obey my rules. In exchange, I offer them a home."

"Why the camouflage?" asked Dom.

"We've had a few Scourge flyovers. The visitors weren't very nice. The camo helps keep them out."

"You're not gathering an army?"

"No, Dominion."

"What's your malady, Luce? Are you Blood Leech?"

He grinned with his lips closed. "My curious black-winged assassin, I like to be enigmatic. It adds to my mystique."

Ely palmed the hilt of a blade in his holster. "I don't like it. The camp has a military vibe to it."

"You've always been a prick, Ely. Don't imagine what you don't see."

"And don't be an asshole, Luce. Ohngel, Remi, Dom, what do you think?"

Ohngel shrugged while Dom stroked his chin with a thumb and forefinger.

With a toothy grin, Remi leaned forward. "I think Luce doesn't want his head lobbed off again, but he looks bulked up from what I remember. Do you lift weights, O fallen one?"

Dom agreed. Lucian's shoulders were broader and his arms thicker, exposed by a sleeveless leather vest.

"Nothing else to do around here. I've never been much of a reader. We have a gym in one of the tents, and you can see the sparring rings over there." Luce pointed toward a fenced-in arena.

Dom scanned the encampment where Luce

claimed to be lying low and being a good guy on the road to redemption. But Ely had a point. The assembled Scourges didn't look like lightweights. Without proof, it was best to keep an eye on the once-golden boy and his assembled army.

The Blood Leech that Lucian had sent on a mission raced back to his side, panting for air.

Lucian flicked a hand through the air. "Well?"

"Nobody knows anything about Praevus, Ike, or Serita."

1. Big surprise. Dom snarled. They were grabbing at clouds, getting only a handful of mist. No leads. No results. His frustration roared to the surface.

2.

Chapter Twenty-Four

Maddy waved goodbye. It was all she could do. Dom had returned home after a visit with Lucian to announce he was off again. A get-together with Michael in Vast. Without answering her questions, he shot out his wings and thundered into the air. No so-long-see-ya. No I'll-be-back-soon to tell you how things went. No why-don't-you-make-my-life-easy-and-plunge-off-the-edge-of-the-cliff.

She watched Dom pick up speed until he was a disappearing black dot, blending into the low, dark storm clouds.

Maddy glanced around the salon. Pulling a pillow close to the lighted fireplace, she flopped onto it, bent her knees, and hugged them.

Alone.

She was facing the worst crisis of her life. Alone. *Yep.* Worse than being a Sycophant. She had no way to reach out to her sisters and Dom had deserted her.

Her birth parents had abandoned her. Her father had deserted his family. Her mother preferred alcohol to caring for her. And even though she suspected the reasons for Dom's escape had to do with his friend Gareth, he had left her.

Maddy descended into the negative thoughts that had plagued her when she was young. Why didn't those she loved stay with her. Was she really so bad? So unlovable? What could she change about herself?

Stop, she shouted. It's not your fault. She hadn't made her father leave. She hadn't forced booze down her mother's throat. And she sure hadn't wanted to be a Scourge.

Besides, though her sisters had moved and made lives for themselves, they had never deserted her. The three were still close, ready to come to each other's aid when needed. The exception was now. Maddy didn't think Fia or Darya could un-Scourge her.

Okay. This is not your fault. You have you. That's enough to get through this.

She heard the tap-tap-tap of claws on the tile.

Freki pounced toward her, the smile on his wolver lips fading once he noticed her expression. "What's what?"

When he cuddled beside her, she stroked her palm along his silky fur, the motion calming, curative.

"You seem different," he said, moaning with each pet.

"Yeah? Fangs and Scourge wings will do that to a girl." She opened her mouth to show him proof. Then, feathers ruffled along her spine. They seemed to be growing bigger.

Freki growled but didn't flinch with her touch, unlike Dom. "You're still Maddy."

"I don't know about that."

Freki rocketed to his four feet. "I do. You smell the same. And my nose is never wrong."

"Tell that to Dom."

"He's all bulk and no brain. Where is the cretin?"

"He ditched me. He's off thinking about whether he should extinct me."

"Scratch that about the no brain. He'd never hurt you. He loves you."

"Don't be ridiculous. Really? How can you tell? Does he frown less often when I walk into the room?"

"Actually, he does. Dom's got issues. But he's been happier with you here, Maddy. Be patient."

"I need a little comforting myself."

3.   "Won't I do?" He snuggled closer.

4.   "Of course you will." She threw an arm around Freki and squeezed him tight.

5.   ****

Serenity Valley, Vast, OneWorld

Dom paced while Remi flipped a knife. Blade. Hilt. Blade. Ely bowed his head in silent meditation, and Ohngel clasped his hands behind his back. They waited for Michael, the OneCreator's Bearer of Death. Why? They didn't know, but the OC had suggested the confab and they were desperate for insights.

Michael's role in keeping Immortals in check was different from that of the assassins. Whereas they dealt with Scourges, the Bearer of Death did business exclusively with Immortals. They were an aggressive lot, requiring a firm hand. Minor rebellions and fighting were regular occurrences.

To the west of Serenity Valley was a clear view of the snowcapped mountains in the Aeries Range and, to the east, the Craggy Peaks. The scenery was a startling contrast to Angor. Here, in a sunny meadow, multi-colored flowers grew amid tall green grasses and low, thick bushes. The clouds were scarce and feathery. No unexpected thunderheads burst, drenching the valley with rain. No winds raged across the valley. Of course, the weather remained consistently boring, interrupted only by light, occasional showers and mild breezes to clear the air.

Michael materialized in the sky, his roan stallion gripped tight between his thighs. He unfurled stark white wings and glided toward the waiting assassins.

He dismounted his stead, both of them splattered with blood. Snapping out his wings, he shook them until they were pristine. The Bearer of Death swatted his horse's rump, sending him to graze.

When the Feard squinted, he toned down the bright glare seeping from his flesh. "Why the fuck are you calling me from my duties?" His piercing gaze settled on Dom.

They hadn't been friendly for millennia. Dom blamed Michael for the role he had played at Gareth's trial. Asked by the OC, the Bearer of Death had served as the prosecutor.

But it seemed Michael had one friend in the crowd. "Hey, Ohngel. Good to see you. Where's your feisty mate?"

"On another job." The fire-winged assassin bumped fists with Michael, all friendly-like.

Dominion jumped into the convo, steering it toward their purpose and a speedy end. "We need answers to questions about abnormal events brewing in Angor." For once, he wasn't trying to antagonize Michael. Pat on the back.

Ely crossed his arms over his chest. "Event one. We're looking for Praevus and Serita. They played a role in confining and torturing a human female in Angor. She escaped. Dom nabbed her off the streets. The Mind Rat took off, and Serita's missing."

Jutting out a booted foot, Michael rested a hand on a dagger hilt, the blade hanging from a belt holster. "Hmm. I can barely remember the last time an Earther was brought to OneWorld. I think it was not too long after Gabriel created them. Some of the Immortals at court wanted to see the new species, and an idiot snagged a *Homo sapiens* to bring to Vast. What an uproar that caused. The OC was pissed. And Vast hath no fury like the boss pissed."

Ely nodded. "I kinda remember. That's when he discouraged travel to the planet."

Dom shifted from foot to foot, wanting to hurry the convo along. "Yeah. This female was not so lucky. I don't think she was a curiosity. Praevus made her a Syc."

"Really? Disturbing." Michael drew his brows tight.

Dom stared. "Obviously."

"I don't deal with Scourges," said Michael.

Ely brushed an errant strand of long hair over his shoulder. It was pale like ice rather than white like Michael's. "Neither Praevus nor Serita can leave the dimension. So who snatched the female from Earth? Had to be an Immortal. You deal with them."

Remi dropped his blade into its holster. "Why did they snatch her? And who the fuck would give her to Scourges?"

Michael shook his head. "Not me. I'd never put a human in the hands of a Scourge."

Dom said, "Not thinking you would. Maybe you know an Immortal who might."

Michael's horse trotted over to nudge his owner's shoulder. The Bearer of Death smiled but sent the steed on his way with a hand smacked to a flank. "I'll look into it. You started the meet by referring to a few events. What are the others?"

Dom scrubbed a fist across his jaw. "Event two. Somebody extincted the Scourge Ike who put us on Praevus's trail."

Michael shrugged. "Don't know him, but okay. You guys, me, and the OC are the only Immortals who make that list of suspects. Should be easy to narrow it down."

Dom continued, "The OC claims innocence. Which leaves…"

Michael stroked his chin with a finger and thumb. "Me? Sorry. Not me, One-eye. I've been busy with a small but bloody uprising in Vast. There's the problem with Immortals. We think a little mayhem is exciting— our injuries healing quickly and the boredom of eternity giving rise to mischief. So, what's a few cuts, bruises, or blood? Of course, that's the good guys, not Scourges." Michael smirked.

"Yeah. Here's the latest kicker. Event three," said Dom. "I tried to take Madeline—she's the human—to Earth after she was healed of Sycophancy. She couldn't pass through the gate. She's becoming a Scourge. Wings. Nascent but growing. Fangs."

He watched Michael's face for a reaction. Bright Boy was surprised. He wasn't faking. Silent, he had the look of someone searching for a memory. The problem with living forever was recall. Sometimes, the brain had to sift through billions upon billions of occurrences.

Finally, he shook his head as if he hadn't pried loose a recollection. "What the fuck have you guys stepped in? Sounds like pure, high-grade horseshit. A Mind Rat can't make a Scourge. It's a malady suffered only by Immortals." Michael shoved his hands to his hips and shifted from boot to boot.

Dom drew a deep breath before letting out an exasperated sigh. "We know nothing more about this shit than we did before."

Everybody shrugged.

Michael whistled for his horse. Afterward, he added, "I've never heard of a Scourge being made."

"Yeah? How about you? Can you make a Scourge?" asked Remi.

"I don't make Scourges."

"Here's more to chew on. When I was headed to the gateway with Maddy, a group of Scourges led by Farce attacked us. Somebody paid to have her snatched."

"Samey-same happened to me over the Razor

Mountains. How crazy is that?" Remi dragged his fingers through his hair.

Michael's attention returned to the conversation. He waved off the steed he had called, saying. "Farce. The guy who used to be in the OC's personal guard?" The Bearer of Death contained the bright light which once again oozed from his flesh. "I never liked him."

"Ditto. He'll never be a bother again," said Dom.

Michael laughed. "Is the OC entertaining court with a game at your expense?"

Dom's upper lip curved into a snarl. "We tossed that around. So, the best guess is the OneCreator is playing us. He brings a human to Angor. Gives her to Serita who gives her to Praevus. Then he extincts Ike for snitching. While everyone is rushing around trying to solve the mystery, the OC's laughing his ass off as he amuses his court. Is that the take?"

"Simplest solution," said Michael.

"Why do I feel the sitch is more complicated?" asked Remi. "I see the OC setting up a game. And hell, if Ike pissed him off for something else, he'd have no problem extincting him. After all, he brought the guy into OneWorld and can take him out of it. What I don't see is his putting a human female through the horror. It's not his style. He's very protective of humans. The weaker species. Self-determination and all that shit he spouts."

"So, where's that leave us?" asked Dom.

"With a mystery whose solution is above my pay grade." Michael's flesh shimmered like a bright star. "Harmony may provide insight into Serita and Praevus."

"Yeah," said Ely. "Been there. Done that."

Remi and Michael were right. Nothing here was simple.

Bright Boy's stallion charged from the meadow, his head down, puffs of steam snorting from his nostrils.

His goal was to knock the Bearer of Death off his feet. Macho horse.

Michael, equally macho, stood his ground, taking the hit. The steed pawed the dirt several times to save face while Bright Boy lunged onto his back. "Rumor has it Lucian is gathering followers again. If you can find him, check him out. I look forward to seeing the assassins next time. Except you, One-eye."

"Asshole." Dom flicked up his middle finger. "Why does everyone bring up Luce?"

His brethren shrugged.

The Bearer of Death swept out his white wings while his stallion shot out his own, snorted, and pranced, anxious to be gone. They took off, their strokes in unison.

The Feard trailed Michael off the ground, taking to the air but flying in the other direction.

Chapter Twenty-Five

Angor, OneWorld

Dom didn't return home after the meet in Serenity Valley. He needed think-time. So he flew above mountaintops and swooped across valleys, trying to wipe Maddy from his mind.

At the top of the steps leading to the yard, she had waved goodbye when he'd told her he was off to see Michael. Dom had ignored her, not returning the farewell. Cowardly? Assholish?

Yep.

But he couldn't muster a response. He was too wrapped up in his repeating past.

Flexing his wings gave him a reprieve from thinking. The exertion when he pushed the limits cleared his head.

He hadn't saved his closest friend. *Damn.* He hadn't even known Gareth was descending into madness. And his trial had been a disaster, primarily because of Gar's behavior in court. The OC, deeming the assassin guilty, doomed him to Angor. While his friend awaited transport, Dom had visited his cell.

"Why should I kiss ass?" Gar had asked, his lips curling into a sneer.

Though annoyed by his brother assassin's attitude, Dom had been encouraging, determined to wait, convinced of his eventual rehabilitation and return to Vast. The copper-winged assassin would once again fly at Dom's side.

After visiting Gar's cell, Dom threw himself on pillows near the fireplace in his home to reflect on the situation. Heavy rain thundered down on the protective shields, soothing and peaceful. Then the OC summoned him for a job.

The boss lazed on his throne as always, his bronze chest bare, his shirt unbuttoned. When Dom reported, the big guy cocked his head to the side. His penetrating gaze unnerving. "I have an assignment for you."

"What is it?" Dom hoped the job was distracting enough to take his mind off Gareth's problems.

"I have chosen you to chase down my copper-winged assassin. He has escaped from his cell. Your task is to capture him and deliver him to Angor. If you can. If not, extinct him."

Silence pounded against the walls of Dom's heart. He wasn't sure he had heard the OneCreator correctly. Or if he had, was this some court game the boss was so fond of?

Dom swallowed hard, the lump in his throat a solid stone. "Why me? Send Michael." He didn't want to volunteer the other Feard. After all, they, too, were close to the afflicted assassin.

The OC waved a dismissive hand through the air. "Michael is dealing with a situation only he can handle. It is you."

Dom considered arguing, but the determined line of the OneCreator's lips told him it would be useless. He accepted the task, his duty as an assassin defining who he was.

Perhaps he was the best choice. He would not harm Gareth, and his brother was likely to come in willingly for him.

Outside the massive Sanctuary Keep where the OC lived in Vast, Dom hovered in the fresh air, allowing his mind to catch up to his task. He had never felt *shrouded in such darkness, caught between his duty and saving his friend's life. If he were smart, careful, and lucky, the two opposing tasks would meld and he would help Gar.*

So he cast out his emotions, something he rarely did because the result bombarded his senses. He allowed them to drift across the dimension, searching for signs of fear, disruptions, and oddities.

Moistening his index finger, he raised it to taste the breeze, focusing his senses on the best direction. At first, nothing. Then a ripple, followed by a scream for help. He stroked his powerful midnight wings downward, lunging into the sky. High above the keep, he angled them for flight, shooting forward, aiming for the desperate pleas.

At The Between, a vibrant valley west of Clearwater Lake and east of the Lakelands region, he found the source of the agonized cries. He was too late, however. On the ground was a body torn asunder, blood soaking into the grass. The arms, legs, and torso of a female were strewn about like trash. On her face, where there should have been laughing eyes, there were orbs that had beheld horror. A nightmarish Scourge leaned over her.

Dom pounded his wings against the air, making certain his arrival was noisy, a distraction for the crazed Immortal. He landed, his long blade already drawn in challenge.

The being swung around, his eyes black lumps of coal. In each fist, he clasped entrails. Dripping down his chin was blood, and in his teeth were chunks of flesh.

Dom's breath hitched. He wanted to scream his outrage. He had come across such sights before. Nothing new. But it was the face of the nightmare that shocked Dom. His heart stopped beating in his chest. He could not swallow. The sword he had drawn hung limp at his side.

Gareth.

His closest friend, the male he'd known since their haven, the one with whom he'd shared adventures and females.

Gar dropped the entrails on the grass and swiped an arm across his bloody mouth, leaving a stain on the sleeve of his tee. "Welcome to the party. I don't suppose I can deny being a Flesh Eater. She is quite tasty. Care for a bite, my brother? Releasing our base emotions is both delectable and freeing."

Dom shook his head, unable to speak. All he saw was the youth who had escaped their haven by flying away with him on an adventure. They were too young. No permission. Yet Gareth always accompanied Dom to keep him out of trouble, to give him a partner in crime. They had flown over the ocean, their wings still not mature. Caught, they were returned to the haven.

As young Immortals in the throes of uncontrollable hormones and youthful curiosity, they had hidden behind a large boulder at a nude bathing pond to sneak peeks at females, water sluicing off their naked bodies. Caught, they were returned to their haven.

Snitching bottles of Demon Scourge from a bar in Vast, they'd drunk their fill behind the stone walls of their haven. Caught, they were returned to their rooms.

In the aftermath of each adventure, his friend stood silent by his side, accepting his share of punishment though the ideas had always been Dom's.

Now, Gar was a Flesh Eater. No longer the honorable copper-winged assassin. A Scourge. And Dom had missed the clues, had missed helping his friend fight the malady, had missed hearing his silent pleas. Or had Gareth never called out for help?

"Right about now, Dom, you are kicking your

own ass. Blaming yourself. Understandable. I was always the docile one, your dutiful sidekick. You broke ground, knowing I'd follow. My turn to take the lead. I am no longer your shadow."

Dom found his voice. "You were never my shadow. You were loyal. Honorable. My friend. Gareth, I never saw you as my sidekick, a follower rather than a leader."

"You were always bigger than life, Dom. The glory-seeker. The barn-stormer. The path-clearer. My role was to back you."

Had his friend so misunderstood him? Had he thought Dom a grandstander? Sure, he had always been his own male, fearless and a risk-taker. Yes. He was strong-willed. He enjoyed the pranks they had pulled. He thought Gar simply took longer to see the merits of a mischievous plan. But he felt they were in their adventures together.

"Now what, my friend?" His eyes diverted to stare lustily at the body parts beside his feet.

Dom shook his head to clear it. "Accompany me to Angor. Do the Ordeals. Reform. Return to Vast." His gaze rolled over the Flesh Eater's form. He had not yet developed any physical signs of being a Scourge. But each progression varied.

Gareth smiled and attacked without warning. He whipped out his copper wings, unsheathing the razor-edged tips. As a backup, he flashed a knife in his fist when he charged.

Though they had often sparred, Dom always showed restraint, realizing he was the stronger of the two. Grabbing Gar's arms, he flung them both to the ground. Landing on his back, he tossed his friend overhead.

"Good one." Gareth shot to his feet. With his

wings flared, the tips arching forward, he rushed Dom. At the last second, he feinted to the right.

Dom fell for the move, and Gar plunged the handheld blade into his eye.

As he swiped blood from his face, Dom realized that Gareth was lost to him, unwilling to go to Angor. He needed to incapacitate his friend. Snapping out his wings, he liberated his sharp, obsidian-tips.

Gareth shouted with glee, "Bring it on, Dom. Finally, a real match between us. Know that I can still extinct an Immortal. Even a moralistic do-gooder like you. Don't look surprised. You led me into pranks, but that's all they were—meaningless, weak games thought up by an Immortal with no real spine. Now we'll see who is better."

Dom shut down, not allowing the mad utterings to reach him. His friend sounded like all Scourges, drinking their personal Kool-Aid.

Gareth's razored copper wingtip sliced into Dom's shoulder before he sidestepped the assault.

"I will never go willingly, Dominion. You have two options—I extinct you and flee, or you allow me to go on my way."

While his once-treasured brother preened over his strike, Dom attacked. His knife-like feathers cut into Gareth's neck, nearly beheading the fifth member of the Feard.

His once-friend slapped a palm to his throat, falling to the ground. His eyes clearing, he reached for Dom, who clasped his desperate hand.

Gareth's words were a low rasp as he faced the injury and his capture. "I guess you took option three, my friend. You brought me to my inevitable end. No remorse. No guilt. Now, do your job."

Dom was too choked up to speak.

"What? No admonitions? No wise thoughts to send me on my way?"

"This is not what I want, Gar."

"Nor I, but here we are." He squeezed Dom's hand. "Remember me as a bright-eyed youth, sparring with my best friend. Remember me as a young assassin with a future, flying wing-to-wing beside you."

Dom swallowed the rock in his throat as he nodded. "You can still accompany me to Angor and heal there."

Gar laughed, a death rattle. "Remember me as a Flesh Eater you had to extinct because you are the honorable Immortal I failed to be. Goodbye, my dearest friend. Now finish the fucking task."

"I cannot." Dom rose, his legs wobbly.

"You must." His eyes grew hungry. "I will regenerate, and I desire female flesh. I will tear a lissome body limb from limb and bathe in her innards. I will…"

Before he finished his tirade, Dom struck, his sword fully decapitating his childhood friend and comrade. He uttered the words, his voice tremulous, "May my blade bring you peace."

Gar's body began the slow process of ashing.

As the copper-winged assassin ceased to exist, Dom felt no victory. He flew from the site to the OneCreator to report on his assignment and to seek aid for Gar's victim. The boss's response was a single nod.

The OC unslung his leg from the arm of his throne, rose to his full height, and strode down the steps that separated him from his subjects. He reached out a hand to heal Dom's eye.

"No. I will keep this reminder."

After hesitating, he rested his hand on Dom's bloodied injury, shooting an agonizing spark into it to prevent it from repairing itself. "What is done can be *undone."*

"Never," swore Dom. He left Sanctuary Keep determined never to allow anyone to get as close to him again.

After he had rid OneWorld of the fifth member of the Feard, Dom forgot how to smile and how to have fun. He distanced himself from his brother assassins or anyone who desired love or friendship. That way, if they suffered a malady, he could do his job. No bother.

Dom changed. No more reckless adventures. He thought through all sides of a situation before moving forward. A part of him longed to be wild again. But somehow, when he'd extincted Gareth, that Dom disappeared.

He blamed Michael for being the prosecutor and for being unavailable when Gar had escaped, leaving Dom to the dirty work of extincting his best friend. He even cast blame on the OC. Mostly, he lay the fault at his own feet for not seeing what had been brewing in plain sight.

Though he had not prevented Gareth's demise, he had learned a lesson. A harsh one he'd never forget. But now, soaring through the air, he questioned the lesson. He had labeled Gar as a victim of his malady, an unwitting sufferer, an unwilling Flesh Eater who couldn't fight the disease. But was that true? Or was his friend responsible for his own actions?

After all, Madeline, once a mere human, had made him promise to prevent her from hurting anyone. "Swear it," she'd said. Her first instinct had been to protect others.

Dom was an ass. Instead of understanding what Maddy was going through, he had withdrawn into his past. She was not Gar. She was not a victim. She was a fighter.

But she couldn't fight alone. She needed him. And what had he done? He'd left.

Madeline was more important than he'd admitted to himself. He would tell her about Gar and how she was different. He'd stay by her side, keep her safe, and prevent her from harming others. Nobody would assign her to Angor's punishments. Nobody would extinct her. While he searched for a cure, he'd be her jailer, reformer, friend, confidant, and lover.

He did, however, begin to see Gar in a new light. Through the centuries, Dom had blamed himself for not recognizing his friend's decline. Yet, never in his fellow assassin's descent into madness had Gar asked for help.

Gareth had lacked Maddy's strength of character.

Dom changed direction and streaked across the sky, heading for home and the female who needed him.

****

Maddy raced into the salon from the bedroom when she heard the shush of wings. She stopped, leaning against the door jamb, cocking one foot over the other. When Dom threw out his arms, she resisted running into them. She was pissed.

Dom clasped his hands behind his back. "I've been an idiot."

She angled her head to gaze into his eye.

"No comment?" he asked.

"None needed. I agree. You've been an idiot." She crossed her arms under her breasts, her posture speaking volumes about her feelings.

"I never should have left you alone to deal with the problems."

Maddy frowned. "No. You shouldn't have, but you did."

"I did. I had my reasons. They aren't good enough ones, though."

"I understand about Gareth, but I'm not him, Dom. You abandoned me when I needed you most. A lifetime of assholes have deserted me. I want someone who'll have my back. It's not too much to ask."

"It's not."

"And yet, it happened. Again. You broke my heart and threw it away as though it were a piece of trash."

He winced. "I never intended to do that. It was my problem, and I was a selfish asshole. What do I need to do to win you back?"

"What if I said you can't?"

"I wouldn't believe you, Maddy. Please let me put your heart back together. I know you've patched mine up."

Was that really how Dom felt? Maddy studied him. He looked sincere. And when he spread his arms wide, she ran into them as if he hadn't been an idiot. She jumped, locking her legs around his waist. "Promise never to leave me."

"I promise. Never again."

She arched her back to stare into his good eye. "That was too fast. Take a minute to think about it because I won't give you a second chance."

"I don't need more time. And you've already forgiven me." He leaned close, nibbling her neck, kissing her jaw, capturing her lips.

"Uh huh," she mumbled as he worked hard to convince her he'd been an idiot.

Chapter Twenty-Six

The next morning, Maddy sat at the kitchen counter, head in hands, when Dom walked in with his hair still damp from a shower. "What's wrong?" he asked.

Madeline was settling into her Scourge form. Unhappily. Her fully formed, fast-growing, uncontrollable wings were her nemesis.

Tilting her head up, she glared at Dom, as if her problem was his fault. "Nothing."

"Really. I admit I'm not sensitive to moods, but a mopey expression means something's wrong."

"I tried to fix breakfast, but these damn wings have other ideas. They're heavy. They drag and twitch, knocking shit onto the floor. I fell earlier because they're unbalanced. Of course, I've got fangs, too, and they keep cutting my lip."

Dom slipped on cracked eggs beneath his boots. Catching himself, he avoided flying ass-first to the tile.

"Watch out for the floor," said Madeline, following his ungraceful movement. "I may have dropped a few things when I tried to fix breakfast." She returned to moping, head-in-palms.

After a quick cleanup, Dom retrieved a carton of unbroken eggs from the fridge. He set the coffee pot to brew and snagged a skillet from a lower cabinet, plopping it on the range. Chopping, dicing, and mixing, he made omelets. Coffee brewed, he planted a mug in front of Madeline, returning to his task.

She curled a finger into the cup handle, lifting the drink to her lips. "Ahh. I still like caffeine. I don't even want creamer and blood added."

Toast ready, counter set, Dom served up two omelets. Before sitting, he pressed his warm lips to Maddy's mouth. "Good morning."

"I guess I forgot to say that, too."

They ate in silence since Madeline was not in the mood to chat.

While she downed the last of her coffee, Dom cleaned the kitchen. When done, he said, "Follow me. Flight training."

She jerked toward him. "I'm not ready."

"You are." He beckoned her to the hallway with a crooked finger.

As she trailed Dom to the gym, Madeline's wings scraped the tile. He signaled her to the middle of the floor mat, surrounded by weights and a few machines.

She frowned, shifting her left shoulder high to lift a damn wing. *No go.* It still dragged. So, Maddy shuffled onto the mat, her damn feathered accessories drooping and useless.

When she stood facing Dom, he spun her around. Though unable to control her new appendages, she felt Dom's touch on them as he examined her.

"Now that I'm looking closely, your wings aren't covered by a smooth leather-like skin."

She twisted her neck to look over her shoulder. "Really? So, no bat wings."

"Correct. You do have some leathery feathers. Not all. Many of your primaries and secondaries are blonde, like your hair but darker near the base and lighter at the tips."

"What does that mean?"

He chuckled, pivoting her around again to face him. "Fuck if I know. Odd. But we'll think about that later. More important things to do now."

Dom shushed out his glorious black wings until

they spanned wall to wall. And the gym was very big. "These are a web of bone and muscle. They allow you to control your flight, tightening or changing shape to give more lift, less drag, greater maneuverability."

"Uh huh." Madeline rounded her shoulders, trying to flip out her wings as Dom had. Instead of complying, they stayed limp on the mat. She thought the right one had twitched, though. "I understand, but I can't do anything with them. Except screw up."

"You can, but..." He swiped a palm down his jaw. "You can't control them with the muscles you're trying to use. These," he tapped her breasts, "will lower your wings." He grinned. "Not your breasts, which are lovely, but the pecs under them. But your supracoracoideus will raise them."

"The what?"

He patted her back. "Think of them as a pulley with a rope that wraps around your shoulder blades. Focus on tugging the rope to lift your wings."

She rolled her shoulders.

"No. It's not your shoulders. The controlling muscles are beneath them. Not above. Concentrate and use them as a pulley. Try again."

Madeline closed her eyes. She envisioned a cord that looped over her shoulder blades and connected to strange muscles. Mentally, she hand-over-handed it until her left wing wiggled, rising slightly off the floor.

"You got it." Dom gave her an encouraging smile.

The wing flopped to the mat. "I felt it for a minute." Excited, Madeline almost jumped up and down. "A kiss would probably encourage me."

Dom curled his hands around her waist and lifted her for a brief kiss.

"That was fast."

"But proportionate."

"Stingy."

Dom grinned, but then turned serious. "Each of your wings operates independent of the other. Each has a separate muscle to raise or lower it."

"How can I concentrate on two of these things? I can't even control one."

"Think of walking. You don't worry about which muscles to use, do you? Your legs operate independently."

"True." Madeline squeezed her lips together to help her focus. Her left wing flicked out to the side.

"Great. Now, hold it there."

For a moment, she did. When she exhaled, the wing flopped to the ground. "That's hard, but I'm getting the gist."

"Of course. You've never used those muscles before." Dom combed fingers through his hair. "Maybe you never had them."

"Okay." Madeline chewed her thumbnail. "Let me practice. Go do something. Stop staring at me while I learn to move these fucking beauties."

The wise man left her alone, wandering over to select a few giant weights from a rack.

Pull on the left rope. Pull on the right rope.

Madeline eyed Dom, distracted by him when he began his workout routine. He curled one arm at a time, his bicep bulging with the effort. His heavily slabbed chest rose and fell. Eventually, sweat dripped down his rigid abdomen. Her gaze flipped to the pulse in his neck. It pounded as blood flowed through his veins.

What the fuck?

With her concentration on Dom's throat rather than her task, her left wing flicked out wildly, tumbling her sideways. Her fangs twitched, and she wanted to sink them into a tasty vein.

Focus.

Madeline closed her lids to erase the image of her mouth on Dom's neck. Determined, she resumed her workout. Hours later, she was exhausted. When the skin on her arms tingled, she glanced up to see Dom leaning against a wall. He'd crossed arms over his chest and was staring. Her wings, which she'd been holding off the floor, collapsed to the mat.

Dom prowled toward her, a glint in his eye. Toe-to-toe, he bent and captured her lips.

Madeline broke off the kiss. "I'm sweaty."

He caressed her shoulders, sending chills along her spine. "I love sweat. Besides, you've done very well and deserve more than a quick kiss." Kicking out her feet, he took her down, making fast work of his clothes and hers.

"Here?" she asked.

"Yep. Here and now."

Madeline got with the program, exploring his sculpted body. Her palms skated across his chest and slid down to his waist, his thighs.

Dom clasped onto one of her hands, guiding it to his heavy cock while he rolled on top of her. When she gripped him and squeezed, he moaned.

She stroked from crown to hilt, sighing at the thickness of his length. "Get on with it. Or are you all talk?" She rested the tip of his shaft at her opening but did not penetrate. "Your move. Fuck me."

Dom teased, nudging her, pushing in, pulling out. Probing.

Two could play this game.

Madeline wrapped her legs around Dom, locking him in tight with her heels, forcing him further inside her. Another inch. Torturous. But sweet pleasure.

Her grim winged assassin tilted his hips. Forward.

Backward. Forward, driving himself deeper. So deep his shaft throbbed inside her moist sheath.

Maddy's inner muscles squeezed Dom as she began a slow undulation, rocking her pelvis upward to meet him.

He drew out mid-way. Then with a single thrust, he seated himself to the hilt. "You feel so good."

"Too slow." Madeline ground against Dom, begging for fast. Instead, he continued to set a leisurely rhythm, each stroke a slow caress. She steadied her hands on his back, shoving into Dom's advances, forcing him to speed up.

Groaning, he clutched her hips, trying to gentle her, his neck muscles cording like stretched cable wires as he rose above her.

"No," she snapped. "Faster."

Dom leaned down to whisper, his hot breath fanning her. "You want my fucking cock, Maddy?"

"Damn it. Yes." She shifted her pelvis.

"Work for it. This is the gym." He grinned.

Wicked, wicked man. A tease.

She bared her fangs and snarled, tightening her legs around his thighs, her nails digging into his ass.

But he obviously insisted on control. He captured her wrists, slamming them above her head. "Don't hurry me. Watch me take your pussy."

She stared at Dom's thick flesh as it disappeared inside her and reappeared slick with her juices. The sight was hot, but she was in no mood for a slow frolic. "Stop playing and fuck me."

"What do you want?" he tormented.

She gasped, "I want to come."

He kept up the measured dance, creating a maddening friction as his cock slipped in and out of her. Madeline groaned and pleaded.

Dom uncoiled her legs, flinging them over his shoulders, opening her wider. Then he got serious. He did what she asked, pounding into Madeline. His grip on her hips tightened, bruising her as he drove deep.

"Your wish, Maddy."

Watching the pulse in his neck throb, she grew wild, meeting him thrust for thrust, wanting to bite, desiring his taste. She bent her head, her tongue flicked out, and she licked his skin. *Delicious*. But through force of will, she didn't sink her fangs.

While her muscles clenched around his shaft, he hammered into her. Once. Twice. Three times.

"Dom. Yes," Maddy shouted, no longer interested in his blood, fixed only on her release. Her orgasm built, rolling through her first as a gentle wave but then as an ocean storm. She cried out his name while he slammed into her trembling body.

Chasing his own relief, Dom rocked his frantic hips up and down. The muscles in his arms strained above her, his pulse banging in her ears. When he exploded, his seed spilled into her. Warm. Flowing. He shuddered, tossed his head back, and roared.

Their gasps for air filled the room. Their chests heaved. Once they calmed, Dom rolled off Madeline, collapsing, spent on the sweat-soaked mat.

After a while, she whispered, "I wanted to bite you."

Dom's eye flicked open. He gazed upon her with sympathy. "Can't happen, Maddy."

"Why?"

"It's forbidden for Immortals to give their blood to a Leech willingly."

"Why?"

"The OC doesn't explain the reasons behind his laws. I always supposed he feared the Leech could transmit his malady." He paused. "Even though we've been told the disease is not contagious." He tugged her close, cupping her head to his chest, her hair tickling his palm. "If I could help you, I would."

"I'll control it."

"You will."

After about five minutes of quiet, steady breathing, he said, "I'm hard again." He clasped his dick, giving it a few tugs. "Get on your hands and knees."

"Is that an order?"

"Definitely."

She rolled to her stomach and pushed up, studying him over her shoulder. "I'm not a Syc anymore, but I'm happy to obey. Like this?" She licked her lips and shot him a wicked smile.

He grasped her hips, positioned her for his cock, and pistoned into her waiting sheath, burying himself in one brutal drive forward, his wings fanning out behind him. "So good. Nobody has ever affected me as you do, Maddy."

He took her harder and faster than he ever had before. His groin hammered into her, his balls slapping against her ass. Dom pulled out and slammed in again. And again.

His fingers found her clit, rubbing and pinching. "Come now," he ordered. She had no problem obeying him. What began as a tingling sensation roared through her as an explosion. Dom's orgasm followed hers.

With both of them panting for breath, Dom rolled to the side, taking her with him and curling a hand around her hip. "Have I told you that you're beautiful, Maddy?"

"I don't remember. If you have, tell me again."

He reached around and kissed her. Soft. Gentle. "You're beautiful."

Maddy's mouth tingled where his lips had

touched her. "Even with fangs?"

"Even with."

"Even with ugly wings?"

"Yes. But your wings aren't ugly. They're fascinating."

"As in weird."

"As in, you're the most unique female in OneWorld, and I care deeply for you."

Was that Dom-speak for "I love you?" She hoped so because she was falling hard for the black-winged assassin.

****

The week passed in a flurry of gym workouts, wing exercises, air-time, weapons training, and sex without Maddy biting Dom, thanks to many silent recitations of the Dewey Decimal System Classification.

Her wings didn't drag on the floor, wobble wildly, or do the unexpected.

Whoopie. Success.

As Dom sat on a bench doing his usual arm curl routine, Maddy did what she always did. She stared. His biceps expanded. Contracted. Eventually, her gaze did what it always did. It slid to his neck, where his pulse throbbed with a rhythmic beat. A Tootsie Roll Pop to a little kid.

Thump. Thump. Thump.

Madeline licked her lips, her tiny fangs tingling.

Stop it! Stop it!

But her self-talk had no effect. When she opened her eyes again, she zeroed in on Dom's pulsing throat, gnawing hunger an ache in her belly.

Madeline sprinted from the gym, calling over her shoulder, "I'm off to the study."

She raced along the tiled floor which led to her favorite room. Throwing open the door, she scanned

Dom's volumes of books, all in their proper place thanks to her OCD. She breathed in the scent of the ancient leather-bound tomes, a soothing odor.

When she'd originally wandered into Dom's library, the books had been shelved haphazardly. She had no idea what organizational method he used, if any. Knocking the place into shape had become her priority. She used the activity to forget her changing life and Dom's blood supply.

Now, with her fists propped on her hips, she strolled from bookcase to bookcase, admiring the extensive and organized collection, sometimes fingering the spines of beautifully bound books. She stopped.

I am not a victim. I will change what I can and accept the rest.

She would never, however, accept that she was evil. She whispered to herself, "I am taking back my life. Not my old one, but a new one. Whatever it is, it's mine. I say who I am, what I am, and what I'll do. I may be a Scourge, but I'm not the villain of my story. So what if I crave a little blood now and again."

Stop the pity party. Start researching.

Madeline grabbed a few books from the shelf. Pulling out a straight-backed chair, she sat at the table, surrounded by tomes, all on the same topic—Scourges.

Growing up, she'd learned it was harmful to hide from problems, to stick her head in the sand. So she accepted she was a Leech even though Dom had explained her wings were unique and her tiny fangs were oddities.

When there was a scratch at the door, Madeline opened it.

Freki prowled inside. "Hey."

"Hey back."

"Don't mind me. Just looking for a spot to close

my eyes. Had a late-night party with a shapely female wolver. She wrung me out." He crawled under the table, plopping onto his belly.

"Why do you suppose I can read these books? Aren't they written in a different language?"

Freki lifted his head. "How the hell would I know? I'm a wolver. Books aren't my thing. Think of me as a lover rather than a reader."

She peeked under the table, grinning with the challenge. "But I thought you were smart."

Freki snarled but gave in. "The written and verbal language in OneWorld conforms to each person. I don't bother to question the process. It just is. Accept it. Now, let me snooze."

Madeline shoved aside a leather-bound, worn book. She'd already read it.

She studied photos in another book. The fangs on the Leeches were huge. Dom was right. Hers were smaller.

She flipped through another volume, the usual banter about the cause of maladies. She didn't care. Was it Chaos's fault or the boredom of eternity? Neither of those reasons explained her situation. Somebody had to write a new book.

Here's an interesting one.

It was about the winged assassins. She read the section on Dom and his friendship with Gareth. Though Maddy had pieced together bits of the story from Dom's comments, the article filled in what had been too painful for him to share. No wonder she was a reminder of one of the worst moments in his very long life.

She opened a history on infamous Blood Leeches, not recognizing any names except Lucian's. The writer called him a beloved Immortal who had surprised everyone when he led a rebellion against the OneCreator.

She read the flowery description of the revolt as recorded by Scribe.

The OneCreator sat on his throne, gloriously resplendent in purple robes. His long, blond hair fell about his shoulders, and his eyes were as knowing as the universe.

As he listened to a plea from a courtier, he turned toward a commotion outside his chambers, a room protected by a sturdy door at the entrance. The clamor grew louder, a group led by Lucian breaking through to enter the throne room.

Snapping his head in the Immortal's direction, the OneCreator's gaze momentarily froze the intruders. "Lucian, explain yourself."

"I've had enough of your rule. Your cruelty knows no bounds."

"And what do you intend?" The OneCreator arched a regal brow.

"To replace you." Lucian drew his sword.

The ruler of Vast shifted in his throne. "Indeed. Think hard on this."

"I have."

"Why?"

Lucian uttered one word, "Kalia."

Madeline paused in her reading. Kalia? *Oh, yeah.* The first Scourge.

"It was Chaos's decision," said the OneCreator.

"You could have stopped him."

The OneCreator neither denied nor agreed with Lucian's accusation.

When the much-admired Immortal lunged forward, the OneCreator leaped from his throne, landing in front of the rebel leader. Before Lucian could swing his sword, his head fell from his shoulders.

Madeline skimmed through the chapter until she

read Lucian's fate.

The rebel was taken to Angor, where he lay healing for one and a half millennia. The beneficent OneCreator, in recognition of Lucian's age and status, did not sentence the Immortal-turned-Scourge to extinction. Rather, he doomed him to a life in Angor.

It is rumored he is a Blood Leech.

She selected another book that cited victims of the Blood Leeches, complete with images following their attacks. Madeline slammed the volume closed, swallowing hard.

Ugly pictures were seared in her mind. Fanged creatures tearing into a neck, blood splattered everywhere. An Immortal's bitten and ravaged body. A Leech, fully maddened, his canines sharp, his eyes wild.

She rested her head in the palms of her hands and cried.

That is not me.

Chapter Twenty-Seven

Dom awoke with a start, Madeline beside him screaming. He shook her.

When she didn't stop, he curled one arm under her shoulders and the other under her legs, lifted her off the bed, and cradled her in his lap. Tucking her tight, he restrained her as she thrashed. He kissed the top of her head, whispering, "Madeline, wake up." No reaction. Louder. "Maddy."

Her eyelids swooshed up, her face a canvas of terror. When he relaxed his hold, she threw her arms around him, snuggled into his chest, and sobbed.

Dom waited, letting her cry it out. Obviously, she'd had a nightmare.

Maddy sucked in large gulps of air, choking on her tears.

"Do you want to talk about it?" He smoothed his hand up and down her back, amazed that he wanted to chat it out.

She tensed, her back straightening. "It was horrible."

Dom said nothing. Rather, he unfurled his wings and wrapped them around Madeline to comfort her. She calmed, relaxing in the darkness of his protection. He waited.

Finally, she inhaled, exhaled, and mumbled, "I had a nightmare."

"About?"

"Blood."

"Go on."

Her chest heaved with shallow breaths as if the story were too gruesome. "We were in a meadow.

Making love." Maddy raised her chin, a small grin curling her lips. "When I straddled your legs, I bent forward and kissed you. With my hand on your chest, I felt your heartbeat. The sound was mesmerizing, exciting. I leaned closer, nibbling your lips, your jaw, your neck. Then I bit."

Her gaze flipped to Dom's good eye as if he'd censure her.

When he didn't, she continued. "My fangs popped through your skin, sliding into a vein. Your blood flowed down my throat. Warm. Delicious. Then everything went to shit. You struggled, but I held you down while I kept sucking. When you fought, I ripped into your flesh, tearing it, blood spraying everywhere." She paused as if the scene were too horrible. "So much of it."

Dom nodded, not wanting to interrupt.

"You convulsed in my arms, but I didn't care. All I cared about was your blood, and it flowed onto the grass beneath you. I threw myself off you. On my hands and knees, I lowered my mouth to the ground and lapped up your blood like a monster. I knew you were dying."

Dom wiped away a tear that rolled down her cheek. "I can't…"

She smacked his chest with her palm. "I know. You can't die, but you were in bad shape. Still, I didn't stop. The more your blood spilled, the more I drank."

He scratched the patch over his bad eye.

She snuggled closer to Dom. "I'm a terrible person."

"It's the malady talking."

"I know, but I'm so thirsty." She ogled his neck. "For you. I've accepted that I can't leave Angor. I've accepted I have strange wings and fangs." She gulped. "What I cannot accept is that I want to hurt you. It has my stomach in knots." When her sharp canines punched from her gums, Madeline slapped a hand over her mouth to hide them.

Dom stroked a palm up and down her back. "You're not alone, Maddy. I'm here. We'll find answers."

"What if we don't?" She sniffled back her tears. "Swear again that you won't let me hurt you."

"I promise."

"And if I try to hurt others?"

"I won't permit that either. I swear."

She nodded.

The malady was tearing Maddy up inside. Her greatest fears were for the safety of him and others. Dom had to find a solution because her pain was his. Though he ached for her, he didn't regret his promise to stand with her. Despite his past, he was happy to be the one Maddy turned to for help. No matter the future, he would be her lover and her protector. They would get through this together.

Dom shared an idea he'd been thinking about. "It's illegal for Immortals to give their blood to a Leech, but Aeternal vampires on Scath can survive on bottled blood."

She jerked her head off his chest. "You think that could work?" She glanced at the pulse in his neck. "God. I'm going to hell."

"No, you're not, and it might. The question is, can we risk your drinking even the bottled Aeternal stuff? It's possible it could make your malady worse, less controllable. It could be the last step in the progression of the disease."

She snuffled back tears. "I think the disease is already under way."

Dom stroked his chin. "True."

He rested Maddy on the bed and swung his feet

over the side. Reaching for his pants, he jerked them on and slid a t-shirt over his head. "Shower. Dress. You'll feel better. I'll fix breakfast."

In the kitchen, he pathed Ohngel. *Can you get me some of that bottled blood vamps on Scath use?*

Do you know how fucking early it is?

I do, but this is important.

So is sleep, and my time with Indy. What's your request again?

Bottled blood.

Ohngel didn't ask why Dom wanted the stuff. Obviously, he'd guessed. *Give me a few secs. I'll teleport Indy to her nephew. He stocks it in his fridge.*

While he waited, Dom mixed pancake batter, put the griddle on the stove, and set the table. He poured two cups of coffee.

When he turned around, Ohngel stood beside the fridge holding a bag of blood. "If you need more, let me know. Later today. Much later." He ported out of the kitchen. Obviously in a hurry. Wings were too slow.

When Madeline showed, she was calmer and gorgeous in jeans and a cropped tee. Though still damp, her tousled, shaggy-cut hair curled around her face.

Dom pulled out a stool for her. "Pancakes. Coffee. Blood." He waved the bag in front of her nose. "Known cures for the morning blues."

With a loud sigh, she flopped onto the seat in front of a plate of pancakes. "If only life were so easy."

Dom poured the blood into a glass. "Warm or cold?" he asked.

"Um, warm."

He heated it in the microwave, setting it in front of Maddy.

She eyed him over the glass. "It doesn't smell good."

"Chug it."

Maddy downed the contents in one swift gulp, resting the glass on the counter when it was empty.

They waited.

Before Dom could ask "How is it?" she jumped up and ran for the bathroom. He raced after her.

As she upchucked into the toilet, he wet a cloth for her mouth. "That's not good." He crouched beside her and brushed a hank of hair from her eyes after she flopped onto the tile floor.

Madeline tucked her legs under her. "What if I want blood but can't drink it?"

"Maybe you just didn't like this brand."

Her gaze fixed on Dom's neck. "That's probably the reason, or you're the only brand that appeals to my tastebuds."

****

Later that day, a sleep-deprived Madeline heard a commotion outside. She rushed down the marble steps to the lawn. In the yard, Oskar shot streams of fire from his mouth while Freki prowled around him, snarling and dodging flames.

On the sidelines, Ohngel watched, his muscular arms crossed over his chest, a scowl on his face.

Indigo, spotting Madeline, shouted, "Aren't they cute? Best buds."

Madeline frowned. "How can you tell?"

"They're playing. If Oskar wanted to, he'd fry the wolver's ass in a sec. So, just goofing off."

"Hmm." Maddy, uncertain of Indigo's assessment, looped a hand through the crook of the witch's elbow, leading her up the steps and inside Dom's home. "You have to see our new additions."

Dom had kept Maddy occupied all day by decorating the salon.

Indigo jumped up and down. "Two couches. Fan-damn-tastic." She flopped onto one, fluffing the back pillow for comfort. "Lovely." She yanked Ohngel down beside her.

Dom strolled into the salon and leaned against the wall. "Glad you approve."

Bouncing up and down, Indigo tested the sofa's stuffing. "It's a good thing Maddy cares about her guests."

Madeline caught the "her guests" comment. It sounded as if Dom and her were a couple who shared the house. *Hmm*. She supposed they were.

"Do you like this color?" asked Maddy, settling into the opposing sofa with Dom. Both pieces of furniture were a soft green linen. A deep-pile rug of earth tones covered the floor between them, everything cozy in front of the fireplace.

Indigo smoothed a hand over a cushion. "What are my choices?"

Madeline pointed at Dom. "Do your thing."

With a slight wave of his hand, he clad the sofas in rust-colored velvet.

Indigo shook her head. "Keep the green."

Madeline signaled Dom to change the color back. He did.

Upholstery approved, Ohngel rested a palm on Indigo's thigh, stretching into the cushions. "No news of Praevus or Serita, but how was the bagged blood I dropped off?"

Madeline curled herself under Dom's arm. She welcomed the diversion of visitors. Still, she wasn't comfortable discussing her thirst for blood. She blushed. "Terrible. I upchucked it."

Dom slung an arm over her shoulders, very brave since she wanted to drain him.

"Too bad," said Ohngel. "It was worth a try. Other than that, how's your Scourge-ness?"

Maddy rose and flicked out her wings. "I'm getting these babies under control. I wish they weren't so weird."

"Be proud of them," said Indigo. "I'd love wings, even the weird variety. No reflection on you, girlfriend. But the OC nixed them. S'okay. He lets me ride my best bud."

"I took my first flying lesson the other day, dropping off the cliff behind the house. I'm still limited to short distances." Maddy shushed her wings in and sank back into the new couch beside Dom.

"Ballsy." Indigo reached across the coffee table, high-fiving her.

Madeline smacked palms with the witch. "Yeah. Well, it took a while for my stomach to catch up. I didn't last long on my first attempt. Dom had to save me. But I got better." She opened her mouth, allowing her fangs to drop. "Then I have these."

Indigo's eyes lit up. "Nice. Sharp but tiny. Vamps on Scath have bigger ones. Of course, bigger isn't always better." She slapped Ohngel's leg. "What am I saying? Of course it is. The bagged stuff didn't work, but do you still want to suck on the black-winged hunk?"

"Yeah." Madeline ogled Dom, the beating pulse in his neck thundering in her ears. She closed her eyes, drawing on her control.

Technology, Arts and Recreation, Literature…

Indigo tapped the side of her throat. "How do you feel about mine? Or the big guy's here?" She jerked her head toward Ohngel.

Maddy stared at the couple, locking on their necks. Her hearing focused on their pulses. *Thump. Thump. Thump.* "I hear blood pumping through your veins." She licked her lips, drawing their scents in through her nose. "You smell good, but the urge to bite you is weak. Very weak."

Indigo and Ohngel exchanged looks, her mate speaking. "Interesting. So, you mostly want to suck on Dom."

"Seems like." Maddy really wanted to change the subject, but this was Ohngel and Indigo.

"My Indy spends a lot of time thinking about the two of you." He smirked at his mate. "Time we could spend doing other things. Which brings us to the reason for the visit," said Ohngel.

Indigo stretched out her legs, encased in leather. On her feet were scuffed motorcycle boots. The witch's taste in clothes was as changeable as Angor's weather. On some occasions, she dressed for a Grateful Dead concert in long skirts, sandals, and tie-dyed shirts. Today, she was decked out for a Sturgis bike rally. You could never be sure who'd show up.

Madeline recast her gaze to her own outfit—the jeans, the cropped t-shirt, the ankle boots. Plain. But Dom seemed to appreciate her style.

Her assassin scraped his fingers through his hair, brushing it off his forehead. "Spit it out, Ohngel."

"It's Indy's play. She has an idea about the whole Leech shit."

Madeline chewed her lower lip. "A cure?"

Indigo scooted to the edge of the sofa. "Maybe. Maybe not."

Maddy's shoulders sank. "Oh."

"More of a containment."

Madeline would grasp any straw. "What's the idea?"

"You know about my nephew Rein. The guy who provided the bagged blood." When Madeline nodded, the witch continued. "He was on the edge of the bludfrenzy, being a super vamp and all. Anyhoo, he mated a human." Indigo tapped her chin. "The chickadee's not so human now. She's a Blood Coven witch, but that's a story for another time."

Ohngel looped an arm around her shoulders. "Get on with it, Indy."

"Sure. They mated and exchanged blood. Rein is lots more stable now. Maybe it's the mate thing. Maybe it's the blood from his mate."

Madeline scrunched her brows. "You're suggesting Dom and I mate? Then I take his blood?"

Indigo shrugged. "It's a thought."

Dom scowled. "A couple of problems. First, giving my blood to Maddy is illegal."

Ohngel, exchanging glances with Indigo, said, "I told you so. It's a no-go."

"Yeah, yeah. But who'd tell, Dom? Not us. Sometimes, you gotta bend a few rules. Roark's strategies to save Aeternals and humans showed his willingness to stray from a righteous path."

"I'm not Ohngel." Dom turned a sorrowful eye to Madeline. "Besides, it could make her malady worse."

Indigo shrugged. "Sometimes ya gotta take a risk."

"Second," said Dom, "Immortals don't mate."

Ohngel grinned. "I beg to differ."

The statement made Dom pause, glancing at Madeline. "I wouldn't know how."

Indigo patted Ohngel's leg. "Neither did big guy. He proposed. I accepted. The mating bug struck. Of course, we were flying above Earth at the time and in the middle of the fight of our lives. But sometimes shit happens and you just go with the flow."

Maddy was dying here, but drinking Dom's blood

was a no-no. The intensity of her urges was growing, even though she fought them. If they grew too unbearable, maybe Dom could extinct her. *No*. She'd never ask that of him after Gareth. She'd continue to struggle. She'd win.

In her head, she tossed around the notion of mating. Was it a step beyond what she already felt for Dom? A stronger tie? Maddy had no doubt that she loved the black-winged Immortal. But how did he feel about her? He cared about her, though all she had to offer was a repeat of Gar. How could she tie the man she loved to a Scourge?

Chapter Twenty-Eight

Maddy tipped her hand above her eyes to block the bright sun while she waited for Dom to appear in the sky. It had been a busy day for the Feard, apparently quite a few Immortals were turning into Scourges.

She spied four growing spots in the distance. "Here they come," she shouted to Indigo who was refereeing Oskar and Freki.

Dom had invited the Feard for drinks, always finding diversions to keep Maddy busy and unfocused on blood. Indigo had arrived earlier with her gryphon.

Soaring into the yard first, Dom's shadowy wings pounded the air until he landed beside Maddy on the grass. He pecked her cheek.

"Aw. That's sweet," said Indigo, tapping her mouth when Ohngel dropped down.

A dark cloud formed overhead, sleet and heavy rain pelting them. They raced for the cover of the house. The returning Feard gathered in Dom's salon, sitting on the new couches and chairs.

Accustomed to Oskar and Freki, Maddy ignored the yaps, howls, and snorts from the two creatures outside while she served mulled wine to the visitors.

With a drink in his fist, Dom relaxed, his boots kicked up on the new coffee table.

Maddy poked his ribs, giving him a squint-eyed glare.

"What?"

"Off the table. We just got it."

"I can always zap us a replacement."

"Dom. Off."

He obliged her, the guests staring.

Remi angled against the fireplace mantle. "Big guy, never thought I'd see the day. You not only took your boots off the fucking table, but you barely grumbled. Maddy, you work wonders."

Dom growled. "I've never been as grumpy as everyone says."

The disbelieving smirks refuted his statement.

Ely turned the convo to business, but nobody had anything new to add about Praevus or Serita.

Madeline perched on the edge of the couch, combing fingers through her hair. It was getting too long. She preferred her raggedy, chin-length cut. They still didn't have any answers. The assassins had met with the OC. They'd met with Harmony. They'd met with Lucian and Michael.

Almost swinging his feet back onto the coffee table, Dom stopped, arching his brows and grinning at Maddy. "What did you think of Lucian?" He fixed on his brother warriors.

Indigo moved to the edge of her seat, obviously also interested to hear about the famous Scourge.

Remi responded first. "I don't trust him. Despite what he said, he's building an army. For what? Who knows. His actions scream rebellion."

Dom nodded. "And the OC and Michael seem hesitant to elaborate on his powers."

Ely asked, "Why?"

"Cause they're assholes," said Ohngel.

"Hey," popped off Indigo. "The OC and I are buds."

Maddy rested an arm on her knee. "I'm a little confused about Luce…"

"Who isn't," interrupted Ely.

She continued, "Is he a Blood Leech, like me?"

"Hard to say," said Dom.

"Does he do the Ordeals? Other Scourges do."

They all shrugged.

Maddy chewed her lower lip before adding, "Why don't you check him out with Harmony? He should be on her list. Right, Ely?"

"Uh. Didn't think of it. I'll get back to her. She might have more insight into Mr. Enigmatic."

"Here's a biggy," said Dom. "The OC claims he can't make Immortals into Scourges…"

Maddy's mouth dropped open. *No.* She interrupted. "I've been so distracted by what was happening to me, Dom, that I forgot to mention this. The OC said he DIDN'T create Scourges, not that he COULDN'T. He said it exactly that way. You need to pin him down on his wording."

"Great catch." Dom patted her thigh. "Now that I think about it, those are the same words Michael and Luce used. Not 'I can't' but 'I don't.'"

"That's the kind of shit they all pull," said Ely. "The OC, Michael, and Luce."

Maddy grabbed a notebook off the coffee table. She flipped it open in her lap and tapped a pen on a page. "And I make lists. It's a minor compulsion. See if I've got everything. One, an Immortal kidnapped a human on Earth." She patted her chest. "Me. Two, an Immortal, maybe the kidnapper, brought said-me into Angor. Couldn't have been a Scourge. Three, somebody gave me to Praevus, along with nice digs and a dismissal from his punishments, most likely Serita. Four, Praevus and Serita are MIA. Five, someone killed an unkillable Scourge, Ike. Six, an asshole … excuse the language … gifted me with fangs and ugly wings, but we don't know who or how."

Maddy's shoulders slumped. Seeing all the unanswered questions at once was troubling. "Is the list complete?"

Dom sighed. "Almost. Add seven and eight. The unnatural geological problems in OneWorld and the OC's health. Also, we don't know the end game. Is that an item or an aside?"

"The only problem solved is that I'm no longer a Syc. Another aside, I have a really, really big personal question." Maddy drew a deep breath, her chest expanding. When everyone's curious gaze fixed on her, she asked, "Now that I'm a Scourge, am I immortal?"

Dom scratched his jaw. "I never thought of that one." From the group's puzzled expressions, he wasn't alone.

Adding another jig-saw piece, Dom shrugged and asked, "Is Maddy really a Scourge? I've been thinking about it. Her wings are not entirely like a Scourge's. Her fangs are tiny." He glanced at Maddy, a sympathetic look softening his dark eyes. "And she only wants to drink from me. I'd say that makes her ... unusual."

Ohngel shot a hole in Dom's positive thinking. "But she can't get through the gateway. That pretty much says it all."

They bounced those thoughts around for a while until Dom cleared his throat. "I have something else to say. For centuries, I have been," he glanced at Remi, "grumpy, distant. But that was wrong. You're..."

"Assholes?" offered Ely.

Ohngel chuffed, "Better looking?"

Remi crossed his arms over his chest. "More skilled lovers?"

"No," said Dom. "Friends. Brothers. Family. And I ran from that. Tha…"

"Don't finish that statement," said Remi. "We'll get all teary-eyed and want a group hug or some such shit."

Indigo shared a glance with Maddy who shook her head. "They're such men."

****

Remi didn't go home after leaving Dom's. Restless, he strolled into his favorite BDSM club in Stupool.

Right now, the evening was young, and the serious shit hadn't started. After asking around about Praevus, he stood in a corner watching a dominatrix straddle some Scourge, sticking a giant dildo up his ass and proceeding to spank him with a flat board. Though his cheeks were red and most likely painful, he moaned in ecstasy. He enjoyed the action so far, but things would change. Let the guy get his jollies while he could.

The female changed instruments, snagging onto a flogger. Not a nice ribboned, feathery one. *Nope.* This whip had leather straps ending in metal barbs. Each lash cut deep into the victim's skin until he oozed blood.

Nonetheless, the guy shimmied his hips to rub his cock on the rough mattress, trying to orgasm. Never gonna happen. That was part of the fun here. Brought to the edge but no jizz.

The dominatrix glanced Remi's way, her white eyes ablaze. A Rat. Nice. She was in her victim's head, convincing him he'd blow his nut if she just kept up the punishment.

She shooed her victim away and sashayed over to Remi's corner, giving him a come-hither. She was naked except for thigh-high, ankle-breaking black boots, gartered stockings, and chains crisscrossing her chest. Her pussy was shaved.

"How about I show you a good time?" She pointed to a contraption with chains.

A little bondage play might be welcome. *Yeah.* Face it, he was a bit depraved. Or a whole lot depraved, depending on perspective. Remi found that it took more and more stimuli to get him off. He only orgasmed when pain was involved. Lots of pain.

But duty before pleasure. Right now, he was on the job. So, to avoid taking the dominatrix up on her offer, he asked, "Seen Praevus?"

When she said, "No," he sauntered toward the door no wiser than when he'd arrived.

Action on his left caught his attention. A female Flesh Eater was chained to a contraption that held her legs spread wide, her arms overhead. She wore nipple and clit clamps. When a male applied a cane to her back, she cried for more.

Her punisher dropped a hand to the front of his pants to diddle his bulging dick.

Damn.

Some of the shit here gave Remi a hard-on. Well, until things got too gross even for him.

He stomped outta there, shaking off his urges to get down and dirty. Resuming his search for the hard-to-find Praevus, he curved his bronze wings and landing on solid ground in Violence Village. He packed his feathered goods at his spine. If he gave the Rats an hour's reprieve from the craziness here, he figured they might be grateful enough to spill their guts.

From the middle of the main street, Remi watched the Scourges run helter-skelter armed with swords, knives, baseball bats, or makeshift weapons. The goal of this Ordeal was for the participants to beat the shit out of each other. A mind game. Or a win-win, as he saw it.

Among the screams and blood, he sought Scourges who might keep up with the rumor mill. He sidestepped a blade-wielding crazy. When the female missed, Remi snapped out his bronze razor-edged wings and slashed her upper arm. She barely winced before she scampered off, looking for an easier victim. Remi ducked as a long sword swiped above his head.

Fuck.

Now he was pissed. Didn't the Scourges know who he was? Lesson forthcoming. Remi drew both knives from the holsters strapped to his thighs. This place was good practice for an assassin. He joined in the frivolity. A tall, skinny Rat challenged him, a bat gripped in both fists and raised overhead. Anticipating the guy's swing, Remi sliced the soft flesh on the insides of the guy's arms. As the Scourge rushed off screaming, the bronze-winged assassin chose another Rat. Before he could slice and dice the guy, though, another attacker pounded Remi's head with a crowbar.

Lucky hit.

Wiping blood from his eyes, Remi saw he was surrounded. About ten against one. Time to show the assholes what a winged assassin could do. Fisting two knives and flicking out his wings, he took down four Scourges with a simple three-sixty. The remaining attackers worried their lips. But Remi didn't give them a moment to think about the error of their ways. Lunging forward, he plunged a blade into a chest, stabbed a neck, and used his sharp feather tips to gut another. After doing a backward flip, he ran at the last three. With unfurled wings, he took down a double and finished the final attacker with a knife.

Remi had drawn a crowd. He threw his fists into the air, bouncing around Rocky style. Then just to mix things up, he shouted, "Yippee-ki-yay, motherfuckers. My homage to *Die Hard*. A great movie if you haven't seen it yet. Who's next?" *Damn.* No takers. He re-sheathed his blades and strolled along the middle of the main street, Scourges sprinting out of his path. This stop was proving to be more fun than he'd expected. A little action to soothe his restlessness.

Cowering in an alley, a Mind Rat caught Remi's eye. He signaled the assassin to follow him deeper into the passageway.

The Rat's eyes were white and nearly spinning. Violence Village did that to them, making them delirious as they thrived on delivering and receiving pain. Remi waved a hand in front of the guy's face. "I need your attention. Focus on something other than burrowing through my brains or joining the fun."

The spinning halted long enough for the Scourge to concentrate. "I hear you're looking for info on Praevus."

"Yep. What do you know of him?"

The Scourge peeked around Remi, trying to keep up on what was happening in the street. "Haven't seen him for a while. Heard he ran into some good luck."

"I got that much. What kind?"

"The kind that won't land him in Violence Village. Lucky fuck."

"Who could do that for him?" asked Remi.

The guy shrugged, his eyes going for a spin again. "Another Scourge. One with power. One who is out of the punishment game."

Remi thought that would make the Scourge pretty important. A trustee.

"That's the rumor." The Rat sniffed, his nose wrinkling like he had post-nasal drip.

"Got anything else?"

"Saw him flying toward the Razor Mountains once with Serita. Real friendly."

Remi had stopped his search there when four Scourges had attacked him. Had they meant to divert him?

He supposed he should be a nice guy in trade for

the intel. "You wanna ride home?"

The Mind Rat's spooky white eyes did a funky dance again. "I'll bide my time here." He bent to the ground and picked up a metal bar, a smile creeping across his face.

The informant sprinted out of the alley, returning to the main street while Remi took to the air to search the Razor Mountains thoroughly. As he dipped through valleys and wove around peaks, he filtered energy through his hand to flood the dark surface of Angor with light. After hours of searching, he was about to give up.

Just before he veered off, he spotted an isolated cabin, nearly hidden by trees.

Landing in front of it, he kicked in the unlocked door to announce himself. It was empty and tidy even though the furniture was threadbare and sparse. The only litter turned out to be recognizable remnants of Praevus. A head. A decomping torso. No regeneration going on.

Remi raised a hand, fire shooting from his fingertips and incinerated what remained of Praevus, making the Mind Rat ashes on the wood floor. The guy had been extincted at least a few days ago given his state of degeneration.

Fuck.

Remi searched the cabin, finding male and female duds in the closet and a bunch of shit on a dresser. Makeup. Lotion. A brush with strands of dark hair in it. Not the Mind Rat's. So, Praevus and a female had stayed here.

Then there was more. Cuffs were attached to the bedposts. Remi leaned over to sniff the sheets. Madeline. Her scent was faint. It had been a long time, but she'd been here.

Outside he was about to path the Feard when he heard a soft whimper. Traipsing through the underbrush, he found the source. A female, moans coming from the mouth on her nearly decapped head. Given her coloring, she was likely the source of the dark hair in the brush.

He crouched beside her, a hand to her bloody neck. "Serita? What happened?"

Her eyes widened, but all she rasped was, "Help."

Decapitation, or even near decapitation, was a painful recovery for an Immortal. Most opted for extinction rather than to go through the process. How Luce had endured was a mystery.

Remi telepathed the OC. This was his territory.

What's Serita's role in all this? was the boss's response.

I think this was her cabin. Praevus was extincted here. Looks like he'd been squatting for a while.

Will she speak to you?

Remi glanced toward the body parts. *A lot of pain.*

Get answers if you can. Then give her a choice.

Once the OC's voice was gone from his head, Remi asked, "Serita, what do you want?"

She moaned, her eyes pleading. "E-e-extinct."

"If you give me what I want. Tell me about the human."

"Mine. Praevus did this. Took her."

Remi said, "I need more than that."

Her voice was so weak, he leaned close to her lips. "Mine. From Malacour. Rebel leader. Angor."

Malacour. The bar manager and trustee. "He can't leave this dimension. Who was the Immortal who delivered the human to him?"

Her words came in breathless starts and stops. "Don't. Know."

"What else?"

"No. Thing." Serita's lids slid closed. With such a severe injury, she could be out for hours or centuries. He opted to grant her request, believing he'd learned all he would. Remi unsheathed his sword, severed the strip of skin connecting her neck and head, and said, "May my blade bring you peace."

Done, he pathed to the OC. *Malacour's who we want.*

Some bodies ashed faster than others. Serita's had already begun.

Chapter Twenty-Nine

Just when Ely had fallen asleep, the OC tapped into his head. Short and sweet. *Bring in Malacour.*

He flew toward the trustee's bar in Angor. No doubt about it, Scourge misbehavior was on the uptick. More fights than usual spilled onto the streets. Gangs of miscreants wandered the city, smashing whatever was in their paths. Weaker Scourges ran from the stronger rampaging malady-stricken. Shit was stirring.

Ely pushed through the front door, shoving through the crowd to get to Malacour's office. It was empty.

The patrons were rowdy, high on rumors of a rebellion as Ely cleared a path to the bar. His gaze swept the room while he listened for intel or news of Malacour. Nothing definitive on either.

Ely may have been as excited as the Scourges. A rebellion was something to consume time. The chatter around him was speculative. No one was named, other than Lucian, who popped up often. Guesswork or knowledge?

Some of the patrons were eager for the Singer in the Velvet Cage, as she was billed. Despite the pain they'd feel from her song, her voice and beauty were worth the agony.

Ely agreed. Even with no real intel coming from the Scourges, he planned to stick around for her performance before he searched for Malacour.

The crowd's anxiety ratcheted up, a sure sign she was expected.

The room quieted. A spotlight beamed onto the stage. Her cage descended from the ceiling. That was new. He guessed her popularity warranted an expensive gadget. As before, she was in a swing, her back to the audience.

Fiery red hair hung to her waist while her hands gripped the chains of the swing. Two Blood Leeches rotated the cage, the bars wrapped in velvet. She faced her fans.

She was stunning in a strapless, black gown, a snug bodice of shimmering sequins, its full skirt showing only the tips of her matching shoes and a slit revealing a shapely leg.

Her flesh was lightly golden and dotted with freckles like her face. Her makeup was artfully applied, red lips, blush, and mascara-ed pale, translucent eyes. They were almost like a Mind Rat's but more subtle, more beautiful, more hypnotic, and the soft green of the palest sea glass.

Despite his revulsion, Ely's heart thundered with emotion.

Her song was deep-throated and bluesy. Something about a two-timing lover. The crowd was silent, lips parted, intent on the singer and her song.

When that tune ended to uproarious applause, she sang "I Will Always Love You," made famous by the human Whitney Houston.

Listening to her, Ely felt more alive than he had for millennia. Maybe ever.

Then the Scourges clutched their heads and cried in pain. She'd dug inside their minds and twisted. Though Ely sensed an intent to enter his brain, it was only a twitch, easily blocked.

Her gaze locked on him. She unfolded from the swing and gripped the velvet-covered bars of the cage. With her sea-glass green eyes wide, she pleaded with Ely. "Do something. Help," they begged.

He turned away from the attractive Mind Rat. The bartender, a trustee who was shifting from Scourge to Immortal, was obviously feeling the singer's effects.

"Got any Demon Brew?" asked Ely, breaking through the pain.

"On tap."

"A pint."

The guy winced, slapping a hand to his temple. "You paying?"

Ely tossed a few creats onto the bar. "Who's the singer?"

"Some oddball Scourge Malacour picked up. But she's a looker, huh? Great for biz."

"Speaking of your boss, is he around?"

"Somewhere." The bartender's gaze surveyed the room. "There he is."

Ely spied the manager near the stage chatting on a phone. No telepathy for the guy since he was a Scourge, albeit a trustee. Malacour still had to use the device to communicate. All nervous like, he glanced around the room. Spying Ely, the guy dropped the device from his ear and melted into the crowd.

Ely ignored his drink and sprinted into the crush of patrons, tossing bodies out of his way to get to Malacour.

Was this his eternal life? Chasing down Scourges? Maybe it was time for him to rest again, to hibernate, to go into stasis at a retreat until OneWorld was new again. If not, he feared he would be on the road to contracting a malady as Gareth had. It was said that the pressure of eternity could cause madness.

"Outta my way, assholes." Ely jumped on top of a table. His gaze darted left. Right. Ahead. He didn't spot Malacour.

There.

The front door was closing, the trustee scurrying outside to the street. Ely charged after him, ignoring the ruckus he'd caused in the bar.

When he spied Malacour, he pounded down the sidewalk. Gareth had been an asshole. Ely didn't think of himself as asshole material. Maybe sometimes, but not always. He was just bored out of his mind.

He did have to admit that Dom, Madeline, and the unexplainable events stirring up OneWorld were noteworthy. Maybe shit would get interesting enough to shake him out of his stupor. Though chasing Scourges around was biz as usual, earthquakes and the enigmatic Maddy were kinda exciting.

He took his mood temp. *Yeah*. He was feeling a bit livelier. A bit more interested in seeing what was coming. The redhead in the cage pinged his curiosity. Too bad she was the thing he hated most.

At a corner, he looked around. No Malacour in any direction. He angled his head to the sky. He hadn't left on wing. Where the hell did he go? Ely had failed to catch him, his mind focused on other shit.

****

Long after their guests had gone, Madeline lay beside Dom on the bed, staring out the open roof at the stars. The night was amazingly clear and warm. For the moment. Comfortable, she snuggled against Dom's arm which was looped under her neck. But she heard the blood thrumming through his veins. Her chest bounced up and down with panted, panicked breaths while she struggled with her urges.

Philosophy and Psychology, Religion, Social Sciences...

But Maddy's recitation did nothing to curb her hunger for the black-winged assassin.

She'd conquered the traumas of childhood, led a

good life, had a great job, and was independent. Praevus disrupted all that, making her a slavish dupe. That problem erased, her focus now narrowed to a beating pulse in Dom's neck.

She closed her eyes to concentrate on happy moments, such as the last time she'd been together with her sisters. They'd gathered in St. Louis since it was in the middle. Darya had flown in from New York and Fia from Los Angeles. They met at a long-running restaurant, Lombardo's Trattoria near Union Station. Madeline had ordered the rigatoni with seafood, her usual.

With a scallop poised on her fork, she asked, "How's your dance studio, Darya?"

Though her sister had trained to be a ballerina in New York, an automobile accident had ended that career path. The resilient Darya, however, picked herself up and opened a dance studio for determined young performers. She never looked back.

"I have some talented youngsters. One kid, in fact, was just accepted into the Dance Theatre of Harlem. I was sorry to see him go, but it's a big step up. Anyone want the last piece of focaccia?"

Maddy shook her head.

Fia, whose career as a lounge singer was hitting big, waved her sister on. "I was approached by a record producer at the nightclub. When I get back to LA, I'm going to meet in his studio to go over his ideas. What about you, Maddy? You're the brains of our outfit. What's new?"

"I'm starting my masters, beefing up my creds in special collections and research."

The happiness of the get-together had stayed with Madeline, a celebration by three young women who could have been damaged by a bad childhood. Instead, they'd tackled life and won.

Good times.

Now Madeline cuddled up to a winged Immortal in a dimension somewhere in the universe, thinking about sucking his blood. This sure wasn't grad school.

No blood sharing. No mating. Dom had nixed Indigo's idea. In desperation, she'd even tried bottled blood. Nope. She'd thrown up what she swallowed.

Now she was hanging on by an un-manicured nail. And losing her grip. If she didn't manage the cravings soon, they would control her. She refused to put Dom in harm, although he'd assured her she couldn't kill him since he was Immortal.

That may be, but she didn't want to severely injure him either. Like drinking all his blood so that it took centuries for him to heal.

Twisting toward Dom, Madeline stared at his masculine face with its hard angles, firm jaw, and lines that said he'd seen sadness. A man she was falling in love with. *Hell*. She'd already fallen.

He was gruff. He was impatient. He was a survivor like Madeline. He'd tackled life and won. But there was more. Despite a less-than-cheerful outlook, he was kind and caring. It didn't hurt that he had a body women wanted to fondle.

Would she be his downfall?

Dom opened his good eye, fixing on her, his black hair loose, a silky swath resting on a thick pectoral muscle. He caught her ogling him. "What?"

"Nothing. This is nice. The two of us. The starry sky." She felt the flush of embarrassment on her cheeks.

He smiled, something Dom didn't do nearly enough, but when he did, well, ladies hold onto your knickers. And in his smile was an equal dose of love and assassin confidence. A lethal combo. She felt it to the tips of her toes.

Dom suddenly went still, a sure sign he was listening to a telepathic conversation. He growled. Apparently, the news was not good.

Maddy grabbed a book from the bedside table.

T.M. SMITH

Chapter Thirty

Dom mentally disconnected after he and the other Feard listened to Remi's newspath. He leaned against the headboard and gazed into the distance while putting the info in order. On this side of the gateway, an unknown Immortal had given Maddy to Malacour. He handed her off to Serita. Then the trustee Scourge's Mind Rat employee, Praevus, had chopped his boss into little pieces and stolen the prize—Maddy. One puzzle solved.

Ely added his tidbit. Sent by the OC, he'd found and lost Malacour. Tough break.

But somebody had extincted Praevus. Two mysteries. Ike and Praevus extincted. Malacour, the apparent rebellion leader in Angor, was in the wind. But he couldn't ash a Scourge. That left the same suspects. The OC, Michael, and Luce. Harmony was a powerful Immortal with major responsibilities, but her skills were nowhere near those of the others.

Realizing he was spinning and nowhere near getting answers, he shifted and kissed Maddy's cheek. Dom shared the news with her, interrupting her read on Blood Leeches. She probably knew more about the malady than he did. Of course, he'd never cared to know the deets about stricken Immortals.

He wondered again whether he'd ignored Gareth's descent into madness or his friend had hidden it well. Whatever his history, Dom had already decided he would be more attentive to Maddy.

While her nose was in the book, he studied the human-turned-Scourge. Or was she? Too many oddities. Still, it was hard to dismiss the wings, fangs, and inability to get through the gateway. At the very least, she was a hybrid of some kind.

With her chin tilted down, her hair fell around her face and her expression changed with each passage she read. Sometimes she bit her lip. Sometimes she wrinkled her forehead. Sometimes she nodded.

Dom didn't know when it had happened, but it had. He loved her. The connection he'd felt the first time he'd seen Madeline huddled in that abandoned car in Stupool had only grown stronger. He could no longer deny it. *Damn.* He didn't want to deny it. A thin but unbreakable thread from his heart reached toward her. If Madeline accepted him, it would bind them together, tethering one to the other. He no longer ignored the truth. They were mates.

Ohngel was right. Dom didn't have to understand the particulars of bonding. When it happened, it happened. And he was good with that. *Fuck.* He was ecstatic. Maddy completed him.

Once he spoke those words to himself, a door he had shut long ago opened. Dom no longer wanted to keep Madeline at arm's length out of fear. Rather, he wanted to live beside her as long as he could. He suddenly understood why Ohngel was goofy for the witch Indigo.

Rumors had floated around Vast that many millennia ago Immortals had formed bonds with their true loves. But no one stepped forward to bear witness, to fess up. At least not during his existence. So the belief faded, becoming a rumor. A myth. But every bone, every nerve, every inch of his flesh shouted out for Maddy. Something ancient in his psyche told him it was the mating call.

And Fate had a sense of humor, didn't it? His best friend had developed a malady. Now, the female intended as his mate was oddly infected.

While Maddy was still lost in her book, Dom explored his options. One, he could allow her to sink further into her malady, confining her so she couldn't harm others. Perhaps he'd need to do this later. Two, he could desert her to the illness as he had done Gar, eventually sending her off to extinction or a life of Ordeals. That was a no-go. Three, he could find out how to undo her troubles. Unlikely.

Or, four, he could bind Maddy to him and give her his blood in the way of Scath's vampires. Could it eliminate her cravings? Or could it be the last step in her deterioration?

He knew one thing for certain, though. The OC would not tolerate a violation of his law.

Enough thinking! In his heart, he knew Madeline was his mate. He'd bind them together without exchanging blood. Perhaps the mating alone would help her. Decision made.

Dom twisted toward her to find the book closed in her lap, a finger marking a spot. She was ogling his neck while she licked her soft, enticing lips.

When Dom rolled toward Maddy, she scrambled out of bed. "Stay away from me. I'm having a moment."

"What are you thinking about?"

"I'm thinking about biting you."

Dom reached out, locked onto Maddy's wrist, and dragged her back onto the bed. "You're strong. I'm strong. We'll be careful."

He rose onto his knees, slipped the thin nighty over her head, and yanked the matching panties down her legs, tossing them to the floor.

Dom hooked his thumbs in the waistband of his loose-fitting black pants. Off.

Instead of going for her, he leaned against the headboard, his heavy cock jutting out. "Let me distract you."

Her throat bobbled as she swallowed and

mimicked his pose, her thighs spread.

Though he wrapped a hand around his aching, swollen dick, he didn't move his fist. Tilting his head to the side, he rasped, "I expect a show." When she didn't move, he added, "I'm waiting. Touch yourself."

Maddy's fingers shook as they trailed down her stomach toward her sex. When they dipped between her folds, she moaned, her eyes fixed on Dom's hand.

He grinned, loving a good challenge.

"Knees up, Maddy. I want to see everything. That's it. Now stroke yourself."

Dom's lids were half-masted as he slid his own palm from crown to base, at first slowly and then quicker. When her fingers played back and forth through her pinkened, moist flesh, he whispered, "Faster."

She complied, despite the blush on her cheeks.

"Take a breast in your other hand."

"Like this?" Madeline taunted him, flicking a nipple. Then she alternated between pinching it and circling it with her finger.

Damn.

"That's nice." His hand stroked faster, his balls like heavy weights.

Madeline stared, her mouth falling open to bare her fangs.

Gorgeous. Thirsty for him alone.

"Oh, yeah. Put your fingers deep inside. Stretch yourself for me." Dom moaned, his hand tugging on his dick.

Madeline licked her sharp, pointed teeth as she invaded herself, penetrating her sex with two fingers while she continued to massage a breast with her other hand. "This feels so good, Dom."

She is hotter than hell, spread out for me. Her breath hitching. Her lips parted. Her skin pink. Even the fangs are sexy.

She fucked herself harder, faster as Dom pumped his swollen cock until it was about to break.

When her hips bounced in time to her hand rhythm, she arched off the bed, her head banging against the headboard.

"Fuck. Pinch your clit with those soaked fingers."

"Dom, I can't last much longer."

"I'm thinking of my cock stroking in and out of your tight pussy." He fisted himself hard. Up. Down, stopping for a moment to massage his aching balls. Frantically, Dom's ass rocked in time to Maddy's motions. His hand felt so good as he watched her enjoy herself. He imagined her wet mouth sucking him, her tongue licking his aching shaft. His nads tightened. He was close. His cock thickened. "Come with me. Damn. You're beautiful."

She shouted his name, an orgasm jolting her off the bed.

"Fuck. Yes." Dom's stomach clenched as he worked himself. He popped his hips forward when he spewed.

****

With her breathing jagged, Madeline dragged a willing Dom flat to the mattress. She rolled on top, straddling his thighs.

He grinned, licking his lips. "I'm gonna need inside of you."

She gripped his still hard cock, rose onto her knees, and dropped down inch by inch until she was full.

They both moaned.

When Madeline leaned over his broad chest, Dom cradled her breasts. Lifting his head, he sucked a nipple into his mouth. Then the other. He licked and nipped, driving her crazy.

She drew back to focus on him, rising onto her knees until only the tip of his shaft was inside her. Then, both hands clenching his shoulders, she dropped hard.

With a groan, Dom said, "Damn good."

But since he had to be in control, he flipped them until she was the one on bottom. Her nails drew blood on his arms. She thought about licking it, but her attention was elsewhere. "Move, Dom."

"Oh, yeah." When his hips undulated, he created an intense friction inside her.

Hell, yes.

Tilting her chin up with a finger, he captured her lips. His tongue invaded, pushing in, sliding out, keeping time with his hips.

When it slid across her fang, drawing blood, Madeline tasted Dom for the first time. An accident. Surely it didn't count, but the sample was delicious. She jolted back, fearing what she would do next. "No."

He settled his weight on her. "Be my mate."

Tears streamed down her cheeks. Dom was deep inside her, offering her what she wanted. Him.

"This is us Madeline. Do you love me?"

"Oh, yes. So much I can barely breathe."

"Then accept me as your mate. I'm waiting for you." Dom slid almost out of her. He tilted forward again. In. Out. Slow.

Trembling with need as his tight grip bruised her hips, she nodded. When she did, a wave of energy slammed into Madeline. It was a live wire. That was the only way she could describe what happened. She gasped as the power blasted through her.

Dom threw back his head and roared, his body trembling atop her. Recovering, he gripped the back of her head, pressing her lips to his neck. "Feed," he ordered.

Madeline kissed the pulse in Dom's neck. Unable to control her thirst, she bit, her fangs penetrating skin and vein. *Pop*. His blood flowed into her mouth, warm, succulent. It flowed down her throat, feeding her, pleasuring her, giving her life. His blood was ecstasy, but it was also connection. Love.

As she drank deep, Dom's hips slammed forward. Backward. With his shaft hard as steel again, he pistoned into her while his balls slapped against her flesh and the bed shook with their fury.

Her orgasm built while she gorged on him, their bond growing stronger and stronger. She sensed the tie that connected their hearts. Separate but not alone. Two but one.

She released Dom's neck, crying out his name, her body shuddering, tightening on his cock like a vise.

He pulled out to his crown and thrust in hard and deep, grinding, pounding into her, every stroke a pleasure. "Yes. Maddy. Yes." He gripped her hips as he shouted, his black wings punching out, surrounding them in darkness as they struggled to catch their breath.

When her breathing steadied, she shouted, "No. Oh, no, Dom. What have I done?"

****

Sated, Dom sank his weight on top of her. With a grunt, he drew his wings to his spine and rolled to the side. Then it hit him. In his desire to take the pain from Madeline, he'd allowed them to break the law. And the OC would know.

"What have I done? I've condemned us," she said, tears dripping down her cheeks.

"It was my fault, Maddy. I offered myself."

She wiped moisture off her face. They lay quiet for some time until she said, "We're in deep shit, right?"

"The deepest."

"I feel ... strange."

Dom shot up onto his elbows. "I hurt you. Are you okay?"

"I'm not hurt. The intense thirst is gone." She glanced at his pulse. "I still want to bite you, but the feeling is more of a wish than an uncontrollable craving."

"Is that all?"

She clapped a palm over her heart, thinking. "No. I just can't process the feeling. I'm changed. I don't know how. It's too much to think about. I need time."

"Stand up. Let's see your wings."

Madeline popped off the edge of the bed, unfurling her wings. "Look. Are they better?"

"Turn around," said Dom.

When she did, he touched her feathers. "The same. Nope. Wait. Something's different."

"What? Tell me."

"Your wings are more ... exotic than ever. They're the same except, here and there, you have streaks of midnight black." His brows pulled down tight. "My color."

She curled a wing around her waist until she could see part of it. "They're kinda pretty."

Letting it snap back, she opened her mouth and dragged a finger across her teeth. "Ouch. Still got fangs. Oh, no. I'm so selfish. Open your mouth."

Dom complied, showing her his teeth. "No sharp pearlies."

"Your wings. Let's see."

He rose from the bed and snapped out his midnight wings. Still the same.

"Thank God," said Madeline. "You didn't change. You're not a Blood Leech."

"I told you. Maladies aren't infectious."

But they had broken a law, and they would be

called to account.

He tumbled them to the bed, pressing her head on his chest. "You're my mate. We're bound together. That's what's important."

"How do you know? I mean, I felt something, but…"

Dom searched inside his body. He envisioned a thread. "Our hearts are tied together."

He felt her lips curl up against his skin. A smile. "Are you okay with that?"

"I love you, Maddy. We were already one."

But what should have been a cheerful moment was shadowed by gloom. Though he wanted to protect Maddy, he had, instead, put her in jeopardy.

Chapter Thirty-One

The next morning, Maddy propped herself on an elbow to stare at the still-sleeping Dom. Her mate. After a sinful amount of time ogling him, she slipped on her robe and sneaked out of the bedroom. Padding across the salon, she walked down the steps and flopped to the grass on the side of the house.

Last night was big. She and Dom had mated. She'd drunk his blood and broken a law. Maddy waited for her OCD to kick in. But, surprise, she was not compelled to re-organize the canned goods in the kitchen or recite the Dewey Decimal Classification System. Her quirks had faded.

Maddy stretched out her legs and leaned back on her hands. A warm breeze blew across her face, ruffling her hair. She tilted toward the rare sunshine.

A warm, furry body curled up beside her. "Hey, Freki. Isn't it a little early for you?"

"Yes, but I'm in charge of the pack runts today. Brought them on an outing."

Maddy glanced across the lawn to the edge of the cliff. Sure enough, five wolver pups ran in circles, play-attacked, and piled atop each other. "Cute."

"Trouble."

Without warning, the ground shook and rolled, not as bad as sometimes, but disorienting. Maddy stumbled to her feet, throwing out her arms for balance. The pups yelped and howled. When she glanced their way, they bounced frantically, calling for help. She and Freki raced to the cliffside. A pup had tumbled off the edge, lying crumpled on a rock below with its head twisted at an unnatural angle.

Freki called out, "Bolt."

No answer.

Maddy fell to her stomach and reached as far over the side as she could. She wasn't able to grab the unmoving ball of fur. "Just a little more. Freki, you and the pups sit on my feet. I think I can scoot far enough to grab him."

"Too dangerous, Maddy. You could slip over the side."

She had to try. "No. I think I'll be okay." The pup still hadn't moved.

Freki whistled. "Pile on, runts." He stretched across Maddy's calves, the young wolvers also taking positions on her legs.

She inched forward, her upper body stretching farther over the cliff. "A little more." She wiggled until her fingers touched fur. Taking her eyes off the pup, she stared down. A fucking long fall. But she squirmed nearer, hoping a pile of wolvers could keep her from falling.

Finally, she grabbed a chunk of fur and a bit of skin. Maneuvering backward, she cleared the edge, pup in hand.

Maddy rolled into a seated position. Bolt didn't move, his body lifeless. The other pups whined while Freki used his snout to nudge the injured juvenile wolver.

Nothing.

Freki's sad gaze met hers. He howled, his cry plaintiff rolling through the air.

When she cradled Bolt to her chest, a tear fell from her eye and landed on his golden fur. Her hands heated, and the warmth passed to the small, broken creature.

She thought, *If only...*

Bolt stirred. He shuddered. When Maddy opened

her hands, he jumped from her grasp, jacked onto four legs, and shook, ruffling his fur. The pup dropped to the ground and curled into a ball beside her as she stroked his back to the sound of his soft whimpers.

Maddy's gaze locked on Freki, who said, "What the fuck just happened?"

"I don't know."

She continued to pet Bolt. "My blood got very hot. Then the heat seemed to travel to my fingers and into Bolt."

Freki blinked. "Pretend I'm scratching my head because what you said is crazy."

At home, birds hit glass windows all the time. Stunned for a time being, they sometimes awakened and flew away. Surely, that's what occurred in this case. Nonetheless, she couldn't shake the feeling that something more significant had happened.

"Maybe Bolt was just stunned from the fall." She gave words to her thoughts.

Freki's snout bobbed up and down as if he agreed. But slowly he changed direction, shaking his head. "He was dead, Maddy." He said to Bolt, "How ya doing, champ?"

The pup yipped. Off he scampered to play with the others, careful to stay away from the edge of the cliff and slightly wobbly on his feet.

Maddy chewed her lower lip. "Do you think Dom can explain all this?"

"Sometimes he's smarter than he looks."

Despite her worry, she chuckled, stroking a hand over Freki's head. "You love him. Admit it."

"I tolerate him."

That was all she'd get from Freki. She returned to puzzling the strange occurrence. Her blood had heated, warmth flowing through her and into the animal.

Impossible.

How could she use that word after everything she'd been through in OneWorld?

Pushing to her feet, she waved as Freki disappeared with his charges. She strolled across the yard to the gardens where flowers thrived in the morning sun. She bent forward to smell one that looked like a daisy, albeit blue and huge.

Maddy touched the bloom and drew in the fragrant scent. When her blood cooled, frost spread to her fingertips. She gasped as she stared at the flower. Shocked, she moved from plant to plant, getting the same result each time.

As a test, she cradled a bloom in her palm and allowed warmth to travel into it. The desiccated flower sprang to life, as sweet-smelling as a moment before. She experimented again and again. Cold. Heat. Dying. Living.

Oh, shit.

****

Dom called out, "Hey," when Maddy didn't answer to her name. She was focused on some bush in the garden.

Then she turned, broke a flower off the plant, and sprinted barefoot into his open arms. With her grip tight around his neck, she waited. And waited. Silent.

"What's all the commotion out here?" he finally asked.

She popped her head off his chest. "You need to see for yourself." She opened her hand to reveal a dead flower.

"Okay."

She arched a brow but didn't speak.

"Uh … I'm not up on plants. Disease? Not enough water? Too much water? End of the season?"

"Me," she said. "Watch."

The blossom sprang to life as if it had just bloomed.

Dom's stare flipped from the blue flower to Maddy's eyes.

"Wait for it." She killed the flower, showing him its sorry remains.

He shook his head. "I don't get it."

"I don't either. Freki and I thought you might."

Dom sank to the grass, Maddy dropping beside him. "You're telling me that you can kill plants and bring them back to life?"

Her hands twisted in her lap, having tossed the flower onto the grass. "That's not all. Freki dropped by with some rowdy young ones."

"And?" He leaned back onto his elbows.

"And I brought a dead pup back to life after he fell over the cliff and broke his neck."

Dom jerked upright. "Impossible."

"It happened. So, you don't know any more than I do?"

"No. Are you sure the wolver was dead?"

"Positive."

Dom held very still. First, they broke the OC's law and now this. He feared Maddy's new powers might not sit well in the halls of Sanctuary Keep.

"What are you thinking?" she asked.

He didn't share his real worries. "I'm wondering if you can extinct Immortals."

She gasped. "I have no intention of finding out."

"Whatever you can do, Maddy, it's important to keep it under wraps. For now. Until we figure out what the fuck is happening."

"I'm good with that. We'll just forget about it for a while." She sat quietly. "I need a distraction."

"We'll try the gateway."

"What? No."

He unfolded from the grassy lawn and stretched his hand out to Maddy. "We have to. Where's that fearlessness your famous for?"

"I'm a chicken. Let's test my Scourge-ness other time."

"I'll carry you. I don't want you crashing into the gateway on your own."

She sighed, taking Dom's offered assistance and rising to her feet. "Let me fly on my own for a bit. The physical exertion will push this craziness out of my head." Maddy snapped out her wings.

The sun was still shining, though a dark cloud threatened to dull it.

"Wait," shouted Dom. He wiggled his fingers, clothing her since a robe wouldn't do. With another motion, he donned his usual black garb and teleported his weapons from the house before he joined Maddy in the sky above the house.

Your wings are beautiful, he pathed.

She stalled but then resumed flying. "Did you just talk in my head?"

He nodded.

She chuckled. "Mating seems to be the gift that just keeps giving. Prettier feathers. Life. Death. Telepathy. I should be overwhelmed. And maybe I am but don't know it." She pursed her lips and blew out a long breath. "Let me try." Maddy squeezed her eyes closed as if that would help. *Dom, I love you.*

Message received and back at you. He soared straight up, flipped, and beelined for the ground, head down, wings back. Just before plowing nose-first into a snow-packed mountain peak, he pulled up, smiling, bumping a fist into the air.

"I want to do that," pathed Maddy.

"When your wings are stronger."

Instead of obeying, she angled her neck, tucked her wings, and arrowed toward the peak.

Dom's heart stuttered. He raced to catch up, to save her if needed. But he couldn't pass Maddy. *Damn female.* She was fast. Dom yelled out when she neared the ground.

At the last moment, she arched her wings and shot upward, laughing. Pulling alongside him, she said, "Did you see that?"

Dom growled. "You could have been splattered on the mountain."

"But I wasn't."

"You're damn fast. Add that to your list of mating perks. But no more stunts. My heart can't take it."

They flew side-by-side, taking in the sights below, skimming the ice-capped White Mountains and Loneliness Desert.

Now that we can path, can you read my thoughts? asked Madeline.

Can you read mine?

She furrowed her brows. *No.*

And I can't read yours, either.

Good.

Why? Are you planning to keep secrets?

Just some. To maintain my feminine mystique.

Dom grinned.

How close to the gateway are we? pathed Madeline, looking pleased with herself.

He pointed ahead to a shimmer in the air. *There.* He dropped beneath her. "Pull in your wings."

When she did, he caught her in his arms and inched forward.

With her arms tight around Dom's neck, Madeline closed her eyes and muttered, "Please. Please. Please."

When she opened them, she asked, "Well?"

"We made it, Maddy. The gateway didn't read you as a Scourge." She was a hybrid. The passage out of Angor proved it.

She rubbed her hand on his chest, begging, "Let's go further, Dom. Can we fly to Vast?"

He wanted to please her. It might be his last chance. "I don't see why not." He tossed her high, and she flicked out her wings with a squeal and shot forward.

They approached from the south and Contemplation Bay. When the Lakelands were below them, Maddy hovered in place, taking in the new dimension. "Everything is so green. The grass. The giant trees. And the blue sparkling water is vivid, almost neon."

They passed a few Immortals who nodded at him but stared at Madeline. She smiled and waved.

After they spent hours exploring the dimension, the horizon glowed as the sun dipped lower in the sky. "Let's go home, Dom."

A pleasant silence accompanied them on their return journey. This time Maddy flew through the gateway on her own. She was an anomaly Dom didn't understand. His mate was unique among the beings in OneWorld. While glorying in the observation, he also stewed over it. What would the OC make of the new Maddy when he saw her? He expected that to be soon.

As they floated into the salon, she asked, "Do you think everything I can do now is because we mated?"

"I don't know, Maddy."

Inside a welcoming committee awaited them. His Feard brothers. Grim expressions all around, and Dom knew why.

He pathed Maddy, *Remember, we'll keep your new-found skills to ourselves until we understand them.*

Gotcha.

Madeline greeted the visitors, chattering about her new, improved wings, flicking them out for all to admire. She prattled on about their adventure through the passageway and on to Vast. He didn't have the heart to stop her. Let her enjoy while she could.

Freki loped up the steps and into the salon. "Great. Visitors." He snuggled alongside Maddy on the sofa.

Dom circulated with hot cider, appropriate since storm clouds roiled above the house. Afterward, he sat on the other side of Madeline, looping an arm over her shoulders and glaring at the wolver who made himself at home on the couch.

Freki tossed his snout in the air. "Maddy said I'm allowed on the furniture if I don't shed."

Having bigger problems, Dom accepted the answer and faced his brothers. "Why are you here?"

Ohngel sipped his drink. "Can't it just be a friendly visit?"

"I'm not catching that vibe."

Remi scrubbed a fist along his jaw. "You need to stay calm, Dom. We're here at the order of the OneCreator."

Dom's muscles tensed, preparing for a fight.

Ely said, "Don't go battle mode on us. We gotta take you in."

"Is that why the OC sent three of you?" he asked.

Ohngel smirked. "We tried to talk him out of the whole routine, but he wouldn't listen. He was on a rant, screaming about how you broke the law. He said he'd come for you himself or send Michael if we didn't bring you in. You gave Madeline your blood. And how damn stupid are you, Dom? You both flew over Vast, where every asshole Immortal reported the presence of a

Scourge-like female."

Remi added, "You know I enjoy pushing boundaries, but blood?"

"I forced him," said Madeline.

Dom patted her shoulder. "Hush. I made the decision. Willingly."

Ely shrugged. "I don't think the OC gives a shit about the whys. We're to bring both of you to him."

Dom shot from the couch, spread his feet apart, and flung his black wings out like two giant weapons.

Madeline ducked under one to stroke his arm. "We have no choice, Dom. We knew the consequences." She looked at the three Feard. "What happens now?"

"You'll get a trial, but we'll be there every sec to make sure it's fair," said Ely.

"Who's the judge?" asked Maddy.

Dom's feathers quivered with his anger. After all these millennia of serving the OC, this was his payment. "The OneCreator is judge and jury."

"But I'm cured," said Madeline. "I can fly through the gateway. Surely, he'll see that as good. Right?"

"He's unpredictable," explained Ohngel. "And intolerant when it comes to his laws being broken. I've never seen him so angry."

"I could promise never to take your blood again, Dom," said Maddy.

"What if that's the only thing keeping you from being a full-fledged Scourge? If that's so, I will do it again." Dom flicked his gaze to Ohngel. "We're mates."

Ohngel nodded.

Remi said, "Impossible. Immortals don't mate."

"Is it impossible, Ohngel?" asked Dom.

The fire-winged assassin smiled. "You know it's not, Remi. Indigo is my mate."

"I thought you just said you were mates. A way of staking claim to your witch."

"That's part of it, but I can see and feel the bond with Indy. It's unbreakable." His focus flipped back to Dom. "How do you know Madeline is your mate?"

Dom sank into the sofa again, a smile twitching his lips. He drew a deep breath and exhaled. "I see the tie."

Maddy tapped her chest as she stared at him. "He's right here."

"Well, shit," said Ely. "You're making eternity interesting, Madeline."

Freki jumped off the couch. "Am I getting this straight? Madeline fed on Dom. She's better. She even…"

Dom gave him a slight shake of his head.

"Never mind. The OC, a cantankerous bastard, is pissed because they broke one of his lame laws. He's ordered you to bring them in for a trial, after which he'll pass judgment. What are the possible sentences the prickly bastard can dole out?"

Remi ticked them off. "Not guilty. In which case, they go merrily on their way to suck and fuck. Guilty. In which case they could be condemned to Ordeals in Angor. No. I don't see that happening since Dom isn't a Scourge, and Maddy is … I don't know what. He could order their extinction, or stasis is an option."

Freki bounded off the couch, growling. "Nobody's taking them." He pulled back his gums, revealing very sharp canines.

Maddy reached out to pet the wolver. "You're sweet."

"Not true. Who's gonna feed me?"

She chuckled, "I think it's more than that."

"Believe what you want, but you are not leaving

with the three asshole assassins."

"Enough, Freki. They're right. We have no choice." Dom unfolded from the sofa, offering Maddy his hand. He had a plan. He stared down his assassin brethren. "I'll be pissed and very non-compliant if you try to net us. We'll fly to Vast under our own power."

Before the Feard could answer, the foundation of Dom's house started to rock and roll. The motion was so severe that he snagged onto Maddy to steady them both, his feet spread for balance. "Again?"

"Worse than last time," said Ohngel. Soaring through Dom's open roof, he beckoned the others to follow.

Flying alongside Maddy, Dom pointed at the shoals below. The ocean savaged the rocks, upset from the quake.

Chapter Thirty-Two

Vast, OneWorld

As jails went, Madeline and Dom were in a great one while they awaited the trial. At least she assumed so, never having been in the slammer before.

Their room in the OneCreator's Sanctuary Keep was a luxury suite with a sitting area, kitchenette, bedroom, and well-stocked bathroom. Their clothes were in the closet. The only snag was they couldn't leave, not even if they tried. Dom said his abilities were muted. She wasn't certain about hers and sure in hell didn't plan to test them.

Madeline was okay since the place was loaded with books, but Dom struggled with being locked in. He needed flight, a gym, a Scourge to chase, or somebody to extinct. He needed action—his words, not hers.

A knock on the door.

Dom stormed to it and yanked it open. "Great. Bright Boy. That's all we need."

She latched onto Dom's elbow before he imprinted a fist on Michael's face.

The white-winged warrior shoved inside. "I'm here on OC business."

"Even better," said Dom. "Don't bother to sit. You won't be here long."

Madeline hip bumped Dom aside. "Nonsense. You're Michael?"

He stuck out a hand. "Yes. Nice to meet you, Madeline. I must say life is a bit more exciting in Angor and Vast since your arrival."

"I'd rather not have stirred up so much interest. Take a seat." She pointed to a chair, relaxing on the sofa herself. She patted the cushion for Dom.

Growling, he joined her. "Make it fast, Michael."

The very gorgeous, very tall man brushed white-blond hair away from his face, an inner light shining through his eyes. She knew he and Dom had a past, but he acted trustworthy.

Michael crossed an ankle over his opposite knee. "You're not gonna like this, Dom. But it is what it is. When the OC says fly, we ask how high."

"Get on with it."

"I'm your defense counselor."

"Holy Angor. No." Dom jacked to his feet, nearly upsetting the coffee table.

Madeline stroked a hand along the back of his thigh to calm him. "What does that mean for us?"

"It means I will be standing between you and judgment."

Dom flopped onto the couch and took her smaller hand in his. "It means we're fucked."

Michael stared at their clasped palms. "Tell me why you gave Madeline your blood, Dom. I need the whole story if I'm to mount a defense." He eyed her. "It doesn't look as though you devolved deeper into being a Leech because of it. That's supposedly the reason for the law." He scrubbed a fist across his chin.

Dom pathed a reminder to Maddy, *Don't reveal your gifts to Michael.*

I know, dear. I'm neither stupid nor forgetful.

Sorry.

Dom summarized for Michael—Maddy's kidnapping, escape, Sycophancy, cure, atypical Scourge-ness, and Indigo's idea to curb blood hunger.

Michael stared. "We don't mate."

Madeline and Dom exchanged glances as he mumbled, "Tell that to Ohngel."

"Ohngel and Indigo claim to be mates. Everyone lets them get away with the statement."

"Are you sure?" snarled Dom. "Maddy and I have been drawn to each other since we met. When I asked her to accept me, she did. A bond snapped into place. We are mates."

Michael dropped his foot to the floor, leaning forward in his chair. "Let me think." He paused, intermittent light seeping from his skin. "Long ago. Eons. I remember Immortals who claimed to be mates. But the notion fell out of favor." He flicked his gaze to Dom. "How do you know you're mates?"

"I can see and feel the bond," explained Dom.

Let me do the talking, he pathed to Maddy.

I'm your mate, not your Syc. I'll talk when I want.

Dom chuckled in her head.

Michael nodded. "This could be a defense. I must find out more about Immortals and mating. If it is … or was a thing, perhaps we can prove your attraction to Madeline was so great you couldn't help yourself." He paused before his following announcement. "Tetrys has been appointed prosecutor."

"Fuck," said Dom. "I might as well just extinct myself now."

"Why?" asked Madeline.

"'Cause he has his lips so far up the OneCreator's ass, they're permanently puckered."

Michael shrugged.

"I'll confess. I'm guilty of talking Dom into giving me his blood."

Maddy, stop, Dom pathed.

No.

Dom shot to his feet again. "She will not take the fall for me. Understand, Michael? I want your promise that it will never happen. Now."

He hesitated. "Calm down, One-eye. I swear I will not allow Madeline to accept the blame."

"You can't make that promise, Michael," said Maddy.

Both men stared at her as if she had no say. She sputtered but remained quiet. She'd sacrifice herself for Dom in a heartbeat. They couldn't stop her.

Michael continued, "I have a lot to research before I can mount your defense."

Still standing, Dom said, "Then I guess you better get going. Be sure to note that Maddy was never a typical Scourge. Even now, she's a hybrid who can pass through the gateway. Unique among us." He signaled for Maddy to rise. "Show him your feathers."

She flared out her wings.

Unfolding his large frame from the seat, Michael asked if he could touch them.

"Yes," said Maddy.

Dom clenched his jaw as Michael ran a palm over her glorious feathers.

"Some are leathery, similar to a Scourge's but not. Most are blonde, and a few are black. A combination of both of you. Quite unusual."

"Are there rules about wings?" asked Madeline.

Michael shook his head. "And your teeth. I understand you have fangs. Show me." He approached her again, Dom unable to smother the growl passing his lips.

After demo-ing her canines, Madeline rubbed her mate's shoulder to calm him. A lot of good that did. He still looked ready to strangle their only hope for a solid defense.

After escorting Michael to the door and closing it behind him, Madeline asked Dom, "Why don't you like him?"

"He was the prosecutor against Gareth and enjoyed his job too much."

****

Maddy's gaze swept the courtroom, which didn't look like a courtroom. She figured it was more appropriate for a medieval king's throne room than Judge Judy's chambers. "Who's testifying for us?" she whispered in Michael's ear.

"Dom's Feard brothers. The witch Indigo. Her brother. A few surprises. Your damn pet, Freki."

"Don't ever call him a pet to his face," warned Madeline. "It's demeaning."

Michael chuckled, leaning forward, one elbow on the table, to talk to both Maddy and Dom. "My research into Immortal mates is turning up some interesting tidbits, but I'm not ready to review them with you."

Perched on a dais in a royal high-backed chair was the OneCreator. He was decked out in a long, purple-velvet robe, open to reveal a massive, bronzed chest. Bare feet peeked beneath flowing black pants when he lobbed one leg over the arm of his throne. His hair, the color of a golden halo, fell down his back almost to his waist. His face was patrician, but his smile was mischievous. He was so glorious Madeline had to clamp her lips tight to choke back a sigh. She was nearly blinded by the power that seeped from his body.

Without straightening from his slouch, the OC fixed his gaze on her, a barely perceptible shift softening his eyes.

In a thunderous voice, he shook his head and announced, "For the sake of our visitor, Scribe, please stand." A man sitting at a desk to the left of the throne rose. "This male is a court appointee who documents all important events. He will record the trial and report on it to my Immortals."

Like the OC, Scribe was rocking a robe, a billowy brocade of pink and purple flowers on a navy blue background. He smoothed a palm across the top of his hair, careful not to flatten the dark blond pompadour. With one arm curled in front of his waist and the other behind his lower back, he bowed with a flourish when introduced.

When the OneCreator waved his hand as though he were starting a car race, a man flowed from his chair behind a long table to address the court.

His hands fisted the lapels of his black robe. "Tetrys for the prosecution." He nodded to the throne and the audience. "My case is simple. First, a Blood Leech fed from a willing Immortal." He pointed. "The female is the Scourge. Dominion is the Immortal. Second, the act violates the law."

Tetrys neglected to say that Madeline was not your typical Scourge. She guessed that fact didn't matter to him.

Michael rose and unfurled his wings, a bright white luminescence blazing from them and his skin. Everyone winced, shielding their eyes from the light.

The OC was the exception. He drew his mouth into a smirk and said, in a booming voice, "Enough."

"Sorry," said Michael. "Sometimes I forget."

"Sure you do. Get on with it. And no theatrics. That's my thing." The audience applauded, earning a slight grin from the OC.

Michael paced back and forth before the OneCreator as he laid out his case. "Tetrys's opening was okay but not spectacular. Not even completely accurate. I will present four arguments with witness testimony followed by a summation of logical conclusions."

With his hands clasped behind his back, he paused in front of the OC. "First, Madeline was brought to OneWorld against her will, a human outside your laws. Second, she was never a typical Scourge, hence not a true Blood Leech. Third, the bloodtaking resulted in still more change for the hybrid human-Scourge-Immortal. Fourth, neither she nor Dom should be held accountable for their actions since they are true mates. I think the court will be entertained."

The OC's eyes flashed surprise while mumbles bounced through the courtroom audience.

Madeline guessed the mate defense was a heavy hitter.

Michael glowed with the response to his surprise announcement.

Tetrys, looking somewhat deflated after Michael laid out his plan, presented the prosecution's case first, calling Librarian to testify.

A thin man, wearing what Madeline thought of as a black toga, carried a huge leather-bound book when he approached the OC's throne.

Tetrys said to Librarian, "Please read the law as it applies to Immortals freely giving their blood to a Leech."

The OC rolled his eyes when the witness had difficulty standing and opening the evidently heavy book. He snapped his fingers, summoning a bookstand. Librarian rested the tome on it to read a passage which clearly stated that an Immortal was forbidden to feed a Blood Leech.

Pretty clear.

Michael asked only one question on his cross. "Where are the laws pertaining to mates?"

Librarian looked to the OC for an answer, but his boss's expression was inscrutable, his face that of a marble Greek statue. The witness said, "I know of no laws pertaining to Immortal mates."

"Because none exist or because none are recorded?"

Again, when the OC failed to give him direction, Librarian said, "I do not know."

"Thank you." Michael let a spark of light shine from his body but reined it in again with a twist of his lips.

The OC smirked.

Tetrys then called on Dom. Apparently, in this court, you couldn't plead the fifth.

When asked, Dom said, "Yes. I gave Madeline my blood."

"Did you know it was illegal to do so?" asked Tetrys.

"Yes." His gaze swung from Tetrys to the OC. "Madeline is a human from Earth who was unaware of our laws. She should not be held responsible for my disobedience."

Madeline jumped up, her fingers splayed on the table. "Not true. I did know. Dom told me."

Michael pushed her into her chair while the OC pointed at her and drew a finger across his lips, zipping them. At the end of Dom's testimony, Michael stated he would question the black-winged assassin later.

But Dom did not sit. Instead, he said, "OneCreator, I formally petition that you release Madeline." Snapping his fingers, he produced a sheet of paper, which the OC teleported into his own hand. "I am the Immortal. I broke your law. As your subject, I alone should be deemed guilty."

After reading the document, the OC angled his head toward Dom. "Your petition has merit."

When Maddy tried to rise, Michael grasped her arm to restrain her.

The OC frowned, cautioning her to stay seated

and quiet. "You know the law, assassin. You are aware that I enforce my laws, and you expect stasis or extinction as punishment."

"True to all," replied Dom.

Michael shot to his feet. "Hear the case before you judge."

The OC rested an elbow on the arm of his chair. "Why should I do that? My assassin has confessed and is willing to accept punishment."

Light blazed from Michael's eyes. "Because true justice demands you hear me out. Even Dominion does not have all the facts."

The OC smiled at his Bearer of Death. "Very well. Petition denied, my black-winged assassin. Gladly. I, too, am interested in following this case to its conclusion."

When Dom growled and nearly leaped forward, Michael body-checked him. "Sit. The OC has ruled."

The courtroom remained quiet for several moments. A dejected Dom slumped into his chair, Michael pressed his lips into a thin line, and Maddy twisted her hands in her lap, angry with her mate for the end-run.

Tetrys broke the silence by calling Madeline to testify. She admitted to biting Dom and drinking his blood, heaping blame on herself. "I forced him to feed me."

Leaning forward, an elbow on his knee, the OC puzzled his brows. "How did you force Dominion? He is bigger than you."

"I ... I begged him. Made him feel guilty."

Michael held Dom in his seat. "No," he whispered. Rising as if to cross-examine Madeline, he announced he would question her about the incident when he called her to testify.

At that point, Tetrys rested the prosecution's case. "The verdict is simple. You have heard the law, and the defendants admitted to violating it. What could be clearer? Only one conclusion can be reached." He glanced briefly toward Madeline and Dom. "Both are guilty. Of course, the decision and punishment are yours, beloved OneCreator."

The OC flipped an errant strand of blond hair over his shoulder. "Yes, it is. Thank you for stating the obvious."

If the judgment were as easy as Tetrys said, Madeline conceded they were fried.

Chapter Thirty-Three

The room tilted. Dom grabbed onto Maddy's chair to keep it from toppling to the floor as Michael rose to introduce his case. The Bearer of Death slammed his hands onto the table to steady himself. Even the OneCreator's throne swayed along with other furniture in the room.

The OC clutched his temples with his palms and roared.

Dom didn't miss his pained reaction. Nobody could deny the quake's effect on the OC as he jumped to his feet, flinging out his arms. His voice traveled far beyond the walls of the throne room. "Cease!" he bellowed.

All ground movement stopped, but his face reddened, his eyes narrowing into angry slits and his lips curling into a snarl. In an unexpected rage, he flew across the room, grabbing Dom by the throat. "You have broken my law and brought this upon OneWorld." He squeezed.

Dom gasped for air, only moments from extinction.

Maddy wrestled with the OneCreator's arm. When she touched him, he cast a stunned look at her, seeming to notice her for the first time. "What...? What the hell...?" he spit out, backhanding her in his fit of temper, sending her across the room. At the last moment and with an obvious change of mind, he cradled her fall with a cushion of air.

Michael intervened, a blinding light streaming from his body. He tugged on the OC's fingers to pry them loose from Dom's neck.

The OneCreator glanced at his hands as if he were

surprised by his anger and actions. He released Dom. Maddy sat up as though nothing had happened.

Rushing to Madeline, Dom crouched beside her to check for injuries. "Are you okay?"

"Yes. He didn't hurt me. I think he actually softened my fall."

The OC stormed toward the exit, pausing in the doorway to shout, "Court is in recess until we find out what the fuck is happening." He pointed at Michael and the Feard. "You, you, you, and you, with me now."

Assured Maddy was uninjured, Dom rubbed his throat, rasping to the OC, "I can help."

The boss stared. The anger cleared from his eyes. "Okay. You, too. Outside."

"Return to our room, Maddy. I'll be back in a bit." Dom lowered his voice. "Did you try what I think you tried with the OC?"

She chewed her lower lip. "I couldn't help it. I thought he was going to kill you. Obviously, it didn't work, but I think he realized what I was doing."

"Not a smart move."

"Excuse me! I was a little worried about you."

Dom smiled and crushed his lips to hers. Breaking away unwillingly, he said, "I appreciate the gesture. Now, get going. I'll catch you later. This earthquake was strong. It must have done a lot of damage."

He was right. Outside the keep's walls, homes had crumbled to the ground.

Displaced, frightened Immortals ran toward the snappish OneCreator. "Don't bother me. I know nothing more than you do. But I will."

He gathered the Feard and Michael around him. "Angor has storms and unpredictable weather. Vast has breezes and sun. But OneWorld does not have geological disruptions. We'll each take different zones in Vast and fly above to assess the damage. Come back to report to me."

The OC seemed perplexed, as if he didn't understand what was going on. That was something for the tight-lipped bastard who claimed to be all-powerful. Though Dom was angry with the OneCreator, he acknowledged that his temper tantrum had been out of character.

The Feard, Michael, and the OC took off like six spokes of a wheel. Dom's assignment took him over Contemplation Meadow and the Aeries Range. Maybe an eighth of the homes in the grassy meadow had tumbled down.

He dropped into the valley to chat with the Immortals gathered there. They were worried, clamoring for answers. The black-winged assassin had none.

He questioned a female who stood in the rubble of her home—fallen timbers, collapsed walls, cracked steps. Her wings flicked in and out. She was nervous.

"Sorry about your place," said Dom.

"Do you know what happened?"

"No. Have you felt the other earthquakes before this one?"

Both turned toward a noise as another portion of her roof caved in. "Last week, the ground shook a little. I thought it was my imagination."

Leaving her to mourn the destruction, Dom soared into the air again. After counting the collapsed homes in the meadow, he moved on to the Aeries Range. The area was expansive, and his flyover took some time. He saw no permanent damage. Of course, the Immortals who lived here resided in rocky but exquisite cave-like dwellings. They were intact, though the residents were shaken.

Once he finished with his grid search, Dom

rejoined the others outside Sanctuary Keep. Only Remi reported widespread damage in the city of Farfield to the south. The bronze spike-winged assassin detailed the destruction. Whole neighborhoods collapsed. Immortals buried under wreckage. Others helping to dig them out.

The OneCreator listened, closed his eyes, and drew a deep breath. He held it for some time before he exhaled. "The buried are uncovered. The homes are restored."

He leaned forward, his palms on his knees, as if he were wobbly. Dom had never known the OC to be exhausted. Or violent as earlier.

Straightening, the OneCreator tapped his ear, obviously carrying on a telepathic conversation. "Harmony needs help. Groups of Scourges are running amuck in Angor. It seems they had a similar quake. She's got her hands full. Ely, Remi, Ohngel, rein them in."

As if reading Dom's mind, he said, "No. Return to Madeline. You must prepare for court tomorrow." When all but Michael had flown off to assume their duties, the OC latched onto Dom's shoulder. "You know what she can do?"

"She told me, showed me a bit, but I don't know if I believe her."

"Believe."

"Did you give her these abilities?" asked Dom.

"I did not. And know that I would have destroyed her if I doubted her character, her propensity to do what is right. Still, time will tell if she can handle such power."

"Can she extinct Immortals?"

The OC nodded.

Dom feared what the OC might be thinking. He added, "She can handle the gifts. Maddy's strong."

"She is."

The OC released his grasp as Michael looked on,

confused. Later, when the Bearer of Death confronted Dom, he learned Maddy's secret.

****

The last trial Dom had attended was Gareth's. That hadn't turned out well. He hoped he and Maddy fared better. His petition to accept full blame for the bloodtaking had been denied. His mate's response had been a frosty night of silence. Now they were at the mercy of the OC, and the guy was behaving erratically.

Dom crossed his arms defiantly over his chest as today's arguments proceeded. Michael called Maddy to testify.

He asked her to retell the story of how she came to OneWorld. Maddy captured the audience's sympathy with her harrowing account of being kidnapped on a street in St. Louis and rescued by Dom.

When she finished, Michael faced the audience and raised his arms as if victorious. "So goes my first argument. A human forced to enter OneWorld is not under the OneCreator's laws."

The OC popped that optimistic balloon. "One could also argue that anybody in OneWorld, regardless of how they arrived, is under my law."

Michael shrugged. "On to the next point. Madeline, when you were supposedly a Scourge, what did your wings look like?"

"Leathery primaries and secondaries layered with blonde feathers."

"Hmm. Not typical. How about your fangs?"

"I was told they were smaller than usual."

"Did you crave blood?"

Her gaze flicked to the floor as a blush creeped onto her cheeks. "Yes."

"Anyone's?"

She jerked her head up. "No. Just Dominion's."

"So your wings, fangs, and blood cravings were oddities. And though you couldn't pass through the gateway out of Angor, you may never have been a typical Scourge."

He asked Madeline to unfurl her wings. When she did, the audience gasped.

"Spectacular and strange, aren't they," said Michael. "A few leathery primaries but many blonde feathers now joined by ones similar to the black-winged assassin's. Thanks, Madeline. Your fangs, please."

She opened her mouth.

"As you can see, they are present but small. Quite unlike a Blood Leech."

While Madeline stood silent, Michael continued, "So what do we know? Here is a human who resembles a Scourge. We don't know why or how. We do know she isn't conventional. And may I repeat, she was human— not an Immortal who could suffer a malady. Madeline, why is it you believe you are no longer a Scourge?"

"Mostly because I can fly through the passageway out of Angor. Well, that and the added color in my wings."

Once she had answered, Michael said, "Whatever had affected her does no longer. Since drinking Dominion's blood, Madeline is a strange blend, seeming Immortal as she had once seemed a Scourge." He fixed his gaze on the OC, who leaned forward, listening intently. "Most importantly, if she never was a Scourge, never a true Leech, no law exists to prevent Dom from feeding her his blood."

The OC's only comment was "Hmm."

"Thank you, Madeline. Please return to your seat."

Michael stroked his jaw, appearing to contemplate his next move. Then he acted. "I have a question for the

OneCreator. It pertains to my case."

The OC nodded. "Unusual but granted."

"Does Madeline have other abilities that make her unique in OneWorld?"

The OC squint-eyed him but answered. "She does."

The Bearer of Death, the male standing between them and the OC's judgment, glanced at Dom, who nodded his approval. Maddy, though, was pale and stunned by his question. "What are they?" asked Michael.

His expression neutral, the OC said, "She has the power to extinct and give life."

The rumblings in the audience grew to a roar.

"Did you give her these powers?" asked Michael.

"No."

"Do you know where she got them?"

"No."

Michael clasped his hands behind his back. "So Maddy is truly not a typical Scourge. In fact, she is a unique creature in OneWorld."

"She is a rare being whom I will keep a close eye on," said the OC.

Michael's cat-lapping-milk grin said he was happy with the direction of the proceedings. He called Indigo to testify. A good idea since she was a favorite of the OneCreator's. A little brown-nosing never hurt.

Indigo toodled a wave at the OC as she approached his throne. "Hey, big guy. Nice to see ya."

He grinned, looking instantly happy, adding for the audience's benefit, "I will announce to all that I find favor with this Aeternal witch. She will in no way, however, sway my judgment."

"Not fair." Indigo turned toward Michael. "Okay, Bright Boy. Ask me about the sitch. I'm itching to tell everything I know. And," she glanced at the OC, "it's a hell of a lot. Very sway-worthy."

"I'm sure," said the OC.

"I'm digging the pants. New, big guy?" she asked. He nodded.

"Well, on you they work."

Tetrys jacked to his feet. "Can we get on with this?"

The asshole prosecutor lost points with the OC for that question.

Michael looked pleased, his lips curling. "The human Madeline had traits suggesting she was a Blood Leech." He paused. "I have, however, shown she is not nor has ever been a Scourge. Tell us about the idea you proposed to curb her desire for blood."

"No problemo. On Scath—that's my realm—it is well-known that mated vampires don't get the bludfrenzy as frequently as the general pop. The whole mate-to-mate thing tampers the craving."

"So you proposed that Dom let Madeline drink from him?" asked Michael.

"I did. I thought, 'Hey, Indigo, what works for vamps might work for Maddy.' And it did." She batted her lashes at the OC. "So kinda all my fault." She waved her finger at him. "Just don't get any crazy idea to punish me."

"I wouldn't think of it."

Michael excused her.

"Anytime, Bright Boy. Ta-ta, big guy."

Tetrys rose from his place behind the prosecution's table, gripping the lapels of a long black robe. "Hold on, witch. Did you make Dom and Madeline do as you suggested? Did you cast a spell to force them?"

Indigo tapped a finger on her lips. "I could have. I can be a bit forgetful."

"Did you?"

"Could have. I get brain farts. Once, I found my bra in the fridge." She tucked a finger in the neck of her tee. With a glance down, she said, "Uh-oh. See?" She flicked a wrist. "Better."

Indigo swaggered toward a seat beside Ohngel in the audience, the hem of her patterned skirt swishing on the floor, her bracelets tinkling as they bumped each other.

The OC cocked his head to the side. "Let me get this straight, Michael. If breaking one of my laws solves a problem, then disobeying me is okay? Is that the gist of your argument?"

"Not quite, since I've claimed the defendant is not and has not been a Scourge. But in part, yes. Be patient. I'm getting there."

"Get there faster. The gods and goddesses are throwing a party tonight. I want to show up and bust a few dance moves." The OneCreator shifted in his throne, looking recovered from his previous out-of-control behavior.

"I call Indigo's brother, Alarik, to testify. He's a mage mix with solid knowledge about bludfrenzy."

Tetrys rose. "What is all this talk about bludfrenzy? The female on trial with Dom is not an Aeternal vampire."

Michael twisted his body toward the prosecutor. "She also isn't a Scourge."

The OC waved his hand. "Okay. Enough drama. I'm interested, Tetrys. So, continue, Michael."

Alarik strode into the court, quite official in a long dark robe. He nodded to the OC.

"Give us your credentials, please." Michael stood beside his witness.

Alarik cleared his throat. "I am the director of the Ministry of Well Being on Scath. On my realm, I am an

347

accredited healer."

"Why, among vampires, does feeding from a mate alter blood cravings?" asked Michael.

"Scientists working for me have studied this effect. According to their research, the brains of mated vampires undergo a chemical change. That alteration moderates the violent desire for blood."

Michael spoke directly to the OC. "That seems to be what happened to Madeline once she fed from Dominion, your black-winged assassin." He glanced at Tetrys. "Even though she isn't an Aeternal."

"Alarik, have you examined the human?" asked the OC.

"Yes."

"Did you find a chemical change?"

"My examination was inconclusive because I had not examined her prior to the bloodtaking."

"So, Michael, Alarik's testimony, though interesting, is meaningless. He cannot prove Madeline underwent a chemical change. Besides, once again, I ask if a positive outcome means my laws may be broken?"

"Bear with me. Alarik's testimony will help build a foundation for my next argument."

Like the audience, Dom was interested in where Michael was going. But his defense was interrupted when the OC recessed the proceedings for the day.

Chapter Thirty-Four

Back in their cell at Sanctuary Keep, Madeline and Dom brushed their teeth side by side, not talking. After spitting toothpaste into the sink, she walked out, slamming the door behind her, hoping it showed just how really pissed she was.

Maddy crawled into bed, curling onto her side to face the wall.

The mattress dipped as Dom got in beside her. "You're still angry."

Maddy tossed toward him, locking the sheet under her arms. "I'll probably stay that way."

"For an eternity?" he teased.

"No one really knows if we'll have that long, but if we do, yes."

"I had to try the petition, Maddy."

"No. You didn't. You promised never to abandon me. You broke your promise. I told you I wouldn't give you a second chance."

"What I did wasn't the same."

"Yes. It was. I can't live without you."

He grinned. "But you can spend eternity not talking to me."

She drew her brows tight. "Yes. No. What were you thinking?"

"I was thinking I could accept any punishment as long as I knew you were safe. Remember, you tried to take the blame, but I'm still talking to you."

She snarled. "My attempt was half-assed. I didn't know I could submit a formal petition."

"I had to do something to save you, Maddy."

"And what if the OC had accepted your petition?

349

Did you think about what that would do to me?"

"You'd be safe. You're my mate. My heart beats for you. What happens to you, happens ten times worse to me. I could handle my stasis. Not yours. You have to be free to live for both of us."

Dom seized her lips for a kiss, stifling any objection. He released her. "Please don't be angry with me."

"I can't stay that way. I love you, Dom. But being apart would tear me up worse than any stasis."

"You're unique. We don't know how you'd handle sleep. And I can't even consider your extinction."

She curved her fingers around the nape of his neck, tangling them in his long, dark hair. With her lips pressed to his, she slipped her tongue into his mouth. He sucked on it, making her dizzy from the passion.

When he released her, Maddy stroked a palm across his solid, bristly jaw. "Whatever happens, happens to both of us. If not, you've failed me. You've abandoned me like my birth parents. Like my father. Like my mother who lost herself in a bottle."

"Madeline, if you could live one more day, I would gladly offer my life. You've given me more in weeks than I had for centuries. Millennia."

"And I can say the same. Except the centuries and millennia part. But you must swear that our fate will be together. No matter what it is. Good or bad. If not, Dom, we mean nothing."

"We mean everything." He sighed, his breath catching before he said, "Together, then. In life. In death. In sleep."

"Thank you." She snuggled closer, nibbling his chin, jaw, and lips before she returned to his mouth. Her heart thundered against her chest. Her body warmed in his embrace. But before giving in completely, Maddy pushed Dom away. She curled to the side, rising on an elbow. "About Gareth."

Dom was still panting from the kiss. "I'm not sure I want to talk about Gar right now."

"Well, we might not have many more chances."

He rolled toward her, adopting her pose. "What about him?"

She shook her head to concentrate on the conversation rather than on Dom's incredible bare chest. "You know about my mother's abusive alcoholism."

"I do." Dom stroked a palm along her naked thigh.

She shivered from his touch. "After my sisters moved out, I attended Al-Anon meetings. There, humans having similar problems discussed their situations. Anyway, one of the big lessons I learned applies to your relationship with your friend."

"What was the lesson?"

"Al-Anon 101. You cannot help someone who does not want to help himself."

Dom closed his eye. Moisture seeped from it. Wordlessly, she watched as centuries later her mate came to grips with the loss of his best friend.

The black-winged assassin, her gruff lover, pulled her on top of him, his arms lashing around her. "You are nothing like Gar. He was vain, selfish, and unwilling to change or control himself. I know that. Now ride me, mate. Ride me into oblivion."

Forgetting their troubles for the moment, she laughed. "You say the most romantic things. I'm not a Syc anymore, but I'm happy to follow your order, O bossy one."

Madeline straddled Dom's thighs, rose to her knees, and massaged her breasts, plucking on her nipples. With a wicked grin, she grasped his hard cock, sat down on it, and rode him into oblivion. Though her fangs punched from her gums, she did not drink his blood for fear they were watched. She hoped the jailers reported her restraint.

In the early morning, a knock woke her. Very polite. Why didn't the visitor just walk in? After all, they were prisoners.

A sleep-rumpled Dom stumbled to the door, stepping into his pants on the way. The voices were too whispered for Madeline to hear, but her mate returned, his expression all business.

"The OC has called the Feard out. It seems I'm still active even though he wants to hang me out to dry. Anyway, we're splitting up to quell problems in Angor."

Maddy hopped out of bed and rushed to the closet, pulling out leather pants, a shirt, and a lined jacket. "I'm going along."

"No."

"Yes. I can be lookout."

"No. We don't know if you're Immortal. And you don't know how to use your abilities yet."

She fisted her hips and tapped a foot. "Our relationship will not work unless we're equals."

"Maddy. We're not equals. I'm a winged assassin of the OneCreator. I've also been at this for a few more millennia than you have. You have new gifts, but they're untested."

Frowning but determined, she said, "Not equals that way. I know you're bigger and stronger. I mean in the decision-making process."

"You're right. If we survive the trial, we'll talk."

She chewed her lip and her shoulders sank in defeat. "Okay, flyboy, I'm giving in this one time. Get out of here. Stay safe."

"Always. Besides, I'm saving myself for a good

spanking from the OC."

"I don't think you're sufficiently worried about the trial."

He kissed her cheek. "I'm worried about you."

She flashed her most confident smile as he left, hiding her fears. Their time together was slipping away. *No.* Dom had promised they would face whatever the future had in store—together always.

He had saved her, but what she felt for Dom went way beyond gratitude. He was her lover, her confidant, her north star, her best friend. He had seen her through the most drastic changes in her life and stood with her. She clasped a hand to her chest. He was her mate.

****

Court resumed when the assassins returned from Angor. Yawning, the OneCreator rested an elbow on the arm of his throne. He was in a quandary about Dom and the once-human. Though he enforced his laws consistently, this case had him stymied. "Now, where were you, Michael? Oh, yes. You were pointing out that it's all right to break a law if it works out okay or if one of the miscreants is unique. Do you have anything else?"

"I do. I was promising that the testimony to this point would help my next argument."

He called Alarik back to finish his statements. Michael asked, "As a healer, you examined the defendants?" He spun toward the OC. "With their permission, of course."

"Yes," said the Aeternal from Scath.

"What did you find?"

"Their hearts are linked by a thread that binds them together, similar to our mated Aeternals."

The OC rubbed his jaw. "Similar but not the same."

"True, though…"

With a wave of his hand, the OC silenced Alarik.

Michael continued to plug away at the mate defense. "And Ohngel and Indigo?"

"The same. I saw the thread, the mating bond." The Aeternal mage flicked his gaze to the throne, probably expecting to be stifled again.

Michael surrendered his witness to the prosecution.

Tetrys rose. The male was pompous but loyal. And boring. He gripped the lapels of his somber robe. No color for him. "How can you be sure the thread you see is a mating bond?"

Alarik shifted from foot to foot. "I cannot be one hundred percent positive, but both couples have similar connecting threads—heart to heart."

"But you are not one hundred percent certain?" Tetrys faced the crowd, performing for them.

"No. But…"

"Thank you. You are excused." With a flourish of his robe's hem, Tetrys sat.

Michael called Freki to the stand, an irritating creature who was never at a loss for words. "Why the fuck are you calling my wolver to testify? My first. One of my flawed creatures." He muttered so low, most could not hear, "I did better with Unicorns."

"I heard that," said Freki. "A bunch of sissies. Too busy primping their manes."

Michael glared at the witness until he stopped talking. "I called Freki to testify because wolvers are well acquainted with mating bonds."

"We are," said the wolver, plopping onto his haunches. He growled at the OneCreator. "And I am not flawed. You just don't like lip. Even when it's the truth."

Michael began quickly as if fearing the response. Or a lightning strike. "How does mating work?"

"Can't tell you how. Only that it does. A male wolver can be going along minding his own biz. *Pow*! A female struts by wagging her tail, and the bond snaps into place. When it does, neither can fight the attraction. They mate for life."

"Has it happened to you?" asked Michael.

Freki's snout dipped toward the floor. "Yes," he rasped, his voice halting.

"Where is your mate now?"

Freki cleared his throat. "She was killed, shredded by a Flesh Eater a century ago."

Madeline gasped and slapped a hand over her heart, a sympathetic tear streaking down her cheek.

"What would you have done to save her?" asked Michael.

"I would have offered myself to the Scourge. I would have done anything necessary."

"What if there was a law forbidding it?" asked the Bearer of Death.

"There is no law beyond the mating law."

The OneCreator cocked an elbow on each knee, his heart sad at the wolver's loss. He softened his tone. "There are my laws."

"Who knows what drug you snorted when you wrote them. Some of your rules make less sense than others."

The OC rested his chin in both palms. "A reminder to all. Freki is a wolver. Dom is an Immortal. Madeline is a … something. But they are all under my rule."

Michael called Ohngel to testify. "How do you know you and the witch are mates?"

Indigo shot to her feet from the audience section, "I'll field this one."

Ohngel glanced at the OneCreator and shrugged.

"Roark…"

"Who?" asked the OneCreator, suddenly a tad snarky. Everyone wanted to be an expert on mating. He'd outlawed it millennia ago.

Indigo slammed her fists to her hips. "We've covered this whole name business. Anyway, Roark here asked me to be his mate at an inappropriate time. We were in the middle of a battle. I said, 'Yeah,' and the goddam thing snapped into place and almost took me out. I was speechless."

"If only," said the OneCreator.

Indigo blew him a kiss. Cheeky female, but she entertained him, and he admired her spunk.

When Tetrys declared he had no questions of Ohngel before he returned to his seat, Indigo smirked. "Cluck, cluck, cluck."

Michael questioned Dominion, who also saw the bond he shared with Madeline, the mystical manifestation of their love. Once he finished with the black-winged assassin, he turned toward the spectators, announcing in a booming voice, "I call Jasmine and Terrell to testify."

The audience whispered and even the OC flinched, unhitching his leg from the arm of his throne.

He opened his mind, searching for a memory of the two Immortals who were among his earliest creations. If he could sort through all the data in his head, he might remember them better.

The only memory he extracted from buried recesses was that Jasmine and Terrell had retired from court society, gone off to live somewhere, and had never been seen or heard from again.

All eyes in the courtroom, including his own, followed the two Immortals as they strode forward hand-in-hand.

"Let's get to the point. Are you mates?" asked

Michael once they stood in place to testify.

"We are," said Terrell.

Jasmine nodded.

"How do you know?" Michael asked.

The female Immortal said, "We see the bond."

"How can we be certain what you say is true?" asked Michael.

She bristled. "Other than our word?"

"Yes." Light seeped from Michael's skin. He quickly sucked it in.

"The OneCreator could look inside our minds to view our truth. I am aware he is reluctant to use such powers on his creations, but such would be possible," said Terrell.

The OneCreator avoided Michael's questioning stare. He was not ready to invade their minds. Besides, law was still law.

"Why did you leave the court millennia ago?" asked the Bearer of Death.

"We knew we were different. And by then, the OneCreator," Terrell swallowed as though he had a fist in his throat, "had announced mating was a thing of the past. Along with others of our kind, we sought a place to live in peace. We call it The Retreat."

Had he grown sloppy in his management of OneWorld? Had he spent too much time at court, entertaining frivolous gods and goddesses who had the attention spans of a Vast nat? *N-a-t*, not *g-n-a-t*. Why would Earthers add a *g* to the name? He didn't know.

Anyway, an entire colony lived off the grid, unbeknownst to him. But the law was still law. The case was not about mates. It was about an Immortal, a Leech, and blood. But does the hybrid Scourge have a malady?

"What is life like at The Retreat?" asked Michael.

"Similar to that anywhere with a few exceptions."

"We'll get back to those exceptions in a moment. What do you know of a book of laws for mated pairs?"

Jasmine kneeled on the stone tiles to riffle through a huge tote bag. "I have a copy." Retrieving it, she held it up for all to see.

The court wide-eyed the OneCreator as he pressed fingers to his temple, trying to remember. Had he written laws for mated beings? He couldn't recall. There had been so few bonded Immortals. Even then. Hadn't there?

"May I read it?" he asked.

Jasmine appeared reluctant to put it into his hands.

Acknowledging her hesitation, he said, "Do not fear me, child."

After some thought, she stretched out her arms so she did not have to climb the steps to his throne.

Taking it, he studied the cover, sensed the ancient tome's age, and set it in his lap. "I shall peruse this after we recess today."

Michael paused, likely for effect. Over the millennia, his Bearer of Death had pleased him. He had grown into his power. Other than a tendency toward showmanship, he sorted out other Immortals with equity. He was a child to be proud of.

"Let's return to those exceptions you mentioned earlier, Terrell. How is it different where you live?" asked Michael.

Terrell flicked his gaze to the throne, as if to judge reaction. "Younger mated couples have joined our group."

The OneCreator schooled his expression. Matings still occurred? He'd thought Ohngel an exception because of the Aeternal witch. He doubted Dom and Madeline's claim.

"Other irregularities?" pursued Michael.

"Some of us have borne offspring."

The audience, including Dom, Ohngel, and Indigo, gasped. Madeline probably did not understand the gravitas. Murmurs of *not possible* and *untruth* made their way through the court.

The OneCreator shot from his throne. "We are in recess. Leave now. I will announce my verdict tomorrow. Begone," he bellowed.

He thundered from the room with Jasmine's book under his arm. He needed to think, recall, and read. Changes were rocking OneWorld—geological disruptions, his declining health, his mood swings, disobedience of his laws, and an entire community of mated couples and livebornes.

He slammed into his personal chambers, angry at himself. Fearing the spread of the malady, he had sought to control Immortal DNA by calling an end to mating and producing liveborne. Or so he thought. It had been so long ago that he barely remembered. Chaos and his sisters had stood with him then. Aeternals and humans had not existed.

He had also worried about overpopulation. The creation of Immortals had to balance their extinction. Such was mandatory with eternity. Otherwise, in time, OneWorld would be overrun.

Though he had failed to eliminate the mating urge, a bigger problem niggled in his mind. How did Madeline come to be?

Despite his distaste for the invasion, he might need to crawl into a few heads.

He was slipping.

T.M. SMITH

Chapter Thirty-Five

Scribe cleared his throat with a nod from the lord of OneWorld. "Hear, ye. Hear, ye."

The OneCreator sighed, something he did so well. As he did all things. "Get on with it," he said, his royal glare a warning.

"Yes, sire. My pleasure, sire." Rustling his cloak with a flourish, Scribe turned toward the audience which packed the throne room. "Today, our esteemed lord will pass judgment on the black-winged assassin called Dominion and the human Scourge-maybe-not-Scourge Madeline of Earth. They stand accused of breaking a sacred law of the OneCreator, who knows all, sees all, is all."

"Today, Scribe. We're on a clock. Give us the short version." The lord of all of us lobbed a graceful, though masculine, leg over the arm of his throne, leaning into the back of his seat in what some would describe as a royal slouch.

As always, his form was magnificent. Scribe took a moment to document the OneCreator's attire on an electronic pad, his thoughts controlling the keyboard.

The lord of Vast was clothed in soft, velvety black trousers hanging low on his masculine hips. On this judgment day, he had donned a brocaded satin robe in hues of blue and purple, the likes of which Scribe had never seen. Its fabric was thick. Its folds soft. Its royal cloth tumbling to the floor.

He glanced at his sire. Though the OneCreator was without flaw and always correct, Scribe had imagined a lengthy formal process to precede the announcement of the verdict—an introduction of important parties, a statement of accusations, a summary of the testimony. All would lead to the OneCreator's most-wise verdict. "Sire. There is a script we follow in these proceedings."

"Who wrote it?"

"I did, my lord."

"Rewrite it."

"Certainly." Scribe entered a few notes into his pad, reminding himself to edit future court procedures. He did so without malice, though each word he had written for the occasion had been perfect. Later, he would think long and hard on an appropriate revision. Setting his device aside, he opened volume seven of the *OneCreator's Laws*. "It is written that no Immortal may offer blood to a Blood Leech Scourge." His gaze scanned the crowd. "Though I have read the shortened version, the law is clearly written. Praise be to the OneCreator in his wisdom."

Waving Scribe aside, the greatest being in the galaxy unfolded his masculine form from his throne, pulling himself up to his nearly seven-foot height.

Scribe entered his sire's actions into his pad.

When the OneCreator stood, his robe parted to bare his bronze, wide chest. He shook his head, his blond hair falling straight down his back, a waterfall of bright sunshine, an appropriate frame for his purple eyes. His feet were bare, his legs mighty, his shoulders broad, his height towering. He was glorious.

Along with the others in the crowd, Scribe awaited the OneCreator's judgment.

His regal voice thundered across the throne room, holding all gathered in its thrall. "I have heard testimony for and against Dominion and Madeline. I have studied the law of which they stand accused of breaking. I have read the once-lost *Laws for Mated Pairs*, turned over to the court by the bonded Immortal Jasmine. In those ancient rulings, much latitude is granted to mated pairs."

Tetrys rose, his fists tugging on the lapels of his robe. His tenor voice spread throughout the courtroom. "I object."

The OneCreator arched his god-like brows. "How can you object when I have not stated my judgment?"

The prosecution wisely took his seat.

"I have listened to all testimony. I heard that the human may not have been a Scourge. Likewise, my black-winged assassin and Madeline claim a bond, a thread ties them to one another, making them mates. I believe them. So, which law prevails? A mate may take any action deemed reasonable to save a mate? Or no Immortal may willingly allow a Scourge to drink their blood?"

As the attendees held their breath, he announced, "Dominion and Madeline are deemed mates and, therefore, not guilty. And since the hybrid Madeline was never a true Scourge, I will not hold her accountable for being a Blood Leech. Henceforth, they are set free."

The crowd roared. Scribe nodded at the most-wise ruling while a few booed, though quietly so as not to offend the OneCreator.

Dominion and Michael, longtime enemies, shook hands, appearing to mend their centuries-long rift. The Bearer of Death, today the defense, hugged Madeline, a unique being in OneWorld.

The OneCreator pulled Terrell and Jasmine to the side. Scribe, who must know Vast's business in order to document it, moved close to listen in on the conversation.

"How many young are in your camp?" asked the sire.

Unfortunately, since Terrell lowered his voice to a whisper, Scribe could not hear the answer, but the

OneCreator arched a royal brow.

As the courtroom began to clear, the grand sire handed the *Law for Mated Pairs* to Scribe. "Please document this book and pass it to Librarian to be housed in the Hall of Time."

The OneCreator signaled for Dom and the hybrid Scourge Madeline to remain behind. Again, for the sake of his duty, Scribe tried to listen in but was shooed off. Obeying, he tucked the *Law for Mated Pairs* under his arm and hurried to complete his worthy task.

****

Maddy preferred to go home, but no one ignored the OC, certainly not a human-Scourge-Immortal whatever. So she laced her fingers in Dom's and approached the throne.

The OC cocked his head to one side, studying her until she shifted from foot to foot nervously. She bit back a "What?" Then she felt a thousand probing fingers exploring her mind. Her knees weakened, and Dom's arms came around her to keep her on her feet.

"Stop," her mate commanded.

The OC halted. "Madeline," he said, "OneWorld has not treated you well."

She steadied herself with a hand on Dom's shoulder. "Not at first. But I think life is looking up." The OC was correct, up to a point. Her kidnapping and torture had been horrible. She could do without wanting her mate's blood or the trial. But finding Dom was worth all the unpleasantness. And she was accepting her physiological changes. Al-Anon's three Cs. "I didn't cause it, I can't control it, and I can't change it." For once, she was happy for her childhood and its lessons.

The OC rested his elbows on his knees. "Somehow you have obtained gifts along with your unique hybrid form. You can heal and extinct."

"I'd give them back if I could."

"I believe you. Do you wish to use these gifts in service to OneWorld?"

"No. Hell, no. I mean, I wouldn't mind healing things, but not the rest. I don't want to be an assassin and kill Immortals who become Scourges. Never. That's not me."

"I see that, Madeline. You have a sympathetic heart."

No time like the present for her question. With confidence, she asked, "Since I'll be sticking around, there's one job I'd like."

"What's that?"

"I want to be a librarian again."

"Angor or Vast?"

She glanced at Dom. "Angor?"

He nodded.

"Angor it is. I am uncertain how you became what you are or why you are here, but I am satisfied you are worthwhile. I have no inclination to kill what I do not understand. I do have an inclination to keep an eye on you and to find answers to my questions."

"We want answers, too," said Maddy.

****

Dom tapped his mate on the shoulder. "I'll be just a moment. Wait for me outside." He added, "Please."

She dawdled out of the throne room, probably curious about why he stayed behind.

Dom had a request. It was time. *Damn*. It was past time.

The OC relaxed into his throne, his elbow on an arm. "You are gonna ask for a vacation, aren't you? Granted."

Dom shook his head. "No, but I'll take it."

The OC looked at him askance. "Are you thinking

you can quit your job because you are pissed at me? I will not allow that. Be as angry as you want, but you will remain an assassin."

"Nope. Not gonna quit. And I'm not really pissed. I expected to be caught and punished. So the not-guilty verdict is an appreciated reprieve. I'm down with it."

"Then what the fuck is it? Do not keep me waiting. I have courtiers to entertain." His eyes flicked to the side, dark circles under them making him look tired. "I also have female Immortals who make it their life's pleasure to entertain me."

"A request," said Dom.

"Spill." The OC pointed at the I-giveth-I-taketh-away reminder written above his throne as if any of the Feard could forget it.

"Once, I asked for a permanent reminder of my extincting Gareth. You let me keep my wound, and I thank you. I needed it. Now I realize the best of him is in here." Dom tapped a finger to his temple. "The early Immortal. I'll not forget who he became, but I'll remember a legendary warrior and assassin, too. My friend. But it's time for me to heal so that my memory of him is of the whole male not just the damaged Flesh Eater."

Dom fixed his gaze on the OC. "First, I have a question. Why did you send *me* after Gareth? You must have understood its impact. In part, you played a role in my guilt."

"Not sure you'll understand."

"Try me. I've grown wiser."

"You're a great warrior, Dominion, with a strong sense of right and wrong. An ethical right and wrong. Not a legal one. And you are stubborn."

Dom rubbed his bad eye. "I can see that."

"I did not seek to give you guilt. I sought to show

you truth. You needed to experience the complex being Gareth had become, his strengths and weaknesses. Without that picture, you would never have believed he was unable to survive a malady. I sent you after the truth. You found it, but in your stubbornness, you did not accept it—until now."

"It was a hard lesson."

"Harder than I had foreseen, but worthwhile truths often are."

"I have carried the shadow of Gareth inside me. He was guilt, a darkness that ate away at me. Madeline shone a light on that darkness. She helped drive it away. Do you ever question your choices?" asked Dom.

The OneCreator smiled, shifting a bit in his throne.

"No answer?"

"To question my judgment would mean I do not see the future. To question my decisions would mean I do not see their impact on my Immortals."

"That isn't an answer."

"Yes, it is. It just isn't the one you want. The answers to our questions are not always clear. So back to your request. Do you no longer need a reminder of your betrayal?"

"I no longer believe I betrayed him. You cannot help someone who does not want to help himself."

"A wise perspective on the matter."

"A good person told me this."

"Approach, Dominion, my onyx-winged assassin."

When he did, the OC barely waved his fingers. Dom's patch fell away. "May you be as free of the past as you wish. May you remember my troubled copper-winged assassin as he truly was. As I remember him. The good and the bad at odds. Yet, strangely, they made him whole."

The light was brighter. Dom hadn't realized that in seeing from only one eye his surroundings had dimmed.

The OC shooed him out.

Dom pushed through the door, his path clearer, his future shinier, and Maddy waiting for him on the steps of Sanctuary Keep.

She slapped a hand to her mouth but was unable to smother her gasp. "Dom," she cried out, her eyes watery. "You didn't do that for me, did you? I loved you as you were." She paused to smile. "I also love you as you are. I guess I just love you."

"I would have done it for you, but no. I asked the OC to heal me because I no longer need to carry guilt. You made me see I never did, but I'm a slow learner."

On the return home, Dom saw OneWorld with two eyes again. The view was almost blinding, despite cloudy skies.

When he and Maddy landed, Freki raced up the steps and into the salon, crashing into his mate. Laughing, she ruffled his fur. With what passed for a wolver's smile, he jumped and twisted, tail wagging, happy to see them.

Scratch that. Freki was happy to see Madeline. He greeted Dom with a bounce of his snout and a "Hey."

After Madeline fed the wolver and whispered in his ear, she disappeared into the bedroom. Freki stilled for a moment, his eyes moist, before he returned to chowing down.

Dom said, "After you eat, get lost."

He paused. "Why?"

"We'll be celebrating our release."

"I don't need the deets. Got a gal wolver waiting for me to play hide the hot dog with her. Didn't plan to stick around and watch you fumble your dick with Madeline."

Dom snarled. "Just be sure to get lost."

"Don't you want to know about my love life?"

"No."

"Sad. You could use a few pointers."

Dom shook his head but paused in the doorway, staring over his shoulder. "I'm sorry about your mate, Freki."

The wolver stopped eating, his eyes tearing up again. "Time does not heal all wounds—but they scab over." He bounced his nose and returned to his task as if his stomach were as empty as his heart.

T.M. SMITH

Chapter Thirty-Six

Dom woke from a deep sleep the next morning, the world a little brighter. Maddy was curled up, ass to his groin. But instead of getting time to continue the celebration of their release from custody or getting that vacay as promised, the OC interrupted with a path. So much for Maddy-and-Dom time.

He had nearly slipped out of bed undetected when she said, "What's up?"

"The OC has ordered me to bring Lucian in for a chat."

She rubbed a hand across her eyes and stretched. "I'm going with." She swung her legs over the side of bed.

"No. You're not."

Standing naked, which was unfair in any argument, Maddy crossed her arms under her breasts. "I am. I want to meet this Luce guy. I've heard so much about him. It's like he's a celeb in OneWorld." She grinned. "I might even get his autograph."

"No."

"Rethink that." She stormed toward her closet, her shapely ass swaying.

Stubborn female. Stomping off to his side of the closet, Dom shoved his legs into black cargoes and tugged an equally grim t-shirt over his head.

On a sudden impulse and needing a way to deal with his frustration, Dom pathed Ohngel, *I've got a question.*

Yeah?

How do you control Indigo?

Ohngel laughed. After a pause, he said, *Oh.*

You're serious?

Yes.

You've seen us together. Do you really think I control Indy? Do you think anyone does?

Dom supposed not. *But how do you keep her safe?*

I'll deny I said this, but if Indy's life were in danger, fuck what she wants. I'd overpower her, kicking, screaming, and swearing never to talk to me again. But only then. Otherwise, I kinda like her the way she is.

Having a stubborn mate's hard, said Dom.

Not so much. Listen to what she says. More importantly, learn when to laugh and when to shut your mouth. Of course, there's that nastiest of words— compromise. Learn how to do it.

I don't know, Ohngel.

Exactly. You don't know. I don't know. And who the fuck cares. Just enjoy the ride. They're worth it.

I'm going after Lucian and his merry band of Scourges. Maddy insists on going along.

Luce won't hurt a female. Ohngel chuckled. *Besides, he's probably partying with other Scourges in some valley, throwing back a few drinks, hitting on celebs in Angor, and getting jiggy with the latest pop hits?*

I'm impressed with the jingo, Ohngel. You're starting to sound like Remi.

Yeah. Been watching too much TV with him. Good luck. I'm helping Ely hunt for Malacour. The bastard's proving elusive.

Dressed, Dom found Maddy waiting in the salon. He decided this was one of those compromise moments. *Wow!* He was turning into a great mate.

"Come on if you're coming." He soared into the sky, beckoning her to follow. He angled his wings to veer left, glancing over his shoulder at Maddy.

She mirrored his moves, smoother, stronger than ever. She might even be able to beat him in a head-up race. He wasn't jealous. *Hell no.* He was happy since speed was her friend. It could get her out of a tough situation.

Madeline caught up, a satisfied smirk on her lips, probably because she'd won the argument. Might have been their first real disagreement. *Yeah.* And he'd lost the tiff. It didn't set a good tone for the future, but it had allowed him to compromise.

Dom issued Maddy another order. Not that she'd obey it. "We're heading over Harpy Plains. Keep an eye out. The hags attack from the air, but they keep to lower altitudes, flying in squadrons. If you spot them, call out. I'll handle it. Stay on this course while I drop down to search for Lucian."

Below, he saw no signs of Luce's encampment. Intel said the guy had relocated his camp to this general area. When he rejoined Maddy, he angled toward the east. She kept pace.

Dom said, "We'll cross the Rushing River of Blood in a moment. Again, stay up here while I check out the banks." Following the river to the lake, he spotted a camouflaged camp, a cluster of huts with netting thrown over them.

Ballsy. Since it was near Outcast Tower, the seat of Angor's government.

Lacking gonads, though, had never been Lucian's problem. The dust-up with the OneCreator had not been the guy's only transgression. *No.* A few centuries after he had recovered from his beheading, he gathered some of the evilest sonsabitching Scourges he could find. Armed, they cut a bloody swath through Angor before Dom and Remi had caught up with them in Loneliness Desert.

On that day, Lucian and his followers took a stand

where the desert met Mortus Peak in the Razor Mountains. Though Dom and Remi had called in the rest of the Feard as back-up, the battle raged for days, maybe a week. He had to hand it to Luce. The male was an asshole, but he was a great soldier and dedicated to causing havoc.

After that rebellion, the OneCreator had again not issued an extinction order. Lucian and his followers had been chained, staked, and left to shrivel in the sun. But once the rebel lost fifty percent of his body mass, he slipped his chains and hid out somewhere to recover.

Ascending, Dom rejoined Maddy above the encampment. "They're in the valley where the lake feeds the river. You stay…"

Before he could finish, she interrupted. "I'm coming along. I thought we settled this."

"You settled it. I'm iffy. Lucian is dangerous, and the village is filled with Scourges. We don't know yet if your body has settled into Immortality or if you can use your gifts at will."

"All I hear is blah, blah, blah." She laughed, arched her wings, and bulleted toward the encampment.

He had no choice but to catch up, and she was damn fast. After a soft landing, Dom glared at Madeline, certain he'd get gray hair unlike any other Immortal. Then he took a quick look-around. Nobody was storming toward him.

He shoved his mate behind him, swooping out his wings as a shield, unsheathing his razored onyx-bladed feathers as a just-in-case. A crowd gathered slowly, likely most of them recognizing him.

When the mob parted, Lucian strode through a pathway, a confident swagger, his golden hair glinting in the rare sunshine and whipping around his face in the wind. He stopped directly in front of Dom. Catching a glimpse of Madeline, he asked, "Who's your new partner?"

"None of your business."

"Anybody in my encampment is my biz."

Dom rested a palm on the blade holstered at his hip. He'd laugh at Luce's hubris if the guy weren't such an asshole. "You are not a warlord in Angor. You're under the OC's rule as is every Scourge. Disobey and face punishment."

"Uh-huh. I'm shaking in my shitkickers."

"Are you looking for trouble, Luce?"

"Never. Especially not with such a pretty female here." As Madeline slipped around Dom, Lucian stretched out his arm and offered her a hand.

When she put her palm into it, the ballsy rebel kissed the back of her fingers. A grin crawled across his face. He said, "I am fascinated."

"Oh," she said, flipping her gaze to Dom and shrugging.

What? he asked his mate.

I think Lucian's in my head and knows my gifts.

Impossible.

Just a feeling that's snaking through me while he holds my hand, pathed Madeline.

Dom snatched Maddy from Luce's grip. "She's my mate, asshole." He gave no warning before he drew back a fist and knocked Luce on his ass. "Stay out of her head."

Lucian rose, dusting off his pants, a slight grin curling his lips. "Got me. But I won't fall for that a second time." He wiggled his jaw between his thumb and fingers.

The rebel's eyes ping-ponged from Maddy and back to him. "I heard a rumor that you mated an unusual Scourge but didn't believe it. You know how the malady-stricken like to gossip. Anyway, why are you here?"

"Crazy shit's going on in OneWorld. The OC's worried about you."

"You mean the earthquakes and the volcanic disturbance?"

"Volcanic?"

"Yep. South of Necrosis Valley. At this moment a mountain is burping smoke, but who knows what the future holds."

Dom combed worried fingers through his hair.

More shit.

Luce studied Madeline. "So you were human."

Maddy smiled, her tiny fangs peeking from her lips. "Yep. I was human. Then I wasn't."

"You already know her story. What about the riots?" asked Dom.

"What about them?"

"Your doing, Lucian?"

"Nope. I'm more interested in your mate."

"Don't be," snapped Dom.

Luce asked Madeline, "You escaped Praevus?"

"It was more like he let me go after he made me a Syc. I was cured. But then... Bingo, I was kinda a Scourge."

Luce fixed on Dom's two eyes and grinned. "No patch. Hmm. I won't ask how that happened. What are you thinking, assassin? I flew out of Angor, went to Earth, kidnapped your future mate, and dropped her off with a Mind Rat..."

"With Malacour."

"The trustee and ex-wing commander?"

"The same."

Luce paused, rubbing a fist across his jaw. "Interesting. So you're thinking I dropped this lovely human off with Malacour? After that sleight-of-hand, I made her a Scourge, or hybrid-Scourge, for shits and giggles? Then, as if I weren't busy with all that showmanship, I returned to lead a rebellion…"

"Malacour is the leader," interrupted Dom.

Lucian laughed. "And I follow that asshole? Okay. That's a good one. But let's go with your story. After all that I created geological disruptions in OneWorld and made her whatever she is now? No offense, Madeline. I think you're lovely. In fact, if you want to desert this asshole… Anyway, why would I do that? How would I do that?"

"Don't know."

"What if I told you I'm not guilty? In fact, other than the OC, I don't know who could do all that."

"He says he didn't bring this on."

"That's what he said, huh? He's been known to dodge the truth."

"The OC wants a chat with you, Luce."

"Fuck the OC," he said, his stance widening, as he prepared for a fight.

Dom shoved Madeline behind him with a warning to stay there. "You can go along or you can be dragged along."

"You against me and all my happy followers?"

"You want a war? I can have the Feard teleport here in an instant."

The crowd of Scourges went crazy, shouting, jumping up and down, jamming their fists into the air.

"They'll be extincted, Lucian. The same fate may await you." Dom drew his sword but kept it at his side.

The rebel glanced over his shoulder at his followers. "I don't want them hurt because of me. They sought shelter here, and I gave it. Besides, I know what the big guy wants. Lead on, brave Dominion."

Lucian swooped out his wings, grinning. They

were not leathery like a Scourge's. By way of explanation when they stared, he said, "I glamoured them. You see what I want you to see."

Can he glamour his wings? pathed Madeline.

Obviously.

And so they flew to Outcast Tower, where the OneCreator waited outside the entrance.

The OC momentarily fixed on Madeline, probably wondering why she was on a fly-along. Then the ruler of OneWorld turned a menacing glare on Luce. He powered toward him, moving so fast that his loose golden hair streamed behind him. He curled his palms around Lucian's neck, the biceps in his arms bulging. Dom had felt the OC's hands on him. It was something to take seriously. He lifted the Scourge off the ground, Luce's boots dangling in the air. "What have you done, asshole?"

Lucian struggled in his grasp, his voice a strangled gurgle. Eventually, the OC released the rebel who, staggering, rubbed his throat. "I've done a lot, I'm sure. But what in particular?"

"The geological disasters. The riots in Angor. The whole shitstorm surrounding this human. Malacour."

"I wish I could take the credit for all of it, but I can't."

Lightning crackled around the OC. He snapped out his wings. At first, they were a brilliant white. In a second, they morphed to black, touched with specks of gold, blending into the oncoming darkness like a starry night. Overhead, deafening thunder rumbled.

Lucian, in response, slicked out his wings. His golden wings.

They each stood, legs wide, awaiting a fight. Luce blinked first. He shushed his wings to his back, where they disappeared.

The OC settled down. With a deep breath, he waved away the lightning and thunder while he folded in his once-again-brilliant white wings. "You remain irreverent, Lucian. Such will not fare well for you." His hands flew to his temples, and he howled in pain as the ground beneath their feet began to roll.

Dom grabbed Maddy's arm to steady her.

Adopting a wide-legged stance for balance, Luce tapped his head. He glanced at Dom. "Is this what you meant?"

"Yep. Most often the OC's pain comes and goes with some geological shit."

"Okay. So I had contact with Malacour. He stopped by and met with a couple of my Scourges."

The "my Scourges" got a raised brow from the OC. Since he'd created Immortals, he probably figured Luce couldn't claim any ownership, even of those infected with the malady.

Lucian continued, "He told his contacts he was off to check out the gateway. Personally, I hope he tries to get through and fries his ass. Never liked the guy."

Stiffening his spine, the OneCreator breathed deep, wiping the grimace from his face. Swaying, he waved the three visitors off. As they prepared to leave, he shouted, "If I discover you are at the center of or even on the periphery of this situation, Lucian, your punishment will be extraordinarily painful and long. I suggest you have a chat with *your* Scourges. Be fucking gone now."

Before Dom took to the air, he asked Luce, "Is there any truth in your words?"

The rebel laughed. "I am telling the truth. Of course, if I'm a liar by nature, my statement may be false."

"That makes no sense."

"Neither does OneWorld right now." Luce

ascended in a blaze of golden feathers, lighting up the sky, his speed faster than Dom could track.

"I don't trust him," Madeline said as he disappeared. "What will you do now?"

"Path the Feard about what happened and watch him."

Dom closed his eyes, sharing intel with his brothers-in-arms.

Fucker, said Ely.

Ohngel pathed, *They both play games.*

Remi said, *Keep your friends close, but your enemies closer.*

When nobody responded, the movie-watching assassin added, *It's from* The Godfather, Part II.

Snapping out his wings, Dom signaled toward the sky. Madeline took flight alongside him, the tips of their feathers almost touching. It was a closeness Dom had not known he'd desired. Now that he had his mate, he could not imagine eternity without her. Even if she was stubborn and threw herself into dangerous situations.

Damn. He was one lucky assassin.

Chapter Thirty-Seven

Malacour flew fast, his wings struggling in a strong headwind.

He'd finally received a call from the male he trusted most in all of OneWorld. No packed bags. No tearful goodbyes. He left after they had talked, only stopping off at Lucian's encampment to leave a few instructions for two Scourge followers.

Praevus, who had stirred up all this shit, had been a minor and accidental character in the game. He'd been nothing more than a gofer for Serita, an honored member of the rebellion. Malacour was fortunate the Rat's screw-up hadn't messed with his chance to advance in the cause, but his trusted ally who was high in the ranks still had faith in him.

He cast a worried glance over his shoulder. No one was following.

When he'd seen the ice-winged assassin in his bar, he thought for sure he'd get nabbed. But no, he'd dodged the Feard by hiding out at a different place each night.

Then the trusted caller told Malacour it was time to disappear, to take up a new job. An exciting one, he'd said. Malacour was ready for his reward. The caller had instructed him to escape from Angor through the passageway. All was set up for his safe exit.

Though Malacour was a trustee nearing the time of his release, he had taken risks out of duty to the Immortal he respected, the one to whom he would always pledge his allegiance. Besides, he suspected he'd never fit in back in Vast. He liked this life. Cutting corners. Being his own boss. *Yeah.* Can you say recidivism? He'd never make it in the dimension of flowers and blue skies.

Rebellion was a better fit.

Not having traveled far for some time, Malacour's wings were weak. He threw them into overdrive, though, determined to escape. He could collapse later.

He flew above the Rushing River of Blood, Harpy Plains, and Hallucination Woods. He climbed the high Razor Mountains. Beyond them was the ocean and the exit from Angor.

The gateway shimmered in front of him. Drawing a deep breath, Malacour treaded air. He'd either get out of this dimension or fry. Time to see how much power his trusted ally had.

He soared into the flickering current of wind. With ease, he flew through the passage. He was free. On the other side, he punched a fist high, humming with the confidence that his deeds would be justly rewarded.

"Null, here I come," Malacour shouted into space. "It is time for new leadership. The OC has had his turn."

Before he could celebrate, a blinding spark shot toward him. As it coalesced into a shape, Malacour beat his wings hard, zipping across the sky away from the light. But the Immortal blocked his path. "Michael."

"Malacour."

Unable to escape the Bearer of Death, he confronted him. Malacour faced Michael like the warrior he was. With honor and pride.

"A few questions," said Michael.

"Some I may answer. Some I may not." He wondered if his escape from Angor had been a ruse. Was the Bearer of Death part of the rebellion sent here to extinct Malacour because he had allowed Praevus to fuck up?

No.

The male to whom Malacour owed allegiance

would not do that. Would he?

Michael's questions were simple. "What is your role in the rebellion?"

Was this a loyalty test?

If so, Malacour failed. Light shining from Michael ate through his flesh, the pain unbearable. "I coordinated rebel activities in Angor as instructed."

"How did you get Madeline?"

He screamed. The pain was searing. "I received her from an Immortal inside the gateway and gave her to Serita to care for through the transition."

"What transition?"

"To hybrid-Scourge."

"So, it was known from the beginning that the human would change?"

"I suppose."

"The name of the Immortal who gave her to you."

Malacour steered the conversation away from the name. "I arranged for Remi's attack above the Razor Mountains to divert him from Serita's cabin where Praevus was hiding. I sent Scourges to recapture the human from Dom. That didn't work out. Of course, I didn't extinct Ike or Praevus."

"Who is the Immortal who gave you Madeline?"

"Followers are awakening. I know names." He rattled them off but still held back the name of the male he felt honor-bound to protect. He owed him. Pain loosened his lips but didn't destroy all of his pride.

Michael was dogged, though. "The Immortal?"

When the Bearer of Death pointed the tip of his sword toward Malacour, his flesh burned until he could no longer bear the torture.

Malacour revealed the name of the one male in all of OneWorld who meant something to him. But he withheld a secret. At the gateway, he'd been given not only Madeline but another human as well.

Michael let loose his sword and, with one blow, sliced off his head. The last words Malacour heard were, "May my blade bring you peace."

The sensation was odd. He felt the cold steel of the Bearer of Death's sword slide into his neck. He even felt part of his body crumble to ash.

His final thought was "Have I failed the loyalty test? Hence, extinction?"

Then nothing.

****

When Dom strode into the bedroom, Maddy was showered and shiny. Not bothering with a nightie, she'd eased herself against the headboard, her breasts perky and one leg cocked up, giving him a great view.

"Fuck," said Dom, hopping on one foot to remove a boot. Then the other. He stripped off his pants and ripped his tee over his head. Naked and horny, his cock saluting his mate, he prowled toward her. "What do you want, mate?"

"I want joy, an orderly life, and sun on my face." She reached toward him. "Mostly, I want you."

Dom had his own plans. He grabbed onto her bent knee and made room for himself between her thighs. He glanced up at her and grinned. "I can give you me."

"What are you waiting for then?"

He groaned, lowered his head, and flicked out his tongue. When he licked between her folds, with lazy, slow strokes, she squirmed. He pressed a hand on her stomach to hold her still.

Maddy's fingers tangled in his hair as she guided him where she wanted.

He sucked and nipped on her clit. Flipping his gaze to Maddy's lust-soaked eyes, he licked faster. When he moved his hand off her stomach, she jacked her hips off the bed, screaming out his name.

But he continued to torture her until her fingers unwove from his hair and her arms fell lifeless to the side.

Dom backed off, asking, "Good?"

She opened one lid. "Incredible."

He prowled up her body to seize her mouth in a rough, claiming kiss.

Maddy's tongue slid inside to brush against his as her hands caressed his back, her palms soft and warm against his skin.

Having other plans, he released her lips. Dom raised onto flexed arms so she could see his cock. "Go on. Put me where you want."

Madeline reached between them and grasped onto him. She moaned, nudging her entrance with his shaft.

Dom rocked forward, inching into her wet warmth. "You're mine."

She latched onto his hips, driving him deeper. "And you're mine."

Being in the mood for slow and torturous, Dom resisted her urging.

"Please," Maddy begged. So sweetly. So urgently.

"Please what?"

"I want all of you, Dom."

He jammed his hips forward burying himself deep, his flesh throbbing inside Madeline. He pulled out to the tip of his cock and hammered back in, lost in the feel of his mate. He withdrew. Pushed in. Out. In. Faster. Harder.

Dom's rhythm was steady but rough. No more slow and gentle. "Bite me," he ordered.

When she paused as if uncertain, he raised his voice. "Do it."

Maddy's tiny fangs sank into Dom's neck. He

jerked from the pleasure as she fed on him. About to lose it, he whispered, "You better come now, mate."

She did, releasing his neck, locking her feet around his thighs, and digging clawed fingers into his muscled shoulders. "Yes. Yes."

That was all Dom needed. He hammered his hips. Up. Down. Faster. He threw back his head, his balls tightened, and he spilled into Madeline, roaring his release. His stygian wings swooped out uncontrollably, curtaining them in shadows, protecting their bodies and hearts, shielding the bond that united them.

****

Madeline loved lying in bed with Dom after sex, her cheek to his chest, his heart a steady beat, and his wings sheltering her. But her thoughts were weighty. "Dom, I'm afraid."

"Of what, Maddy." His voice was still raspy-raw from sex.

"Of what I'm becoming."

He stroked her hair. "You're becoming you."

She rolled to the side, propping her head in a palm, her elbow bent. "Me on steroids, maybe. Life and death are heavy for a mere librarian."

He grinned. "You were never a mere anything. I'm sure of that."

"Thanks. My ego appreciates the boost, but you know what I mean. What if I accidentally kill someone? How do you deal with all your powers? How do you keep from slipping?"

"You're most concerned about the ability to extinct others?"

"Of course. Healing is cool, but the flip side is evil. I'm like a black mamba or a poisonous scorpion."

"Maddy, you've always had the ability to kill others. Guns. Swords. Hammers. You didn't then, and you won't now."

"But it's easier now. I need some Immortal wisdom."

Dom curled an arm under his head. "Hmm. Never thought much about it before. Our gifts are like muscles, I guess. We flex them. Extend them. Retract them. Doing anything out of the ordinary, though, requires a conscious command. You don't accidentally slap someone, do you?"

"No."

"The same with your powers. They don't jump out of you willy-nilly and do whatever. If you want to perfect them, train, but you won't kill someone unintentionally, Maddy."

"I don't want to kill anyone at all."

"That's good because you won't be joining the assassins."

"Fine by me. The OC promised me a job in Angor's library. I intend to make sure he follows through." She rested her cheek on Dom's chest again.

After they lay silent for many moments, she said, "I need to contact my sisters. They must be worried." It was time to reach out to Fia and Darya, though she was still unsure what to tell them.

"Ohngel has a lot of dealings on Earth. I'll see if he knows an easy way." He closed his lids to contact Indigo's fire-winged mate.

When he opened his two shocking green eyes, he lifted an index finger. "Just a minute. Wait here." He climbed out of bed to drag on his pants before heading toward the salon.

She heard voices. Dom returned with something in his fist. A cell phone. "Ohngel says this will do the trick."

"It's an iPhone. Does he have some kind of a deal

with Apple? Like a cell tower in Vast and Angor?"

Shucking off his pants, Dom slipped into bed, leaning his back against the headboard. "He keeps up on Earth shit. Has friends there."

"What about you?"

"Not so much. I watch some Earth TV. Not since you arrived and not as much as Remi. He's obsessed with television and the movies. Quotes shit all the time."

"You have a television? Where is it?"

"Wherever I want it to be." He snapped his fingers, and a widescreen television appeared on the bedroom wall. It was tuned to a cooking show.

"Hmm. I wonder how … never mind. It's magical or technical. In either case, I don't want the particulars." She palmed the phone. "Should I punch in their usual area code? Is there an international number?"

"I don't know what the fuck you're talking about. Try."

"Simmer down. We can't all use telepathy." Maddy scooted upright in bed.

"Don't see why not. And you're stalling."

"True. I didn't ask about phoning them before because I wasn't convinced I'd live. It was better to let them believe I'd disappeared. Cruel but kind. Now, I'm not sure what to tell them."

"The truth."

She snorted. "Ha. They'll think I'm crazy."

Maddy punched in the country code and number for Darya. She smiled at Dom when the phone rang, but she listened to a message that said the mailbox was full. "Strange. Never happened before. She's not deleting her voicemails."

Dom's lips curved into a smirk. "Still not sure what you're talking about."

Entering Fia's digits, Maddy waited. "Now I am

concerned. Both boxes are full? Something's wrong. Maybe they're looking for me. They must be worried sick. I have to reach them. Can we go to Earth?"

Dom angled his head toward her. "Not a good idea yet. Fangs. Wings. Blood urges."

"Yeah. I need to be sure I have control. How about Indigo or Ohngel?"

"Worth a try."

Dom went still.

When he relaxed, Maddy asked, "Well?"

"I told Ohngel you couldn't reach your sisters. Something about their voicemail being full and them not answering their phones. He told me he had the entire U.S. Army at his disposal and would get back to me."

T.M. SMITH

Chapter Thirty-Eight

Remi was quelling riots in Angor while Dom took time off from the job.

The bronze-winged assassin hovered above a bunch of Soul Suckers, escapees from the Slough of Despair. He herded them together. "What the fuck's wrong with you? You're adding to your sentence with this shit."

"We heard voices," said the spokesfemale, a typical Sucker with puckered lips. Her long dark hair was tangled as if she'd been pulling on it. Obviously, the Ordeal had done a number on her. "We started running."

"Whadda ya mean? Voices?"

"The Slough makes us sad. We wanna pound our chests, cry, and tear out our eyes. Kill ourselves if we could. But a voice called out, ordering us to run."

"Do you still hear it?"

She shook her head.

"I don't know anything about a voice. So beat feet back to the Ordeal before I extinct a few of you as an example of stupid."

She turned toward the Slough, eyeing it warily. When she took one step and then another, the others followed.

Remi soared into the sky again after monitoring their retreating backs. He dropped low beneath storm clouds to search for the next crazy rioting Scourges.

When he skimmed above Fear Mines, hundreds of Mind Rats rushed from the entrance, holding their heads and bellowing. They stampeded toward Loneliness Desert.

Here I go.

Remi began roundup maneuvers again. He circled the Scourges, driving them into a group. Eventually, they came to a halt, their hands falling to their sides, their caterwauling fading to moans and, finally, to silence.

Descending to the ground, his boots kicking up dust, Remi shouted, "What the fuck are you up to? Where ya going?"

"The screams," said one. Another shook his head. "No. It was loud, screeching music." "Both of you are wrong. The OC yelled for me to run." A fourth said, "Drums pounded in my head. They were so amped up my brains rattled. I took off to escape the noise."

"What do you hear now?" asked Remi.

They all shook their heads. "Nothing," mumbled a couple.

Remi blew out an exasperated breath. He'd faced down rioting Scourges before, but their reasons had never been so bat-shit crazy.

"Then get your asses back to the mines. You're wasting my time."

Flying above the Valley of Doom, Remi spied a large gathering armed with knives, axes, and clubs.

He adjusted the long sword sheathed at his spine and tapped the hilts of the two blades jammed into his hip holsters. Strafing the ground, he shot bronze-daggered feathers from his wings, dropping a few Scourges but not extincting them.

In a voice that shook the land, Remi shouted, "Throw down your weapons and sit on your asses. If you don't, the next shots will result in extinctions. Decide now."

Lacking any leadership, the Scourges complied, looking as puzzled as Remi felt. Who'd gathered them? Who'd armed them?

What the fuck?

He floated to the valley floor, his sword drawn, his wings ready to release razor-edged feathers. But he got no lip and no resistance. The Scourges sat on their sixes, their weapons in a pile.

As he strode among them, he shouted, "War is Hell."

When they stared at him, their eyes empty, he said, "Don't you watch the movies? It's a line from *Full Metal Jacket*. Gotta see it. One of the best action flicks ever."

A Scourge raised his hand.

"Yeah?"

"I seen it."

"Good for you. Now, let me guess, guys and gals, something in your head made you do this, but how'd you get the weapons?"

The film buff said, "They were in a pile over there." He pointed toward a tall shrub.

With no answers from the other Scourges, who seemed content to sit on their asses as ordered, Remi called for Angor's henchmen to clean up the mess.

Tasks complete, he kicked into high gear, angling his wings to take him to the big city where he hooked up in a BDSM room with a lovely Scourge who enjoyed asphyxiation play.

She loosened up the kinks in his shoulders and elsewhere, but the relief didn't last long. On his flight home, three of the OneCreator's Immortal winged squadrons sped from behind dark clouds to surround him. Remi studied their faces. He recognized a few of the males. Their pose was aggressive. Odd since they were all on the same side.

Hovering, Remi touched the hilt of his sword. Better cautious than not. "Hi, fellas. Perfect timing. The Feard already settled shit."

The biggest male spoke up, an insignia on his arm indicating he was a wing commander. "We're not here for clean-up duty, assassin."

"Yeah? What are you here for then? My boots are dirty. They could still handle a good spit polish."

The big guy bristled, his feathers ruffling. "Wrong."

The three squadrons of Immortals tightened the circle around him.

Remi drew his blade, yelling, "Well, gentlemen, when the shit hits the fan, some guys run, and some guys stay."

Their eyes blanked.

"Doesn't anybody watch movies? *The Scent of a Woman*? Al Pacino. I'm surrounded by cretins." He curled his fingers, waving them. "Come get me if you can."

Remi couldn't figure out why the good guys from the OC's elite winged squadrons would be after him, but their body language spoke for them.

It wasn't a fair fight. Something stung his arm. His wings collapsed, and he plummeted, the wind of his fall thundering in his ears.

Then, lights out.

****

That night at home, Dom leaned against a pillar at the edge of the salon, gazing down on the shoals and the sea beyond. He and Maddy had made love, eaten a late dinner, and talked about her future in OneWorld.

Now, they stared at the beautiful view. Then she gasped. "Dom. Look."

She pointed south toward a mountain. It had blown its top. A volcanic eruption.

He looped his arm around her waist.

They watched fire and ash spew from the peak.

Rivulets of red lava creeped down the mountainside, heading for the valleys.

Madeline sprinted to the side of the house overlooking the expansive lawn. "Where's Freki?"

"Hunkering down if he knows what's good for him."

When a cloud of thick ash spread outward, encroaching on their home, Dom waved his hand through the air to drop shields around their place. The sky grew dark, a twisting, impenetrable black haze.

Dom approached the protective barrier, inhaled, and released his breath. The toxic volcanic gases and debris moved on. "That was fun," he said. "Don't go out without me, Maddy. Things are getting…"

"Wack?"

"Sure. That works."

"Check in on our friends," she said.

"Our friends?" asked Dom, a pleased grin curving his lips.

Maddy gave him a hesitant nod. "Yes. They're my friends, too." She raised her arms and laced her fingers around Dom's neck. "This is my home. This is my life. I have friends, and I have you."

Dom pathed the Feard.

After verifying that he and Indy were safe, Ohngel added, *No sign of your mate's sisters. And the army's pretty thorough. But they'll keep an eye out for them.*

Damn. She's not gonna be happy about that.

When Ely reported in, Dom said, "Everybody's fine except I haven't reached Remiel. And bad news. Ohngel's Earth contacts haven't found your sisters."

"But they'll keep trying?"

"Yes."

She leaned her cheek on his chest. *I love you,*

Dom.

I'm sorry your life has turned upside down, but I'm not sorry I found you.

She tilted her head to stare into his green eyes. *If everything I've gone through was necessary to bring me to you, I'm good with it.*

He kissed Maddy's choppy blonde hair. *Perhaps happiness comes with a cost.*

You sound like a philosopher.

Fuck. Don't tell the Feard. They already think I'm getting soft. Best not to overload them.

Do you think life will settle down with Malacour dead?

Doubtful. He can't be the big rebellion leader.

She sighed. *I'm gonna use my mouth to talk now. My brain's tired.*

"I'm in favor of you using your mouth whenever the mood strikes," he said to Madeline, drawing her into his arms and folding his wings around her gorgeous body.

****

Vast, OneWorld

The OneCreator shared the evidence from Dom and Madeline's trial with Harmony, who had been busy keeping the explosive lid on Angor's boiling pot.

"Interesting," she said, flicking an errant strand of honeyed blonde hair over her shoulder.

"You have a way with understatement, my dear." The OneCreator coughed into his hand, the fit so bad he ceased talking.

"You like her."

Harmony and the OneCreator were so in tune that he didn't need to ask who "her" was. "Like the witch Indigo, I see something special in Madeline."

"And her gifts?"

"We have talked. I lectured her on using her power ethically. She listened. She is a good being."

"Did you see her coming?"

He leaned into the overstuffed chair in his office to stare at Harmony. She was old. Older than Michael and Lucian. A contemporary of Kalia. She knew all the dirty secrets and kept them to herself. She had flirted with being a Scourge and won, but the memory of her cruelty had stayed with her. He'd appointed her to manage Angor in his absence because she had insisted on doing more time there. Guilt.

But she was his only confidant now.

He had no Siblings. He had no one to remember who he was at the beginning. And without anyone to remember who he was, rather than what he had become, he was slipping. He was losing touch with a profound part of himself. It was only his steel will that held him together. His will and his love for the Immortals who depended on him.

Harmony crossed her legs, lovely beneath a short skirt. He admired them, his gaze sweeping from her feet to her thighs, the ardor they'd once briefly shared flickering inside him. Now, they were simply close friends.

She said, "No answer may be an answer. On another note, Ely asked me if Lucian attended Ordeals. He asked what malady the rebel suffered."

"What did you say?"

"I said my list was corrupted. Happened during the whole Madeline-Serita-Praevus-Malacour thing. I was working on reconstructing the files. I'd get back to him."

"Good save." The OC hacked into his palm, another bout of coughing overcoming him. He rubbed his aching chest.

Harmony waited for the paroxysm to stop. "Sadly,

you are no closer to knowing how Scourges come to be than you ever were."

"The root cause is beyond my vision. Of course, I can create Immortals with Scourge-like characteristics, similar to Madeline and without deadly urges."

"But you have never done so?"

"Never." He relaxed into his chair, crossing an ankle over a knee. "Perhaps I should have extincted Kalia's livebornes once we learned the mother was an abomination, the first Scourge."

"They were not Scourges. And there is no sign either has turned."

Clearing his throat, he said, "New mated pairs and offspring. Right under my nose. I never sensed the births even though they occurred in Vast. And, other than Ohngel and Indigo, I had no knowledge of other recent mates. I have readjusted my awareness and intend to be more cognizant of my Immortals' comings and goings."

"You had good reason to discourage mating and livebornes. You not only feared those with the malady in their DNA could have Scourges as offspring, but you feared overpopulation."

"Yes. And if the trend becomes popular, we will outgrow the space which is OneWorld."

"Create another dimension."

"I shall have to." He stroked his chin with a thumb and forefinger. "Let's put aside the problem of Scourges, mates, and progeny for the moment. What else do we have?"

"A tsunami slammed into the west coast of Angor. Violence Village took the worst hit. Repairs are moving more slowly than I'd like. We could use your help." She studied him as if he might be too weak.

"I think I can get it up to repair the village," he snapped. After a slight wave of his hand, he said, "Done."

"Simmer down. I didn't mean to question your masculinity. We still have the same line-up of suspects. The Feard, Beatrix, and Yosef. Michael and Lucian. And, of course, me."

Harmony? A suspect? No.

Ignoring her name on the list, he said, "Beatrix has made her anger known for millennia. She was my sister Melodia's frequent lover and has not forgiven me for my Sibling's departure from OneWorld. The love-besotted female never realized she was just one of many. And Yosef is a sneak. He plasters on a smile in my presence, but beneath it is seething hatred for me since his adored Prima left."

"Why do you keep him on?"

The OC worked around holes in his memory, the tangle of events. A few more had to uncoil before he could reply.

"He is an able supreme commander of my winged squadrons. But it is irrelevant. Neither Beatrix nor Yosef is powerful enough to cause these problems."

"Unless new skills have spontaneously generated."

"Without my knowledge?" *Click.* A memory untangled. Possible?

"Yes. You missed knowing about The Retreat. What else?" Harmony arched her brows.

He shrugged and explored other suspects. "For centuries Dominion was angry about Gareth, but he is not a male to seek revenge. Elysium worries me, but he is only a danger to himself. Eternity weighs heavy on his shoulders. He is too mired in his own problems to do this. My sister Lumia mentored and trained Remiel." He paused, grinning. "For a time, they were lovers. Of course, she drew paramours to her like Vast sunflies to ambrosia. Then she rejected Remi for Cael, whom my bronze-winged assassin had to extinct later when he turned Scourge. But Remi never seemed to blame me for the troubles. Ohngel could be pissed because I put him in stasis. I doubt it. And none of my winged assassins can make a Scourge."

"Unless new skills have spontaneously generated."

"Is that going to be your answer to everything?"

"It's a good one."

"That leaves Michael and Lucian. And to borrow your explanation, Harmony, I ask whether they have developed gifts of which I am unaware?"

"To hide such strength takes willpower, planning, and malice."

The OneCreator lobbed a leg over the arm of his chair, his most comfortable position for thinking. "Lucian has rebelled before."

"Such is his nature, but beware the monster who hides behind an innocent, shining mask. The perpetrator could be Michael. He was hasty to extinct Malacour without getting answers from the Scourge. Perhaps he had good reason."

The OC nodded. Was he forgetting something important? Michael. A memory twisted as he explored a path. He could not retrieve it.

Harmony shrugged, recrossing her shapely legs. "How did Malacour get through the gateway out of Angor unharmed? He should have fried. Another mystery. If only Michael hadn't acted in haste." Harmony tossed out a surprise question unrelated to the conversation. "Do you miss them?"

Again the OneCreator understood who she meant. He combed fingers through his golden hair, giving himself time to consider. "I do. Terribly. They are always in my thoughts. I miss Prima's exuberant dances. I miss

Melodia's voice. I miss Lumia's wit. I miss my brother Chaos, his grim but sage wisdom. His sly humor. They were my rocks. They were the only beings like me. When Kalia and Chaos were no more, my sisters provided solace." He leaned forward, his elbows on his knees. "I am bone tired, Harmony, as if an infection runs through me."

"Though you cannot be ill, you somehow are."

"Indeed. Back to our list. No one on it can create a Scourge or a hybrid Scourge like Madeline."

"Unless their powers have exploded spontaneously. And you refuse to consider me. I'm insulted. I should be on your list. Michael, Lucian, and the Feard are the most powerful Immortals in OneWorld. And I am nearly their match. In these many millennia, I have grown." Harmony's voice rose to punctuate his omission of her name.

"Have you gained gifts of which I am unaware?"

She tapped her chest. "Sometimes, I feel a strange vibration here, as if I am growing. As of now, nothing else."

"Life is a gift, Harmony, whether it comes at my hand or from the love of two beings. Growth is part of that gift. You are not who you were eons ago. Neither am I. Joy has exited our lives, and sometimes has entered. Change is to be expected, to be treasured."

"Not when it's bad. You need to get into our minds. Read our thoughts."

He shook his head. "What if I don't like what I find there? I could not bear betrayal from some of my beloved Immortals, your betrayal. I missed my friend and confidant when you were a Scourge those many centuries. The days were dreary. The nights long. I have lost a brother and three sisters, but still I treasure the Immortals I fashioned. And you, among all, are loved."

He patted her hand.

She gasped, her chest expanding with a rapid intake of air. "What did you just do?"

"I gave you the power to extinct."

Harmony shot to her feet. "Are you insane? After what I told you?"

"I trust you without question, whether or not I see into your mind, and I need strong fighters. I fear what lies ahead may be the biggest challenge OneWorld has faced. Now, congratulations. What shall we call you?"

She resettled in her seat with a resigned sigh. "As your representative in Angor, I am known as the Dispatcher. That works as my new title, as well."

He paused, his chin dipping to his chest. "So be it. I am weary and must lie abed."

He sensed Harmony's worried eyes follow him as he left the room. They had once had an affair. It had burned too brightly and too fast. She was not Kalia, but in his ignorance or hubris, he'd not seen that. He had seen the lush body but had missed the keen intellect, the wit, and the heart.

Never before these days had he felt the burden of ruling. The mantle was heavy. And he was... He paused, searching his memory.

What am I? Oh, yes. I am ill.

The End

EVERNIGHT PUBLISHING ®

www.evernightpublishing.com